I0535728

Bad Elements: The Hybrid Unleashed

Book III

Lynn Mullican

This is a work of fiction. The characters, names, incidents, places, and plot are products of the author's imagination or are used fictitiously. Any resemblance to actual persons, companies, or events is purely coincidental.

BAD ELEMENTS: THE HYBRID UNLEASHED

COPYRIGHT THE HYBRID UNLEASHED © 2013 LYNN MULLICAN
GRAPHIC DESIGN © BY VIC WEIFORD

ISBN: 0985547138
ISBN-13: 978-0-9855471-3-4
Published by
Cryptic Bones Publishing
Phoenix, AZ 85022

No portion of this book may be reproduced, stored in a retrieval system, or transmitted in any form or by any means – electronic, mechanical, photocopy, recording, scanning, or other – except for brief quotations in critical reviews or articles, without the prior written permission of the author or publisher.

All rights reserved.

PRINTED IN THE UNITED STATES OF AMERICA

Also by Lynn Mullican

BAD ELEMENTS SERIES:
Crystal Dragon
Blood for Blood

Sacrificial Blood
The Awakening

DEDICATION

For my family, Patrick, Cassandra, Bridget, Joeseph, Martha, Rich, Aeva, Zoe, Rhea, Asher, and Grayson, friends and fans - Cherish those that you love and let their laughter, warmth and spirit fill your heart.

AWAKENINGS

Rapid gunfire spread throughout my living room, penetrating the walls to where my children would sleep, had they been in bed. Instead, they screamed, cried, and clung to me. My son, Robert, was ten years old, and my daughter, Jennifer, was only four. We huddled together in the corner behind the oak entertainment center.

Bullets riddled past, striking the wall to the right of us. The suppressor on the gunman's rifle kept its noise to a minimum. Dressed in black, the gunman swept the room with his rifle. Then, he turned and pointed the gun at me and my children.

Tears flowed down my cheeks. "No!" I screamed. I squeezed my children tighter, pressing their heads against my chest.

"Please no!"

The gunman grinned. As he readied himself for another shot, my husband Wayne, rushed through the front door. His footsteps resonated throughout the house.

The gunman whipped around. As he turned the rifle on my husband Wayne grabbed the barrel, yanking the rifle and the gunman, at an inward angle, toward him, the barrel pointed at the floor. The gunman jerked forward, his finger still on the trigger.

Another succession of bullets fired into the Spanish tile floor sending pieces of the tile flying everywhere. Then another bullet struck the television and the stereo system to the left of us. Sparks shot everywhere, igniting a fire to the entertainment system.

Jennifer's screams died down to a coughing, crying fit as Robert's echoed throughout the room.

I was afraid to move.

My home was no longer my safe haven. It had been intruded upon, and I was scared. If I didn't do something to help my husband, we might all lose our lives.

Robert and Jennifer needed to know mom and dad were here to protect them. But, huddling here in the corner was not protecting them. I had to step up and do something even though I had no weapons in my hands.

A fight ensued between Wayne and the gunman. Wayne spun around, driving an elbow into the man's ribcage. Snarling, he ripped the gun out of the man's hands and tossed it to the floor. The werewolf within Wayne came forth, revealing his large canine fangs.

If we made any noise, we might attract the werewolf's attention. That was the last thing I wanted to do, so I tried to keep the kids silent. I pressed my finger to my lips to indicate they needed to keep quiet. Robert understood. Jennifer did not. She was too young.

Wayne's fingers transformed into claws. They dug into the man's arm. Blood oozed out from the wounds. Then Wayne latched onto his head, his fangs penetrating the man's skin. The gunman screamed.

"Mom..."

I clamped my hand over Jennifer's mouth as she wriggled in my arms. The man's cries overrode her voice. Thank God. My heartbeat raced.

"Shush," I whispered.

To our left, the fire traveled up the walls and onto the floor. Next, it would be us. We had to get out of the house. The nearest exit was our living room window, so we crept over to it. I motioned for Robert to keep quiet as he opened the window and scrambled out of it. Tears streamed down his face.

My adrenaline sped up, my heart beating faster by the second. The werewolf was too busy with his kill to notice us.

Trembling, Robert reached through the window and grabbed his sister. Without hesitation, he covered her mouth, turned, and ran away toward our neighbor's house.

I hesitated, contemplating grabbing the gun, or immediately following my kids. At least with the gun, I could shoot whoever attacked us.

Then two figures emerged from the shadows. They moved toward my children.

"No!" I screamed.

I grabbed the windowsill to jump out of it. Behind me, Wayne growled.

Glancing back, I cried, "Somebody's after the kids."

Our children screamed.

Snarling, Wayne leaped at the window. I backed away as he crashed through the glass. It shattered everywhere.

Just then the entertainment center erupted into a full blown fire. It was growing out of control. I couldn't wait any longer. My only chance of escape was through the window, so without question, I grabbed the windowsill. Broken shards of glass penetrated my skin. Shit!

Groaning, I glanced out at my children. They struggled against the two men who fought to control them. As Wayne leaped at the man who held Jennifer, another figure emerged from the darkness. In his hand, he held a Taser.

"No!" I screamed.

An electrical current shot out, connecting with Wayne. It sent my husband into seizures as he fell to the ground.

Heads turned toward me.

Fuck!

No time to wait! I snatched up the rifle. When I spun around to aim it, an electric current shot through me. The rifle fell from my grip. As if in slow motion, I fell to the floor. Red and orange embers danced, gracefully and rapidly moving in toward me.

The back door opened, and in strode a man with dark-colored boots. Though I was unsure and fearful of who stood over me, I could do nothing about it. My body was paralyzed and before I knew it, I lost consciousness.

Awakening from a deep sleep, I bolted upright. I glanced around. My dream was a distant memory. My hair was wet and it clung to my face. When I touched my cheek I found my fingers soaked with blood. Bloody tears streaked my face.

Memories of my past were coming back.

§

Woodrow and his friends had masqueraded in the underground fighting circuit for quite some time to avoid the clutches of the Underground Secret Service aka the U.G.S.S. Yet, Woodrow stood here in the basement of an old, abandoned correctional facility where several prison cells had been built, below ground floor level cells. This was where it all started, well, at least, for him and his cohorts.

Distant memories invaded his mind.

Though Woodrow had worked for the U.G.S.S. at one time, it was over the moment his employer decided it was best to start the real experiments with one of their own, Jace Templeton aka J.T. He had become the first successful creation with the controversial DNA that had been found, confiscated, and maintained within the agency. Mortals had already been experimenting with medicinal science, but now it was time for the immortals to make the plunge; the only two differences between them was that the agency was going to use it for international war and the DNA they were using didn't exist anymore, at least, not in the mortal world. The U.G.S.S. was going to become the first agency to create medicinal scientific hybrids.

Debate had already started over the controversial matter, but the U.G.S.S. was the first, and as far as they knew, the only agency to raise the bar on international warfare with the hybrids.

So, in order to progress with the testing, it began small, and moved to larger subjects, resulting in an odd and horrid array of deformed creatures, many of whom were either put to death or escaped when a security breach happened at the laboratory.

Woodrow and Jace had been the doctors on hand to assist with the unsuccessful experiments, but when it was suggested one of them volunteer to become a part of the experiment, Jace decided it was time to back off.

When Jace attempted to flee the premises, strict orders from upper command demanded security personnel capture and detain him for his part in Project Hybrid.

"Strap him down. And, get on with the procedure," Lagunas demanded. Repeatedly, he jabbed Woodrow in the chest.

Rage boiled up inside of Woodrow as he thought back to that day.

Jace's friend, David Wineberger, who was part of security personnel, assisted in strapping Jace down to the surgical table. Woodrow Myrddin was the surgeon on duty.

It was in Woodrow's final days with the U.G.S.S. that he understood where their mistakes with Project Hybrid had lain. So when he came to the table to complete the procedure, he knew exactly what he was doing, but in doing so, he also came to the surgical room with their escape plan to leave the facility permanently.

With the assistance of David and several other staff members, the plan was set forth and escalated right after the procedure. These men, in turn, would become Jace, Woodrow and David's friends. Their friends would assist them with helping to find fighters in the underground fighting circuit for their own genetic hybrid medicinal mutation, something the U.G.S.S. had been intent on before Jace and Woodrow's departure.

Though their escape wasn't as easy as they had expected, they made it out alive, and with Jace intact, healthy and more volatile than ever. Despite the outcome of the procedure, it had not been as successful as they had predicted, which put Woodrow and Jace back to the drawing board. For all of the hard work they put into the project at the agency, Jace's hybrid creature never emerged. Instead, it remained hidden beneath his flesh.

Once the agency found out the rogue vampires had stolen the DNA, they sent out elusive agents to find them and confiscate it. In the search for them, several agents had been killed by Jace and his men prompting a massive yet elite hunt to find and capture them, dead or alive.

In the meantime, the U.G.S.S. continued their own research on Project Hybrid with other DNA and new doctors, thus increasing the numbers of malformed beasts. But with one disappointment after another, they were apt to move on. Many of the deformed monsters were put to their death and disposed of in the surrounding canyons near Flagstaff, Arizona. They were committed to providing an alternative should they never recover the so-called secret DNA which they so highly regarded.

Woodrow's unsuccessful procedure led Jace and his men to believe the DNA had been either tainted or not contained efficiently, which may have led to other problems, thus eluding him to the fact the DNA they stole from the agency was worthless. But Jace prompted Woodrow to continue his research. It took time. They completed multiple surgeries, resulting in failure after failure. Even then, Jace and his men trudged onward, continuing with their research and experimentation.

Woodrow mulled over their past with the U.G.S.S. while he investigated the damage that had been created in the correctional facility. He needed no light to be able to see in the vast darkness, for his eyesight was exceptional. Periodically, his eyes would shift, dilate and refocus on the abnormally bent steel bars, the broken cement walls, and the hole that led to the black sky.

Blood spattered the floor, walls, and ceiling, obviously from the injuries the creatures sustained in escaping their scientific home. In the middle of the floor lie two dying experimental winged creatures. Blood leaked from their wounds. A battle had been forged here. The strong had won and the meek lay dying, but thankfully, they were still alive. Jace would need them.

Jace stirred within his prison cell.

Woodrow walked up to one of the crying beasts. Without any remorse, he snagged one by the back of the neck and dragged it to the cell where Jace lay healing from the injuries he sustained in the fight with Crystal. Blood trailed along the floor behind the injured creature.

Jace hadn't moved. He was healing, but he needed to replenish his strength and regenerate his energy.

As Woodrow opened the cell, Jace spun around, fangs bared. Woodrow held up the defenseless creature. Jace lunged for it, tearing it from Woodrow's hands, and gorged on it. The creature's shrieks echoed within the concrete walls.

Woodrow was eager for Jace to fully recover. They had work to do.

§

I sat on the roof of our house, overlooking the forest. Though my memory was slowly coming back, I had not regained one hundred percent of it. In due time, I would remember everything including why my ex-husband Wayne held me prisoner for almost five years in an underground prison cell, and why he had forced me to fight to the death with vampires and werewolves in attendance.

I laid back, recalling my latest memory, and stared up at the night sky. Why had somebody come into our home and tried to kill us? And why couldn't I recollect much of my life since then? I closed my eyes and tried to force the memories to come forth. But, the shooter and the fire remained a vivid visual.

My reunion with my family snuck into my head, along with the reminder of our fire loss. A small section of the house had remained untouched, that portion included my bedroom. After my disappearance, my parents moved my children to the Munds Park area near Flagstaff, Arizona. Since then, they raised my children until they passed on. Then, my children inherited the house, of which they still lived in. After being reunited with my family, I moved in.

The clouds loomed overhead. A pale face appeared above me. Tristan, my lover, stood there. Deep lines and scars, primarily the one by his eye accentuated his middle-aged face. Most who met him, on first glance, might be deceived by his hardcore biker style—but I knew him better. Tristan was trustworthy and respectful. He was a man of honor and valor, and would lay his life on the line for many, but very few, in his eyes, deserved it.

Though my children and granddaughters were cursed with the werewolf bloodline, the vampire in Tristan was still able to respect that. He had even put his life on the line for them. He was centuries old, but through those years, he had learned to control his thirst for blood and his distaste for his natural enemy, the werewolf.

Had he been part of a vampire clan, he most likely would not have been able to control his appetite. Even though Tristan had built a rapport with my family, there was still some primitive vampire/werewolf tension.

As for me, I was a hybrid baby in this underworld. Three creatures lived beneath my flesh—vampire, werewolf, and another one, which had not revealed itself. Until then, it remains hidden.

I gazed up into his intense blue eyes. Then he offered his hand, of which I accepted. As I stood, he swept me up into his arms. My hair clip fell, allowing my long auburn hair to flow down my back.

Then he kissed me. The passion between us invoked the strong burning desire to bed him but it was not the time. We were hungry.

Instead, it was time to hunt.

§

Filled with renewed energy and vitality, Jace fled the old correctional facility with Woodrow fast on his heels. His clothing was still scorched, bloody and torn from the night he fought Crystal. He had wanted her for her fighting abilities, agility, stamina, and her mortal womanhood but since she was no longer mortal, he debated on whether to kill her instead, especially since he found out she was involved with another U.G.S.S. agent other than her ex-husband Wayne.

Wayne? Wait, yes, where was he, by the way? And where the hell was the other U.G.S.S. agent, Warrant? He didn't recall seeing them inside the building. As a matter of fact, it was desolate.

Jace came to an abrupt stop. Eyes red, he glared at Woodrow.

"Where is he? Where are they?" he spat.

Woodrow halted. "Who?"

"The agents, Wayne and Warrant. Where are they?" Jace demanded.

Woodrow bit his tongue. "They escaped."

"How in the hell…?" The scent of a dead carcass lay nearby. He drew in a long breath. The smell was invigorating.

"Listen, Jace…"

"What the hell happened?"

"The hybrids got out. I think they got in a fight and destroyed part of the building. There was a huge hole. I imagine that's how the men got out, too."

Jace's eyes shifted rapidly.

"Jace, are you okay? You seem…"

"Just continue." Jace snapped his head to the right and looked around.

Woodrow looked him over. "Uh, um, yeah, they were getting stronger by the day. With the DNA they had in them, maybe it was just a matter of time. They're smart, almost too smart." He followed his gaze. "Maybe that was something we didn't think about. Anything could have happened."

Jace whipped his head back around.

Woodrow stared at him. "Hey Jace, I heard through the grapevine there was a security breach at the U.G.S.S. recently. I think we have a problem. Our hybrids and theirs are on the loose. We need to do something."

Jace sniffed the air.

Woodrow patted him on the shoulder. "Are you listening to me?"

Jace gazed back at him but remained silent.

"What's wrong with you?"

Fangs bared, Jace said, "I smell…burnt flesh."

He stared past Woodrow's shoulder.

Woodrow glanced behind him. Nothing. When he turned back around, Jace was gone.

§

Deputy Torrance stared down into the large pit. It had to have been well over one hundred feet deep and thirty yards wide all around. Remnants of two burnt cars and human remains lie at the bottom. Most of the skin had been burnt to a crisp. The fresh scent of charred flesh wafted up his nostrils. The fire had died down to a crack and pop in the night.

The sheriff's office had received a call complaining about the deathly smell from somebody driving en route to the lake. Dispatch had asked the driver to stop and wait for the deputy to arrive, but apparently, the driver decided it wasn't worth his while.

Had it not been for the overwhelming stench, Deputy Torrance may never have found the bodies, but now, he stood alone over the dump site and scanned the area. Though the dark forest near the pit was pushed a little further back, it closed in on him.

Deputy Torrance unsnapped his holster, ready to draw his gun. The wind picked up. The decomposing stench overwhelmed him. He gagged, covering his mouth and nose with his hand, barely stifling the urge to vomit. There were too many bodies to count, and at this moment, he really didn't want to be alone. Unfortunately, burnt bodies were becoming a normal thing lately, and there were more questions than answers in the investigation.

He debated on calling his partner, Robert, but decided against it since Robert had taken a vacation day. So, Torrance didn't want to disturb him.

Robert wasn't just Torrance's partner, he was also Torrance's best friend and lately, Torrance worried about him. Robert's family was going through some personal issues, but he didn't know the extent of the problems. Torrance would be there when Robert was ready to talk, though.

Unable to peel his eyes away from the pile of bodies, he straightened up. Another gust of wind blew the unpleasant smell toward him again.

The violent urge to vomit overtook his body. He fell forward, onto his knees, in the dirt, his dirty blonde hair spilling over his face, and resisted the urge to take another breath.

The wind spiraled. Another odor wafted up his nostrils. Only this scent was the Grim Reaper himself.

Sensing a presence behind him, he reached for his gun and turned around, throwing himself to the ground. He tucked and rolled, pulling his gun out.

The spot where he had stood was empty. A knot formed in his throat. Nervously, he surveyed his surroundings. His eye twitched. It was not a figment of his imagination. Death's odor still lingered, making it difficult to move.

Oh, how he really wished Robert was with him, primarily because Robert was a werewolf. Robert would be able to detect if there were supernatural forces at work. Unfortunately, Torrance didn't have that gift.

§

Tristan disappeared into the night on his own hunt, searching for something of larger size for his appetite. Had we hunted together, our combined scents would have scared off the animals, which would make it difficult to stalk our prey.

So, it didn't bother me that he went out on his own. Besides, it gave me time to think things over.

My thoughts drifted to Wayne. What was the reason behind my captivity? Also, who was behind the attack on our home? And why did they come after our family?

Something rustled behind me. I turned. Wings fluttered in the trees, the pitter patter of paws moved in the brush, and the scent of badger filled my nostrils.

My stomach grumbled.

The badger wasn't enough to suffice me, so I walked on by, shedding my clothes and climbing the nearest tree, so I could camouflage myself in the night.

About fifteen minutes later, a wounded bull elk appeared. Mid-stride, he stopped and fell forward.

The scent of his blood filled my nostrils. It triggered muscle spasms to ripple throughout my body as the hybrid in me came forth. I leaped. My body took on full transformation in midair.

§

As Deputy Torrance took a step forward, something grabbed his rear ankle. He fell, almost dropping his gun. Whoever it was drug him backward, toward the pit. Hand still on the pistol, he kicked back, but all he found was air.

What the hell, he thought.

The hand remained wrapped around him. There was no way he missed, not unless…

Shit! Torrance swung his right arm behind him and shot at the assailant. He glanced back. It disappeared. The bullet ricocheted off the rock below.

"Fuck!" he yelled.

As Torrance grasped at vegetation and rock to keep from going over the edge, he lost his grip on the gun. It bounced off the terrain and into the darkness below.

"Motherfucker!"

Groaning, he grabbed onto a rock that was embedded in the dirt wall. He started to pull himself up when the rock broke free, causing his hand to slip off of it. Then he lost his footing. His heart leaped into his throat.

With one hand on the rock, he slammed against the dirt wall. There he hung suspended above the pit, desperately searching for something to hold onto.

Wait…there! Yes! He secured his toes into a niche. It wasn't much, but just the ability to stand gave him some relief. The jolt from the fall had torn something in his shoulder, making it more difficult to hold on.

Painstakingly, he reached for a deeply embedded rock. The moment he grabbed it, his other hand slipped, threatening to cast him into hell.

As he gained hold of another rock, his shoulder fought against him. The jagged edge cut his hand.

Carefully he climbed, moving from one rock to another, his arm and shoulder nearly disabled. The jagged edges of the rock left deep cuts in his hands. Blood coated his skin.

Slowly, he ascended the dirt wall.

When he reached the top, Tristan whisked him up and bared his fangs.

"No! Let me go!" Torrance struggled, punching him in the face.

Oh, shit!

The man's blue eyes darkened. The vampire attacked.

§

The carcass lay before me, the skin and muscle torn away from the elk's bone. The internal organs hung from its stomach. Its blood coated my body. I wiped my hand across my mouth to wipe the blood from my lips. Instead, I spread it across my face.

A chilled breeze brought in the scent of pine, rain, blood, meat and...Tristan. My long, dark red hair swept up into the wind and smacked me, sticking to the bloody mess.

My hunger was satisfied. His massive body was sufficient to provide me with the nutrition I needed. I caressed his antlers, my fingers trailing along the rough edges of the broken piece, and then my gaze fell on his glassy eyes. The poor bastard, he didn't know I was there until the last moment but when he did, it was too late. Yes, I felt remorseful, every goddamn time I took a life. But was it my fault? To some degree yes, yet I blamed the bloodthirsty beasts inside of me, the ones who made me kill.

Rain fell from the clouds. A bloody, stringy mess was entwined around my fingers. With a snap of my wrist, I flicked it away.

Tristan approached from behind, wrapping his arms around my bare waist. I drew in a deep breath, inhaling the scent of his victim. It was familiar, yet I couldn't place it. Maybe it was the human aspect that was obvious but that didn't matter right now. Only Tristan mattered.

I turned my attention back to him. His strong but gentle hands lingered below my breasts, caressing me.

Growling, he said, "You smell yummy."

His tongue slithered up my neck.

I grinned. "Do I?"

"Yes, you smell like..." He sniffed again. "Beef jerky."

"Oh, how romantic," I said.

The breeze picked up. It sent chills down my spine. Tristan slid his hands over my breasts, rolling my nipples between his fingers, enticing me. Then, his fangs grazed my skin. I melted into him. Every detail of his hardened body stood defiant against mine.

"Oh, yes," I moaned.

I spun around and latched onto him, my mouth on his. His fingernails dug into my skin as he grabbed me by the hips, prompting me to wrap my legs around him. As I did, he picked me up and pinned me to the tree.

The intensity of the storm increased. Rain poured down upon us.

Tantalizing me, he licked and nibbled on my nipples, eliciting a mixture of pleasure and pain. The tree cut into my back as he moved further down my stomach, licking off the blood. With a firm grip, he pushed my hips up toward him and flicked his tongue across my clit. The pleasure and pain erupted a fire deep within.

Moaning, I pressed him harder against me. His tongue provoked every crevice of my sexual being, intensifying the need to have him inside me. Rain splashed down upon my breasts, sloping into a waterfall upon his dark hair.

"Oh, Tristan," I moaned.

Then he stood, his hands wrapped beneath my legs. He drew me in fast and hard, plunging deep inside. The taste of his victim was still upon him. As the storm escalated, so did our adrenaline. My beasts allowed his dominance to supersede ours, allowing him the opportunity to taste our blood. But soon, the beasts within would take control, sexually gratify, and feed from him.

As he drank of my blood, I wrapped my legs around his waist. I couldn't control it any longer. I needed him…every morsel of his being. My fangs pierced his skin. The blood sharing between us during our climax was like a lifetime of bonding.

§

The fresh scent of blood and death permeated the air but the odor of charred human remains lingered.

Jace stood near the edge of the pit. His gaze fell upon the bodies, which lie amongst the burnt rubble. One body, in particular, stood out, the deputy. Fresh blood was splattered across the uniform.

A gust of wind picked up. It carried the scent of the vampire who had killed the deputy, Tristan. Jace recognized the aroma. He leaped into the pit and advanced upon the dead body.

Kneeling down, he leaned in and drew in a deep breath. Yes, it was Tristan. Tristan was a current U.G.S.S. agent, one whom Jace was a bit unsure of.

He glanced around. Tristan had been by recently…

A little too recent that Jace could have passed him by without realizing it.

Nowadays, the U.G.S.S. was hiring agents who had exceptional gifts or talents, ones that if Jace wasn't careful, could kill him. He would have to be on guard with Tristan.

§

"Something has been bothering you," Tristan said. "And I want to know what it is."

Oh, cripes!

"Talk to me."

He could only be talking about my obsession with my children's father, Wayne. I had not been open with him regarding the fact that he was their father. I wasn't sure how he was going to take it, or the fact that Wayne was my ex-husband.

Already dressed, I sighed and looked at the ground. I really didn't want to talk about this right now but I guess it was a better time than any to discuss it.

Just where the hell was I going to start? Well, yes, of course, there was only one place to begin.

I peered up at him. "Do you remember when I was in my cell?"

He nodded. "Yes, of course, I do."

"Do you remember Wayne, my captor…?" My voice cut out. The stress and tension from my captive days came back, bringing back every vivid horrific detail.

A questionable look arose on his face. The crease in his forehead deepened.

"Yes, I do."

"He's the father of my children."

I remembered the day I awoke in my prison cold; alone, beaten, and frightened, and my ex-husband was partly to blame for it, let alone forget Tristan was a part of it as well. Tristan was an Underground Secret Service Agent hired to do a job but there was much more that had been held secret. The one thing I truly didn't understand was Wayne's position in it.

I fought to keep my emotions in check for it was still hard to digest. My adrenaline sped up.

His eyes widened. "How do you figure that?"

"Robert was helping me get all of my important papers. When I requested my marriage license, I found out there were two of them. Wayne Devereaux is my first husband. My second husband is Chris Pent. Wayne has to be their father because I was married to him when the kids were born. I didn't marry Chris until years later." My heart raced. "I found pictures of Wayne and Chris in my lingerie drawer. The one of Wayne was a younger picture of him."

I paced. "I almost didn't recognize him. His face was different. I couldn't figure out why, until now. I think he may have had facial surgery. It just looks different."

Tristan cocked his head. "What are you talking about?"

"What I mean is there's a difference from the photo to what he looks like now. He looks like a normal person, but if you look carefully, you can see it's the same man." My voice rose.

"The eyes are the same." I pointed at mine. "But something about the rest of his face looks different. I'm positive he had surgery on his face."

Tristan shook his head. "It can't be. You must be mistaken."

"No, it's him. It's him," I stammered. Had Wayne been in an accident of some sort and needed reconstructive surgery? Or was there another reason his face was altered?

Tristan paced. It was obvious he was concerned. He rubbed his chin.

"Tristan, it's him. I found a goddamn picture of him when he was probably in his early twenties. It's him! He's their fucking father! Now, if that's the case, why the hell did he do that to me?" I struck my chest. "And everything that I've been told is bullshit! So, don't tell me it was because of gambling debts," I spat. Tears welled up.

"And why the hell did he imprison me? And why the hell did he say he was going to kill my son…our son…who obviously was never even kidnapped, and neither was my daughter. What's up with that?" The heat rose in my face. "She went to the hospital for anxiety issues right after I disappeared. So, what the fuck?" I yelled. I threw my arms up in the air.

Tristan stared at me.

Then, it struck me. I was woozy. Memories overwhelmed me.

"Oh shit, that makes sense." I fell to my knees.

The trees spun around me, moving faster by the second. I was dizzy. I tried to focus in on Tristan. His eyes merged into one and then grew apart. The spinning slowed, but not before his eyes shifted and merged back out again.

He knelt down.

Because of the confused look on his face, I was sure he didn't know the truth. I had to presume it was a front to kill Chris and get to me, but why? What had I done to deserve this? I looked away.

"What makes sense to you?" he asked.

I swallowed hard. "Wayne would never let me see my son. He would never let me talk to him. It was like he was keeping him in the dark."

Tears rolled down my cheeks. "I began to doubt that I actually had a son, and he never mentioned Jennifer. Not once did he speak her name. Now, why would he do that?"

Tristan scratched his chin. "It sounds like he might have been protecting them. He could have used your son as a distraction, but from who or what, I don't know."

"So, he throws his wife, the mother of his own children, into an underground fighting circuit. What kind of a husband does that? Something is not right about this whole thing. You're a cop. What do you...?"

More memories invaded my head. I stared through him and forced myself to relive my past.

MEMORIES

Toward the end of my captivity, in some odd way, it was as if Wayne was protecting me. Also, why would a kidnapper bother to memorize a birth date if he didn't have to? If it were not for Wayne, I would never have found my son or my family.

I remembered the night vampires and werewolves chased us through the corridor of the underground facility. They had broken through the barricade separating the arena from the audience. Once we were locked inside a stock room, Wayne told me my son's birth date. I recited it repeatedly so as not to forget it.

Then the image of a grueling fight popped into my head. It questioned my loyalty of Wayne. If he were my ex-husband then was he trying to come clean the night we were forced to fight each other? He tried to tell me something during our fight, but couldn't. Was he going to tell me the truth about my captivity? Or was he going to tell me who he really was? Then something horrific struck me, something that stung…and hard.

I wrapped my arms over my chest. My heart ached.

"Oh shit, Tristan."

Several vampires and werewolves crossed the barricades that separated the arena from the spectators. David emerged from the audience. Unsure of his intentions, I backed off.

David approached Wayne, who lay on the ground. Even though I despised Wayne, I hoped that he was dead and wouldn't have to suffer from the hands of David.

I did not want to witness the horror David was going to deliver on him, so I turned away. The glass before me shattered. I cast my eyes upon the fans. The vampires and werewolves in the audience began their transformations.

In fear for my life, I ran for the hallway. Behind me, the creatures bore down on one another. Hesitantly, I glanced back. The vampires who were clearly set on getting me were confronted by the four-legged beasts. For the wolves, it was one of their own who had lay bleeding. The scent of blood had attracted the attention of the bloodsuckers.

My eyes settled on the ground where Wayne had been. Only now he was gone along with David.

"Tristan, who are these men…err, vampires? Who are they really? What do they want? David was one of Jace's henchmen. He took Wayne. Why didn't he just leave him there to die?"

Tristan stared at me. He knew where I was going with this. I was sick to my stomach of the thought of *Jace.*

Jace Templeton went after one man I had grown close to, Warrant. We thought Jace had killed him, but he did not. Instead, Jace turned him into a hybrid, a creature of more than one species. He was already a werewolf, but whatever Jace had merged Warrant with, had never revealed itself. So, its identity was unknown. I presumed that when Warrant and Tristan turned me into a hybrid, I had taken on the third beast but I wasn't sure, for it remained hidden. If a third creature resided within me, it was either hibernating or hiding.

I was convinced why David took Wayne. It was not to kill him or torture him, instead, Jace was going to create another hybrid like he had with one of his experiments, Ezzie. Only, this time, he was going to use Wayne. My throat tightened.

Wayne was out there, somewhere, alive. I was convinced Jace would attack again, but using Wayne this time. My heart was heavy. I glanced back in the direction of my house.

"Oh God, not my family," I muttered.

"We need to get you home," he said.

The evening changed into something ugly and horrifying. My past was not going to leave me alone. It was going to haunt me in every twisted and horrific way. As we headed home, another memory wormed its way into my thoughts.

I swore I had been asleep for hours when Wayne turned me onto my back. I must have slept hard because I didn't detect him entering my cell. My eyes shot open. One of his hands forced my head back onto the cot. The weight of his body held me down. He forced his other hand onto my mouth. A gush of fluid filled my throat. The taste of Wayne's blood made me gag. His wrist covered so much of my mouth I could barely breathe.

"Breathe, Crystal."

Eyes wide, I stared at him. I tried to calm myself. As I swallowed his blood, I gagged.

"I'm not trying to hurt you. I just want to help you, Crystal."

He put more of his weight on me, his head hung low, next to my neck. My body recognized his blood. Only this time my adrenaline moved rapidly. His breath was hot in my ear.

"I'm sorry I had to do it this way. It's best you not see it coming, otherwise, you would have fought me and not drank my blood," he said.

I closed my eyes, and concentrated on his breathing, feeding from the open wound on his wrist. Gradually, I relaxed. His blood would heal the wounds I sustained from the fighting. Knowing this, I pulled his wrist tighter against my lips. The taste of his blood was disgusting, but if I was going to survive this nightmare, I needed it.

Usually, Wayne diluted his blood before feeding it to me. But, tonight, he did not. The undiluted blood sent my body into convulsions. Wayne pulled his hand away and stayed atop me. Tightly, he held me down by my wrists, confining me to the cot. He drew in a deep breath.

I tried to fight the convulsions that ripped through my body. But Wayne told me to let it go. There was no stopping it.

My breath became short and erratic. He locked his feet around my ankles. Wayne's tongue lapped across my cheek to my lips. Our eyes met. I swallowed hard, unsure of where this was going. His tongue slithered over my cheek again, only, this time, from my lips to my ear. His heart beat faster and stronger by the minute. I closed my eyes and pulled my head further back into the cot.

I relinquished my neck to him. His tongue slithered over my jaw line and back to my mouth, refraining from touching my lips with his. What was happening was not purely sexual, even though there was an intense desire to have sex with him.

Like an animal, he used his head to turn my face to the other side. Then I realized, he was licking up the blood that had spilled from my mouth. His tongue slithered in my ear, raising the intense desire to bed him.

Instead of fighting him, I pressed his face to mine.

"Oh, Wayne," I moaned. What the hell was I doing? Yet, I could feel it. An unidentifiable emotion stirred within me. His breathing became heavy. A low rumble started within his chest. Then it erupted into a growl. I moaned. His hands roamed, studying every inch of my body. The urge to bed him grew stronger but I told myself no, he was my captor. I could not give in. Like a hungry wolf, he pressed his nose to my throat and inhaled my scent.

I tried to stifle my moans. Grabbing me by my hips, he pulled me up onto his lap. I gasped in surprise. The hardness of his manhood stood defiant against me. The scent of his testosterone wafted up my nostrils, throwing my hormones into overdrive. I had to have him. His fangs grazed my shoulder.

Remembering the last attack, I winced and curled into him. I was leery of having sex with him. Yet, I still wanted him.

Our eyes met. I wanted his lips on mine, to taste him, to revel in our intense sexual exploration but as I moved in to kiss him, he pulled my face into his neck. I ran my tongue up his throat. His manhood throbbed against me for he wanted me just as much.

He moaned.

I touched his chest. His taut muscles flinched beneath my fingers. I kissed down to the hollow of his collarbone. I unsnapped his jeans. Then, he pushed my hand away.

"No, we can't," he mumbled.

"You can't tell me you don't want me," I said, my lips against his chest.

I slid the zipper on his jeans down. Again, he pushed my hands away.

"No, Crystal."

I whispered in his ear, "Look, I don't know the last time I had anything, but I can guarantee it's been a while. Fuck me, Wayne."

He glanced at me. I moved in fast, my mouth enveloping his. For a moment, I thought it was definite but it was not. He had responded, but just as quick as it started, he pushed me back.

"You don't understand…"

"No, obviously you don't understand. I need somebody to show some compassion toward me, even if it is just a one-night stand. I don't give a shit, Wayne. I'm not asking for a fucking relationship with you. You're my fucking kidnapper. Just give me something, anything…Please. All I ask is that you don't bite me."

Hesitantly, he allowed me to push him back on the cot but the moment he was down, he latched on and held me tight against him, not allowing me to do anymore. I fought for him to release me, but he wouldn't let go.

I cried. I needed something other than this hellhole, other than the need to fight for my life. I needed some sort of comfort, regardless of what it was. As I lay in his embrace, something stirred within me and I detected it in him as well. It was something I should have recognized but didn't. At first, I thought it was a mutual physical attraction, but it was not. The physical attraction was still there, but it was much different.

Then it hit me—that un-defining emotion was an old love. I cringed, for I remembered what he had put me through in the prison. I despised him, wanted to bury him in my past, but couldn't.

Somewhere, Wayne was still alive. He was a product of Jace's diabolical experiments. Whether Wayne's conscience knew it or not, he would come after his family to kill them, including his children.

Had Jace been alive, he would have come after me too. As for David and Woodrow, they disappeared after Jace died. Where they went to I didn't know, it was as if they had disappeared. They were twice as dangerous. I worried they would reappear in our lives. The only question was when and where?

PROBLEMS

"Listen bitch, are you going to play or what? You're like dead fucking weight around here. You might as well just leave the court," the blonde girl snapped.

Jennifer took a moment to refocus on the game. It was one thing trying to keep her strength and power under control, yet, it was another to not let the snotty nosed girls on the other side of the net get to her. If Jennifer had her way, right now, there would be no volleyball, better yet, there might be some nose crunching fighting going on.

Wait, what the hell was she thinking? Stop it, she told herself. You're not like that and never have been. Well, at least she wasn't until the change. Now, it brought on her more primeval side. That wasn't a good thing. When she was younger, doctors tried to convince her family she had anxiety and anger issues. It was only recently that she came to learn she didn't suffer from either problem. It was much deeper than that.

As they switched up positions, one of her teammates threw her the volleyball. She held her tongue, refraining from verbally retaliating. As her brother once told her, keep your emotions under control, it helps to control the beast within. If you don't all hell will break loose. Her dark eyes narrowed in on the blonde teenager. Bitch!

Grinding her teeth, she stepped into the server's spot. She bounced the ball in her hand picturing Michelle's head instead. Dammit, stop it. The werewolf in Jennifer was determined to rip the girl's head off of her shoulders. She thought about walking over and punching the blonde. Just then, Jennifer's fist connected with the ball, sending it full force, over the net, and right into Michelle's face, striking her in the nose.

Michelle howled in pain, clamping her hand over her face.

"What the fuck?" yelled one of Michelle's teammates. "You did that on purpose, you stupid bitch."

Surprised that she nailed the girl dead on, Jennifer played stupid by throwing her hands up in surrender. She bit her lip, trying to stifle a smile, even though she knew what she did was horrible. Stop it, Jennifer.

A couple of Michelle's teammates ran to Michelle's aid.

Don't fuck with me, bitch. I'll get even with you one way or another. This was perfect, too! Nobody could say she really did it on purpose. If the girl can't hit the ball, that's her problem, not mine. Jennifer's alter ego needed to tone it down a bit.

"Uh…sorry, it was an accident," Jennifer yelled, glancing around.

Everyone was staring at her. That was one hell of a serve. It caught everyone by surprise, even Jennifer. She shrugged her shoulders.

One of her teammates, Raelin, put her hand over her mouth, to hide her smirk.

Jennifer tried to ignore it. It wasn't deliberate. Who are you kidding? Your alter ego doesn't like Michelle any more than you do. Stop it! You're one and the same. You can't blame your alter ego for everything, can you?

The gym teacher's voice echoed throughout the gym. "What is going on, ladies?"

It was about time Miss Ross came back. Had she not been tending to an important phone call, the girls wouldn't have opened their traps.

"Jennifer intentionally hit Michelle in the nose with the ball," Michelle's friend yelled.

Miss Ross rushed over to Michelle's side. "Let me see. Move your hand."

"Really? How do you figure that?" Jennifer asked.

Michelle's friend snapped her head around to stare at Jennifer.

Jennifer rolled her eyes. "I did not."

"Girls, stop it! Accidents happen!" She turned her attention back to Michelle.

The moment Michelle moved her hand blood gushed from her nose.

The girls screamed.

The teacher turned to Michelle's friend. "Stephanie, take her to the nurse."

As Stephanie took Michelle's hand Miss Ross spoke up again. "Make sure she keeps her head tilted back."

"All right," Stephanie said. As Stephanie led Michelle out of the gym, she sneered at Jennifer.

Miss Ross glanced back at Jennifer before turning to the rest of the class.

"Back to the game, ladies!"

A tall busty blonde threw the ball to Jennifer. "Not so hard this time."

Jennifer caught the ball. Yeah, not so hard this time. Keep your werewolf under control.

§

I awoke to Robert and Rebecca arguing downstairs. The girls wailed. Their cries hurt my ears. Unsure of what was happening, I jumped out of bed, and threw my clothes on, glancing back at the spot where Tristan would sleep if he had been human. Luckily, I could sleep in my bed, one of the few things that made me feel like a human. I was thankful my gift allowed me the ability to walk in the sun. The one thing it kept me from enjoying was the smell and taste of human food. It made me sick to my stomach.

One of the girls wailed again. The high piercing screech made me cringe. I dashed downstairs. The living room to the left of me was empty, so I turned toward the kitchen. The smell of bacon made my stomach churn. I fought the urge to vomit.

The sun lit up the room. The rays bounced off of the white walls and tile floor. A crisp, cool breeze drifted in through the window. The curtains danced about.

Rebecca and Robert looked at me.

"Sorry, I didn't mean to interrupt you two," I said, glancing from one to the other.

Their faces were red and heated from the argument. They stood near the kitchen sink, glaring at one another.

"How convenient of you," Rebecca said, cocking her head.

I didn't appreciate her hostility, but at the same token, I wasn't about to argue with her strictly because she was Robert's wife.

"Listen, I'm sorry…"

If looks could kill, Rebecca's gaze would have done it. Her long dark African curls fell in her face.

"Rebecca…"

"No, it's because of you that we're in this situation," she said, turning toward me. "I warned him, told him not to find you. I explained to him that you would bring bad elements with you…to us…to our family. I can't believe the situation you got us in."

Her voice rose. "I tried to take you in, tried to become friends with you, but no, you make it difficult. You and your immortal lover and friends," she said.

I tried to keep my mouth shut, but now she was crossing the line. She had every right to be upset, but it was not all my fault and she knew it.

"Rebecca, you apologize to my mother right now. That was totally uncalled for, and you know damn well that we've been having problems way before that! Way before my mother came into the picture," he snapped.

My eyes fell on the gun on his uniformed hip. He was a good deputy and he made me a proud mother. I was thankful he was level headed and not rash, like some individuals. Like…Rebecca?

As if reading my mind, she snapped her head around to stare at me. The girls sat at the table, tears drenching their face. They gazed up at me.

"Rebecca, I just want the kids. Please let me take them out of here," I said.

With a weird obscene twist of her mouth, she forced out one word, "Sorry."

There was no sincerity in her voice, but that was fine for the moment. My priority was the children. I was surprised Rebecca hadn't taken them into account for she was a great mother. She always reprimanded the adults when they cursed around the children. So, I was surprised she was arguing with Robert in front of them.

"We'll talk later. I have to go to work," he said, turning away from her.

"Yes, Robert, let's do that. Sometime when you're not always working," she said with sarcasm.

"Come here, girls." I waved the children over.

Hesitantly, they climbed out of their seats but once they were down, they scurried over to me.

"Not now," he said, walking away. "We'll talk later."

"Just keep me in mind whenever you have time. Which is never very much, by the way," she yelled.

I hurried the kids into the living room. "Come on, girls. Let's go watch cartoons."

Robert walked up to me. "I'll see you later, mom."

He hugged me. "Try not to let her get to you. Hell, get out of the house if you can. She is a witch, you know. She may try to cast a spell on you," he replied.

"Yeah, okay," I said, biting my lip.

"I heard that," Rebecca said. She stood in the entryway to the kitchen, her eyes on us.

"I know you did. I meant for you to," he said, rolling his eyes. He kissed me on the cheek. "I'll see you later."

"See you later."

Once he left the house, Rebecca glared at me. Standing at five foot eight, she towered over me by five inches. With her statuesque figure, she was very intimidating, not only on an influential level but also on a female competitive level, regardless of her witchery, which only added to her mystique.

Staring at me, she crossed her arms.

I didn't want any confrontation with her so I changed the subject. "Did Jennifer get off to school already?"

Her eyes narrowed in. "I don't know, I'm not her mother," she spat.

Sighing, I turned. The girls were in front of the television, watching some horrendous girlie cartoon. Since they were focused in on the show, I turned and approached Rebecca on her terms.

I kept my voice low, to avoid the kids listening in on our conversation.

"Listen, Rebecca, I don't want to have any issues with you. You're my daughter-in-law. I'd like to be friends with you, or at least keep a civil relationship with you. So, why don't you back off and act your age! Act like a grown woman."

Her nostrils flared.

I turned to leave the room. No, wait, I had one more thing to say. I faced her one last time.

"By the way, I'm getting tired of the, 'I'm not taking care of your daughter' remarks. We both know I was not able to take care of my children. That was not something that was a choice for me. I'd appreciate a little bit more respect, and your husband is busting his ass working for you while you sit here and take care of the girls," I said, pointing at her. "Try being a little appreciative that you can stay home with your kids. Not every mother can. This is an important time in their lives. They need both of you, and they need to learn from both of you."

With that said, I walked into the hallway.

In the kitchen, Rebecca slammed dishes around in the sink.

I followed the hallway past the staircase to my left, stopping in front of Jennifer's door. My daughter was sixteen and usually got to school on time, but since I was up early, I decided to check on her.

I knocked on her door a couple of times. No answer. Presuming she already left for school, I opened it. As usual, her room was a mess. Glancing around, I caught sight of a crumpled up framed photo. I carefully trudged through her room and picked it up. It was the same photo of me Robert had used during his missing person's search.

I hated Wayne for the time I missed with my children. I hoped that one of these days, my full memory of my life with my children would come back. I despised him for that too. Sighing, I put the frame back on the nightstand.

§

Jennifer walked out of the gym. Raelin followed behind her. Her footsteps echoed on the concrete. More than fifty feet away, the gym door closed behind them. Teenagers spilled out of the doorway.

"Hey!"

Jennifer ignored her.

Raelin hurried to catch up with Jennifer, her long, strawberry blonde ponytail bouncing up and down. Her curls remained resilient, despite her workout in P.E.

"Hey, slow down a minute!" Raelin's voice pierced the air again.

Spinning around, Jennifer balled her hand up into a fist.

Raelin threw her hands up in surrender. "I don't mean any harm. I'm not like those other girls," she said, putting her hands down.

Raelin had observed how Jennifer's speed, power, and strength had grown from the time the school year began until now. She was stronger, powerful, and faster than any girl her age, much more than the typical teenager. Lately, Jennifer was more in tune with her inner being, more like her earthly or spiritual side.

Jennifer was also going through physical changes like weight loss, body toning, and strengthening. Raelin recognized it for what it was. Anybody else would say she was exercising and dieting but Raelin detected something else, for her nose told her so.

She knew about those changes, for she had her own secret and she would gladly keep quiet about Jennifer's as well. Lord knew she didn't want to get on Jennifer's bad side, so she would rather make friends with her and besides, they had a lot in common. After the volleyball incident, Raelin knew her instincts were right.

"Friends?" she asked, extending her hand.

When Jennifer's anger shifted to surprise, Raelin caught the color change in her eyes. Where her eyes had been brown before, a yellowish hue glazed over, and then faded.

Raelin kept her defenses down, for she knew better than to make the stronger creatures angry.

"Yeah, sure," Jennifer said.

Once they shook hands, Raelin smiled and relaxed a little.

"Listen, I'm sorry if I freaked you out. I know you don't have many friends here, but I'd like to be your friend," Raelin said.

A vague smile flashed across Jennifer's face. "Oh, crap! I'm going to be late for class. I have to go," Jennifer said, walking away.

Raelin kept up with her, her legs matching Jennifer's speed.

"I'm going to be late for math. It's my worst subject," Jennifer said.

"I'll race you," Raelin said with a sly grin.

Their eyes met, but only for a second. Jennifer quickened her pace. Raelin matched her speed. Their walk erupted into a run.

As they came to a halt outside one of the buildings, they exchanged looks. Neither of them was sweating, nor breathing hard. The average person would have been winded.

Jennifer raised her eyebrow. "Who are you, anyway?"

Just then, two teenage boys walked by them, so Raelin whispered, "Not now. But I'll show you later and only if you show me yours."

Jennifer recoiled. "Look, I'm not into…"

Raelin laughed. "You're funny. That's not what I'm referring to. I like boys, not girls."

Blushing, Jennifer laughed. "Sorry, I thought—"

"Don't worry about it."

§

"Have you heard from Torrance?" Sheriff Peterson asked. The short burly man sat behind the desk, his arms folded behind his head. The Venetian blinds on the window stood open, illuminating the deputy's bald head.

Robert looked at him. "No. Why, isn't he here?"

"No, he's not. Nobody's heard from him since last night." As the sheriff leaned forward, the chair squeaked beneath his weight. He rested his elbows on the desk. "We sent him out on an investigation just east of the freeway, round about Lake Mary/Mormon Lake Road. It was his last call, and he never checked back in. We sent Ramos in to check it out, but he said he didn't find anything."

Robert removed his hat and glanced up at him. His dark glasses obscured his eyes from the sheriff. He knew the area well, including the pit.

"When did you get the call?"

"Close to midnight."

"I'm going out there." Robert grabbed his keys and headed toward the door.

"Hey!"

Robert stared back at him.

"Do you know where he is?"

Lying, he answered, "No, but I'll look. You said east of the freeway right, off Lake Mary/Mormon Lake Road, right?" He had a sneaky suspicion he knew where Torrance was, but he wasn't eager to find out. Worried, he turned away. His heart raced.

"Yeah," the sheriff replied. Suspiciously, he eyed Robert. "Robert?"

Robert's hand remained on the doorknob. "What?" He peered over his shoulder.

"Let me send somebody with you."

"No, I'll be fine."

"Robert, let me send somebody with you," he urged.

Robert eyed him, warning him to back off.

"Robert, we've had too many killings here lately. The burnt bodies are making me nervous. I'll go with you."

"I'll be fine," Robert said, pushing the door open. The sun filtered in through the door. It awakened the beast within.

The sheriff spoke up again. "Be careful and don't do anything stupid."

Robert rushed toward his car. He wished that he could transform into his alter ego but that was not a good idea. Too many witnesses were nearby. As he peeled out of the parking lot, he reminded himself to keep his emotions in check. Doing anything crazy in this town might alert the townspeople he was onto something dangerous. People would start talking.

And where the hell was Torrance? Fuck, really, the pit? He knew not only where it was but what it was. It was just a dirt pit in the daytime, but at night, it became a fighting arena for the immortal. If Torrance had come out here last night, there's no telling what happened to him. The thought horrified him. Hands glued to the wheel, he drove onward. It didn't take him long to get to the pit.

Pulling off of the road, he drove into the forest, scanning the terrain around it. He rolled his window down and proceeded through the deserted area. The overcast sun beat on him. Nothing stood out. At the base of the small hill, he turned off the ignition.

Robert sat there a moment longer. The scent of two immortals lingered in the air. Their scent overpowered that of anything mortal.

Reluctantly, he got out of the car. A few feet away he found two sets of footprints which led him to the pit. As he followed them, the glint of objects in the dirt caught his attention. Kneeling down, he scooped them up and shook them. Dirt filtered through his fingers to expose the objects in his palm.

Frowning, he inspected them. Then he shoved the police issued nine mm empty casings into his pocket. They most likely belonged to Torrance. After all, who else would it have been? Afraid of what he might find, he cautiously approached the pit. Robert took a deep breath. The hint of a recent fire and the strong aroma of oak permeated the air. He prayed that whatever he would find in the pit was anything but foul.

Two more steps took him to the edge of the pit. His throat locked up. It wasn't the two burnt cars that caught his attention, instead, it was the body that lay in between.

Unfortunately, the pit was a known area for abandoning stolen cars, so he was used to finding burnt and bullet-ridden vehicles in it. What he wasn't used to finding was lifeless bodies, especially those from the sheriff's department. The beast inside of him pulsated with life, fighting to gain control. Mixed emotions rippled through him.

Robert let the creature take over part of his physical being. The werewolf pushed his body forward as he leaped off of the edge, landing in a crouched position next to his best friend. The blond man lay face down. He told himself it wasn't Torrance.

Afraid to accept the inevitable, he inched in toward him, his fingers creeping along the ground. He closed his eyes and forced himself to turn the deputy over.

When he opened them, he stared into his friend's cold dead eyes.

Tears streamed down his face. Disturbing the evidence at the scene of his death was the furthest thing from his mind. He broke down crying, his fingers curling into the material of Torrance's jacket.

"No, no!"

He pulled him up against him, cradling his head. Looking him over for his injuries was the least of his concern. All he wanted was time for his grief.

"No, goddammit, no!" he screamed, his voice echoing within the pit. Tightly, he held his friend against him. Tears spilled onto Torrance's face.

"No, no, no…!" he cried, fighting the beast inside. For the time being, he was able to stifle the creature back, but soon, he wouldn't be able. He buried his face in his friend's shoulder, crying, muddying the dirt that coated the man's body.

§

I spent most of the day away from the house, including Rebecca and the girls. Despite the fact I would have preferred to spend time with the kids, I decided otherwise. My beasts were still adapting to being around the children. My inner wolf was calmer around the kids than my vampire, most likely because the girls were part werewolf too. Regardless, the vampire within me fought to take control when we were together. So, I made the decision to spend less time with them unless I had another immortal nearby. Though Rebecca could cast a spell to refrain me from hurting the girls, we made the decision her spells were our last resort. Everyone, including Tristan, agreed I had to learn to control my beasts.

Instead, I spent my time alone in the woods, hiking the mountainside near our home. It was best I avoided any conflict right now. Besides, I needed time to myself, time to piece together my life and my memories.

§

Jennifer gritted her teeth, hoping the pain would subside. Her abdominal muscles contracted again. Another spasm ripped through her body, causing her to double over in pain.

Groaning, she grabbed the cafeteria table. It hurt so bad she wanted to cry. What the hell…? She hadn't done anything that strenuous.

Volleyball came easy to her, so she knew it wasn't that.

The piece of hamburger she was eating lodged in her throat. Choking, she grabbed at her neck.

From behind, a young man wrapped his arms around her midsection, yanking her to her feet. A fist contracted hard just below her sternum about five times. A chunk of hamburger flew from her mouth, clearing her airway.

As he set her down, her legs wobbled. She half ass leaned back against the guy. A deep voice boomed over her shoulder.

"Are you alright?" he asked. The large teenage cowboy stared down at her, his brownish hair sticking out from beneath his beige cowboy hat. He had large pleasant eyes and a friendly face.

Jennifer's eyes brightened at the sight of him.

A cheesy grin spread across his lips, revealing his bright teeth, which stood out against his tanned skin.

Oh, was he cute. No, not cute…hot! Jennifer gazed down at his body. With his farmer's tan and his large frame, she was sure he tended to his family's farm. Regardless, she returned his warm smile, alluring him with a flirtatious glint in her eye. Her eyes fell on his broad shoulders and powerful muscles.

Although he was muscular, his muscles were broad and large, and not so defined as some of the teenage boys. The muscles beneath his t-shirt flexed, stretching the cotton fabric that was tight against his body. His jeans barely covered his hips. The waistband of his boxers protruded over them, exposing his sloppy side. But did she really care? No, she didn't.

He leaned down, his stubbly beard brushing against her face. "Are you all right?"

"Yes, I'm okay. Thank you," she muttered. Spasms ripped through her stomach again. She tried to hide the pain by biting her lip.

"You don't look all right. I think you need to sit down." He held her hand as she sat down. Then, he took a seat next to her.

"Thank you," she said. She tried to spin around but his long legs restricted her from turning around.

"Sorry, my legs get in the way sometimes," he laughed. The cowboy spread his legs further apart so she could move around them. Another pain ripped through her, only, this time, the gut wrenching pain ripped not only through her abdomen but through her groin.

"Is something wrong? I don't have a hole in my pants, do I?" he asked. He pulled his jeans tight across his groin, searching for a hole.

Jennifer latched onto the top inner portion of her thigh. What the hell was wrong with her? She blushed, the heat rising up as she finally understood what was happening. The female werewolf in her was responding to the cowboy.

"I have to go," she said, grabbing her purse.

As she stood, he looked up at her. "What's wrong? Did I say something to offend you? If I did I'm sorry!"

She ran out of the cafeteria, her arm around her midsection.

Seconds later Jennifer stood in the bathroom. The dirty white porcelain tile on the restroom walls and floor made her gag. Toilet paper, spilled make-up, and feminine product packaging lay on the floor.

How she hated coming in here. It was disgusting. She refused to use the school bathrooms unless absolutely necessary, and if she did, it was primarily to fix her make-up, but even that was a chore. Notes and stupid comments were written in lipstick and eyeliner on the mirrors. The newest comment, *Mrs. Reddick is a bitch,* stood out in bold red lipstick. Sighing, she rolled her eyes.

The faint yet apparent scent of someone's menstrual cycle lingered in the room. Gagging, she held her breath, turned and examined herself in the mirror. Her cotton shirt rippled against her stomach like a small tidal wave. She pulled her shirt up and stared at it. As she went through hormonal changes, she shed some of her fat. The abdominal muscles were becoming well-defined and prominent since her first transformation into her beastly alter ego.

Her brother had warned her about this. Since her inner werewolf's metabolism was picking up, she would need to consume more food to exceed the required calorie intake. This worried her. She didn't want to hunt and feed on the wildlife, much less, people like her brother did but it was inevitable.

Footsteps entered the room followed by a teenage girl laughing.

Jennifer yanked her shirt down and gazed into the mirror. The rounded wall behind her blocked the view of the entrance.

Michelle, dressed in her cheerleader uniform, walked around the corner.

Jennifer stared at Michelle in the mirror. Dammit, she muttered to herself. Why her? Why now?

Michelle sneered, her face, nose, and eyes bruised from the volleyball.

"Well, look who we have here, the little bitch who tried to break my nose."

Three more cheerleaders followed Michelle. Their feet scraped against the floor.

Jennifer rolled her eyes. Hesitantly, she turned to face them. The painful ripples intensified. The tension between her and Michelle was unavoidable. It was time to leave, hopefully, with the avoidance of the bitches. Jennifer moved in their direction.

Michelle straightened up.

One day, she would have to take Michelle down, but not now, for she feared her werewolf's reaction to the situation.

As she and Michelle came face to face, several girls walked into the bathroom, bumping into the cheerleaders and knocking them off balance. As the cheerleaders gazed back at the newcomers, Jennifer took advantage of it. She ran out without a fight.

§

Wayne stood before me, his lips against my ear. "You know I'll always love you and I will always protect you and the kids."

Closing my eyes, I buried my face into his neck. Yes, he was mine. He was the only one for me, and he would always stand by my side.

I was both right and wrong about that. Wrong, in the fact, he would always be by my side. Yet he would be the only man to father my children.

His goatee scratched my face, leaving a rash I would awaken to ninety minutes from now.

"Make love to me."

He hesitated. "But the children?"

"I put them to bed an hour ago. They're asleep, we're not. Make love to me."

He grinned and nipped at my ear.

"Make love to me, Wayne," I moaned.

Teeth nipped at my ear again, too hard this time. "Ouch, that hurt."

"Sorry, you know how I get," he groaned.

I pulled back. My excitement turned to fear. A chill shot down my spine. I stared into my husband's eyes. The bedroom scene shifted to a moment in my prison cell when Wayne stood over me, blood dripping from his lips.

I had drifted off to sleep in my favorite spot on the mountainside. Now, the sun slipped behind the mountains, leaving a fiery crest just at the peak of it.

My mind drifted back to the dream. They were becoming more

vivid. At this point, I believed they were memories, not false visions. Above me, the tree leaves rustled. The breeze caressed my face, brushing my hair gently against my skin. Dusk settled down upon the earth. Then, I sensed the tension.

Something was wrong. I needed to get home. I bolted to my feet and ran, the darkness following close behind. My feet pounded across the rocky terrain as the wind whistled past me.

Within seconds I was home. As I opened the door, voices filled the air. I stood in the brightly lit room, the eyes of my family upon me. Tears streaked their faces.

Robert and Rebecca sat cradling one another with two of the girls on their laps and the other laying against them. Jennifer sat on the opposite end of the couch, her nose red. Tears streaked her face.

"What's wrong?" I asked, worried something might have happened between my lover and my family. Then I remembered he was not awake, not yet.

Tristan stirred upstairs. After the recent vampire attack, he had been spending his nights with us to help protect my family and our home.

I half expected Robert to be the first to speak up, instead, it was Rebecca.

"Torrance is dead," she said.

Torrance? That was…

"Robert's best friend, his partner," Jennifer said.

Oh, yes, Torrance. I remembered him.

"Oh my God, Robert, I am so sorry," I said. I sat beside him on the arm of the couch, and took him in my arms. I wanted to take his pain away.

Robert had spoken very highly of him. He clutched onto me, his tear-streaked face against my shoulder. My heart ached. If only there was something I could do to help him.

Just then, I detected another presence, Tristan. He stood on the stairs, his hands in his pockets.

"Robert, I am so sorry. Torrance was a good man," I said, trying to remain strong for him. Tears leaked from my eyes.

"He was…" he muttered, "my best friend."

Tristan rested his hand on Robert's shoulder. "My condolences, Robert."

Now, who would have thought a vampire and a werewolf could not be exchanging friendly words.

Robert gazed up at him. "Thank you," he said.

I peeled his tear streaked hair from his forehead. He had taken a shower, yet I detected another scent on him, possibly Torrance.

"No problem, Robert," Tristan said. "A man of valor deserves a friend like you, somebody who's been willing to put his life on the line for him, to protect him, to serve him, to trust him with his heart and not to betray the code of ethics in which he lives by."

Where the hell did that come from? I glanced up at Tristan. Oddly, he was out of place, as if he were not himself. Normally, his eyes were an ocean blue, but now, they were darker, almost opal. I sensed a change in him.

As if sensing the same thing, Robert sat up. He shot me a puzzled look before thanking Tristan one last time and then leaned against Rebecca.

Tristan sat down on the recliner, his eyes shifting to Rebecca, who consoled her husband. Then he glanced over at Jennifer, who sat solemn on the corner of the couch, the girls now on her lap.

Katie sat close to her mother, holding her hand.

"And you, are you okay Jennifer?" Tristan asked her.

"I'm fine. Thank you for asking," Jennifer answered.

Robert's eyes were bloodshot.

"What happened to him, Robert?" I asked.

Robert broke down crying.

THE PREDATOR AND THE PREY

"Hey Yolanda, bring me another beer!" Bryce yelled. Orange embers danced up from the burning wood and into his face. He recoiled, almost knocking his chair over.

"Bryce, I told you not to put too much wood on the fire," Gloria said.

The wind blew her dark hair around her face. As she brushed it out of her eyes, the fiery smoke wafted up. Her eyes burnt. As she rubbed them, a pair of dark skinned masculine arms reached around her chair and grabbed her from behind. She screamed.

In a heavy Spanish accent, Carlos whispered, "And I told you to not get so close to the fire if he did."

She gazed back at him. "Don't scare me like that."

"Sorry baby," he said, kissing her. Carlos grabbed her chair and pulled her away from the fire.

"You're warm," she said.

"Oh, you're cold, baby. Do you want me to get your coat?"

"Please," she said, batting her eyelashes at him.

"Woman, don't even try that. God knows you're not innocent," he said, walking away.

Gloria turned to stare back into the fire, but the awkward way Bryce was sitting caught her attention. His head lolled backward, his eyes closed.

"You alive over there?" she asked, jokingly.

The wind blew his shoulder length blonde hair about his face. He didn't move.

Where the hell was Yolanda with their beer?

"Hey Yolanda, can you bring me a beer, too? I'm out." She threw her empty can into the fire.

Gloria was thankful Yolanda and Bryce had brought their parents RV so nobody had to sleep on the cold, hard, rocky ground. Another cool breeze swept through camp. A couple of the empty cans that lay near Bryce blew across the ground.

Gloria glanced over at him. Was he sleeping? Usually, it took a few beers to knock him out. She was sure he hadn't had that many yet. It was unlike him to fall asleep by the fire, especially after the hot embers hit him in the face.

Behind her, Carlos moved about in the truck. As she listened to him, she leaned her head back and stared up at the sky. The moon and stars hid beneath the clouds.

"I really hate how dark it gets out here. It's kind of creepy, you know," she said, wrapping her arms around her thin frame.

"Hey, Bryce, are you awake over there?" His feet were too close to the fire. The glowing streaks slithered out further along his feet.

"Bryce? Hey, you're going to catch fire."

He didn't move.

"Bryce!" She stood up.

The can he held fell to the ground.

Damn him! Gloria hated it when he played jokes on her. He had played too many on Yolanda to fool her anymore, so Gloria had become his secondary prey.

"Hey, asshole…" She kicked his foot away from the fire.

Again, he didn't move.

Then, she leaned over and shook his arm. It was cool to the touch.

"Dammit, enough with the jokes." She gazed back at the RV. "Yolanda, tell your boyfriend to stop playing around! It isn't funny anymore!"

Why the hell wasn't Yolanda answering her? Standing, she yelled, "Yolanda, tell your fucking boyfriend to knock it off!"

Her eyes drifted over to Carlos, who stood in the shadows, struggling with a bag by the truck.

"Carlos!" Gloria peered over her shoulder at Bryce, half expecting him to leap up and scare her. "Carlos!"

"Woman, what are you screaming about?" he yelled, his voice faint in the wind. The ferocity of the wind picked up. It blew the chair over that she had been sitting in.

"Dammit," she said, turning toward the chair. As she bent over to pick it up, a heavy gust of wind blew it further into the night behind Bryce.

Gloria stared into the heavily wooded area surrounding them. It was dark and too quiet. A lump formed in her throat. Turning to get Carlos, she ran into the chair Bryce was seated in, and fell over it, her face in his lap. As she pushed herself up, Bryce bolted upright, shouting in her face.

She screamed, falling over backward.

Bryce's drunken laughter echoed in the night. Then, Carlos ran over, grabbed him and pulled him to his feet.

"What the hell is going on out here?" Yolanda stood in the doorway of the RV, beers in hand. "I was in the fucking bathroom!" The wind blew her blonde hair around her face.

"What the fuck, man…! What the hell is wrong with you?" Carlos screamed. Fingers entwined in his friend's shirt, he yanked Bryce toward him. "Do you have no respect for my woman?"

"I was fucking kidding, dude! Now, get your hands off of me," he snapped. He pushed on Carlos' chest but he didn't move.

With his hands still on Bryce, he spat, "That's my woman. She doesn't like it when you do that shit."

Bryce puffed his chest out. "You want to go? Is that it? You want to hit me? Go ahead…!"

Then, Carlos punched him in the nose. Bryce retaliated by hitting him in the face. The fight escalated.

"No! Stop it, you two!" Gloria yelled.

"Stop it!"

Yolanda ran out of the RV, her foot missing the second step. She crashed to the rocky ground, dropping the beer cans. One of the cans struck a rock, spewing alcohol. A gust of wind picked up the dirt and spray of alcohol. The mixture burned her eyes prior to the sand blinding her. Groaning, she rubbed her eyes.

Gloria scrambled to get to her feet. "Stop!"

Bryce fell over backward into Gloria, pinning her to the ground. Blood gushed from his nose.

Yolanda bolted to her feet. Then something moved in the darkness.

A winged creature emerged from the brush. The oddly deformed dragon struck her with its dark leather scabbed wing. It sent her flying backward into the RV, tearing a hole in the side of it. Twisted metal shrieked in the night.

"No!" Bryce screamed.

Carlos stood with his back to the creature. As he turned to face it, the dragon's tail whipped around. The pointed end punctured his chest. Blood sprayed the campground.

Gloria and Bryce screamed.

Bryce bolted to his feet. "Come on!"

Her gaze fell on the RV. Did Yolanda survive the horrid attack? She wanted to go check on her but Bryce grabbed her hand and ran, pulling her alongside him.

"Move!"

The dragon tossed the dead man's body into the fire. Then, it peered up in the direction they had run.

As they ran into the forest, Bryce let go of her hand. Desperately, she rubbed her eyes. She couldn't see for shit because of the dirt that had gotten in them back at camp.

Fuck! She stopped and rubbed them, trying to get the dirt out of them.

"What the hell are you doing?" he yelled.

In the near distance, the dragon stared back at them.

"I can't see for shit!" she said, stumbling forward. Blindly, she searched in the darkness, and then fell on her face.

Bryce ran toward her. The dragon came after them. He barely grabbed her arm when the dragon buried its talons in him.

"No!" he screamed.

She was next! Heart racing, Gloria ran deeper into the forest, not knowing where she was going.

§

I hunkered down in the brush, naked. The thirst for blood overpowered me. My transformation was taking effect, the muscle mass enlarging, defining my feminine body.

A whiff of blood came from the south. Then, the stench of charred remains filled the air. It aroused my curiosity. I would investigate it but not now, my hunger was more important.

I slinked out of the brush in my werewolf form. My stomach cramped up again.

Oh, yes, it was feeding time.

§

The ground beneath Gloria gave way, throwing her down a rocky ravine. Bryce's blood coated her, dirt sticking to the mess, muddying her skin and clothes. As she tried to regain her footing, the bone in her ankle cracked, tossing her to the ground. She fell and struck her head on a rock.

Gloria came to a standstill next to a small creek. Blood erupted from the open wound. The pain in her ankle grew. Weak and scared, she was afraid to move, fearful she would catch the dragon's attention. Maybe if she remained still, it wouldn't find her.

A distant splash in the creek caught her attention. Only it came from the opposite direction from where the dragon was. Weakly, she lifted her head. Though the werewolf's splash had been far-off, it now stood in front of her. Her jaw dropped.

Its canine face lowered, saliva dripping from its mouth.

Face to face with it, she lowered her gaze. All she wanted to do was bury her face in the creek and pray that it would go away. Something else splashed in the nearby distance. She presumed it was the dragon. It moved away, its footsteps softening. Maybe it found something else to pursue.

In the meantime, here she lay, prey to the werewolf above her. Tears welled up.

The werewolf growled. Its saliva dripped as it inched in toward her.

Trembling, she gripped onto a rock underwater. It was her only weapon. Rock in hand, she spun around, hitting it on the side of the head but it didn't stop the beast, instead, it latched onto her jugular. She lifted her arm to swing at it, but she was weak. Her arm fell to the ground, her life draining from her body.

§

"Put the word out, we need another man," Special Agent Lagunas demanded.

Tristan gazed back at him, cringing. "How many is that now?"

"Fourteen, way too fucking many," Lagunas spat. In the dark hallway, he stopped, turned and stared at Tristan. "We have to kill them. Even with the rogue experiments, we don't have these issues. We might lose one or two agents tops, but not fourteen."

"Yeah, you're right," Tristan said, folding his arms over his chest.

Tristan thought about the special agents who had watched over Crystal during her fighting days. Those men and women were dead, their lives taken by some experimental paranormal creatures.

He stared up at the red beacon light which hung from the ceiling. It was the only light that lit up the darkened hallways.

Lagunas leaned in toward Tristan, his face inches away. "I don't care what we have to do or who we have to get. They need to be killed. Get some help, Tristan. I know you have connections," he said, tapping Tristan's chest.

Tristan unfolded his arms and straightened up, his eyes widening at the thought of his brotherhood. Oh, yeah, he knew who Lagunas was referring to.

"Oh no, not…"

Lagunas rubbed his chin. "Yes, I'm talking about your men. They may not be agents, but I don't give a shit. You're the one I count on most. Get your men. I know they're sloppy, but that's all right. We can always hide the evidence," he sneered. "It's not like it hasn't been done before."

"I left that life behind me. Do you know what's going to happen if I call them out?"

Lagunas' eyes darkened. "I don't give a fuck," he snapped, pointing at Tristan. As he spoke, his lips parted, revealing abnormally sharp teeth, his chiseled features deepening. "Get your men!"

"Lagunas, it's not just that…,"

"I know what it is and I don't give a fuck! You get Sabol and his men out here. I don't care what issues you two have had before, you're going to fix them and you're going to get his help. This issue needs to be dealt with, and now," he said. "And while you're at it, get your lover and her son to help. I'm sure they can do the job. Hell, they might not be as sloppy as your men."

Tristan's eyes narrowed in. "She's not helping."

"Yes, she is."

"She doesn't work for you and she's not going to."

"Don't push me, Tristan. She needs a job and this one would be perfect," he snapped. "She might even be better than you."

Tristan's heart raced, his eyes darkening.

"Ah, did I hit a nerve, my man," he said, his beady eyes focusing on Tristan's. "You shouldn't let your emotions get in the way of your job. Too many agents have lost their lives, and even their jobs, because of it.

She may have better control of hers than you have of yours. Do you love her?"

Tristan remained silent.

"Does she love you?"

No answer.

Lagunas raised his eyebrows. "Or are you two just fuck buddies?"

The heat in Tristan's face rose. Fuming, Tristan snapped, "That's none of your business."

"Not that I'm opposed to fuck buddies, especially after a bad day. It just makes the sex even more exhilarating, doesn't it Tristan?" He cocked his head. "Angry sex, isn't that what they're calling it now? Regardless, I have my ways. Don't make me use them. Keep in mind that if I don't use them, the big guy will," he said with an evil grin.

Tristan didn't like it. In a split second, he grabbed the man by his throat and slammed him into the steel wall. The loud boom echoed down the corridor.

His dark pupils turned red. "I'll fucking kill you if you go near her," he hissed.

Lagunas laughed. "Really Tristan? Do you think your threats scare me?" He pushed Tristan off of him, throwing him into the wall behind him.

Straightening his shirt, Lagunas continued. "I suggest you get your men, your girlfriend, and her son to get the job done," he stated, tucking his shirt into his pants. "They'll be paid well. If you decide otherwise, you better watch your back. Or it may be Crystal we send to kill you, without even her knowledge. I've done it before. You better think about that."

Again, Tristan hissed. He could kill him, but if he did, he knew the consequences. There was no escaping the clutches of the man in charge. The big man would send a rogue posse after him, Crystal and her family. They would be killed. Unfortunately, killing him wasn't an alternative, however, he, Sabol and his brotherhood could retaliate. Those consequences would put everybody's life in jeopardy. He had others to think about, though, which included Crystal's extended family—Rebecca and the children.

Tristan started down the hallway.

"By the way, I like that hot little thing in their house," Lagunas said.

Tristan stopped and glared at the man. Oh, how he wanted to destroy Lagunas.

"You know that hot little teenager? Mm, she'd taste mighty good…"

Tristan shoved him into the wall, driving an elbow into his throat. "You touch one member of her family, and I'll rip you to shreds. Trust me, the big man won't find you because nothing will be left."

Lagunas sneered. "Just get your fucking men, your woman, and her son."

Tristan's fist connected with his face.

"Next time, you're dead." With that, Tristan walked away, fading out of the dimly lit corridor.

§

Scowling, Lagunas wiped his hand over his mouth. Blood adorned his hand. Tristan was a motherfucker when he was pissed, but that was what Lagunas wanted out there in the field. The agency needed Tristan and his brotherhood. They were a force to be reckoned with, but Lagunas was willing to put up with it to get the job done.

§

Robert sat across from the sheriff.

"We're going to miss him, Robert. We all loved him and cared about him." Two puffs on the cigar lit up the opposite end. He didn't care about the non-smoking policy, especially now.

Robert leaned back in his chair, his eyes bloodshot. He didn't want to discuss Torrance, yet it was inevitable. Better to get it over with.

"Thank you," he said, looking away.

"Robert, you know his family. I'll let you talk to them."

"Not a problem." The tears were building up again.

"We'll help with whatever we can…"

"Yeah, I got it." Let's just get this over with.

"Robert, stop being short with me, I know the pain you're in."

Robert looked at him. "Look, I'm sorry, but I really don't want to talk about it."

"Listen, the Medical Examiner's office and I want an autopsy done. We need the approval from his family. Since you're practically his family, I'd like you to talk to them."

Robert stared at him. "Autopsy?"

"Yes."

"I thought it was a clear-cut case."

The sheriff looked him over. "I know you don't want to deal with this," he said, sighing. "Listen, I've put Barracus on the case."

"Bullshit!" Robert exclaimed. "He's my friend, my partner, goddammit…!"

"And that's the exact reason you're not working on it."

"Fuck you! You're going to put me back on it."

"No I'm not Robert."

"Goddammit, yes you are."

The sheriff leaned forward, his finger pointed at Robert. "Robert, you're a good deputy and a great man, but no, I'm not. This case is too personal for you."

Robert glared at him, pissed. "I have the right to work this."

"No, you don't and as of now, consider yourself on leave." The sheriff stood up.

Robert's jaw dropped. "What? Why? I don't want to take leave."

"Stop it, Robert. It's standard procedure."

Sighing, he looked away. "So, what's up with the autopsy?"

A puff of smoke escaped the sheriff's lips. As the sheriff sat down, the chair squeaked beneath him. His potted face wrinkled beneath his thick, dark eyebrows.

"Due to the condition of his body, we're requesting an autopsy, plain and simple."

Robert glanced at him. Of course, the sheriff wasn't going to say anything. It agitated the werewolf inside, pushing his adrenaline to pump faster. He needed to calm himself down before his alter ego decided to reveal itself.

"We all know it was an animal, Sheriff."

"We're aware of that. There's another issue, though. So, an autopsy does need to be completed."

"Yes, sir," he melted back against the chair. "I'd like to apologize for snapping at you, Sheriff."

"Accepted." The sheriff snuffed out his cigar.

"Can I request something, though?"

The sheriff's gruff features hardened. "And what would that be?"

"Can you please not put me on leave?"

The sheriff looked up at him. "Robert, it's quite apparent that you need some time off. You'll be compensated."

"No, sir, I'll be fine. I promise." He sounded like a child. Dammit.

"Deputy…?"

"Sir, I'm asking you to please let me work. I'll hurt worse if I'm left alone to grieve. I can't do it. I'll go off the deep end if I do." Great, that sounded worse.

The sheriff stared at him. "You're already having personal issues at home."

"Even more reason I need to work. Sir, I need to stay busy. The more time I spend doing nothing, the more time I spend grieving and worrying about everything. Please, Sheriff. I have to stay busy. It's how I deal with things. I'm not the same as everybody else." Boy, wasn't that the truth?

Silent, the sheriff stared at him, studying him, rolling his snuffed out cigar between his fingers.

Robert took a deep breath.

"I can't have you fighting back or snapping. There's a reason for this procedure."

"I understand."

The sheriff looked him over.

"And besides, you just said you wanted me to talk to his family. I can do that. I'm like a second son to them."

Robert's mind shifted back to the Medical Examiner. He needed to get his friend's body out of there before they cut into him. The last thing the mortals needed to know is that vampires and werewolves did exist. It was best it remained hidden.

"Fine, but if you do one thing out of context, you're on leave. And I'm getting you a new partner."

"Sheriff…"

"Don't argue with me, Deputy. If I'm going to let you work, I'm going to place you with somebody. Besides, they may help keep you sane while you're working."

"Yes, sir." With that, Robert shut up.

"I already have somebody in mind for you. Peterson's leaving us and we've been interviewing for his replacement."

Robert took a deep breath. "Where's Peterson going?"

"He's moving back to Nebraska come the end of next week. So, I'm going to partner his replacement with you. I'll find somebody else to replace him. Besides, I think Deputy Miller would be good for you."

"That's fine, sir. I'll partner up with the man. Just send him my way when he comes on. I'll show him the ropes."

Robert stood up.

"Good." The sheriff smiled. "On that note, you make sure you treat her with the same respect you did Torrance."

Robert's eyes widened. "You're teaming me up with a woman?"

Robert and Torrance received the more violent crimes, so for him to team Robert up with a woman meant one of two things. One, that Robert was going to have to worry about a woman dealing with some of the morbid issues Robert was already used to. Or, the sheriff was going to restrict the cases Robert was going to receive. Either way, Robert wasn't happy about it.

"Yes, I am. I think she'll be good for you."

Robert approached the desk. "Sir, I don't think that's a wise idea."

The sheriff leaned in toward him. "And why do you say that, Robert?"

"I've been the one working most of the killings around here, and I'm not sure a new deputy, or a female, for that matter, can handle the shit I've seen."

The sheriff scowled at him. "Robert, do I need to put you on leave or not?"

Robert regretted his remark. "No, sir."

"Then go back to work. I'll let you know when she's ready." The sheriff gazed down at the papers on his desk.

"Yes, sir."

§

Her blood coated the inside of my stomach. It was invigorating. As I scrambled up the side of the ravine, the smell of burnt flesh lingered in the air. I followed the scent. Not only did I smell blood and burnt remains, but I also detected something else, something different.

Not too far away, I found the remains of a man ripped to shreds. The meat was torn partially from the scattered body parts. Something powerful had torn him apart. I sensed it was not a vampire or werewolf. As I looked the situation over, the illumination from a campfire caught my attention.

Cautiously, I approached the camp, unsure if the creature that destroyed the man I found was nearby. The remains of a man lay burning atop the fire. It was his charred remains the wind had carried in the night.

Chairs and beer cans lay scattered on the ground as if something had attacked the camp. Then, I noticed the RV. A gaping bloody hole was torn in the side of it. Twisted metal exposed a small section inside of the RV where a bloody body lay visible inside.

The wind blew the fire in my direction, warming my right flank. I continued past it, slunk up to the hole, and gazed inside. The woman wasn't dead, instead, she lay there, trying to breathe. Twisted metal was stuck in her stomach, pumping blood from the wound.

Stealthily and quietly, I jumped inside the RV. As I crept up around her and the jagged metal, she coughed, choked, and coughed again. Then her eyes widened at the sight of me. She tried to scream but couldn't. More blood filled her mouth, choking her.

Growling, I lapped up the blood where it pooled around her.

The thick piece of metal kept her confined to the floor but as I moved in closer to her, she flinched.

Then, I attacked.

ADMIRERS

The next day, Jennifer and Raelin sat at the cafeteria table eating lunch.

"So, did you see that hot guy in dance?" Raelin raised a single eyebrow at her.

"Oh, yeah he's hot," she agreed.

A masculine hand patted Jennifer on the shoulder, catching her by surprise. It must be the cowboy. Raelin confirmed his presence by grinning and winking at her. With that in mind, Jennifer turned to face him.

"So, how are you feeling today?" the cowboy asked.

Her face flushed and her eyes gleamed with delight. "I'm feeling much better. Thank you."

"Good. I apologize I didn't get to introduce myself the other day. I'm Tyler. What's your name?" he asked, offering his hand.

Jennifer accepted his hand. "Jennifer and this is Raelin."

"Hi," Raelin said, shaking his hand.

"Nice to meet you," he said, glancing at his friends. "I should probably go. The guys are going to give me shit if I'm not over there pretending to be a womanizer like them. Maybe we can talk later when the guys aren't over there acting like asses."

Raelin and Jennifer glanced over at the table. One cowboy had his lips puckered and his arms wrapped around his chest, imitating a make-out session. Once the girl's gaze met his, he stopped and straightened up. The other cowboys laughed and pointed their fingers at him.

"You got caught, asshole," one laughed.

"Oh shit," Raelin said, looking them over.

One of the cowboys winked at her making her blush.

"Yes, that would be nice," Jennifer said.

"Hey, asshole, get over here!" one of his friends yelled.

The girls glanced back at Tyler.

"Nice," Raelin said. "They're a wild bunch, aren't they?"

"Just a little," he replied. "Sorry about that." He turned back to Jennifer. "Listen, I'll have to catch you later. Hope you don't mind," he said.

"No, not at all," Jennifer replied.

"Thanks," he muttered.

"See you later."

Walking away, he kept his eyes on her, flashed her another smile, tipped his hat, and tripped over somebody's bag. He nearly fell to the floor, but somehow regained his footing. Then, he winked and walked away.

Raelin stared at her. "Who the hell is that?"

"I really don't know. I just met him the other day."

They glanced at the table where his friends sat. They were giving him shit for almost falling in front of her.

Jennifer dug into her food. "He happened to walk by while I was eating. Good thing he did, though, because I choked on my food. He kind of saved my life," she said, blushing.

"He and his friends are kind of cute, in a country boy kind of way." Raelin took a swig of her drink and wiggled her eyebrows. "You'll need to introduce me to them."

"I don't know them. Heck, I barely know him." She took a bite of her apple. "And he's not cute. He's hot."

§

Later that day, after changing their clothes, Jennifer and Raelin ran into the dance room. The rapid drum and bass beat of a hip hop song boomed loudly. Half expecting the teacher to yell at them, Jennifer glanced around. The teacher was nowhere to be seen so they ran across the wooden floor, and threw their backpacks to the side. The backpacks slid across the floor and hit the wall as the girls joined the class at the mirrors.

As they drew in a deep breath and propped their legs on the ballet bar, the new student walked in.

He was about six foot and had blonde hair that hung loosely around his face.

He glanced around the room, brushing his hair back with his hand.

Raelin was right, the new guy was hot, and he was also not in Jennifer's league.

Then, his gaze fell on hers. Oh, shit. Had she been staring? She looked away. After a few seconds, she glanced back at him. He was still staring at her. She blushed. She had been staring, she was sure of it.

Raelin leaned into her. "My, are you popular today. I think he likes you."

Jennifer whispered, "Shut up."

Raelin smiled and waved at him.

Jennifer's face turned red. "Oh my God, I can't believe you just did that." She was unable to look at him anymore, instead, she stared at her friend. "You bitch."

"All right, everybody, line up!" the teacher announced.

As everybody took their positions on the dance floor, Jennifer's eyes fell on him again. Their eyes met, and her mouth fell open.

Smiling, he turned to face the front.

Raelin pushed Jennifer's chin up to close her mouth. "Don't let your mouth hang open. He's watching you in the mirror," she said.

Jennifer clamped her lips tight. He could easily attract any of the girls in the room, but he's looking at me. She peered up at him in the mirror.

He took advantage of the mirror, and slicked his hair back, his eyes casually falling on her. Music bellowed out of the speakers.

Jennifer's hips gyrated with the music. As she danced across the floor, her eyes remained on him. The heavy smell of testosterone filled the room. It was strong, masculine, and penetrating.

As she spun across the floor, she became dizzy. Jennifer turned her attention to the mirror and gazed at her reflection. The lights in the room flickered on and off. Despite the electrical disturbance, she stayed focused on her moves.

Voices carried through the room, throwing some of the dancers off-balance.

The teacher moved in front of the mirror, blocking her reflection.

"Keep it going! Keep it going!" she said, her eyes focused on Jennifer.

"Think of this as a test. If you can continue to dance while there is an electrical issue, you can do this on stage!"

The teacher walked toward the new guy. "James, you're doing great! Keep it up! Michelle, get that leg higher." She turned toward Jennifer. "Jennifer, you're looking good, keep it up!"

As Jennifer danced toward the side of the room, Michelle and James danced toward the center of the floor.

"Michelle, you need to jump higher, otherwise, James is not going to catch you! You are going to fall on your face! Higher now! Try that again!"

She attempted the jump again, her long lean legs sprinting a little higher in the air but it wasn't enough.

"You need to jump higher!"

"Sorry, Miss Ellis, my muscles are tight. I didn't stretch out enough," Michelle said, resuming her position before the jump.

Miss Ellis frowned. "Again, Michelle!"

Michelle backed up further. She ran, leaping higher and spreading her legs wider than she did before. This time, James caught her, one taut arm wrapped around her midsection, his other arm pulling her leg back, stretching it out, straining the muscle.

She screamed.

As he released her leg, she curled up in a ball in his arms and cried. Carefully, he set her down.

"I'm sorry, Miss Ellis, I didn't mean to…" he stammered.

If Michelle would have stretched out before class, then maybe she wouldn't have hurt herself, Jennifer thought. She hid her smile.

Miss Ellis ran to Michelle's aid. "What's wrong?"

"I…my legs are cramping up," she cried, tears streaming down her face.

James and Miss Ellis helped to turn her over on the hardwood floor. "My knee hurts now. Oh god, it hurts."

James was tentative to Michelle's leg. Oh, how Jennifer wished he was attentive to her needs.

Then he picked Michelle up, a horrendous groan escaping her lips. Her limp leg hung awkwardly over his arm as he headed toward the door.

Everybody stared after him.

"Everybody practice your moves for now. I'll be right back," Miss Ellis said, following him out of the door.

"Well, that was interesting," Raelin said. "I kind of wish I was her right now."

Jennifer replied, "Yeah, I guess so."

"What do you mean you guess so?" she asked, glancing at Jennifer.

Jennifer stared at the door. "Yeah, kind of."

"Bullshit, you wish you were in his arms. Don't tell me you didn't think about that," Raelin blurted out. "By the way, what the hell was that, dancing with your eyes closed and shit? Who the hell can do that without bumping into something?"

"I've been practicing."

"Bullshit." Raelin leaned back against the wall, sliding down it to the floor.

Jennifer followed her lead, along with a few other students. The smell of sweat hung in the air.

"What are you doing later?" Raelin asked.

"I have some homework I need to get done. After that, I don't know," she said, draping her arm over her knee.

"Yeah, what is it?"

"Geometry. I can't stand that class."

"You need some help with it?"

"No, I think I got it."

"Are you sure?" Raelin asked. "We can go to a movie before you do it."

"Yeah, we'll see."

"Fuck it, come on, let's go after the dance," Raelin said, perking up, her eyes glistening in the light.

"I want to see that new vampire movie. Then, maybe you can stay the night at my house? Or better yet, maybe I can stay at yours? What do you say?"

Jennifer frowned. "I don't know about that."

"Oh, why not?" she pouted.

"Well, my family…"

"I'd like to meet them. Besides, I have something I want to show you later. Oh, come on, Jennifer?"

She smacked her in the arm.

"It's really cool," she snickered. "But I can't show you until later."

Jennifer was worried her brother, mother or Tristan might want Raelin for dinner, literally.

"Let me talk to my mom, all right?"

"You got it."

It satisfied Raelin for the moment.

§

"Girls, knock it off!" Rebecca screamed. She threw her arms forward, freezing the children in place. Their eyes peered up at her, their bodies frozen, each in a running position.

"I just need some peace and quiet. You all need to listen to me. Once I'm done with you, you are all going to play nice and quiet. Daddy is not here, so I need you to calm down," she said, her thoughts drifting to Tristan who slept upstairs in Crystal's room.

Tristan had to be the reason for the children's extreme sense of anxiety and energy. They didn't use to be this energetic until he arrived.

"I really can't deal with this anymore," she muttered. She freed the kids from their frozen position.

The girls fell to the floor, laughing.

"It's not funny. Momma's tired. Come on, let's go to the park. You can wear yourselves out there."

VISITORS

Harley engines roared on the darkened highway. Their groans echoed through the forest that surrounded it. Dark threatening clouds loomed overhead as rain pelted down on the bikers who invaded the town.

Geared up in black leather and bearing the mark of the reaper, the Hell's Changelings rode through the night. The lullaby of howling wolves put the bikers at ease as the wind ripped through their hair. Through dark glasses, they gazed out at the lonesome highway.

§

Robert knocked on the door of the country cottage. Oh, how he wished he didn't have to do this. He shook his jacket to get the excess rain off of it when the door opened.

An older woman in her fifties opened the door, her grayish hair in her face.

"Robert, is that you?"

"Yes, Mrs. Torrance, it is," he said, his face grim.

"Oh, honey, please come in out of the rain."

She opened the door wider for him, allowing him inside.

"Thank you," he said, glancing about the small, quaint home. The cottage was primarily built for a couple of people, yet this was the home Deputy Torrance grew up in, one that Robert knew well. He took his hat off.

"Sorry to come at such a time, Mrs. Torrance. I would have come earlier, but I got caught up in some paperwork. I apologize."

"Oh, Robert, that's quite all right. It's only eight o'clock."

"Well, I know you and Mr. Torrance usually go to bed early."

"Oh, Robert stop. It's all right," she said, leading him into the living room.

"Dear, Robert is here! Won't you come out and visit with him!" she yelled. She turned back to Robert. "Let me get you some lemonade."

"No, that's all right," he said. His heart ached.

"But Robert, you always have your lemonade when you come over. Please let me get it for you." Without hesitation, she went into the kitchen.

Maybe it was the warmth and comfort of home that he needed, so he allowed her to get him the lemonade. He needed comfort right now, and so did they.

Mr. Torrance came down the stairs, his knees wobbly from years of construction and logging work.

"Well, hello there, Robert. Sorry, I'm so used to calling you Robert."

"That's okay, Mr. Torrance."

He offered his hand but Mr. Torrance pulled him in for a hug instead.

"How is everybody doing? The wife, kids? How is Jennifer doing?" Mr. Torrance sat down.

"Everybody's good, sir," he answered, sitting down on the chair opposite him. "Thank you for asking."

"I bet the girls are getting big?" he asked, smiling.

"Yes, they are."

Mrs. Torrance entered the room, lemonade in hand, her gaze settling on his uniform. Her smile faded.

Robert glanced back at her, his eyes tearing up.

She gasped, the blood leaving her face, as it turned white. Tears brimmed over as the glass fell from her hand. It shattered on the Spanish tile floor.

"My dear, what is wrong? Look what..." Her appearance was all it took. Mr. Torrance gazed back at Robert. His heart raced.

"Robert, what are you here for?"

§

Sabol, the leader of the Hell's Changelings, opened the door to the bar. Heavy metal blared throughout the room. Chains rattled off the side of his pants, and his thick boots made a heavy thud as he walked across the wooden floor.

Across the room, the band played on stage, the guitar wailing through the speakers. Tables, chairs, and barstools occupied the space to his left and the bar to his right overlooked the room.

Uwe banged his head along with the band his long blonde hair flying around.

"Yeah!" he screamed. "Fuck yeah!"

Ratliff rolled his eyes. "Would you shut the fuck up?"

"Fuck you!" Uwe said. The bartender behind Ratliff caught his attention.

"You mind keeping your men in line?" the bartender asked.

Sabol turned to face him, his shoulder length dark mane hanging down around his face, his devilish smirk widening.

"You want me to keep them in line? That's like asking the devil to stop leading hell."

Ratliff spoke up, "Yeah, he's enjoying himself. What the fuck?" he asked, glancing at Sabol. "What do you say?"

Grinning, Sabol said, "Have at it."

Sabol's sergeant in arms, Ratliff threw himself over the counter, burying his fangs in the man's neck. They fell up against the mirror, knocking bottles to the floor. Blood and alcohol spewed all over.

The rest of the Hell's Changelings gazed about the bar. Several onlookers, of whom Sabol guessed were mortal, stared at him—their mouths agape, and their faces ashen gray. Christian, the Hispanic among the bikers, approached one of the tables.

"Got a problem?" he said.

Three couples stared at him, their gaze switching from him to the bartender. The smell of blood, alcohol and death saturated the air.

Sweat beaded on one man's forehead. Nervous, he stammered, "Uh...no, no, sir. We just came here to have a good time."

Christian slammed his hands down on the table, knocking over two of the drinks. The women yelped. He glanced from the man to the women, his long dark hair falling in front of his face. As he leaned on the table, his tattoo-sleeved muscular arms flexed.

"You got some good looking women there. I might suggest getting them the fuck out of here before we fuck them and then fuck you up," he said, sizing up the biggest man.

"Not a problem," the man said, pushing his chair back.

Christian straightened up, folding his arms across his chest.

Once the couples turned to leave, Uwe and Sebastian blocked their exit. The tallest of the bikers, Uwe who stood six foot four, stared down at them.

The shorter but broader man Sebastian grinned. "It's dinner time."

§

One isolated light sat on a table in the corner of the room. Jace really didn't need it due to his immortal vision. He had only turned it on out of habit more than necessity.

Sitting with his back to the door, he reached inside the stomach of a naked woman. Bloody splotches stained her recently cleansed skin. His fingers worked diligently within the nearly dead body. As he tried to remain focused on his work, his mind drifted to a discussion he and Woodrow had recently.

The discussion surrounded the assumption Woodrow had been followed when transporting Jace to the dilapidated correctional facility, yet Woodrow was unable to confirm the identity or confront that individual.

Jace had also experienced the same thing.

He was sure it was the Underground Secret Service. The U.G.S.S. would do anything to get Jace, Woodrow and David back dead or alive, preferably alive. If brought back alive, they would be able to complete Project Hybrid and The Genetic Experiment, which entailed impregnating women for hybrid breeding.

The Genetic Experiment required strong fertile women who had a higher pain tolerance, immortal or not. The U.G.S.S. was going to create stronger, faster, bigger, and more efficient monsters through daily nourishment, vitamins and injections to sustain their vitality and immortality. Once the children were born, the mothers and infants would be contained within steel rooms, separate from one another. There, they would be monitored every second.

Jace coordinated the same plan. Only, his project involved a more delicate process, by implanting DNA in strong fertile women, mortal or immortal.

Crystal was going to be his first project for she was strong, fierce and had the physical attributes he was looking for in the mother. What better place to find the right woman than the underground fighting circuit? She was perfect, even in hybrid form.

As he thought about her, he wondered if he had impregnated her.

Had he accomplished his mission? It hadn't been that long since he had sex with her. It would still be early in the gestation process, but either way, he had to know.

§

Jennifer and Raelin sat down in the dimly lit movie theater; popcorn, candy and soda in hand. As advertisements played on the movie screen, they made themselves comfortable.

"Are you really going to eat all that?" Raelin asked.

Hesitantly, Jennifer looked at her. "Yeah, I am. I'm hungry, all right."

Raelin turned to face the screen. "Sorry, you've just been eating a lot lately."

"I know. It's like my fucking hormones are in overdrive right now." Jennifer stuffed popcorn in her mouth.

"Yeah, I've noticed. And how the hell do you eat like that and not gain weight?"

Jennifer shrugged her shoulders.

"Honestly, you look like you've been losing weight." Then, she glanced at her, eyes wide. "Oh my God, are you pregnant?"

Jennifer cringed. "Hell, no," she cried out. Immediately, she glanced around, lowering her voice. "I've just been working out a lot lately."

Jennifer did work out, but not enough to justify the sudden physical changes in her appearance. Her hormones were working overtime but it was the werewolf inside that her body was adapting to.

Jennifer shoveled more popcorn in her mouth.

Then, a male voice spoke up behind her. "Hello."

Dammit! She really needed to get better attuned to her werewolf senses. With that, she turned and stared at James. Oh, shit! Whipping back around, she plopped back down and stared at the screen, accidentally biting her lip. Ow!

What was she going to say to him? From the corner of her eye, she caught Raelin giving her a questionable look.

"Well fine, don't say hi," he said, propping his feet up on the armrest between her and Raelin.

Raelin peered over at Jennifer, her head cocked.

James put his feet on her armrest. What an ass. Jennifer glanced back at him.

"Do you mind?"

"No, I don't mind."

"Get your feet off my seat," Jennifer said.

"Only if you say hi James."

As she turned back to the screen, her blood boiled. What a...?

"Hey, listen, asshole, move your feet," Raelin spat.

"I don't go by asshole, as a matter of fact..."

"Hello, James," Jennifer said sarcastically, her eyes still on the screen.

"Now, see, that's better," he said, lowering his feet. Then, he leaned forward and whispered in her ear, "I think you're hot."

What...? Jennifer's jaw dropped, her eyes widening as she peered over her shoulder at him.

Several teenage boys piled into the seats beside him. Then, James winked at her.

§

That little voice inside Rebecca's head told her something was amiss. Whenever it spoke, she listened. Something dangerous lurked in the night but little did she know what it was.

Cradling her children against her, she walked them up the stairs, tucked them into bed, and kissed them on the forehead.

She shouldn't have to be on guard all of the time, not like this. If she was going to raise her children the way she wanted, there had to be a change.

Swaddling them within the confines of their blankets, her mind drifted to the most recent vampire attacks on their home. Her children needed protection. Staying in this house was not an option. She and the kids needed to get away, at least until shit was straightened out.

The Devil was going to rear his ugly head, and Rebecca wasn't going to stand for it. Fear crept through her body.

"You girls get some sleep," she said, trying not to think about what might happen. The girls were good at sensing when something was wrong.

"We will, mama. I love you," Leah said, peering up at her mom.

"I love you, too, honey." Rebecca turned to Tisa, who stood in the crib to her left, her arms extended out to her mom.

Rebecca picked her up. "I love you, Tisa."

"Wuv you too!" Tisa pursed her lips.

Rebecca started to smile when a vision unexpectedly invaded her head.

A mental picture of Tisa in a cage screamed at her, her daughter's eyes teary, crying out for her mom. Dressed in dirty clothing, she extended her arms out, her arms filthy and grimy, her fingernails crusty, as if she had been scraping to get out of something.

Rebecca stumbled backward, barely managing to stay on her feet, her daughter safe in her arms. Then, Rebecca found herself picking at Tisa, looking for any sign of physical trauma she had envisioned. She pressed Tisa tightly against her and glanced at the other girls.

"What's wrong mama?" Leah asked.

"Nothing honey, nothing," she lied, her eyes trailing over to Katie.

Katie stared at her, her eyes wide with fear. "Mama, is Tisa going away?" Tears leaked from her eyes.

Rebecca was breathless. Goosebumps spread over her skin, the hair on the back of her neck stood, and a shiver ran down her spine. Cradling Tisa to her chest, she sat down on the edge of Leah's bed, comforting Katie as well as herself once she found her vocal cords.

"What gives you that idea?" she asked, afraid of the answer.

Katie scurried to her mother's side. "Tisa was in a cage in my dream, you know, like a cage that an animal goes into."

Rebecca stared at her. She let Tisa climb onto the bed where Leah slept.

"And why would you think that your sister is going away?"

"Because I have dreams like that," she said, climbing onto her lap.

Her heart lurched into her throat. "Why would you have dreams about your sister in a cage?" She tried to smile, but the subject tugged at her.

Katie leaned against her mother's side.

"Katie?"

"I just do," she said.

Katie's big brown eyes stared up at hers. Rebecca wiped her tears away, and pressed her daughter against her, smoothing her hair back while she stared up at the ceiling. She needed to do something and fast. They needed to leave Munds Park, whether Robert joined her or not.

Rebecca glanced at the princess walls. "You know what? Mama's going to sleep in here with you girls. What do you think about that?"

Happily, the girls screamed. What a wonderful sound it was. "But you girls need to let mama do something first. You girls need to lie down and try to get some sleep. Once I'm done, I'll be in here. Okay?"

Tisa and Katie jumped up and down with excitement on Katie's bed, their glorious voices threatening to awaken Leah.

"Shh, enough, you're going to wake your sister, and you know there's no jumping on the beds," she said. "Remember, soft voices, it's bed time."

They sat down.

"Okay, we'll be quiet," Katie said with a smile.

"Yeah, quiet," Tisa repeated.

Rebecca motioned for the girls to be silent. "Shush, now lay down. I'll be back in a little bit."

They were full of sweet smiles. Rebecca turned off the light, and stepped out, leaving the door ajar. The nightlight lit up the princesses on the wall.

Snow White smiled down at them. Cinderella swooned, her dress flowing about her feet, exposing her glass slippers. Small, adorable bunnies, birds, and other furry creatures adorned the wall with them.

Once downstairs, Rebecca sat crossed legged on the living room floor with a single candlestick. It was enough light for her to see as she chanted words of protection and love. An aura of spells and witchery filled the room. Different colors swarmed the air. They stayed within her sight for several seconds before trailing up further into the air.

§

Sabol and Ratliff walked out of the bar into the cool night air, the scent of savage werewolves drifting by.

"There really are some territorial issues around here, aren't there?" Ratliff asked.

"Yeah," Sabol said, chugging down a bottle of beer.

"How can you drink that shit?"

"It's good shit. Hell, are you that old that you can't remember a good beer when you taste one?" Sabol chided, grinning.

"Yeah, and I always thought beer tasted like rat's ass. Now, give me an aged whiskey back in the day and I was good. Now, that's some great shit."

Nearby, wolves howled. Ratliff whipped his head around and stared into the night.

"That and a good fight," Ratliff said, eyeing the dark forest.

"Yeah, guess we better call the boys out here. Looks like we may need the backup," Sabol said.

"Fuck 'em, come on bro, you and me, you know we can do it alone.

Just like the old days."

"Back in the day, Tristan was by our side, too. You remember that, the three amigos?"

"Fuck Tristan and fuck you, too. I'll go it alone," Ratliff said, walking toward the woods.

"Dammit, Ratliff," Sabol muttered. "You're not going this alone." Like a baseball pitcher, he threw the bottle at the nearest tree.

The bottle crashed against the aged bark, spilling the last of the alcohol. Before a drop of liquid or glass hit the ground, a pack of werewolves ran from the forest. They ran at the bikers.

Sabol bolted toward the leader of the pack, his body beginning the transformation.

Ratliff ran for the tree where the glass broke, nearest the wolves. Baring his fangs, he ran halfway up the tree trunk. As his upper body twisted, he grabbed the thick branch sticking out above the pack and swung his body around. The werewolf lunged at him. Ratliff slammed into two of the wolves. A third wolf, which had barely passed him, turned and latched onto his jacket, tearing him from the limb. Ratliff slammed into the ground, dirt and pinecones flying up and around him.

Sabol jumped up, as did the werewolf in front of him. Chest to chest, they slammed into one another, Sabol hooking his claws into the neck of the lead wolf and throwing him down. Sabol landed atop him. Though he had taken on the form of the wolf, his skin had not. His fangs were longer and sharper than the typical werewolf or vampire due to the mixed breed of the Lycan and vampire inside him.

The werewolf threw Sabol off, but Sabol's bloody claw remained intact within the werewolf. He ripped his claw from the wolf's throat and turned to find another werewolf coming straight at him.

The creature snapped at Ratliff, who was atop him. He moved his head to avoid getting mauled as he struggled to flip the aggressive beast onto its back. Then, he hugged it, burying his fangs in the furry flesh. The werewolf's claws ensnared his skin, stripping pieces of it away. Ratliff screamed both in pain and in defiance. As he fed from it, blood and fur stuck to his face.

Behind him, Sabol stood in his human form. The werewolf he had fought lay dying next to him. Two other werewolves stood nearby, snarling at him, saliva dripping from their mouths.

"Go on, be gone, you piece of shit, or I'll kill you too!" he yelled, waving his arms at the beasts. "Go! You want me to fuck you up?"

They backed off.

"Yeah, that's what I thought! Get the fuck out of here!"

Hesitantly, they left their pack behind.

"Hey, asshole, I think he's a goner."

When Ratliff didn't back off, he poked him. "Hey, I said I think he's dead."

Ratliff gorged on the creature.

Sabol grabbed his shoulder to pry him off. "Hey, dickhead, get off that furry fuck, otherwise, you're going to suck up some of that nasty hair."

Once he pried Ratliff off, he backed off. A gory mess stuck to his friend's face.

"That's what I thought. You got fur face, stupid. Go fucking clean up! We need to get into town. Tristan needs us."

Sabol glanced at the bar where his men stood near the entrance, arms folded across their chest.

"You guys need some help over there," Sebastian said, chuckling.

Ratliff walked toward them, wiping his forearm across his chin. Blood smeared across his face even more.

The rest of his friends burst out laughing.

"What the hell are you guys laughing at?"

"Jesus, man, you should see yourself. If I were you, I'd start hunting putty tats. At least you would have pussy fur on you instead of dog fur. That's just wrong, bro," Christian said, putting his arm around Ratliff's shoulders.

"Get the fuck off me, man. I have to clean up." Ratliff shook off Christian's arm as he walked inside the bar.

"Let's clean up, guys," Sabol said. "Tristan needs us."

§

When the ground level window crashed to the floor ten feet below Robert decided to wait for a couple of minutes. When nobody arrived he dropped in through the open window frame, landing on his feet.

The scent of death filled the room. As he stood, his arm brushed against the cold steel frame of a gurney. Then Torrance's aroma caught his attention, drawing him in toward his friend.

Robert stared down at the sheet covered body, afraid to undrape it. Emotions overwhelmed him, ripping at his soul. He was afraid that if he uncovered Torrance that Torrance's killer would have left the man with a new internal gift, the ability to change into a vampire or werewolf.

Slowly, he pulled the sheet back, revealing a cold and lifeless face. He ground his teeth. Oh, how he wished Torrance would just awaken for he longed for the friend he knew and loved. Robert would give anything to listen to his sarcastic comments.

He fought back tears, his legs wavering beneath him. The dimly lit room threatened to swallow him up as he braced himself against the side of the gurney.

Casting all doubt aside, he touched Torrance. The coldness of his skin reminded Robert of his dedication to his friend, of his promise to keep his friend's wants and needs as he would want them. Torrance would not want to live as an immortal.

Afraid that Torrance could easily turn at the drop of a hat, he put him in a body bag and zipped it up.

§

James and his friends wouldn't shut up. The girls were irritated by the time the movie was over. Jennifer swore they were intentionally trying to annoy them, so after it was over she turned to say something, but they were gone.

As the girls left the theater, Raelin asked, "What the hell was that all about?"

"Hell if I know," Jennifer snapped. "Come on, let's get out of here."

From behind his steering wheel, James kept his eye on the girls. Once they pulled out of the parking lot, he followed them.

IN THE MIDNIGHT HOUR

Jennifer stared ahead, her heart racing. The Mustang's headlights lit up the forest as memories from the vampire attack on her home filled her head. She didn't want to come across or fight any vampires out here in the wilderness.

"Why are we here?" she asked.

Raelin detected her nervousness. "What's wrong?"

"I just don't like being alone in the woods," she said, forcing a smile.

"Are you scared? Of all people, you shouldn't be scared."

"What…?"

"Oh, look, it's raining again. I love the rain," Raelin said with excitement. "Come on, I want to show you something."

"What is it?" Jennifer asked.

"Come on. We have to get out for me to show you." With that, Raelin got out and shut the door.

Jennifer sat there a moment longer, peering through the windshield as Raelin took her shirt off and threw it on the car. Great, she probably wanted to streak through the forest. This was not Jennifer's idea of a fun time, besides her nerves were on edge.

"Fuck," she muttered, getting out of the car. "Hey, I'm not really interested in streaking, if that's what you are up to."

"Well, I guess, in a way, you could say it's streaking." Raelin took the rest of her clothes off. "But it's not what you think." Lastly, she removed her shoes.

Jennifer glanced away. "And I'm not into girls either."

Raelin laughed. "Neither am I. We're just going to have fun." She set her shoes on the car and stepped back.

"Now I'm going to have to wash my car to get your nasty ass residue off of it." Jennifer wasn't amused. She looked around, fearful somebody would see them. "Your clothes are going to get wet."

"You sound like my mother." Raelin smiled.

"So, what is it you want to show me?"

In the bright moonlight, Raelin's body painlessly transformed into an elegant mountain lion.

Jennifer's mouth dropped. She wasn't expecting this.

The mountain lion slinked forward, running its head under Jennifer's hand. Jennifer pulled back. Then it struck her, this was the same mountain lion she had petted on a few occasions, the same one who had rescued her niece and brought her back to the family. How else could Jennifer have connected with the mountain lion? It all made sense now.

Bravely, she touched it, running her hand down the head, neck and back. She didn't know much about shapeshifters, except that they could change into animals.

Raelin changed back into her human form. "Do you remember me? I brought your niece home the night your family got in the fight with the vampires."

Jennifer leaned back against the car. She didn't know what to say.

Raelin stepped back and pulled her blonde hair forward to cover her bare breasts.

"I want to thank you for trusting me. Not everyone would, especially as a mountain lion." Raelin smiled. "You're the only one I trust to keep my secret."

Jennifer stared at her. Should she share her secret? No, Robert told her to keep it under wraps.

Raelin continued, "I know your secret too, along with your mom and your brother."

Jennifer frowned. She had preferred to keep that private. "Don't…"

Raelin put her hand up. "Wait, hear me out. Just because I saw everything that night, doesn't mean I can just un-see that stuff. I want to be able to share our secrets with each other. You don't have to tell me everything about your family. I totally get keeping that stuff private. So, I'm cool with that. I just thought we could be friends on an immortal level."

Jennifer stared at her. Deep down in her heart, she knew she could trust her but she didn't want to drag her into any dangerous situation which could arise if any asshole vampires decided to attack.

"Your nieces are special, too. I don't know exactly what they are, but I do detect a hint of wolf in them."

Jennifer straightened up.

"As for your mother's boyfriend, I know he's a vampire. I'm still not sure what to make of your sister-in-law, though."

Jennifer decided to leave it there for she had no intentions of revealing Rebecca's secret.

"And what secret do I have that you know so much about?"

"You're a werewolf. We've played near your home before. Bet you thought I was the real thing, didn't you?" She snickered. "Oh, come on, Jennifer. I just want to have some fun. You know you can trust me."

She was right. A faint smile spread across Jennifer's face. "I'm sorry. I'm just leery since…"

"Yeah, I know, the vampires. I get it. Now, can we be friends with shared secrets?" Raelin offered her hand. "I'm really trying here. We can even seal it in blood if you want."

Jennifer's smile widened. "No, that's okay. I'm good with a handshake."

They shook hands.

It would be nice to have a friend Jennifer could confide in but she would still have to watch what she said around her.

"Now, come on. Let's go for a midnight run. I'm always in this area, and I've never run into anybody."

Jennifer sighed. "All right, fine but if we run into anybody, I'm kicking your ass," she replied.

She glanced around before taking her clothes off. After putting them away, they changed into their alter egos.

Jennifer's bones elongated, jutting out at points to accommodate the growth of the muscle mass. Groaning, her jawbone expanded, the skin tightening around it.

Raelin winced and turned away to peer into the woods.

Once Jennifer's change was complete, she growled, alerting Raelin that her change was done. The mountain lion turned to face the werewolf.

Alert to their alter ego senses, they bound off into the woods, unaware they had a follower.

Behind Jennifer's car, several yards away, James sat unmoving, hunched by a large tree that lay on the ground. Snickering, he rested his head on the decaying tree.

§

Dressed in only jeans and a t-shirt, Warrant awoke to the smell of fire. Droplets of rain splashed down on his face, reminding him that he was no longer in his prison.

His mind drifted back, prior to his escape. The last thing he remembered was a fight between some dragon-like creatures in a correctional facility. Had it not been for the hungry beast, he never would have made it out alive.

The dragon-like beast had repeatedly rammed the prison bars with his head when Warrant awoke. In a state of confusion as to where he was and what was happening, he stared at the ungodly creature.

Somebody cursed in the cell next to him, alerting Warrant to his presence. The metal screeched. Warrant exchanged looks with the other man, Wayne. The steel bars bent beneath the monster's power, echoing throughout the room.

As they bolted to their feet, the winged beast burst into Warrant's cell. The momentum of the powerful creature carried it through Warrant's prison and into Wayne's. There, it slammed into the brick wall, head first.

Outside their prison, other dragon-like monsters forced their way through the confines of their bars. A fight erupted between the monsters that had escaped their prison cells.

Wayne ran for Warrant's cell as the creature turned. It smacked Wayne with a dark leathery wing, throwing him into the beast's prison. He barely avoided being impaled by a protruding steel bar and slammed against the cell bars separating Warrant's prison from the beast's cell where it had been housed. Wayne fell to the ground.

Other creatures slammed against the bars which separated the men from them. The fight amongst the mass of monsters turned into a feeding frenzy. Blood permeated the air. The creature shrieked and other monsters wailed.

Warrant winced, clasping his hands over his ears. The sound was deafening.

The creature inside Wayne's cell whipped around, shooting fire out of its mouth.

Warrant and Wayne ran for the beast's prison, the heat from the fire following them inside, as they ran for the corner and propped the metal framed bed up before them. The mattress slid down, exposing their faces. The bed was their only source of defense as the creature snapped at them. The metal frame of the bed barely kept them out of reach.

Its eyes rolled back, fire erupted from its mouth.

The men hunkered down. Fire scorched the brick wall above them, leaving the wall to remain intact yet scarred.

Blood from the creatures fighting splashed onto the beast. It turned, ramming its head repeatedly against the prison bars. When the bars gave way, it escaped the cell.

The men remained still.

With the last barred wall separating them from the other creatures gone, anything could get in now.

The men glanced around. No windows. What was the only entrance into this dungeon was blocked by the monsters. Even if they could sneak passed, there was no telling what lie in wait elsewhere within the building. Their only other option was to latch onto a monster's wing while it was fleeing the facility but for now, they would have to be mindful of their actions. Any risky movement might attract unwelcome attention.

As the creatures fought, Warrant and Wayne stood. A dead beast struck the concrete wall above them. Debris cascaded over the men. They jumped to avoid the falling beast. They glanced back at the deformed winged monsters, who continued to fight.

The men glanced up at the gaping hole where the dead creature had hit the wall. It was large enough for a human to crawl through. No words were needed. This was their only chance of escape.

Wayne was the first to peer through the hole. The chill of the night air leaked into the building. He stepped on the head of the dead beast, grasped the sides of the hole, pushed the slab wiring down, and pulled himself through. Particles of concrete and other debris fell into the prison behind him. Then he turned to help Warrant, his eyes falling on the monsters behind him. The beasts were staring at him.

"Shit," he muttered, his eyes enlarging.

Warrant gripped the bottom of the hole. As he did, he glanced back at the monsters. The men had the creature's undivided attention.

"Fuck," Warrant muttered.

"Come on!"

Wayne grabbed the man's arm. As Warrant scrambled through, one of the beasts tried to grab him. He kicked back, striking it, barely pulling his legs through when it shrieked. Then, fire filled the hole.

The large male dragon tried to squeeze through but it was too large. It shook its head and then bashed the wall around the hole with its head repeatedly until the concrete and debris fell, widening the hole. The other creatures followed its lead.

Wayne and Warrant ran into the woods. Behind them, three monsters broke free of the prison, their shrieks filling the night, and pursued them.

At one point, Warrant had lost track of Wayne as the creatures chased them.

They separated, and then they ran into each other again. Only this time, a fight erupted between the beasts. In the wake of the fight, Warrant had been knocked out.

Now, the beast within him stirred. The scent of life and death was nearby. Somebody lay not too far from him, his head turned. Warrant presumed it was the man from the prison.

Another odor also lingered in the air. It was one of the creatures from the prison, and it carried the aroma of death upon it.

Though his vision was blurry, he glanced about, leery something would emerge from the brush and attack him. His pupils dilated, allowing his beast to focus in on everything that moved—and everything that didn't.

He stood, slowly walking out of the brush, his nostrils flaring as he sorted out the odors that hung in the air, including the scent of post-mortem charbroiled flesh. He wouldn't allow that odor to overtake his sense of smell, though, instead, he drew in another deep breath. Sure enough, the body nearby was the man from the prison.

The strong aroma of death moved slowly but assuredly in his direction. A sense of danger advised him to get the hell out of here, even though the werewolf within him was prepared to fight. He struggled with his alter ego's need to transform but he decided it was best to remain in human form and leave the area.

But where did his duty lie? Was it to save only himself or to help the other man who might lie dying nearby? The man hadn't moved. Was he unconscious? Or was he dead?

It had been in his nature to help others like he had helped Crystal. So, the need to help the man was strong.

Still woozy from being knocked unconscious, he followed Wayne's scent and carefully tread through the brush and the rocky terrain. In his attempt to step over a fallen tree, he stepped on a branch, his full weight on it. It broke off, the branch crunching beneath his foot. Warrant crouched, hiding amongst the trees and brush. Death's odor was overwhelming.

Frozen, Warrant peered over his shoulder. The monster lurked nearby, but where? He blinked a couple of times, hoping it would help clear up his vision, and scanned his surroundings. The creature was adept at hiding, which scared him. It was not like any other beast he knew of.

Maintaining its stationary position, it defiled him. The odor of death, fire and brimstone lingered, making it more difficult for him to find it.

Apparently, it was waiting for him to make the first move. He didn't want to play the waiting game, for he feared it may sneak up on him when he least expected it.

Warrant turned, his foot coming in contact with Wayne. From almost any angle, large brush and trees quarantined him from the hybrid's vision. He knelt down and checked the prisoner's pulse. The man was alive.

Leaves moved, alerting him to the distance of the creature. Then Wayne punched him in the nose.

Recoiling, he whispered, "Stop, I was in the prison." Another fist struck him, deep in the solar plexus.

Nearby, the hybrid shrieked.

They glanced around. The full moon hid behind the tall trees, allowing visibility only for a short distance.

"What the fuck is going on?" Wayne whispered.

"I don't know, but we need to get the fuck out of here," Warrant snapped.

Thunder cracked, and then lightning struck, knocking a tree to the ground. It echoed throughout the forest. As the men bolted to their feet, another lightning strike lit up the trees behind them. The illumination of their figures caught the hybrid's attention.

§

Torrance's dead body resided in the trunk of Robert's car. As Robert drove, tears streamed down his face. He wiped them away as he tried to focus in on the good times.

The blades of the windshield wipers sliced across the glass, wiping away the calming effects of the rain, something that had settled his nerves after kidnapping his dead friend's body.

Rain snuck in through his window, splashing onto his arm and face.

"What the...?" He glanced at the window, which was open about an inch, and began pressing the power buttons until he found the one that powered it shut.

Eyes focused ahead, he clutched the steering wheel, determined to find Torrance's murderer and kill him.

§

The two story log cabin come into view, the full moon casting its light upon it. As we neared the porch, I detected a whiff of brimstone, or so I thought, but as fast as it came, it disappeared.

"What was that?" I asked, looking around.

"What was what?"

"That smell." I wrinkled my nose.

He peered into the forest. "I don't smell anything."

"It was just here. Don't tell me you didn't smell it."

"I didn't," he said, opening the door.

As I stepped inside, he stood on the porch a moment longer, surveying the property before coming inside.

"You did smell it, didn't you?" I asked.

Our gaze met.

Firmly, he said, "No, I didn't."

He walked past me.

"Just so you know, I don't use electricity because I don't need it."

Suddenly, he was colder, as if hiding something.

"That's okay. I don't need it either," I said.

The abrupt change of his behavior was unsettling.

A thin smile crept up on his face. "But I guess if your family ever comes over, I should look into getting it. It would be more comfortable for them."

"They would appreciate it."

"Let me light some candles."

I raised my eyebrow. "Are you okay?"

"Of course," he answered. "Why do you ask?" Within a second, his eyes and his demeanor softened.

"Nothing, I guess. You're just different."

His voice softened. "How?"

I didn't know how to respond so, for the moment, I let it go. "Don't worry about it, I think it's just me."

"Come, I want to show you my house."

As he lit the candles, I followed. I really didn't need the lights for my keen senses were enough. Regardless, I let him take the lead since it was his home.

A black leather couch and recliner occupied the living room, and off to the side, a pool table took up some of the space.

The memory of fighting a female vampire with a cue stick flooded into my brain. It was the night my ex-husband Chris was killed. To rid myself of the memory, I shook my head. As I walked on, I glanced at the fireplace in the corner. With no one to light it, it roared to life. For some reason, it didn't surprise me. It must have been Tristan's way of setting the mood for what was to come.

Tristan then led me into the kitchen, which was to the left of the front door. A large, black, glass top table stood in the dining area with one single amber candlestick holder to accentuate it. Above it, hung a chandelier and antique black leather chairs accommodated it.

Then Tristan guided me out of the kitchen, and to the left, through the remainder of the living room, past the bathroom, and to the wide staircase. The stairs forked, each direction leading to more rooms which were linear with the living room on the first floor.

We progressed up the stairs to the left, where it overlooked the living room below. As I stepped onto the second-floor landing, the wood creaked beneath my feet. A large elk mount, its body fully intact, stood above the front door. It reminded me of dinner.

Tristan caught me staring at it. "Are you okay?"

"It just reminded me of dinner," I said, rubbing the side where the elk had stuck an antler in me. Fuck eating animals. People were a hell of a lot easier to feed upon, especially the injured woman in the creek.

He glanced at the elk. "Was it that good?"

I smiled. "Yes, it was. Damn near killed me, too."

"We all have scars, Crystal. Without them, we wouldn't be who we are," he said, his eyes on mine.

The scent of his testosterone and leather jacket filled my nostrils. The sudden need to bed him overwhelmed me. It took only a second before he had me pressed against the wall, his mouth firmly on mine. I caved into my desire, responding to his every touch.

The door to his room flew open. It slammed against the wall. Tristan backed me into the door, leaving me a full view of his master suite.

"Oh yes," I moaned, exposing my neck to him to seduce and tantalize me.

His lips trailed down my neck as I peered beyond him at the bed.

The large, masculine, cherry wood headboard and footboard frame were designed with large, medium and small rings bound to it. Chains clung to each ring, each encompassed with ankle and wrist bracelets.

My mind drifted off, exploring the possibility of his freakish sexual desires. I had a strong urge to experiment with the chains and bracelets. Then, my gaze fell on the large metal hook that hung from the ceiling above his bed.

What…?

"No bra, Crystal? That's not like you."

I grinned. "I knew you were coming, so I wanted to be prepared." Then, I shifted my attention to the hook. "What is that for?"

A devilish grin appeared. "Do you really want to know?"

"Yes I do, my beast," I said.

It didn't take much time for him to get me on the bed. I was already geared for a night of hot sex. Tristan ripped my clothes off of me, exposing my well-toned body for his pleasure. Before he could discard his jacket, I latched onto it, keeping it within reach. Then, he stripped down.

I shoved his jacket back at him. "Put it back on."

"Why…?" he asked.

I cut him off. "Don't ask questions, Tristan. Just do it," I demanded.

Pulling back, he grinned and slowly slipped one arm inside.

Now, he was teasing me. Fucker. I wasn't going to stand for his slowness. As he slipped the other arm in the sleeve, I jerked him forward by his jacket. It slid tightly up against his back.

His fangs grazed my neck, drawing a thin line of blood. I gasped. The hardness of his body pressed against mine. The endowment of his manhood enlarged.

"Mm Tristan, feed me…love me…oh baby fuck me," I moaned.

Firmly, he gripped my hips and drew me in, pushing his hardened manhood inside.

"Oh, yes!"

He pumped his hips into mine, nibbling on my nipples, his hand enclosing around my neck.

"Are you sure, Crystal?" His blue eyes glassed over, deepening into an opal color.

"Yes," I growled.

Embracing me, he stood. Mysteriously, he found a section of chain and wrapped part of it to the hook, enclosing the steel bracelets around my wrists, stringing me up and wrapping my legs around him. The bindings burned.

"Are you comfortable?" he asked. The smoke from the burn drifted up into the air.

"Yes," I said, the burn feeding into my flesh.

"The burn along with the sexual gratification is overwhelming," he said.

He wrapped his hand behind my neck, bracing me against him, his mouth on me once again. The burn deepened but not too much to the point of a hurtful pain, at least not yet. Holding me tight, he plunged deep inside.

Desperately, I wanted to hold him, to feel the coolness of his face against mine. His fangs grazed my throat. Oh, yes. Moaning, I wrapped my hands around the chains and used them to brace myself. He pulsated within me, his stiff shaft throbbing intensely deep inside.

The zipper, studs and cold buttons of his leather jacket rubbed against my breasts, creating a sensual sensation. The burn intensified. It radiated throughout my body, invoking a sense of euphoria that heightened the prowess of my beasts. Awakening the werewolf within, it stood defiant, more aware of the natural enemy that made love to me. Submission was not a common characteristic, so I had to fight to keep it under control.

Tristan sensed my urge to control it.

With one hand, he held me tight and with the other, he latched onto my jaw, maintaining control of me. My wolf fangs descended. Passionately yet cautiously he kissed me, aware that he was making love to the werewolf. His fangs rubbed against mine, his tongue lashing in and out of my mouth. Beneath his grip, my jaw changed into a more definitive canine mold, without losing too much of the feminine features.

Passionately yet aware, we made love to one another, each remaining wary of our lover's beast. Gradually, our primeval instinct took hold, never losing ground with the temptation of a bloody attack should the other provoke it.

Tristan pumped his hips against mine, his manhood deepening inside, penetrating me harder and faster. The burn intensified within the realm of my pleasure. My werewolf emerged, my pupils dilating and my claws emerging.

It was overwhelming…it was over indulgence of full sexual satisfaction when he bore down on me. Tristan buried my face in his chest, his fangs sinking into my neck. Ah yes, it was wonderful, but my werewolf didn't like the vampire dominating me.

As Tristan reached up to remove me from the hook, a low growl escaped my lips. When our eyes met, it was too late. I buried my fangs in his shoulder. The intensity of his being, his masculinity, and his beastly creature that I desired, overwhelmed me.

The smoke from the bracelets and the smell of my burnt flesh hung heavily in the air as he pulled me off of the hook. I flipped over so that when we fell onto the bed, I was straddling him. With my wrists still bound in the cuffs, I gauged his chest, driving my claws into him.

Tristan screamed, ripping my claws out of his wound. Groaning, he held the cuffs tight.

Blood boiled over. The smell of it ignited my hunger. I snapped at him, ready to feed, when his other hand lashed out, striking me on the bottom. As I whipped my head around to gaze back, he caught hold of my chin in an attempt to control me and force me backward. He climbed atop, confining me to the bed while he drove hard deep inside.

The werewolf within was infuriated, but the vampire beneath the surface hungered for his lips…and his touch. The wolf fought for control, but it was useless. My vampire emerged. The eternal side of me gave in to him.

Moaning, I swallowed up the blood that poured from his chest.

Tristan grinned for he knew which creature he had control of now. He pumped me hard with his hips, pressing his lips to the charred wounds of my wrists, pleasuring and healing me at the same time—for the pain and pleasure I had endured. The softness of his mouth drew a new intense gratification. As my leather studded lover made love to me, he buried his fangs in me, feeding, pleasuring—owning me.

§

With the beast still in pursuit, Wayne ran. The wind blew against him, carrying the scent of two females. One was his own blood, Jennifer. Did his nose defy him? Or was it really her?

What the hell was she doing out here?

Wayne followed the smell, which was slightly below and in front of him. He dodged trees and branches that blocked his path as the other man ran next to him. Debris shot out from under his feet. He charged up a hill and then it dropped off.

Wayne didn't care at this point. His daughter and another woman were nearby. He needed to get them out of the area. With no hesitation, he leaped off of the edge. The other man followed him.

The scent lured him to a mountain lion and a werewolf, instead of two women. Their scent was strong but one was his daughter—the werewolf. They peered over their shoulder in time to see him coming.

The men tumbled to the ground as the werewolf and the mountain lion snapped at them, their fangs and claws grazing their skin. He and the other prisoner were barely able to avoid being mauled.

The werewolf's fangs sliced Wayne's forearm. Blood drizzled from the wound. The mountain lion snapped at Warrant, her teeth grazing his upper arm. A thin line of blood flowed down his skin. The aroma drew in the beast.

The females snarled and reared back.

Wayne's fangs descended as he growled at them, trying to warn them they were in danger, but the females didn't understand.

Then the dragon-like creature shrieked, drawing their attention as they gazed up at the short cliff. It peered down at them, eyeing each one intently. Its green scaly head reared back.

Then Wayne realized what it was going to do. The werewolf and mountain lion froze.

"Run!" Wayne yelled, grabbing and pulling the werewolf with him.

The mountain lion ran, and Warrant ran alongside it.

The werewolf tried to run away from Wayne, but he wasn't about to let her out of his sight. Fire shot out behind the two of them, catching the nearby tree on fire. Jennifer howled in pain. Whimpering, she fell to the ground, her fur burnt, and her face charred.

Wayne threw her over his shoulder and bolted. Within seconds, she changed back into her human form, curling up within his arms, crying and burying her face into his neck.

The other man and the mountain lion disappeared into the night. Rain poured through the trees, providing them with a small amount of shelter which lasted only seconds before he ran across the road in front of him.

§

The windshield wipers scraped across the windshield. A few yards in front of the car there was movement. Robert slammed on his brakes. The car slid across the wet pavement.

"Shit!"

Tightly, he gripped the steering wheel, whipping it to the left to keep it from veering off the road. Then, the car slid. He jerked it back, and the car fishtailed across the asphalt. Robert overcorrected it, slamming it into the mountainside. The crash of metal and plastic reverberated throughout the patrol car, bouncing him off of the driver's side window. The glass window broke, leaving gashes on his face.

Groaning, he straightened up and touched his cheek where some of the broken glass clung to his skin and blood soaked his fingers. Dammit all to hell.

Robert gazed out at the road where someone had crossed. No movement.

"Fuck!"

He shoved his door open and stepped out into the cold pouring rain. The road was empty. Pissed, he kicked the side of the car, caving part of the door in.

"Motherfucker," he groaned, gazing toward the back of the car. The trunk had sprung open. "That's just fucking great!"

He stomped over to the trunk and stared at the body bag that lay there. As if wanting to confirm Torrance was really dead, he unzipped it. The ashen face stared up at him.

"Fuck," he muttered.

A tree branch snapped. He froze. Something large approached him from behind. Its warmth surrounded it, and it had a distinct aroma that wasn't werewolf nor vampire, and it sure as hell wasn't mortal.

Slowly, he reached for the full auto HK MP5 lying next to his friend.

When Robert became a cop, he started re-loading silver ammo and acquiring artillery in order to deal with the immortals. This just happened to be one of those times.

Robert's hand curled around the grip of the gun, his finger nearing the trigger. Frozen, he peered at the creature from the corner of his eye. It was closing in on him. Damn was he glad he kept his silver bullet loaded gun with him.

Enclosing the gun within one hand he spun around, dropping into a crouch and squeezed the trigger, blasting the creature.

Fire shot out of the creature's mouth.

Because Robert had dropped to his knee, he narrowly escaped the fire, so it shot out at the patrol car. The beast shrieked, flared its wings out, and snapped at him, missing him. Bullets penetrated the scaly flesh. Then, it turned and ran.

It must have realized it was no match for the gun. Still in awe of the strange beast, he decided to hunt it down. With gun in hand, he took off after it, his immortal adrenaline coursing through his body.

THE DEAD LIVE

The shriek of the monster and gunfire filled the air. Unsure whether the gunshot was friendly fire or not, Wayne ran on, his injured daughter in his arms. He could have turned around to get help, but he would probably run into the beast. That was the last thing he wanted to do, instead, he continued on.

On the way down the hill, where it curved horizontally into a table mesa, he set Jennifer down. It overlooked a much larger ravine from the overhead cliff. He presumed the other man and the mountain lion disappeared into the ravine, for there was no other sign of life. So, he ran down to the bottom of the steep plateau where he came to an immediate halt.

Rock and dirt broke off from the ground below him. It tumbled down the cliff where the brush, rock, and trees obstructed his view. Voices echoed within the canyon so he was sure they survived the steep decline. Wayne would have pursued them to make sure they were all right, but he had his daughter to tend to. He couldn't drag Jennifer around the wilderness and rocky terrain in the condition she was in, for she had already endured enough pain.

He peered up at the massive clouds. How he wished it would stop raining. This was not the time to be stuck in the mountains, so he turned and approached Jennifer. She sat naked with her back to him, her head hung low and her eyes closed, attempting to cover up her private parts.

Wayne didn't need this shit right now. It was one thing to find his daughter, but like this, it was too much. Sighing, he pulled his shirt off and handed it to her.

"Here, cover up."

While she dressed, he glanced around at their surroundings.

Something garbled came out of her mouth.

"What?" he said, turning toward her.

Thank God, the shirt covered her body, but her face! Dear God, her poor face. His heart skipped a beat and his breath caught in his throat. Her poor face was burnt to a crisp. She could barely wet her lips with her tongue.

"Oh shit, I'm sorry," he said, his voice softening. "I'm so sorry."

Tears dripped from her closed eyes, and then the rain turned to hail. A distorted scream escaped her lips, and then she tried to bury her face in her hands.

They needed shelter from the storm, so he swept her off of her feet.

"I'll find shelter."

Her young, feminine musk filled his nostrils, awakening a sense in him he had long regretted but never forgotten. Visions of his blanketed baby daughter in his arms swarmed into his head. Oh, how he wished he could have remained in her life when she was a small child.

Wayne ran up the plateau, his mind drifting back to Crystal. He would get her back to her mother, and then he thought about how he found her—as a werewolf. A knot formed in his throat.

Jennifer carried his curse. Did Robert carry his curse, too?

§

Warrant ran down the side of the ravine. Then, it dropped off, revealing a steep and dangerous drop down the mountainside as his momentum kept him traveling at high speed with the inability to stop. He and the mountain lion tumbled down the mountain, regained their footing, and then tumbled again onto the plateau. They were lucky to have survived.

Clouds loomed overhead and hail pelted him as he lay on the rock. A young nude woman lay next to him, her eyes wild, and her voice frantic.

"What the fuck just happened?" she snapped.

He stared at her. "Do you really need me to explain what happened?"

"Where's Jennifer?" The wind brushed against her causing a chill to run up her spine. That was when she attempted to cover up her private female parts.

"We got separated, so I assume she's with the other guy," he answered, glancing at her.

She was young and he was a much older man. This wasn't good. As he grabbed the bottom of his shirt to pull it over his head, she yelled.

"Wait a minute, asshole, you're not doing anything with me!"

She kicked him in the groin and ran, groaning from the rock that cut into her feet.

"You're not going to get far."

"Fuck you, asshole," Raelin said, evolving back into the mountain lion.

"I was going to be a nice guy and give you my shirt, but if you don't want it, that's fine," he said. "How long can you stay in form, shapeshifter? I know it's a short time until you start having problems."

Rain drenched them. She tried to stare him down but he wasn't easily intimidated.

"Your paws won't last long on this rock. They're going to be cut up and bleeding by the time you get out of here, *if* you get out of here," he said, accentuating the word, if. "Do you really want to do that to yourself? You're a nice looking girl, and I do say girl."

Slowly, he walked toward her. "Don't worry. I'm no pedophile and I have no personal interest in you. If you want my help, say so now, otherwise, get the fuck out of here and find your own way out."

Snarling, her ears dropped, and her lips peeled back.

"Are you trying to intimidate me, child? I have many more years than you and can tear you up in a heartbeat." He threw the wet shirt aside, and crouched down, his muscular chest glistening from the rain. "We'd be better off finding our way out of here together, but if you choose not to, then so be it."

When she didn't respond, he said, "Let's rock, bitch."

Again, she snarled, saliva dripping from her lips.

"Just remember girlie, you're only a shapeshifter, I'm not." With that, he removed his pants and called upon his alter ego—the werewolf.

As his transformation began, Raelin attacked, her tail whipping around her. They tumbled to the ground as Warrant lashed out, his claws ripping a large gash across her chest. Raelin whimpered and backed off.

Snarling, he advanced on her.

Raelin reared up on her haunches to attack again when the cool rock brushed against her. Great! She had backed herself up into the crook in the mountain with nowhere to go. This wasn't good.

§

Blackened from the flame that had consumed his body, Torrance walked away from the patrol car, his head hanging loosely on his neck. As he swung around to gaze up at the mountainside, his head rolled awkwardly to the side, his vision hazy.

He stumbled to the right, his head rolling forward, dangling against his chest. The growls from the canyon caught his attention. As he neared the edge of the mountain, he swiveled his head around to gaze down. It was too deep, so he couldn't see a thing. Then, Torrance turned and proceeded in the opposite direction of Robert.

§

Drenched, Robert walked back to his patrol car, gun in hand. Though he was happy about his kill, he continued on in silence. How the hell could a dragon have survived from generations gone by?

As he neared the patrol car, the light from the open trunk came within view. Something was amiss. What the hell was it? Closing in on it, he realized the body bag was on fire and hanging over the side of the trunk.

What the hell? His jaw dropped. Where there more of them? And, what the hell happened to Torrance?

§

The strange man set Jennifer down upon the dirt inside the cave and gently pushed her hair aside. The crispness of her charred face was loosening, and then tightening, which meant that her curse was healing her skin. This was a good thing.

"Well, you're looking a little better," he said.

"Am I?" She tried to open her eyes but the pain was unbearable. She winced. So, she kept them closed, for the moment.

"Yes, you are. You should be thankful for your gift. If you were mortal, you may have died from these wounds. They'll heal up soon, though."

Jennifer thought about his comment. Oh, shit! He wasn't mortal either. Her breath quickened and her heart beat faster. Who the hell was he?

She flinched. Trembling, she asked, "Who are you? What do you want?"

She started to get up until he lightly placed his hand on hers. For some reason, there was comfort there.

"Relax. I have no intention of hurting you."

Her face hurt less. Soon, she would be able to see, and then, she would be able to look him in the face.

"Only somebody with this same disease would know that," she replied. The cold, wet shirt clung to her body, making her feel more vulnerable.

§

A strange but comforting thing warmed Wayne's heart—his paternal feelings. Though he loved his children, he had to make a decision when they were young, one that would hopefully keep his wife and children safe from harm. He regretted his actions but if he had not disappeared from their lives, they could have been killed.

"What are you?" she asked.

"I'm a werewolf, like you," he answered. To confirm she was his daughter, he asked, "What's your name?"

"It's Jennifer...Bouchard. What's your name?" Her eyelids fluttered, then she exclaimed, "Oh! Oh! I think..." She opened her eyes.

§

Raelin, in human form, sought refuge in the crook of the mountain as the werewolf advanced on her. How she wished the rain would stop! She already slipped twice, retreated, and slipped again. This time, she slid on the slick surface, slamming face first into the mountainside. She grabbed onto the rugged rock to maintain her position and balance, cutting her palms in the process.

The combination of his growl and the thunder overhead rumbled in the confined space, rattling her bones and echoing within the canyon, making the rock shake overhead.

She was sure she was going to die, but how—by avalanche, or the werewolf?

Then, down she went, grabbing for the nearest rock, burying her fingers in the crevice of it. The weight of her body pulled her down the incline, forcing her fingers to give way.

"No!"

The rainwater swept her toward the canyon. As she slid toward the drop-off, the werewolf changed and the man latched onto her arm, pulling her up toward the plateau.

"Please don't let me go, please," she begged.

Warrant's feet slid as he braced his foot against an overlapping stone. Then he froze, leaving her to hang from the edge of the plateau, his brow narrowed in.

Why did he stop?

His eyes narrowed in on something past her, and then they widened. Something had caught his attention but what the hell was it?

Warrant resumed pulling her onto the plateau, and then whispered, "Put the shirt on now, but be quiet."

As they both got dressed, she gazed out at the canyon. She didn't see anything.

§

Meanwhile, Warrant eyed the rock plateau that jutted out of the mountain on the other side of the canyon. Thick brush hid the cave and the large dragon that had emerged from it. Its dark leathery skin blended in with the night but its eyes did not.

Lightning struck deep within the canyon walls, shedding light on the dragon's wet skin. It stretched out its wings which had a span of about six feet each.

Raelin gasped and took a step back, rock rolling out from beneath her feet.

The dragon turned its head, its eyes narrowing in on them.

Warrant turned and grabbed Raelin, throwing her over his shoulder, and ran back the way they had come—up the mountain.

"Put me down! I can change! I can run faster that way!" she yelled.

"You'll never make it up the mountain!"

"Yes, I can! Put me down!"

"No! We'll get separated, or you'll get hurt! And I won't be able to help you!"

Leather wings flapped in the air behind him. Raelin screamed, pulling back, forcing him to lean in toward her. As she twisted within his grasp, the dragons' claws ripped through his back. Screaming, he pushed himself up the mountain.

Then, the dragon struck again.

§

A jolt hit the ground, catching Robert's attention. He glanced around at the road, bewildered. What the hell was that? It couldn't have been the dragon he mutilated.

He glanced at the patrol car which stood alone on the desolate road.

Was the jolt from the thunder that had struck? Or was it something else?

Screams came from the mountainside.

Who the hell…?

It didn't matter, instead, he ran toward the edge of the road and peered down the cliff. Rocks tumbled down the mountainside. A man scrambled up it, carrying a woman over his shoulder. A dragon lashed out at them from behind.

"Son of a bitch." Robert aimed the gun at the dragon, and gently squeezed the trigger, multiple times.

§

The dragon shrieked, its blood raining down upon them. Warrant froze. The wings stopped, and then the lifeless creature fell into the darkness below. He pressed the two of them against the rocky wall. Were they the next target?

A male voice yelled, "Hey, are you two okay down there!"

"Yeah, I think so!" Warrant yelled. "You're not going to shoot us, are you?"

His fingers were slipping. He needed to get to the top and soon, it not, gravity was going to pull them down into the canyon.

"No, I'm here to help you! Come on!"

Warrant resumed climbing. He had to take the man's word, for he had no choice.

"Hold on tight," he said. "We're not that far from the top."

"Okay," she muttered, clinging to him. His skin was sweaty, and she was losing her grip. As he neared the top, an arm grabbed her from behind. She yelped.

"Let go of him. I got you." The man dragged her onto solid ground.

As Warrant climbed the edge of the mountain, his eyes fell on Robert. Shit! It was Crystal's son.

Half expecting Robert to beat the fuck out of him once he recognized him, Warrant turned away.

§

Robert helped the teenage girl to her feet. "Are you all right?" he asked.

"Yeah, I think so," she answered. "I'm not sure about him, though."

The wind picked up and blew the wet t-shirt against her body. Great! She folded her arms over her chest.

Robert gazed at the man, who turned away. The stranger was probably in his forties and wore only jeans, yet, the girl was no older than sixteen, and she was barely dressed. This didn't look right.

Robert's eyes narrowed in him. "Are you okay, sir?"

"I'm fine," Warrant said, without looking at him.

"Sir, look at me," Robert said.

Warrant gazed back at him. "Where's your car, Deputy?"

Robert's eyes widened. It couldn't be Warrant, for he died the night he attacked Robert's mother.

"*Deputy*, where is your car? The girl needs to go home."

"It's on the road. Where's your identification?"

Raelin glanced at them. "Hey, this isn't what it looks like. He helped me."

"How old are you?" Robert asked, turning to her.

"I'm sixteen." Her teeth chattered. "But..."

"She's sixteen, you're a middle-aged man, and you're both barely dressed. What's going on?"

"I'm not into teenage girls, Deputy. This is a complete misunderstanding. I saved her life from that fucking thing that attacked us."

"Really?" Robert snapped. "Where are the rest of your clothes?"

"Hey, I'm fucking freezing over here..." she interrupted.

"Watch your language," the men said.

She recoiled from them. Then Jennifer came to mind. Oh, shit! "Oh my God, Jennifer! Where is Jennifer?"

§

Jennifer was more mesmerized by the healing process than him, which gave him the opportunity to turn away. He didn't think she would recognize him, regardless, he preferred to keep it that way, at least for now.

Briskly, he walked to the opening of the cave. "I have to go," he said with his back to her. "You need to go home, child."

"I don't know where I am, though."

"Go up the mountain to your right. Once you make it to the top, go left. You'll find the road."

"You're going to leave me alone, with that thing out there? It will kill me."

She had a point. What the hell was he thinking—abandoning his daughter for the second time? Is that what a father was supposed to do? If he cared, he would make sure she made it to safety. For all he knew, her friend may have been killed, along with the other man. Shit!

"Do you feel up to walking?"

"Yes," she said.

"Good, let's go. We need to get you home to your mother," he said.

Jennifer bolted to her feet.

The rain had slowed down to a drizzle. Now, was the best time to go, so he stepped out onto the plateau. "Follow me."

Jennifer rushed up next to him. "Thank you for not leaving me."

"No problem." He gazed up at the mountain to determine the best course up.

She peered up at the mountain, and then glanced at him. "What's your name?"

He sighed. Great! This was the worst time and place to tell her he was her father.

"Come on, let's go this way." He walked toward a section of the mountain that was not as steep as what they had gone down. "Now, if I tell you to follow me, that means follow me, do not walk beside me, but follow me. Do you understand?"

Jennifer had her mother's big brown eyes, and the same depressed look her mother got when she was sad or upset over something.

Stopping, he asked, "What's wrong?"

She hung her head. "Do you think that thing killed Raelin?"

He wanted to hold her, to let her know everything was going to be all right, that soon she would be safe at home, and that her friend was alive but he couldn't. Holding her would only break him—the same way his heart broke when he held her mother in her prison cell.

"She'll be fine," he said.

"But how do you know that?"

Their eyes met.

He hesitated, clearing his throat. "I don't...miss. Listen, I don't know whether they survived or not but you have a chance for survival. It's not that far. And tell you what… Once I get you to the top, I'll try to find your friend, promise."

"Right," she muttered, gazing up at the rocky wall.

For a second, he stared at her. She wasn't stupid.

"Come on. Let's worry about you right now."

He walked past her and proceeded up the rocky terrain with Jennifer following close behind.

After a few near death slips up the mountain, they came to the top.

Wayne pulled himself up and over the edge when nearby voices caught his attention. He helped Jennifer climb over the edge of the mountain.

She whipped her head around. "That's Raelin!"

"Careful," he said. "Make sure it's her before you make your presence known."

Jennifer approached the trees that stood ten yards away. Cautiously, Wayne walked up behind her. A yelp of excitement escaped her lips.

"Raelin!" She ran through the trees.

Raelin turned. "Jennifer?"

Jennifer froze, her eyes falling on the deputy. Another man stood nearby.

"Jennifer?"

The deputy's eyes grew bigger, and a few curse words escaped his lips. As the deputy approached her, the other man slipped out of sight.

Wayne, too, sought refuge behind a tree and leaned against it. The bark cut into his hand.

"Jesus sis, what the hell are you doing out here?"

Wayne stared at the deputy. I'll be damned if he didn't have his mother's eyes.

As Jennifer explained everything to her brother, Wayne considered revealing himself but decided against it. This was not the time, instead, it was best to talk to Crystal first—to gain her trust but in order to do that, he had to know what she remembered. With that, he might have to jog her memory and there were only a couple of ways of doing it, both of them being quite traumatic if not handled correctly.

Regardless, something had to be said. Crystal had to know she and the kids were in danger, whether she wanted to accept Wayne's apology or not.

The last time he had talked to her, she hadn't remembered

everything. He had to find her, to *kill her*. No, he told himself, he had to save her, not kill her. What the hell was he thinking? He still loved her, and he loved his family, even though he wanted to *kill* them.

What the fuck was wrong with him? He had to protect them. Dammit Wayne, get your act together!

Robert escorted the girls back to his patrol car, cursing something about Warrant. Alone and camouflaged in the night, Wayne followed them to Raelin's car, and then back to his deceased mother-in-law's house.

HELL'S STORM

The motorcycle pipes sang a long and winded baritone as they neared the house. That's when Tristan told me to get dressed.

Healing up, the skin on my wrists emitted a light smoke.

"Who's here?" I asked.

"My brothers," he said.

I brushed my hair with my fingers, walking over to him. "Your brothers? I get to meet some of your family?"

A thin yet disconcerting smile spread across his face. "Yes, I consider them all my brothers, but only one is actually blood. By the way, don't let them get to you," he stressed. "They can be a bit..." He scratched his goatee. "Gruff and aggressive."

"Whatever, you say, master," I said, smiling, kissing and then sucking the blood off of his lips.

He pulled back and laughed. "I think I like that. I might demand you to say that in bed next time."

I thought about our kinky romp. Oh, how I didn't want it to end. Grinning, I kissed him. The deep rumble of several Harley Davidson's stopped outside the house.

The color of his eyes changed from his usual blue to black. How odd. This must not be a welcome visit.

He glanced at the bedroom door. "Can you do me a favor?"

"What's that?" I caressed his cheek.

His gaze settled on mine. "I know how you are, but please try not to overstep your bounds with them. They can be rather persuasive and mean."

I took a deep breath, wary of where this was going.

"They'll do whatever they can to antagonize you. They do it with everyone. Also, I don't want you to cower to them either. You're my woman, but they may try to get your goat—so to speak. So, I'll try not to ever leave you alone with them."

"All right," I said. Now, I wasn't so sure I wanted to meet them. "If I tell you to do something, just do it, please."

Hesitantly, I nodded in agreement.

"Thank you."

Footsteps echoed in the hallway outside his bedroom. Knuckles rapped on the wooden door. With no approval from Tristan, his brotherhood—the Hell's Changelings—opened it.

Tristan glanced back. Then, he let the hounds of hell in.

They stood before me, dressed in jeans, black leather boots, black t-shirts and black leather jackets. Silver chains and knives hung from their waists. The rocker patch on their chest read Hell's Changelings MC in red. Dark sunglasses hid their eyes. Every single one of them turned toward me before turning their attention to Tristan.

"Hey bro, how are you doing?" Sabol asked, his shoulder length dark hair falling over his shoulder. He gave Tristan a tight hug.

Tristan smiled. "I'm doing well, brother. And you?"

"I'm doing good," he said, grinning. "We just got something to eat and thought we'd clean up before we barged in on you."

The smell of blood, testosterone, and...wet dog filled the room. I wrinkled my nose.

Sabol sniffed the air. "Smells like sex, Tristan. You and the lady been busy in here?" he asked, motioning toward me.

The others snickered.

Ignoring their question, he exchanged hugs with them. When he was done, he put his shoulder around his brother.

"Sabol, I'd like you to meet my woman, Crystal."

Sabol leaned forward and took my hand in his. "Nice to meet you, Crystal. I'm Tristan's brother."

I smiled. "It's nice to meet you, too."

As the others followed suit, Sabol and Ratliff looked me up and down.

"Well, any woman of Tristan's is like a sister to me, so I expect to be spending some time to get to know you *well*, Crystal," Sabol said, enunciating the word, well.

I grimaced at the thought of spending time with him, especially after my earlier conversation with Tristan.

Great, I really wasn't looking forward to this. I wondered if the biker clubs in the immortal realm were any different than those in the mortal world. Or did they share the same thought process? I was afraid to find out.

"How about we convene downstairs?" Tristan asked.

The men looked his room over.

"Damn Tristan, you kinky son of a bitch, what's with all of the chains and hoops?" Sebastian asked.

Tristan laughed. "If you can't figure it out Sebastian, then maybe you should go back to school."

Laughing, Sabol patted him on the back. "Sebastian, you really don't know my brother that well."

"Well, it's not like I have sex with him," he said, chuckling.

Laughs filled the air. Tristan and I followed them out.

§

"I swear Robert, nothing happened. We just went out to have fun and these men came out of nowhere. I didn't know they were going to be there," Jennifer snapped.

Raelin sat next to Jennifer on the bed. She chimed in. "Look, I'm sorry, it was my idea. I just wanted to release some of my energy. There was no harm in it. Don't tell me you don't do it?"

Robert glared at her. "Excuse me? Are you questioning me? I'm no..."

"Sorry to cut you off, but I can smell the wolf in you. You and Jennifer are werewolves, aren't you?"

He bit his lip. Jennifer knew better than to tell anybody. So, how did Raelin find out?

"What gives you that idea?"

"I can smell it and Jennifer showed me. Is yours genetic? I mean...the reason why I ask, is because you don't meet too many siblings where both carry the same curse. I'm right, aren't I?"

He glanced at Jennifer. She refrained from looking at him. "Jennifer...?"

"I'm sorry. We just wanted to get out and have fun. It was nice to go for a run in the woods. I know you do it."

Turning away, he put his hands on his hips. He looked at her in the dresser mirror. This wasn't happening. They needed to keep their secrets safe and hidden.

"Who else knows, Jennifer?" He faced her, folding his arms across his chest.

"What?" Her eyes grew bigger. "Nobody, I swear."

His voice rose. "Don't lie to me."

"I'm not. Nobody else knows, just Raelin."

He sighed. "Please refrain from telling your friends."

"You can trust me," Raelin said. "I won't tell anyone."

They stared at her.

"Promise," she said.

§

Wayne lay in the brush beyond the perimeters of the house, waiting. *Kill her, kill them all!* Dammit, stop it, Wayne! Why the fuck do you want to kill her and your family? *Because she's a traitor and a whore! She's been fucking another man behind your back.* Stop it! The voice inside his head was driving him crazy. Where the hell had this come from?

She thinks you're dead, she has for years. It's your own damn fault. If you would have never left her and the kids, the whole family may have been killed, instead, you've reduced yourself to this—another man. You were the one who told her to go to Tristan for help. *And she fucked him! It's still your fault, Wayne-O.*

He smacked his forehead, trying to rid himself of the voice. He needed to talk to Crystal soon, otherwise, he may kill himself if the voice didn't stop with the death threats. The family needed to know the truth about everything. He just hoped they would listen to him.

§

"Do you mind if we bunk here, brother?" Sabol asked, staring at Tristan and Crystal. He sat in the dark corner of the living room, mesmerized by Tristan's devotion to one woman.

Tristan guided her to sit on his lap. She had a feminine yet strong quality and figure, something which he had yet to understand.

Never in his life did he ever expect Tristan to give his heart to one woman, and oddly, he was content with her. Her muscular legs moved over Tristan's. The dark leather chair groaned beneath their weight.

Tristan smiled. "You're always more than welcome. You know that, Sabol."

§

I cringed at the invite. My muscles tightened against his body. How could he turn away his only kin? He couldn't.

"Thanks, we appreciate it."

The bikers smiled.

"The storm's a brewing out there. Mind if we put the bikes in the garage?"

"Go for it."

With that, the bikers left the house to put their bikes away.

Tristan's voice broke the silence. "I'm sorry, he's my brother. I can't turn him away, besides, I need him right now. And on that note, I need to talk to Robert. Can you give him a heads up?"

"Yeah, sure," I answered, peering back at him. "What's up?"

"We'll talk about that later. I really need to talk to Robert though, and soon."

My suspicions rose. "Tristan, what's going on?"

"Now's really not the time," he replied.

Pain struck my heart. Really? Did I have to go through this again? I was getting tired of this shit.

"Now is never the time with you," I snapped, jumping to my feet.

Without a glance back, I headed to his bedroom. Behind me, he muttered something about fucking women.

About the time I walked into the bedroom, Tristan appeared behind me.

"Crystal, we do need to talk, but it's kind of difficult with the pack here."

Abruptly, I turned around, my hair falling in my face. "Do you realize that I'm always put on the back burner? Not only with you but with everyone else I've dealt with in the past few years. This is bullshit, Tristan! I want a man who will keep me by his side and treat me as his equal, not something beneath him or as a prized possession," I said, smacking my chest. "Every time I try to leave my past behind me, something new takes me back to it. I want a normal life, to be with you and my family. I'm sick of all this domination bullshit. You and everybody else have this need to rein control over everything, including my life."

Tristan stared at me. "I'm sorry, Crystal. Please forgive me."

He drew me in close, his lips brushing against my ear. Sighing, I put my arms around him and lay my head against his.

"I'm really sorry, but we need them here right now."

I pulled back. Darkness…the emptiness of his eyes stared back at me. "What the fuck is going on? With you? With us?"

"They have a mission to serve, to protect you, to protect us, everyone for that matter."

"What exactly does that mean?"

"That means they have to meet your family."

"What?" My eyes snapped open. "No, Tristan. There's no way in hell…"

I took a step back.

He took a step toward me. "They have to. They have to be able to protect your family."

"What is it you're not telling me? What are you hiding?"

"I'm protecting you, and I'm trying to keep you out of it."

I shook my head. "No, you're not. You're hiding something."

"I'll tell you later, not now. I have to talk to Robert." He drew in a deep breath. "I need his help."

"Dammit Tristan, you're not pulling my family into something I don't know anything about. What the fuck is going on?" I snapped.

"Just arrange a meeting time for us, please? If you don't do it, I will."

The slam of the door downstairs caught our attention. It was followed by heavy footsteps. The Hell's Changelings had come back inside.

I peered at the bedroom door.

"They can hear us now."

"I know. Listen, just work with me. I'll fill you in later, I promise. Please. I just haven't had an opportunity to talk to you about this."

Anger fumed deep inside.

"What do you mean you haven't had an opportunity to talk to me? I've been here. I've been available. And you've only had the opportunity to fuck me, yet we can't talk? What the fuck, Tristan?" My blood boiled. "Is my family in danger?"

"Yes," he answered.

My jaw dropped.

His brow creased. "But I can't talk to you about it right now. I have to talk to my brothers and your son. Make it happen." He turned on his heels and left the room.

§

After breakfast the next morning, Rebecca sat on the bench in her backyard while the girls played on the swing set. Rebecca's cell phone was glued to her ear.

Her sister Larissa's singsong voice echoed through the earpiece. "I know there are problems when I have bad dreams about you, Becky."

Rebecca's gaze fell to the grass beneath her feet. "Great! That's what I didn't want to hear."

"What's going on, sis?"

"Anything and everything," she whispered. She didn't want the kids to know what their conversation was about.

"Do tell."

"I'm thinking about going back to Phoenix," she sighed. "Just me and the kids."

There was a moment of silence. "What about Robert?"

"I think I need some time alone. He's having his own issues as well. And even though I understand what he's going through, I don't exactly agree with it."

"What's going on with him?"

Her eyes flitted to the girls. "I don't know if I told you, but he found his mother."

Silence, then Larissa asked, "Didn't you say you had visions of her?"

"Yeah, I did. She brought a lot of other issues with her. She's a good woman. I like her, don't get me wrong, but I don't think she's the same woman she was before."

"What do you mean by that?"

Rebecca drew in a deep breath. "I told you there were problems up here, right?"

"Yeah?"

"Well, it's worse than what I thought it was. I haven't really been practicing…"

"We told you to keep using it. You're weakening, Becky. Your magic isn't as strong as it used to be. Mama always said you were the strong one, but now you're the weakest. Why aren't you using it? You were using it when you first met Robert."

"I can't keep using it on the kids. They're kids…"

Larissa cut her off. "So don't."

"That's not the point, Larissa. The point is...umm..." She dreaded this. Larissa was right, Rebecca had always been the strongest, but not now. If anything, she needed to get to Phoenix, not just for her family, but for her gift. Larissa could help her strengthen it.

"You were right about Robert. I tried to deny it, and I was wrong." She didn't like admitting she was wrong. Ashamed, she bit her lip. Rebecca detected the smile on the other end of the phone.

"Now, are you going to listen to me? You put the magic in place to protect yourself from his wild sexual prowess in the bedroom years ago. You haven't taken the protection off since then, have you?"

Rebecca frowned. The last thing she wanted to talk about with Larissa was her husband's sexual endeavors in the bedroom. "Yes, I did."

"And does he hurt you?"

Her cheeks flushed. "No, not anymore."

"What's the worst he's done?"

"He bit me, nothing severe, though. He's never physically changed so it was a human bite, not werewolf."

"It doesn't matter, Becky. The curse courses through his vessels. I know why you love him and I know why he interested you from the beginning. Most werewolves and vamps are wild in that regard. Their high level of sexual aggressiveness is a turn-on, but you've got to keep him under control in the bedroom."

"I know, Larissa. I don't think we need to talk about this anymore, all right?"

"Listen, I know you don't. Do you remember Jet?"

"Yeah."

"Now, that man was a tiger in the bedroom. I know how easy it is to let the magic loose when you're climaxing..."

"Oh, Larissa..." She rolled her eyes. The girls' playful screams diverted her attention.

Her sister's voice rose. "Becky, are you listening to me? Becky?"

"Yes, I'm listening."

"You need to keep yourself in check. Robert may be your husband..."

"Larissa, how does my sexual intimacy play into anything I've been talking about?" she whispered.

"All right..." It was quiet. Then, Larissa said, "The point is, you need to keep practicing, whenever and however it's done. Anyway, come to Phoenix. We need to practice our witchcraft together. We need some sister time."

"Thanks, sis."

"Now, I will add…"

Rebecca interrupted her. "Sis…"

"Don't interrupt me. I need to finish my sentence."

Rebecca rolled her eyes. "Yes, Larissa."

"I know Robert loves you and the kids. That man adores his family. So, bring the kids down here. I haven't seen them in forever."

Just then, Rebecca glanced up. Tisa stood on the top bar of the swing set. Rebecca bolted to her feet, eyes wide.

"Tisa!"

Tisa smiled. "I'm just playing mama!"

"Get…!"

Tisa jumped.

Rebecca threw her hands out, dropping the cell phone in the grass. She froze Tisa in air.

"This is fun, mama!"

"This is not fun. You know better, young lady." Rebecca placed Tisa softly on the ground. "Now, don't do it again."

Katie and Leah stared at their mother.

"The same goes for you two."

Innocent smiles crept up on their faces.

Rebecca grabbed her phone and sat down. "Are you still there?"

"Yes, are the girls all right?" she asked, concerned.

"Yes, they are."

"You don't have control over your life anymore, much less your children's. Get your ass down here, and soon."

She rubbed her forehead. "It's not just that, Larissa. Bad elements are in the air."

"Like?"

"The kids acquired Robert's curse, and I think they acquired my witchery."

The girls took turns on the slide.

Again, it was quiet. It was evident Larissa was smiling. "Hmm."

"Please tell me you're not smiling about that?"

"Who me? Never," she said sarcastically. "You know, that's not a bad thing."

"I didn't think he could pass the curse on genetically."

"Come now. You're lying to yourself if you never thought he could pass on the curse. It's been known for years that werewolves can have canine children…"

"Don't call them that," Rebecca demanded.

"Sorry, sis, but it's the truth and you know it, and well, if they acquired your magic…"

"Well, we all know that's genetic but there's something else."

"What's that?"

"Crystal's boyfriend, Tristan, he thinks Katie has a gift."

"Well, we already know that…"

Rebecca cut her off. "I'm not talking about the magic or the werewolf. He says there's something else there."

"Mm, and who exactly is Tristan?"

"Crystal's boyfriend. He's a vampire," she answered.

"Vampire, huh? How old is he?"

"I'm not sure. I think he's pretty old, though."

"Well, if he's old enough, he may know but what the hell is he doing getting that close to Katie?"

"I don't think he has to get too close to her to know…"

"Either way, even more reason for you to get down here. You don't need your kids turning into his midnight snack," Larissa replied.

"Don't worry. I've been keeping an eye on him when he's here."

"Is Robert usually there when he's there?"

"Sometimes," Rebecca answered, her gaze moving over to the girls. They pushed each other on the swing. "Not too high!" she yelled. "Sorry I yelled in your ear, sis."

Larissa laughed. "Yeah, I'd be careful. That little Tisa might send one of the others to BFE."

Rebecca giggled. "My life is turning into turmoil. Oh, and Crystal's been turned."

"Who turned her?"

"Tristan and one of their friends, Warrant. He's a werewolf."

"Hybrid, huh? You better be careful, Rebecca. They're all over. Somebody said they're making them in a laboratory or something like that."

"Yeah, I'm pretty sure they caught that guy, at least, that's what Tristan said."

"Either way, there's a bunch of those motherfuckers out there."

Great!

"They're concerned about the Mogollon Rim and the large canyons up there. They said that's a good place for them to hide."

Rebecca gazed up at the fence. "Who are you referring to?"

"I have my sources, sis."

"Reliable, I hope?"

"But of course. Do you think I would really tell you bullshit stories just to get you down here?"

Now, that was a stupid question. "Of course, you would."

"Okay, maybe I would. But, either way, it's true. You better think about your children. If there really are issues up there, then you need to get the family out of there. Robert is always welcome, too. And regardless of your problems, he does love you. He's a good man."

"I know he does. I just wish he would listen to me once in a while."

"Just pack your shit up. Let's go. Robert will probably understand anyway."

"Tomorrow."

"I'm not talking tomorrow, I'm talking now. I want to see those kids. It's been way too long besides I want to see what talents they have."

"Larissa!"

"Don't worry. If you really don't want them to have their witchery, I know somebody who might be able to take it away. I can't say that I agree with you not wanting them to have it, but he's good. Of course, I can't promise anything."

"Even if it is genetic?"

"Maybe, like I said, I can't promise anything. I'll talk to him, though, and see what he says."

Rebecca thought about this. Did she really trust somebody to take the curse away? Somebody she never met? What if they screwed up? What if they hurt the girls? Robert would be livid if she even considered it. Though he wasn't happy that the children carried his disease, he also wouldn't trust the idea of a warlock trying to remove it.

"Becky? Are you listening to me?"

"Yeah, sorry, I'm here."

"Did you hear me?"

"No, I...uh, was watching the kids. What did you say?"

"Get down here. I'll try to get a hold of him in the meantime."

"Okay."

"When do you think you can get down here?"

"I don't know. I need to let Robert know, and Jennifer."

"Yes, Jennifer." Larissa paused. "Maybe she can come down with you for a bit."

Rebecca knew where this was going. "She has school, though."

"What about a short vacation for her? Maybe she can see some of her old friends while she's here. She might be game for that."

"It's not her I have to worry about. It's Robert and his mom. I don't think they'll allow it."

"You know, you and Robert have practically raised her. I think you have some say in this."

Rebecca closed her eyes. "Not really."

"Really, Rebecca?"

She used her full first name, which meant that Larissa was growing agitated.

"She's not here very often, but Jennifer is Crystal's daughter, not mine."

"Why isn't her mom there a lot?"

It hurt to think. Maybe Larissa was right in a way. Crystal slept a lot in the daytime, and at night, when everybody was sleeping, she would spend most of her with Tristan. Oh, how her head hurt.

"Listen, sis…"

"I want to know why her mother isn't raising her now," Larissa snapped.

"She's had some issues…"

"What kind of issues? Once a mother, always a mother," she chimed.

"I understand what you're saying, but I also have my own reservations about her problems right now."

"So, explain?"

"It really is a long story."

"I have time."

"Well, I don't…" Rebecca said. She really didn't want to go there right now.

"Well, if she's having issues, why don't you invite her down too? Maybe she needs some time for herself as well."

Oh God, she was going there. Rebecca rubbed her temples. "I don't think that's a good idea."

"Why not?"

Did she really have to say it? And if she did, would her sister take the alternate route and come up here to visit her? She'd come up with a reason to meet everybody and Rebecca wasn't so sure she wanted that, at least, not now.

"Listen, I'll come down there, but I'm only bringing the kids, and I need to talk to Robert first. So, it may be sometime tomorrow before I make it down there."

It was quiet again. Rebecca was sure Larissa's brain was busy calculating all of Rebecca's responses. She was intelligent—a little too smart for her own good, and she was also a bitch at times, which Rebecca was not looking forward to.

Then came her voice, calm and soothing, but different. "That's fine. I'm looking forward to seeing the kids. Maybe another time I can meet his mother and her boyfriend. I would *really* like to meet them, though."

Great! Rebecca swallowed hard. Now, she was dreading going back to Phoenix. She needed to go, though. It wasn't a want, instead, it was a need. She already knew they were going to have mixed company, but when, she didn't know.

Larissa's voice changed back into her sweet singsong melody. "You call me when you're on your way. Then maybe when you're ready to go back, I can go with you."

No, no, Rebecca didn't need that for she already had enough issues. She didn't need her sister playing up the drama with Robert's family. Crystal and Tristan were tough and thick skinned. They could handle the issues. It was the magic she knew her sister would throw at them, and it wouldn't only be with them, it would also be with the sinister evil that recently rode into town.

Maybe this was a good thing; after all, Rebecca did need a break. Larissa would help out with the kids, so that would be helpful although Robert didn't particularly like the girls hanging out with Larissa because of her dramatic and confrontational ways. He also wouldn't be happy about her unexpected vacation.

"I'll call you when I'm ready."

"Talk to you soon, sis," Larissa said.

"Bye." Rebecca hit the end button on her phone.

Hell was calling and right now, she needed to find the alternate path to righteousness.

She thought about her sister's words, *when you're ready to go back, I can go with you.* Maybe she did need her sister with her when she came back. After all, things were getting worse here. It was the children she worried about the most. Did she really want to take away their only source of defense—the werewolf curse and their witchery?

The sweat from her daughter's caramel colored skin glistened in the sunlight. They smiled at her as she reached down into the cooler next to her and pulled out three small bottles of water. As she opened them, they ran up to her and chugged down their waters.

Decisions, decisions.

§

I made sure my hunger was satisfied and my stomach full every time I walked through my front door. Though my grandchildren were my blood, I worried that, someday, the beasts inside of me would try to gain control of my body and attack the children, so I did the obvious, eat dinner and clean up before coming home.

As I neared the top of the stairs, something crashed in the garage. I glanced in the children's room where they lay in bed, sleeping.

Rebecca?

I bolted downstairs to the garage, where Rebecca stood on the ladder leading to the attic. Two suitcases lay on the floor beneath her feet and another suitcase toppled down the stairs, past her, into my hands. As she reached for a duffel bag, another suitcase fell, striking her in the head on the way down where I caught it.

"Ow! Son of a…"

"Witch," I answered.

She peered down at me. "Funny."

"I thought so," I said, smiling.

Rebecca grabbed the duffel bag from the attic.

"I thought you were a witch," I said. "Couldn't you have used your magic to get the duffel bag down? Or whatever it is that you witches do."

She climbed down from the ladder. "Screw you, Crystal."

Apparently, she wasn't in the mood for my dry humor. "Wow, I was just kidding, Rebecca."

She sorted through the luggage.

"What's up with you lately? And what's with the suitcases?"

She took the suitcase out of my hand. "I don't want to talk about it."

"All right," I said, leaning against the SUV. "Can you, at least, tell me if you and the family are taking a vacation?"

Rebecca straightened up.

"I think I deserve to know that," I said. "Especially if you guys are going to be gone."

She sighed. "Listen, Crystal, Brandy, whatever the hell you go by now, not that it matters much to you, but I try not to use my witchcraft a whole hell of a lot. It's my own personal choice."

"All right," I said, glancing down at the four bags of luggage. I presumed there was one for her and three for—the children.

"So, where are you taking the kids?" I asked.

She glared at me but before she had a chance to respond, I straightened up.

"Rebecca, I think I have a right to ask, especially if you're leaving Robert and taking the kids. Does Robert know?"

"He…" Again, she sighed. "No." She paused. "But I'm going to talk to him later when he gets home."

I glanced down at the baggage. "Where are you going?"

"Phoenix, my sister lives there. I'm going to visit her for a little while."

I nodded. "This has been too much on you—me, coming home to my son, to my family."

Our eyes met.

"You don't want me here. You never did." Tension filled the room.

"There are bad elements in the air, and they followed you here," she said. "You brought them here, whether you realized it or not."

She was right. I couldn't deny it. "I'm sorry, Rebecca. None of this was my fault. I hope you understand that." I glanced around. "Tristan's intentions were good when he brought me here."

"Regardless, they have followed you here, and they haven't left."

She grabbed the luggage, tucked it under her arms, and headed for the door.

"Let me at least help you," I said, following her.

"I'm good." She glanced back at me. "Thank you, though."

I sighed. "You're a stubborn woman, Rebecca."

"Excuse me?" She turned around.

"You heard me. You're stubborn. The kids are going to get it from both sides of the family." I smiled. "Lighten up, Rebecca. I'm your mother-in-law, not the devil."

"I'm having some problems right now, all right," she said with a flat tone.

"You are having problems? Or you and Robert?" I asked.

She looked away.

"What kind of problems?"

Again, silence.

"Are they problems you have to run away from because it sure looks like it to me?" I wondered if they were having marital issues, or if there wasn't something else going on.

She turned to leave.

"Maybe instead of running away from your problems, you should stay and confront them. That's what I would do."

"And you're not me. We're two different people. I'm not like you."

I thought she might be hiding something, but what, I didn't know.

"Are you sure about that?" I asked, the beasts stirring inside of me. Then, my adrenaline picked up. It was time to put my energy into something else and by doing that, I needed to create some distance between us to control my beasts.

I began folding up the attic ladder.

"Is Robert working?"

"Yes, they called him in."

"I thought he worked last night?" I pushed the ladder up triggering the hinge mechanism to automatically pull the ladder in and close the attic door.

"He did, but a deputy was killed last night off of I-17. The sheriff needed him in today."

What little bit of exertion I put into closing the door calmed my nerves but it wasn't enough. "You know, Rebecca, he works hard for you and the kids."

"I know he does. What's your point?"

I sighed. "Whatever issues you're having, maybe you need to work them out here, with him."

As Rebecca took in a breath, closed her eyes, and tried to calm herself, I studied her. She loved my son but something else was at work here, something I didn't understand. The expression on her face was part hurt, part pain, yet emotionally disconnected.

"You're a mother, you've raised two children, at least, for the most part," she began.

"Yes?" I responded.

"Did you stay home with your children? Or did you work? Do you remember?"

I thought about this. "I remember I was home with them for a short time, but then, eventually, went back to work."

"So when you were at home with your children, did you ever feel confined? Stuck at home? Felt like you was losing your identity, like you weren't the same person you used to be?"

"It's tough to be a stay at home mom, even more so than it is to be a working mom, either way, your work never gets done. It's hard, I'll agree. Why? Is that the problem?"

My nerves had settled some so I took a step toward her.

"If it is, then I think you need to stay here and reflect on your life. You don't need to leave to do that. Robert needs you here." I offered my reassurance by touching her arm. "He will help. You just need to talk to him. Open your lines of communication."

"That's not all of it. There's so much more, you really don't understand." Her eyes teared up, so she dropped the luggage to cover her eyes.

"I'm sure I don't, but maybe I would if you opened up to me, instead of closing yourself off. You're making our relationship difficult because you won't talk to me and because you won't talk to Robert about whatever it is that's going on with you two."

I made a point to add the two to allow her some room to elaborate since she really didn't want to talk to me.

Rebecca's lips moved, but no sound came out. Silence filled the air, allowing the room to close in on us, making the tension in the room much more volatile and claustrophobic.

I continued on. "All right, I see. It's not something you want to discuss with me. Or is it me you have a problem with?"

Rebecca's gaze shifted.

I got the hint. "You still don't like me…?"

"That's not true…"

I folded my arms across my chest. "Bullshit. You didn't like me before you met me, and now that you've met me, you still don't like me." My nerves were on edge again.

"I've heard you and Robert, everything, from she's nothing but trouble to if she wasn't here, we wouldn't be having this trouble. Thanks for all of the reinforcement you've given my son," I said, pointing my finger at her. The beasts inside threatened to expose themselves.

"You've done nothing but cause my son heartache since I've been here! Granted, I haven't been here very long, but I see and hear the issues you're going through. Maybe you need to tend to your wifely duties instead of fighting them," I stressed, retreating. The beasts within were rising to the surface.

Rebecca's face twisted, her brows narrowing in. "I don't fight them!"

"Bullshit!" I spat, taking a couple of steps back.

"I'm a great mother..." She advanced on me, jabbing herself in the chest.

"I never said you weren't..." I leaned back against the SUV.

Rebecca stopped short, opening her mouth to say something.

I blurted out, "You're a fantastic mother, but you're short on your matrimonial vows!"

"How the hell would you know about matrimonial vows!" she screamed.

She stormed toward me. Step down, Crystal. No, she needed to know the truth.

"From my understanding, your husband cheated on you. Why? I'd like to know. Were you short on some of your *wifely duties*?" Rebecca snapped.

I stared at her. "My second husband Chris turned out to be a piece of shit. Yeah, I told Robert and Jennifer that he was their father. That was because their real dad ran out on me when they were young. Apparently, we weren't good enough for him," I snapped.

My adrenaline picked up speed. "I thought Chris would have been a better father to them, considering the circumstances, but apparently, I was wrong." Tears rolled from my eyes.

"I loved him! I really did love him." Then, I realized I was talking about my children's father, Wayne.

"Oh, God," I muttered. Memories flooded my brain. "Why? Why the hell did he leave?" I screamed. "What the hell did I do to him?" I buried my face in my hands and cried.

Fury raged inside as images of our wedding and our life flooded my head. The wolf within fought to gain control but I tried to force it back down.

"Oh, shit," Rebecca whispered. "No...not here. Not now."

§

Rebecca glanced at the doorway to the house. It was partially open. Even if she could get through and shut it, she feared it wouldn't keep Crystal out.

Crystal's emotional outburst erupted into a violent fit as she slammed her fist into the wall that separated the living room from the garage. Drywall exploded around her. It left a hole through to the living room.

Rebecca took advantage of the situation and rushed through the door, slamming it and locking it. *Get to the girls!* Spinning on her heels, she turned and slipped yet, she regained her footing and ran to the stairs.

Crystal glared at her through the hole, the werewolf within emerging, her red hair spilling in her face. She rammed her shoulders against the hole, breaking it open wider and barging through it.

Rebecca screamed and bolted up the stairs to the girls' room, the werewolf in close pursuit. The girls screamed. Claws raked down Rebeca's back, the force of the strike shoving her forward onto the bedroom floor. Then, the door slammed shut, closing the creature off from them. It wouldn't hold Crystal back... But wait... Who slammed the door shut? Did she do it? Or...?

She spun around. Tisa stood in her crib, gripping onto the railing tears pouring down her small, rosy red cheeks. Katie and Leah sat up in their beds, their sheets wrapped loosely around their legs, staring at her, screaming, tears streaming down their cherub-like faces.

Then, it set in—they were going to die. She had to do something.

The beast crashed against the door, the wood cracking beneath its weight.

If Rebecca could get Crystal to change back into her human form, then she would not hurt the girls. But how? How in the hell was she going to talk her back into her human form? It was impossible.

Rebecca spun around to face the door, her children by her side. Again, the werewolf crashed against it. The door cracked. The kids huddled beside her, clutching onto her.

"Go away!" she screamed, her heart thudding in her chest. She had one other alternative.

The werewolf collided with the door. It caved in and splintered. When the werewolf slammed into the door again, it burst open. Still partially in human form, Crystal walked into the room, her eyes fixated on Rebecca.

"Stop!" Rebecca tapped into her witchery, pushing her hands out before her, creating an invisible barrier, which protected her and the girls from Crystal.

Crystal sneered. Then, she rushed Rebecca, slamming full force into the barrier, the momentum throwing her backward and out of the bedroom door.

The girls screamed.

Katie gazed up at her mother. As if she knew what she was doing, she imitated her mom's movement, cupping her hands together, front to the back of the other hand toward the door, and recited the same chant.

Leah followed along.

Crystal scrambled to her feet and slowly walked back into the room.

"Nana, stop!" Leah screamed, her voice strong and defiant.

Crystal cocked her head and stared at the child.

Leah's lip curled downward. "Nana."

"Crystal, I'm warning you to back down, now! Don't make me hurt you!" Rebecca screamed.

The shield weakened beneath her hold. Oh, no, this was not happening.

Crystal's movements were calculating and more persistent. Something moved beneath the surface of her skin. Slowly, Crystal reached out, her hand penetrating the invisible shield.

Rebecca's jaw dropped as the clawed hand came within inches of her face.

The ultimate decision had to be made, and it was to borrow the girl's magic. With their sorcery combined, she regained her strength to keep the invisible barrier alive, creating a stronger shield of unity. The moment it regained its power, it created a force shield so strong, it alone, sent the werewolf flying out of the room.

Crystal slammed into the wall above the staircase, where she flipped over the railing and onto the floor below.

Rebecca used her witchery to seek out Crystal's mind to determine her next move.

§

Rebecca embedded an image in my mind that horrified me. Then, I realized what had happened, I had attacked them.

I bit my lip, drawing blood. Scrambled thoughts ran through my head. Shit!

The girl's witchery was conjoined with Rebecca's. They didn't understand why I had come after them. What I had feared had come true for I had tried to kill them.

I bolted out of the house, angry at myself for allowing such a thing to happen, for not keeping control of the situation.

Crying mad, I found myself searching for some alone time deep in the forest.

§

Robert walked into the station, the wind slamming the door shut behind him.

"Robert, I really wish you would watch it with that door!" the sheriff yelled.

"Sorry sir, it slipped from my hand!" he lied, rounding the corner.

"Come here, please!"

"Yes, sir," he muttered.

He would have preferred to be anywhere else but here after their discussion the other day but Robert continued on, walking into the sheriff's office. The sun leaked through the blinds behind the sheriff. Before him, a uniformed woman sat in the chair.

Aw, shit, not yet. Groaning, Robert ran his hand through his hair.

"Sir, I need to get back to work. I really don't have time…"

The sheriff leaned forward on his desk, a look of contempt on his face. Dammit, he really didn't have time for this. Not only that, he wanted to look for Torrance's body.

"After what you did to the patrol car last night, you'd better have some time for me."

He grimaced. Yeah, he better give his boss some time. "Sorry about that, sir."

"You're lucky we have other cars available for your use."

"Thank you, Sheriff."

The Sheriff gazed up at him, studying his face. "Well, I can honestly say I've been in the position you were in, but you know the procedure. Though it was a car accident, you should have called for backup. Now, your report said that you were not able to identify what crossed the road. Is that correct?"

"Yes, sir, unfortunately, I didn't have much time for that." Part of his lie was truth, and the other part was a straight forward lie. He knew better, but he didn't want to drag another officer into the problems of the immortal world.

"Uh-huh. Well, we'll have to go over this more, later, just you and I. In the meantime, I'd like you to meet your new partner. Deputy Robert Bouchard this is Deputy Adrienne Miller."

Robert was thankful he had more time to deliberate on his lie. Honestly, how would he be able to explain a dragon? The old man would have Robert pee in a cup for a drug test, and then he would send him to the psychologist.

Robert faked a smile.

The woman stood and extended her hand. "Nice to meet you," she said with a smile.

He shook her hand. "Nice to meet you, too."

"I've heard a lot about you."

"All good I hope?" he said, glancing at the sheriff.

"Yes, all good," the sheriff replied, standing.

Robert looked the woman over. She was older than him, he guessed around thirty years old. Her spiky blonde hair stuck out from under her hat. She had a feminine yet strong physique.

"I've shown her around the office already. I figured, while you're out and about, you can show her around. You can do that, right?"

His gaze shifted to his boss. "Yes, I can."

"Good. Now get to work," the sheriff said, sitting down.

Robert was silent as they walked outside and climbed into the car.

The sun beat down on it, heating up the interior. What was not hot for him was hot for her. As she climbed inside, her plush bottom slid across the seat. The seatbelt buckle grazed her skin. She whimpered.

Robert shut the door, fastened his seatbelt and shook his hand as though he burnt it. He glanced over at her.

"That was fucking hot," she said.

A jolt exploded into the back of the vehicle, throwing them into the dashboard. The screech of metal and plastic echoed throughout the car.

"What the hell...?"

They gazed through the back window. The grill of a large white Dodge truck stared at them. They studied the driver's seat. It was empty. The driver must have slumped over.

Eyes wide, Robert turned to look at her. "Are you all right?"

Mouth open, she stared back at him. "Yeah, I'm fine. And you?"

"I'm okay."

She was already climbing out of the car.

"Well, all right, let's check this out," he said to himself. At least she was a real go-getter. That was a plus.

As they walked toward the truck, a gust of wind slammed against them, threatening to knock them over. Both of them placed a hand on the patrol car to steady themselves. Their other hand went to their guns.

Robert unsnapped the holster with his thumb, glancing at his partner.

She stared back at him, a confused look on her face, brows narrowed in.

His eyes drifted back to the truck. The driver had to be laying across the seat. Ready for an attack, he pulled his gun out.

"Put your hands up and get out of the truck! Slowly!" he yelled.

There was no movement from within.

"Put your hands up and get out of the truck!" he yelled.

His partner approached from the other side, gun in hand. Again, no movement, and silence…*dead silence.*

The beast within him was on alert. Then his beast caught it—the breathing…the heartbeat. It *was* still inside the truck. He took a deep breath and smelled *it.* His partner eyed him curiously. She was going to have to get out of the way. If she didn't, she might be a dead woman. She wasn't immortal, but he was, and so was it.

§

The passenger door flew open. Something inhuman emerged. Though it was part human, it was in transition, wings spread out from its back, its skin naked and leathery.

Deputy Miller's jaw dropped.

The human skin on its face was sagging. The fangs descended from its mouth. Its eyes darkened, narrowing in on her.

As it darted out of the truck, Miller squeezed off several shots. The bullets blasted into the window and the door. Not one bullet penetrated her attacker.

It ran straight for her, and so did Robert. Both were faster than anything she had ever seen. She stood, stunned and petrified, her heart racing and her eyes wide in disbelief. It shrieked. Robert bounded over the patrol car toward her.

The creature slammed her to the ground, its hands hot against her skin. Holes burnt through her shirt where its hands were. Then, it caught sight of Robert and bolted, Robert hot on its trail.

Miller stared in the direction where Robert had pursued the creature. What the hell was that thing? She started to roll over, but the pain intensified. It was as if she had been branded with a hot iron. She hissed.

The sheriff and another deputy ran out of the sheriff's office.

"What the hell happened out here!" the sheriff yelled, running toward her. He stared at the truck, which was embedded into the back of the patrol car. "Son of a bitch!"

She attempted to get up. "I don't really know myself. Oh my God, it hurts!"

They knelt beside her. "You need to be careful," Sheriff Martin said. He pushed her back down and looked the wounds over.

"Oh my…"

She groaned.

The men looked at one another. "What happened?"

Miller tried to raise up, but she couldn't move. The pain was excruciating. As she laid back down, she caught the grim look on their faces.

"What's wrong? Oh my God…!" she yelled.

Their grip on her hands tightened. The burn deepened and spread across her arms like wildfire, eating away at her skin.

"Jesus, what the hell…?" the deputy began.

He glanced at the sheriff, who held his finger over his mouth, shushing him.

The deputy grimaced.

"We need to do something, Sheriff!"

§

Miller's body stilled beneath him. The sheriff lowered his head, frowning. Her sudden passing alarmed him, even as the burn continued to spread across her dead body.

The deputy jerked his hands away from her. "What the fuck…?"

"I don't know." The sheriff stood and glanced around. "Where's Robert?"

The deputy stood beside him, surveying their surroundings.

"He probably took off after the driver."

"Yeah, probably but which direction I'd like to know," the sheriff snapped.

"What the hell was that? It spread like acid, you know like that alien thing's saliva from that movie. You know…uh, what was that called?"

The sheriff chewed on his lip and straightened his hat. "I think it was called Alien. And, yes it was similar to that."

A gust of wind whisked the deputy's hat off of his head.

"Shit," he spat. He chased the hat down and stuck it on his head. Then, he gazed back at the truck. "Did he throw acid on her or something?"

"I don't know. It looks more like a burn but I'll tell you something, we're not touching her again."

§

The winged creature bolted up the mountainside with Robert in pursuit. Abruptly, it turned to defend itself when Robert lunged at it, knocking it down. Robert fell on top of it, his fangs sinking into the creature's thick skin.

It shrieked, and a rush of fire shot out of its mouth, barely missing Robert. The heat burnt his hair, so he shook his head, and rolled them over sideways, sending them down the slope.

Robert fought to keep control when movement caught his attention. Another winged creature, who stood taller than them, camouflaged itself in the woods yet it stared at them, its eyes a wild blue.

What the fuck? Robert lost control of the creature. It scrambled atop him and attempted to pin him down, its talons scraping down his chest, its wings flapping heavily in the wind, tearing branches from the trees.

§

Dark clouds enveloped the sun, bringing hell's storm with it. Above me, the golden sphere peered through a slim crack in the dark shroud, resembling an evil eye. Hell was advancing upon us.

An inhuman shriek in the woods caught my attention, followed by a man's scream.

Robert? No, it couldn't be. The man screamed again. It was Robert! Pain ripped through my heart. I bolted in the direction it came from.

§

Sebastian lay in the darkness, eyes closed.

Tristan's voice filled his head. "Can you check on Crystal? Something's wrong!"

"You got it," Sebastian said, jumping out of his coffin.

Sebastian was the only daywalker within his brotherhood, so if they asked him to do something during the daytime, he did it. He walked out of the house and into the daylight. A forceful wind struck him, threatening to blow him over.

"Not today, motherfucker," he said.

Winds circled in the sky, forming funnels and picking up speed. The wind howled as branches broke and whipped about within the torrential storm. Thunder boomed overhead and lightning struck a nearby tree.

Then, Crystal's scent drifted by. He drew in a deep breath, detecting her vampire, her werewolf, and…brimstone? He knew that scent from…

Wait! She was in danger! He had to find her and fast.

§

Seconds later, I found my son pinned down by a deformed dragon with a wing-span of about three to four feet. Its wings viciously beat Robert, creating further disturbance to the area. Dirt and debris whirled around them.

The unknown beast stirred within me, eagerly rising to the occasion. My eyes changed, fixating on my prey, the creature easing her way to the surface.

As I took a step toward it, the misshapen dragon snapped its head around. It was a scientific experiment gone wrong. It had the dragon snout, body, and wings. Yet, the rest of the face was morbidly horrific. The eyes bulged out, ready to pop out of the socket.

My jaw dropped. "What the…?"

Robert yelled, "Watch out! There's another one!"

A second deformed dragon ran out of the forest behind me. Growling, I spun around. It ran into me, throwing me backward into Robert's attacker, knocking us to the ground.

As we struggled to regain our footing, Robert jumped it. The other dragon lunged for me. Then Sebastian ran out of the woods and jumped on its back.

§

Rebecca had already tended to the wounds on her back. Now, as she moved about the girl's room and shoved their clothes in suitcases, the pain settled in.

Then Larissa's voice popped in her head. *"You need to come home now! If not for yourself and the kids, for your husband! He will need you at your strongest!"*

She tried to clear her sister's voice by shaking her head. Then, Katie walked in the room.

Katie sat down on the bed. Scratching her head, she said. "Mommy, daddy needs you."

She smiled at her. "I know, baby. That's why we're going to see Aunt

Larissa."

"He needs us, though," Katie said.

"I know he does. This is just temporary, sweetie."

Leah looked up at her mom. "What's temporary?"

Rebecca sat down. "It's just for a short time. I need your Aunt Larissa right now, so I can be at my best."

"Yeah, she said you need to be at your strongest," Katie replied.

"Where did you hear that?" Rebecca asked. Then she thought about something Tristan had said about Katie. *This one's special.*

"I heard her mommy. She was talking to you."

Outside, something crashed against the house.

Now what? Rebecca glanced through the window. Wind funnels formed outside, rapidly picking up speed.

Her heart was already racing. This time, her heart lurched into her throat.

"Oh my God."

"Mommy, I'm scared," Leah cried.

"So, are we mommy!" they cried.

Quickly, she gathered up her children and hustled them downstairs to the closet beneath the staircase. Inside, artillery lined the steel insulated walls. She stepped into the deep closet and opened the secret door on the back wall. It opened up to the basement where she flipped on the light switch.

Hesitantly, the girls descended the staircase.

"Mommy, why do we have to go down here? It's scary," Leah asked.

"It's not that bad, sweetie. It's just a little dark," she said, holding Tisa's hand. "Besides, daddy set up stuff down here for you girls, just in case. Now, keep moving."

"In case of what?" Leah asked. She looked up at her mother.

"Leah, you're too smart for your own good. Just keep moving."

§

Warrant was about fifty feet away from the cave when something growled. He stopped and turned to find a mountain lion emerging from the brush.

"Hmmm, have I seen you somewhere before?" he asked.

The feline slinked closer to the cave.

Warrant inhaled her scent. "You're the real deal. No shapeshifter here, right?"

The mountain lion stared at him. Then, something hard struck Warrant in the head. He turned, ready to fight when it struck him again. He glanced up at the sky. Hail pelted him.

"Shit," he muttered.

The mountain lion disappeared into the cave. He waited about a minute before he followed her inside for he didn't want her to think he was a threat. The last thing he needed right now was to get in a fight with her.

"Hey beautiful, where are you?"

A second later, his eyes adjusted to the darkness. The feline lay on a high ledge inside. Emitting a low growl, her eyes followed his every move.

"There you are. I just want to keep my eye on you. I know how you women are," he said, winking at her.

As if understanding him, she snorted.

He sat down near the entrance and chuckled. "Just can't trust you women for shit." He glanced at her and grinned. "It's nothing personal, dear. I learn from experience but, I will warn you, try something stupid and you're not going to like me. Got it?"

As if disagreeing with him, she growled.

"I take it, you're not up for idle chat?"

§

Wayne leaped over the block fence of his family's home. He figured the children wouldn't be playing outside in this nasty weather, so he sought refuge in the girls' playhouse. It was better than nothing.

§

A loud crack bellowed out. A heavy thud followed. I glanced back in the direction where Sebastian and the creature were. "Is Sebastian still over there?"

We stood in a wash near the mountain. The large dead tree and hill blocked our view.

"Who's Sebastian?" Robert asked, glancing back.

"The guy who jumped the dragon," I said.

Robert wiped the blood off of his mouth. "Is he a friend of yours?"

"He's a friend of Tristan's."

Robert rolled his eyes. "Tristan's friend?"

"Yes. Why, what's up?" I looked beyond him at the hill. No movement.

"I remember his last friend."

"Yeah, well, that wasn't exactly Tristan's fault," I said, starting up the hill.

Robert grabbed my arm. "I'll take care of this."

Carefully, he walked up the hill, stopping short of the tree, and knelt down.

I didn't know Sebastian that well, so I was unsure of him and his intentions…and just how the hell did he know I was here? Did Tristan have him follow me? Or did he do it of his own accord? And why?

I followed Robert up the hill and knelt down beside him.

Keeping his eyes on Sebastian, he shook his head.

I followed his gaze. Sebastian hunkered down over the body. The biker club emblem on the back of Sebastian's leather jacket stared back at us.

Frowning, Robert stood. "Hey, what are you doing there?"

Sebastian peered over his shoulder, his face covered in blood. His brooding dark eyes fixated on Robert.

"Jesus, man, you hungry?" Robert folded his arms over his chest.

"What do you want, asshole?" Sebastian stood, straightened his jacket, and then took a step toward Robert.

"Nothing, dickhead. My mother was worried about you. She said you're Tristan's friend."

Sebastian sucked the blood from his lower lip, his eyes falling on me. Sneering, he planted his foot on the tree.

Robert glanced down at the dark green skinned hybrid who lay close by. "What the hell is that?"

Sebastian cocked his head. "That, my friend, is a hybrid, a day walking hybrid, just like your mother."

"And what is that one?" I asked.

Sebastian reached down and grabbed the carcass. Instantly, it disintegrated into dust. Ashes spilled from his hand.

"Well, looks like I won't be able to completely identify it, but it appears its part dragon."

"Dragon?" Robert asked.

"Yes, dragon," he answered.

"You're kidding, right?" I asked, eyes wide. Dragon? What the hell? They didn't exist. Then, of course, who was I kidding. I was part werewolf and vampire.

"Tell me, Crystal why does that surprise you? If we exist, who is to say they don't exist? Hmm?"

Robert and I exchanged looks.

"That explains the thing I saw in the forest the other night," Robert replied.

Sebastian approached me. Alarmingly, he sniffed at my neck.

"Tell me, Crystal, what lives beneath your skin? What ignites your fire?" he asked. Blood stained his chin.

"I don't know," I answered. He was getting too close for comfort so I backed away.

"You don't know? Or you don't care to reveal it?" He leaned in toward me. "Or are you hiding it from your lover and your family?"

"Back off, Sebastian," I spat. Where the hell was he going with this?

He walked around me. "I smell something from years gone by. You hide it..."

I cut him off. "I'm not hiding anything."

"What the hell are you talking about?" Robert asked, his voice rising.

Robert was growing irritated and so was I. My heartbeat picked up again. Then Robert squared his shoulders up and took a step toward Sebastian.

Sebastian held his hand up, stopping Robert in his tracks.

"I'm talking about her third beast. I can smell them, the vampire, the werewolf, and even..." His eyes darkened. Then, he laughed. "Well, even I have a hard time talking about *them*..."

He pressed his nose against my neck and pushed my head against his.

"...for I used to kill them," he whispered. He glared at me.

The tone of his voice sent a chill down my spine. I tried to pull away, but he held on tight.

"But I guess if I were in your shoes, I would have a hard time believing it too. Tell me, does Tristan know? I don't think he does." He rubbed his chin. "Or maybe so, is this his reason for being with you?"

I sneered at him. "Get away from me."

"Oh, I would love to have one as my lover. They are such passionate creatures."

Robert shifted his weight from foot to foot.

"What the fuck is he talking about, mom?"

"I..."

A smirk appeared on Sebastian's face, and then he whispered, "If I get a girlfriend, can you help me turn her? I'd love to have a hybrid just like you."

I had enough. Pushing him away, I spat, "Just get the fuck away from me. I don't know what you're talking about. And I have no desire to help you."

"Oh, but I do. I'd like to know how you became one. They are virtually non-existent." Excitement enlightened his dark eyes and his chiseled face.

I was tired of his game. "All right asshole, then tell me what the fuck I am," I snapped, folding my arms across my chest.

One word escaped his lips.

THE BEASTS WITHIN

After my talk with Robert and Sebastian, I headed back to Tristan's place. Bloody tears streaked my face. Why the hell did I let them do this to me? It was my own damn fault. If I hadn't let Tristan and Warrant change me, I wouldn't be dealing with these fucking beasts inside, and now this? Dragons? What the hell? This had to be a joke.

Something touched my shoulder.

Nobody had followed me, not even Sebastian, or so I thought. Alarmed, I spun around and punched Sebastian. Oh, shit!

Snagging my arm, he spun me around so my back was against him, his arm wrapped around my neck.

"Mother..." I said.

His arm tightened on my throat. "You better thank me, bitch. And next time, look before you swing. That shit pisses me off."

Struggling, I clutched onto his arm. "Let go of me, or I'll kill you. I don't care if you're one of Tristan's friends or not."

"Is that a threat? You better learn your place around here," he said. "I'm the nicest out of the brotherhood, and you want to threaten me?" he hissed. "You better straighten up. Once Tristan's with the guys for a little while, he will start coming back around, so I suggest you...*straighten the fuck up*," he stressed, letting go and pushing me away.

I glared back at him.

"We're going to be here for a while, so you better act like his old lady."

"You're an asshole," I spat.

He grinned. "That's not the first time I've been called that." He took two steps toward the house before he turned and approached me.

I took a step back.

"By the way…"

With one swift motion, he swept two fingers across my cheek. I slapped his hand away. Then he held his blood coated fingers up.

"You might want to let Tristan know what you are," he said, sucking the blood off of them.

My stomach knotted up. Disgusted, I stared back at him.

"Mm, mm, you do taste good. I see why Tristan likes you so much." With that, he disappeared inside the house.

Great! I had issues at both houses now. It was time to find a job or find some hobby to keep me away from Sebastian. If he was the only daywalker among them, he might find a reason to keep an eye on me daily.

Apprehensive, I followed him inside and went straight to Tristan's bedroom.

After my shower, I stood before the mirror, examining my old war wounds from my prior life amongst the vampires and werewolves. The scars were reminders of my mortal life before the change.

My hair fell forward. Water dripped down my breasts. It absorbed into my skin. Was it the heat from the werewolf that caused it to disappear? Or was it the heat from the dragon, the creature Sebastian accused me of hiding?

I studied my face. Nope, no obvious physical sign of the dragon. I opened my mouth, looking for anything to confirm his accusation. Again, nothing. Like the vampire and the werewolf, unless I made the change, there was no sign of it.

Right now, I needed to get dressed. We had Jennifer's dance recital tonight. If I was going to do anything outside of the house, now was the time, for, tonight we would be at the school.

§

When Robert got home, he found his wife and children hiding from the storm in the basement. A couple of futons, chairs, a refrigerator, non-perishable food, water, clothing, blankets, and some toys for the girls occupied the room.

In the dim light, the girls slept on the futon. Rebecca sat beside them, stroking their hair. One glance at Rebecca told him something was wrong. The look on her face was disconcerting.

Quietly, he approached and kissed Rebecca on the lips, and his daughters on the cheek. He swept Tisa's hair out of her face and took a seat beside Rebecca.

"What's wrong, hon?"

Her eyes were wet. "We need to talk, about us, the girls, your mother, everything."

Robert took her hand in his and kissed it. "Let's talk."

§

To occupy my mind, I wandered through the shopping center stores, rummaging through items even though I had no desire to buy anything. Every time the store clerks approached me, I waved them off.

The last place was the comic book store. Vivid colors and art danced before me, forcing my pupils to darken. Fascinated by the art-filled walls and graphics, I picked one of the comic books up and glanced through it. Nothing noteworthy. So I discarded it and grabbed a thicker book under the graphic novel label. The gothic illustrations caught my attention.

"Nice."

"You like that one?" a male voice asked from behind me.

I gazed back at the teenage boy, unable to keep my eyes off of his spiky green Mohawk. It attracted more of my attention than he did. I smiled.

"You like?" he asked again.

"Yeah, interesting work," I replied.

"My brother did that one," he said with a gleam in his eyes.

I peered down at it and flipped through the pages. "It's great work. I'm impressed."

"Don't tell me you're interested in this stuff? Or are you one of those cool moms?" he asked, grinning.

I laughed. "Yeah, I'm one of those cool moms."

"Sweet," he said. "Are you looking for yourself, then?"

I looked him over. His dark gothic pants and his colorful animated shirt captivated me. I thought about my answer as I glanced around at the other patrons.

"I'm looking for myself."

"Well, this section has the paranormal," he said, pointing to the rack next to me. "You know, vampires and werewolves, if you believe in that stuff. Over there, we have DC…"

I cut him off. "Do you believe in that stuff?"

Looking around, he leaned in and whispered, "Personally, yeah. That book you're holding in your hands is based off real events."

A loud laugh erupted from my chest. I couldn't help myself. This poor kid, if he only knew. I scanned a few pages, fanning them rather fast.

"Really, you shouldn't laugh. I'm not kidding. I can show you things you wouldn't believe." He propped his arm on a wire rack.

"Really?" I asked.

Our eyes met.

"And that would be?"

"Lady, just go into the forests around here late at night and you'll see some freaky shit. Hell, just a couple of weeks ago, a friend of mine caught a glimpse of some weird winged creature by that church down the street—in the middle of the day to boot."

He leaned in closer. "I actually heard there's some secret service agency strictly for the immortal and that they go after rogue vampires and werewolves. Can you believe that shit?"

I frowned. What the hell…? The mortals weren't supposed to know anything about the Underground Secret Service.

"Where'd you hear that?"

"Relax, lady. It's nothing to get upset over. I mean, some of us know they're around, but not everybody. You can walk around and pretend they don't exist if it makes you feel better. Or you can start arming yourself and preparing for the worst," he said, fake shifting a gun with his hand. "But remember one thing, they *are* everywhere."

I glanced around. Nobody was paying attention to us.

"You'll never get away from them. So, if you're considering moving, it isn't going to matter."

I snagged him by his shirt and shoved him into the dark corner. His Mohawk didn't move an inch. Behind him, the corner of a small wall rack swung down. One screw held it in place. The comic books inside of it flipped over sideways.

"Where are you hearing all of this?"

He stared at me, wide-eyed. "Wow, you're fast lady!"

"Shut up. Who's telling you all of this?"

His Adam's apple bobbed up and down. "Who are you?" he asked, his voice raspy.

I inched in closer to him. "It doesn't fucking matter."

"Oh, shit!" he screamed.

We caught the attention of nearby customers. I paid them no mind. Yet, he made a point to make a general announcement to the customers. "If anybody needs assistance, you can talk to Ray over there."

He turned his attention back to me. "Wow! I know who you are. Most of your fans think you're dead."

The vampire and werewolf inside were intrigued by his statement. My pupils dilated.

His excitement turned to fear. "Oh shit, you're one of them now." He tried to retreat, but he had nowhere to go.

I tightened my grip on him. "Shut the fuck up."

"Okay," he said, nervously looking around the room.

"Now answer my question," I demanded.

"It's just talk, lady," he stammered.

"Tell me the truth," I demanded. My fangs descended.

He continued on, "I swear, I don't know the specifics. Trust me. I wouldn't lie to you. I know you could kick my ass."

Customers stood nearby, their eyes upon us. I glanced down at the book that now lay on the floor. I let him go.

"Pick up the book," I said.

While he bent down to pick it up, I sneered at the nerdy teenage boys who stared at us. I mouthed the words, "Go home." Then, I flipped them off with a claw.

Their mouths dropped open.

My claw turned back into my mortal finger as the boys hurried out of the door.

He stood up with the book in hand. "Wow! That was crazy. What are you? Your fangs are different than the others."

His eyes were huge.

"I'm a hybrid," I said. I glanced around and tried to remain calm. Nobody else was paying attention to us.

"Oh, cool," he said, grinning.

With one finger, he touched me. I glanced down at his hand as he pulled his finger away.

"Sorry, it's just hard to believe. So, what are you, vampire and werewolf?"

"Yeah, something like that." I kept my eye on the customers.

"What do you mean by that?"

"It means I'm vampire, werewolf and something else. You wouldn't believe me if I told you."

"Try me," he said.

Abruptly, I grabbed him by his arm and led him out back to an area behind the dumpsters. I didn't trust being in the store. There were too many ears, besides, having this little kook as my confidant might be an advantage as he might be able to keep me alert to what was happening in the mortal world. I would have to watch what I told him, though.

"Can you keep it fucking quiet?" I asked.

"Yeah, you don't have to worry about me, I promise. It will be our little secret."

Our little secret? I like that. The boy was growing on me already but I also knew teenagers like to talk, so I would still need to monitor what I told him. I needed a little reinforcement that he would keep quiet, though.

I grabbed him by his collar and pulled him in tight. "Good, because if you don't, I'll come back here and personally kill you."

He nodded. "I promise. I swear on my mother's grave."

I frowned. "Is your mother dead?"

"No, but I swear I won't."

I released him. "I'm part dragon."

"What...?" He stared at me, confused. His mouth hung open. "Really?"

I nodded.

"No." He scratched his head. "Seriously?"

"Yes, seriously. I'm part dragon. Don't ask me how, but I am."

"Wow! That's cool." He paced. "Really, that's just amazing. But how...?"

"I really don't know." I shrugged my shoulders.

"Wow, that's just...crazy," he said, throwing his hands up. "Oh here, take the book. My brother wouldn't mind that I gave a copy to Crystal. My name is Adam by the way."

I took the book. "Nice to meet you, Adam. And thank you."

"You're welcome," he said with a smile. Then his voice took on a serious tone. "By the way Miss Crystal, I'm not sure if you're fighting anymore, and if you are, what you're fighting but keep in mind that all hybrids are individual in their own death. Not every hybrid is alike."

"What do you mean?" I asked, cradling the book.

"What I mean is, because every hybrid is different, they all are unique to their own death. Basically, what may kill a vampire may not kill a vampire hybrid. If you have a hybrid that's half werewolf, half vampire, a stake through the heart may not kill that creature. You may need a steel stake or something else."

Interesting, I thought.

He continued on. "If you run a stake through the heart of a vampire hybrid with the intent to kill, you may not kill that creature. What you think may kill one may not kill the other. You need to remember that with a hybrid, there is always more than one creature within the body so you need to learn the strengths and the weaknesses of that creature. Or you may need to learn exactly what is existent within the body in order to kill them. Does that make sense?"

His words spun in my head. Thoughts of Jace filled my mind. If Jace created hybrids like Tristan and Warrant had said, why would he not make himself one as well? Hybrids would be much stronger and harder to kill, so why not incorporate Woodrow and David in the learning process of creating them. Or were they already assisting Jace in the creation process? Was there more to Jace than what I had seen?

The memory of Jace's horrific vampire face appeared in my head, screaming *"You are mine!"* There was something more than vampire there.

Thinking aloud, I said, "He's not dead." My heart skipped a beat. "Oh God, he's not dead."

"Miss Crystal, are you okay?"

My mind settled on Jace and his crew. "Shit. They're not dead."

§

In the den, Robert sat cockeyed in the wicker chair opposite Tristan, his head on his hand. Tristan leaned forward on his knees.

"I have a huge favor to ask of you, Robert. Granted, I don't want to ask, but I need you. *We* need you." Tristan's eyes darkened.

Great, *something* was up. Ready for the news, Robert leaned back into the chair.

"So, what do you need?" Robert rubbed his chin, contemplating whether to discuss his mother's secret or not. Did Tristan already know her secret? Was Tristan part dragon? Or was it Warrant?

Tristan cocked his head. "What's wrong, Robert?"

"Nothing. Why do you ask?" He should have expected Tristan to detect he was pre-occupied with something but Robert wasn't going to give up the game.

Did Tristan know about mom's third beast? He should have, regardless if it was him or his friend, Warrant. Which man was the hybrid, Tristan or Warrant?

Tristan straightened up. He propped his elbows on the arms of the chair. "Because I can tell that you have something on your mind. Talk to me."

Robert looked away. "You said you wanted to talk to me, so why don't you start."

Tristan rubbed his chin. "There's been some agents killed recently and the U.G.S.S. thinks it's some of the hybrids that killed them."

This caught Robert's attention. "Just hybrids? What gives you the indication it's only hybrids?"

"Not really sure, but evidence suggests its hybrids. I don't have all of the details."

Robert thought about his altercation with the winged creature in the forest.

"Can I ask a question?"

"Sure."

"Have they seen them? The hybrids?"

Tristan raised his eyebrow.

Robert added, "What I mean is, I know the hybrids are out there, but there's more than usual. It's like there's a damn army of those things or something."

Tristan lowered his eyes. "Yeah, maybe."

"I guess I'm just curious why there are so many hybrids and why."

Tristan raised his eyebrow again. "What have you seen?"

Dammit. "I had to chase a couple of dragons down recently. What the fuck, Tristan? It's a little hard to believe these bastards exist."

He thought about mom. Did Tristan know about it? And if so, why wasn't Robert told? Why did he have to find out through Sebastian, somebody he didn't even know?

"Tristan, what the hell is going on around here?" He smacked his hands on the arm of the chair.

"I don't have all the logistics, but what I do know is that we need more snipers. We need to take them out. They've killed too many of our men, which tells us that there's a problem. As you know, most hybrids are stronger than us."

Robert nodded.

"Some of these hybrids are daywalkers, and they're going after the Underground Secret Service," he said, sighing. "Robert, I have a proposition for you."

"What's that?"

"Right now, the U.G.S.S. needs your help. We've recruited some new agents, but we're still shorthanded. We need somebody who will bust their ass to get the job done and wipe these hybrids out. There are too many hybrids, and we can't do it alone. We need more men and women."

Robert glanced at the door. Maybe it was a good thing Rebecca was going to Phoenix. He considered sending Jennifer with her, but she had school unless he and mom could convince Jennifer to complete it in Phoenix. In the meantime, he and Tristan could wipe out the riff raff here. He didn't want to change her schooling, but maybe he and mom needed to put their foot down.

With that in mind, he thought about his mother. Could he talk her into going too? She could use a vacation after everything she had been through but to get her, Rebecca, Jennifer, and the kids to relocate to Phoenix without a fight was going to be a problem. Rebecca and the kids were one thing. His mother and sister were another issue.

"We need your help, Robert. My men are good, but they can also be hard-headed and vigilant. They don't always use their brains."

Robert looked at him. "Why? What's wrong with them?"

Tristan sighed. "They like to work alone. Also, they have a tendency to stand on their own. They will stand behind us and your family but I have to convince them your family is worth protecting."

Robert frowned. "Convince them my family is worth protecting? I don't like the sound of that, Tristan."

He started to stand when Tristan gestured for him to sit. Reluctantly, he sat down.

"They are good men. I need to talk to them. And we need to introduce them to the family. They need to know who to protect, and who to stand behind, if something were to happen."

Robert raised his eyebrow. "What do you mean if something were to happen to my family? If there's something I need to know, you better tell me," he said sternly. He pushed his long sleeves up to his elbows.

"Remember Jace?"

Robert's face hardened. "How could I forget?"

"You know he was creating hybrids?"

Robert nodded.

"We believe some of these hybrids out there were his creations."

"Of course," Robert said sarcastically.

"With that said, would you be willing to help the U.G.S.S. out?"

Robert looked him in the eye. "I'll do it."

Tristan shook Robert's hand. "Great, I'll let my boss know."

Robert stood. "Well, I hate to break up our meeting, but we need to get ready for Jennifer's dance recital. Will you be there?"

"Yes."

"Good, you can help me keep an eye on the family."

§

An hour later, I opened the door to Tristan's home. Tristan stood in the doorway, his brotherhood in the living room behind him. They talked among themselves.

"We need to talk," I said.

"I detect something is wrong. What is it?"

I peered beyond him. As the men sat down, they stared at me, their chains rattling.

"Alone."

Tristan glanced at them. "We'll be back later."

Sabol nodded. "See you later."

Tristan followed me out into the cool night air. "So, why are you upset?"

"It's Jace," I answered.

He gave me a curious look. "I see. And what about him?"

"I don't think he's dead."

"What gives you that idea?"

I swallowed hard. The beasts within crept to the surface. "Just put yourself in his shoes for a moment. If you were him and you were creating these hybrids, why would you not only create them but become one yourself? Wouldn't that make you stronger?"

His eyes darkened.

"Is it true that if you're a hybrid, you become harder to kill?"

"I see you are learning more about yourself," he said with a grin.

"Yes, I am." I placed my hands on my hips. "You didn't answer my question, Tristan. Is it true? Would the beasts in me be harder to kill?"

He put his arm around me and led me to the garage.

"Yes, it would."

"I don't think Jace is dead."

Tristan stopped.

I continued on. When I turned, I caught him staring out into the woods.

Abruptly, he turned and urged me onward, pulling his cell phone out of his pocket. He dialed a number. Then, somebody answered.

"Hey, can you do me a favor? When you guys go out, can you check out the area around here? Thank you. And can you keep an eye on Robert's property, too? I think we might have a problem."

Silence.

"Mm, yeah," Tristan replied. "I think there's more to it than that. We need to get together with her family, later. For now, just keep a lookout for anything and everything. As a matter of fact, I want somebody over at her house, keeping watch."

Again, silence.

"Thank you." Tristan ended the call. He slid the phone in his pocket and climbed on his Harley. It roared to life.

As I slid into the seat behind him, I thought about his conversation. It must have been one of his brotherhood. Who else would keep an eye around our homes?

§

Wayne rummaged through the old box in the girl's playhouse. In the mixture of dress up clothes, he found an old shirt that belonged to his father-in-law and slipped it on.

Leaning back, he thought about his children, about how he had avoided the idea of becoming a father due to his dangerous profession. After Crystal had his children, he had to make a decision, one he feared would change his life forever…and it did.

Wayne swore he would protect her and to some avail, he did, but on the other hand he failed. His life as a U.G.S.S. sniper came to a halt when he accepted another position within the agency. His new job as a security officer was to protect the laboratory and its contents. He knew nothing about what happened inside the lab.

One night, as he and David, the big bald security officer, stood guard by the door, one of the surgeons approached them. His long dark hair was pulled back into a ponytail. Wayne glanced at the doctor's nametag—Woodrow. He recognized the name, but not the face. Woodrow was the morning surgeon, who had gained quite a reputation as the leading surgical doctor in the facility but why he was here at this hour was abnormal. But, then again, life in the immortal world was always abnormal, and for all he knew, something may have happened in the lab that Wayne was unaware of.

Dressed in scrubs, the doctor stood before them, flashing the men his identification. With his assault rifle strapped to him, Wayne allowed the surgeon entrance to the room. The steel door shut behind them, echoing within the dark corridor. They exchanged looks before resuming their position, assault rifles in hand.

About an hour later, David asked, "Hey man, do you know what time it is?"

Wayne glanced at his watch. "It's about ten…"

A blinding flash caught Wayne off guard. David's arm moved, the watch on David's wrist catching the light, almost blinding Wayne. His jaw clenched. The butt of David's rifle slammed into the side of his face, drawing blood.

Wayne tried to shoulder the rifle in the narrow corridor as David grabbed at his gun. He pulled it back, shifting his position, ramming the butt of the gun under David's chin, sending the man backward into the steel door. The thud of the impact echoed through the corridor.

Wayne repositioned the gun, his eye on the scope. He fired one round, hitting David in the chest. A boom reverberated through the steel corridor. The security system went off, sending a signal to the red beacon light on the ceiling. The wail of the alarm drowned out the rest of the noise.

David hit the door. Blood sprayed the walls, but the bullet didn't stop him.

Wayne fired off another round. David turned on him, the barrel of his rifle aimed at Wayne's midsection. One, two, three rounds was what hit Wayne before he hit the ground. Then, David turned his attention to the door and charged it.

It swung open. Wayne fought the urge not to change into his werewolf. Multiple gunshots, screams, and other voices came from the lab.

"You're late, David! The surgery's already been done!"

"What do you mean, I'm late! He never came through the fucking door!" David screamed.

"Jace was already in here! We don't have time to explain everything! Now, let's get him the fuck out of here before everybody shows up!"

David and Woodrow ran out the door, aiding Jace, an overly medicated black man dressed only in white hospital pants. Black, ugly stitches aligned part of his chest and abdomen. Blood still coated his dark, glistening flesh. The men escorted him past Wayne.

Wayne glanced down at his slow healing gunshot wounds. He rolled onto his stomach, his finger on the trigger of the gun.

He stared down the barrel, the crosshairs locked on the patient. There was a reason why they were taking him out of here and Wayne wasn't going to allow it. One shot through the back, narrowly missing the heart, tore the man from David's grip.

David bared his fangs at Wayne.

The dark haired man growled, "We don't have time for this shit, David! Let's get the fuck out of here! We need to get Jace home!" Woodrow hissed.

Wayne took it as a warning to back off, but he knew their hands were tied. All I wanted to do was get the hell out of here. Regardless, he was going to kill them or die trying.

David turned and rushed toward the next door, entering his security code. Woodrow and Jace caught up to him.

Wayne fired one round. Woodrow rushed in front of David, the bullet tearing through Woodrow's back. Then, Wayne fired another shot. The second bullet tore through the doctor's side.

Shit! Still bloody, Wayne stood, propping the gun against his shoulder. The steel door slid opened. He expected agents to be on the other side, ready to fire on the men but he was disappointed—nobody was there.

David, Jace and Woodrow slid into the dark hallway.

Several shots erupted from the end of the corridor, striking Wayne in the torso. Jaw open, he fell.

Determined to not give up, he squeezed the trigger. Several rounds disappeared into the dark hallway as he fell to the ground. The pool of blood splashed up. Ruby red droplets rained down upon him. He wasn't going anywhere, so he lay there, his mind racing with confusion as to what happened.

Were they criminals? Or were they rogue agents? The U.G.S.S. had issues with rogue agents in the past, so it wasn't abnormal for something similar to happen again.

Agents ran into the hallway. Their heavy boots resonated throughout the area. Armed agents hovered over him as his boss emerged from the group.

"Is Agent Devereaux okay?" Sergeant Knox asked.

One of the agents checked Wayne's pulse. "I think so, sir."

"There's a lot of blood," Agent Lagunas said.

Sergeant Knox turned to four of the men. "You four spread out. You two check out the laboratory, and you two check out the hallway. Lagunas, lead the men down the hallway. You know what to do."

"Yes, sir."

The men disappeared, leaving Knox and two men by Wayne's side as they examined Wayne's wounds.

"He's lost a lot of blood. We need to get him to the infirmary immediately."

Deke, the short spiky haired blond looked up at Knox. "He may have, but he'll live. He's not an easy man to put down. I know. I've worked with him before."

As Wayne drifted off, their voices faded into the night. For him, that was the beginning of the end.

§

A car door slammed shut in the front yard. Ecstatic, Leah screamed, "We're going to Aunt Jen's dance recital! Oh, goodie!"

Wayne missed watching his children grow up. So, it would be nice to see Jennifer's dance recital.

As the vehicles left the yard, he followed them, keeping his distance so his family would not see him. Robert, Rebecca, and the children rode in the truck. Crystal and another man followed them on the motorcycle.

Wayne assumed the man was her boyfriend. Anger rose. From this angle, Crystal blocked his view of the biker. He frowned.

Was that a twinge of jealousy? Even if he was, it didn't matter. Wayne hadn't been a part of her life for a long time. The last time he was a part of it, it wasn't exactly their honeymoon.

He regretted everything, from the kidnapping to the beatings to a life of turmoil but it was the only way he knew how to keep her and the kids safe from harm.

After somebody tried to kill them in their home years ago, he made the decision to leave his family. They were better without him. It was the only way to protect them. Then he had to separate her from the children, so no one from the U.G.S.S., or anybody else affiliated with the agency, could track them.

He even went as far as getting facial surgery, so she and the agents wouldn't recognize him. If Crystal got close enough, though, she might still recognize him, so he had to be cruel, cold, and heartless. Any close contact, especially sexual, might restore some of her memory so he had to be careful.

Watching her cling to another man ripped his heart apart.

How he longed to hold her, to make love to her once again. He wanted to restore her sense of compassion, something she had been full of when they met but now her heart was hardened.

Oh, how he desired to bring back the woman he married and loved. It was torture watching her hug another man.

§

As Robert and I sat next to each other in the school's auditorium, Jennifer and a male dancer flitted across the stage. They had chemistry but they were a little too close for comfort.

I frowned and so did Robert.

The dance was too suggestive which made me uncomfortable. My nerves were on edge so I shifted in my seat and tried to relax, when Tristan, who sat to my left, gently grabbed my hand. He kissed it and then laid it on my lap. A weak smile crossed my lips.

I glanced at the girls, who sat on their parents' laps.

The kids' eyes were filled with excitement. Every time Jennifer and her partner pulled another fancy maneuver, the girls clapped and cheered.

As the lights dimmed and the next song started, Jennifer and her partner remained on stage in an exotic pose. Several dancers gracefully danced on stage. Then, Jennifer spun around, lifting her leg, as the male dancer slid his hand up around her hip, embracing her tightly against him.

Robert huffed. "Really, why must they teach them such erotic dances?" he whispered. "You think the teachers would know better. Honestly, there should be more complaints. It's just not right."

Funny, I thought. Robert sounded like a middle-aged man, but he wasn't instead, he and Rebecca were in their early twenties. Their oldest child, Leah, was going on five this year, so Rebecca had to have gotten pregnant within a year or two after high school.

Great! I sighed. Please tell me Jennifer was abstaining from sex.

No sooner had I thought about her having sex, I detected a lingering presence in the back of the room where the parents stood, cameras and cell phones in hand. There was not an empty spot in sight.

When I spun back around, Tristan's seat was empty. He was nowhere to be seen.

§

Wayne stood in the back corner of the auditorium, his eyes on his daughter. She was gorgeous, just like her mother. *Kill them, kill them all,* came the voice in his head. Dammit! Would that fucking voice go away? What the hell was wrong with him?

He shook his head to rid himself of the voice. No, he would not kill her! Wayne clung to the thought of hugging her, to tell her how sorry he was for disappearing out of her life. He was a horrible father for leaving his family behind.

So when he spied the curtain that led backstage, he headed that way, weaving in and out of the audience toward the other side of the room. As Wayne slipped into the dark wing, the song ended. Quietly, he merged in with the stagehands. They were too busy to notice him.

§

Jennifer ran off of the stage into the wing where some of the dancers stood waiting. One of the stagehands handed her a bottle of water. She opened it and chugged some of it down when a presence caught her attention.

Jennifer spun around to face Tristan. "What are you doing back here?"

If Tristan was back here, her mother had to be nearby. His pupils, which were normally blue, turned black. Something was wrong.

Tristan's hand fell on her shoulder. "Where did he go?"

"Who?" She glanced about the wing, unsure of whom she was looking for.

Firmly, he grabbed her arm. "The man who came back here," he answered. "Where is he?"

Alarmed by his change of demeanor, her voice rose. "What man?"

"Listen, Jennifer, I think it's best if you come with me. Get out of the dance show now," Tristan said sternly.

"Look, I don't know what's going on but you need to leave. I'll get in trouble." She looked around for her teacher. "You need to go."

"Jennifer, there's somebody back here. You need to get out of here," he demanded.

"Tell you what, I'll keep an eye out for anything suspicious. Now get out of here," she said, urging him on with her other hand.

She tried to shake him off, but his hand slid down her arm and grabbed her wrist.

He leaned in close and whispered, "Jennifer, I don't want you hanging out with that dancer."

Tristan's demands and his strange demeanor scared her. She was already on edge because of Jace's attack on her family and this wasn't helping.

"Tristan, I like you but you're getting weird right now and I don't like it, you're making me nervous and you're not my father. You can't tell me what to do."

She jerked her arm away.

"Then if not for me, do it for your mother. She would tell you the same thing. There's something I don't like about that boy. He's going to hurt you."

"No, he's not. And I like him…a lot! So go away, and stop with the boogeyman bullshit," she said. "James is a nice guy."

"Jennifer…"

James walked up beside her. "Is this man bothering you?"

Tristan eyed him, his lip curling up.

She wanted Tristan to leave her alone but she was unsure of how to tackle the situation without a confrontation.

Smiling, James asked, "Is this your father or something?"

Without looking at him, she answered, "No, he's not. He's my mom's boyfriend. And he's not wanted here right now." Again, she looked around. "Where's mom, by the way? Why aren't you with her?"

The moment she asked, her mom appeared behind Tristan. Jennifer's heart skipped a beat. She hated it when her mom and Tristan did that. It freaked her out and even put James on edge. A low growl escaped his lips.

"Cool it, wolf. I'm not here for you, I'm here for somebody else," Tristan said, peering at the black curtains that hung around them.

Jennifer glanced at James. "Are you…?"

James shut his mouth. Then, Tristan cocked his head, looking around.

Jennifer threw her arms up in confusion. "What the hell?"

Tristan put his finger against her lips.

"Is it…him?" her mom asked, glancing around.

"No," Tristan whispered, turning to his right.

Jennifer brushed Tristan's hand away. Eyes wide, she asked, "Mom, what's going on?"

§

I motioned for her to keep quiet. Tristan was onto someone, and it wasn't Jace. That worried me. I glanced back at the teenager next to Jennifer.

Tristan slinked away from us.

I started to follow him when his hand shot out, stopping me.

With a sense of urgency, he said, "Get your family out of here."

Angered that he wouldn't tell me who it was, I asked, "Who the hell is it?"

His eyes shifted.

"Just get them out of here. I don't care if she has any more dances or not. Her life is in danger."

§

Something crashed on stage. Screams followed.

Everybody in the wings turned toward the stage. It was Wayne's opportunity to hide while he could. With one last glimpse of his daughter, he rushed out the back door of the building.

§

The bar of lights that had been attached to the ceiling lay across the stage. One dancer lay on the floor, about four feet away from the lights. Two of the dancers ran to her aid. Six other dancers stood against the back curtain, their eyes wide with terror.

Light sparked from the fixture, igniting a fire. Flames reached out toward the dancer as she struggled to get away. A couple of the dancers ran up, grabbed her arms and pulled her away.

Families screamed, their voices filling the amphitheater. Several ran out of the building while others ran toward the stage, including Jennifer but before she could reach the stage, Tristan appeared in front of her.

"Stay away from it!" he yelled, pushing her back.

Eyes wide, Jennifer stared at him. "I'm just going to help them!"

Tristan glanced around. James had disappeared. "Did you drive here?"

"Yes," she answered, glancing at the fire.

"Grab your stuff," he demanded. "Crystal, I want you to ride with her."

My heart raced. I didn't appreciate his forcefulness with my daughter. I understood his concern, regardless he didn't need to get physical with her. My adrenaline picked up, driving the need to control my anger before I lost it with him.

Sternly, I said, "Of course."

"I have to drive Raelin home, too," she said. "She's around here somewhere."

He got in her face. "Hey! Listen to me, we need to go. Find her, now," he said.

More concerned about her friend, she stammered over her words, "But my teacher…"

I grabbed her arm. "Jennifer…!"

"Jennifer, you're just as stubborn as your mother. Get your friend and get the fuck out of here. Now!" he yelled.

I glared at him and hissed. "Back off, Tristan! I can handle my daughter." I knew he was upset, but there was no need to lose his temper with her, and he didn't need to take matters into his own hands, especially with my family.

I turned to her. "You need to hurry up and find Raelin."

"Yes, mom," she said.

HELLS CHANGELINGS

Later that night, Tristan and I stood in his bedroom. His buddies weren't home yet, so I took advantage of our time alone.

Agitated and scared, I snapped. "No, Tristan, I do not want them near my family! I don't trust them!"

"Whether or not you trust them, they need to meet your family," he demanded. "They can help protect them."

"No! How do I know one of them isn't going to attack my family when they're *supposed* to be *protecting* them?" I spat, gesturing toward the door.

The front door opened downstairs. I glanced at the bedroom door. The bikers were here. Dammit!

"I'm not stupid, Tristan! I don't want my granddaughters to become their midnight snack!"

"We need them there to help protect your family. Now, keep your voice down."

Sighing, I sat on the edge of the bed. I buried my face in my hands. "Fuck, Tristan, what the hell is going on? And who the hell was there tonight?"

Maybe I needed to move my family away from this place, away from everything. I couldn't do this anymore.

"I don't know. The smell was familiar, yet it wasn't. It's hard to explain." He took a step toward me. "Listen to me, everything is going to be all right."

I looked at him. "No, it's not."

He took another step.

I put my hand up. "Don't come near me right now. I'm pissed. Don't you ever lay another hand on my daughter again. What the *fuck* got into you?" I demanded.

He lowered his gaze. "I'm sorry. I was trying to protect her. I swear I wasn't trying to hurt her. You know me better than that."

We exchanged looks.

I lowered my head. Yes, I did know him better than that but that was no excuse.

I rubbed my forehead. "I can't deal with this right now. I have too much to worry about, you, your brotherhood, this teenage werewolf bullshit, my daughter, Jace. I mean really, what the hell else is going to happen?"

Tristan sat down and rubbed my thigh.

"Don't worry. My clan isn't the only one you have to worry about…"

I stared at him.

"What I meant…"

I gestured for him to shut up. "I don't want to hear it. I have enough to worry about, including all of the other werewolves and vampires, and now I have to worry about teenage boys, werewolves for that matter, hitting on my daughter. You really know how to console a woman," I snapped.

He tried to wrap his arm around me, but not before I wiggled away from his reach.

"You're not helping me right now." He tried to take my hand in his. I pushed him away. "Stop, Tristan. Really, you're not helping me. It's not working."

"Will you relax? You're going to irritate your beasts right now," he said.

My blood boiled. "Really! You think so?"

§

In the living room, Sabol and his men exchanged looks.

"Sounds like he needs to put that one under lock and key," Ratliff said, cocking his head and gazing up at the second floor. Something banged against the bedroom wall.

"Oh, please tell me no," he said.

Sabol rolled his eyes. "Fuck no, Tristan."

Within a second, Sabol was up the stairs, opening Tristan's bedroom door. Inside, Tristan had her pressed against the wall, his mouth on her neck.

Crystal stared at him. "Really?"

Tristan glared at Sabol. "This isn't the…"

"Don't you have better things to do than barge in here. This isn't a fucking peep show," she screamed.

"Sorry, I thought it was," Sabol grinned.

"Goddammit, Sabol…!"

Tristan shoved Sabol out of the room and against the railing. Part of the wood railing broke apart. Pieces of it crashed to the floor below, along with Tristan and Sabol, Tristan landing atop him.

He threw a punch at Tristan but missed. Then Tristan grabbed him and slammed Sabol into the wall opposite them. The force of the impact sent drywall and plaster flying around them.

§

How rude and disrespectful!

I dropped from the second floor, fangs bared, advancing upon him and Tristan.

The other men stepped in front of me, separating me from my lover and his obnoxious brother. They puffed their chests out.

Tristan's fist slammed into the wall near Sabol, leaving a hole in it.

"Next time, that's your head, jackass!" Tristan yelled.

His men inched toward me, grinning.

I stood my ground. "Tell your men to back off!" I yelled. I was unsure if they were going to attack, so I curled my hand into a fist.

With his hand around his brothers' throat, Tristan glanced back at me.

Sabol smiled. "Looks like you got yourself a fighter there. You might have to put that one in her place. You think you can do it, pussy?"

Tristan growled.

"You use to be able to put the bitches in their place. Can you still do it?" he whispered. "I bet you can't. You like this one too much. She's got you pussy-whipped, doesn't she? Huh, pussy?"

Damn him! I moved toward them. Uwe and Ratliff grabbed me. "Get your hands off of me!" My beasts rose to the surface.

Tristan snarled, "I'm not like you, Sabol."

Sabol leaned his head back. "I think your old lady has a little more testosterone than you nowadays."

Tristan punched him in the face.

"Hey sweet-cakes, you might be Tristan's, but you better learn your place. You're making him look bad. You really want that for him?" Uwe asked.

His eyes met mine.

On a normal basis, Tristan wouldn't have said a damn thing to me but with his family here, I hesitantly backed down. In their world, women stood behind their men, not in front of, or beside them. I could be the death of him.

I gritted my teeth. With one last glance at them, I walked away. I was too angry to sit down, so I stood by his chair, my heart racing, my blood boiling, and my beasts ready to attack.

"Nice, Tristan," Sabol said, sarcastically. "You want to have it out, let's go. You're the one who invited me here, yet you try to put me in place. You haven't been nor are you in the brotherhood anymore. You chose the life you lead now. If you want us here, then you fall back into line just like everybody else." He nodded toward me. "And the same with your woman."

Tristan leaned in. "You're in my house. While you're here, you'll follow my rules, and another thing, Crystal is MY woman. Anybody touches her, they're a dead man."

All eyes fell upon Tristan.

"She has shown her devotion to me and only me. She is not to be shared with the group, and I have already left my mark on her," Tristan said sternly.

He released Sabol and took a step back.

"Yes, so we have noticed. We also noticed others have left their mark on her as well," Sabol said, straightening out his jacket. "Does she truly belong to you, Tristan? Or are there others who have a vested interest in her? From what I've heard, there are others."

Sabol took a seat opposite us. "Please sit, my dear brother. We need to talk, alone preferably."

He glanced at me. "Am I allowed to talk to him alone? Or are you going to assert that feminine yet masculine temper toward me?"

I sneered. "You're an asshole, Sabol."

With a smirk, he threw his hands in the air.

"So I've been told. You're not the first and you won't be the last."

The others snickered.

Tristan sat down. "Stop being a dick." He peered up at me. "Crystal, would you mind?"

I shot him a look of disdain. Was he fucking kidding? When Tristan didn't say any more, I sighed.

"Fine, I'll be in the bedroom." I jumped up to the second-floor landing.

Behind me, one of the men said, "Exactly where a good woman should be."

I gazed back at him.

"Sebastian, Ratliff, you two keep an eye on her," Sabol demanded.

My jaw dropped. I turned around.

Tristan was the first to speak up. "I don't think so."

"I have my reasons. You two get up there, and keep your hands to yourself."

Within a second, Ratliff and Sebastian were at my side.

Tristan turned to Sabol. "Talk to me."

Huffing, I stomped into his bedroom. The men followed me inside, shutting the door behind them. At the foot of the bed, I turned around, my arms across my chest. They were just a couple of feet within proximity.

"You can sit down," Sebastian said.

"Like I trust you guys! No thanks. I'll stand."

"Stop acting like a man, or I'll treat you like one," Ratliff spat. "I'll put you in your fucking place if you don't straighten up."

"I believe Tristan and Sabol told you to keep your hands to yourself," I said, gritting my teeth.

Sneering, he clenched his fists.

Hesitantly, I took a seat on the edge of the bed. If they tried anything, I was going to kill them.

§

Not much was said on the way over to my house. Tristan didn't care to talk, and neither did his friends. Resentfully, I took place within the clan and kept my mouth shut.

I rode on the back of the Harley, resting my head against his back. Oh, how I wish I hadn't left the mortal world. I enjoyed my time with Tristan, yet I resented letting him and Warrant transform me.

I closed my eyes. The vibration of the bike put me into an intoxicating euphoria. The coolness of his leather jacket lay against my cheek.

As we rode through the enveloping darkness, the cool night air blew my hair about my face. The motorcycles sang a deep, hearty baritone. It could have put me to sleep but I didn't want to fall off of the bike, so I opened my eyes.

Trees whizzed past us. To my right, a dark figure emerged from the trees. I did a double take. The man was alone. None of the bikers caught sight of it, for they were focused on the road but I stared at him and his deformity.

Wait! Something about him was familiar. I let go of Tristan and reluctantly, I jumped off the back of the motorcycle.

I kept my eyes focused on him and walked in his direction. The figure staggered. The motorcycles screeched to a halt behind me, yet, I continued toward the figure. It stopped and so did I. It wasn't Jace. Awkwardly, he moved again. It wasn't David or Woodrow either. Who the hell was it? It was different than anything I had seen before.

Tristan grabbed my arm, catching me by surprise. My breath caught in my throat.

"Crystal?"

The others were behind me, the lights of their bikes illuminating the pavement.

I moved forward and then it turned toward me. What was wrong with it? It was human but the head was cocked strangely to the side.

Tristan called out my name again, "Crystal!"

I twisted out of his grasp and ran toward the figure. It was Deputy Torrance.

The roar of Tristan's bike was upon me. The headlights zeroed in on Torrance as I came to an abrupt stop, my heels digging into the asphalt. Oh, hell, no! Deputy Torrance stretched his arms out toward me, his partially decapitated head lolling about on his shoulder. His skin and bones were deteriorating and his eye sockets sunk into his zombie-like appearance.

My heart leaped into my throat. What the fuck happened to him? I turned and ran toward Tristan. His arm slipped around my waist just as a motorcycle grazed past us. Tristan whisked me onto his bike.

Uwe reached over his shoulder and wrapped his hand around the bone handle of a machete hidden within the confines of his jacket. The skull devil face on the emblem grinned at me. The large red blade stood defiantly within his hand. Swiftly, it came down upon the zombie.

The head rolled off of his body, and across the road. I turned away in disgust. Then I understood why I had not detected his human scent, he was already dead. He wasn't a vampire and he wasn't a werewolf. Instead, he was a living corpse.

I laid my head upon Tristan's back, my fists locked around his waist. Periodically, he would pat my hand.

Uwe rode up next to us, machete still in hand, licking some of the zombie residue off of the blade. The wind tore some of the flesh off of it.

"Would you like some, Crystal?" he yelled, holding the blade out toward me.

Disgusted, I turned away from him. The beasts in me detected the deathly scent. They rose to lay claim on the blade but my humanity took reign. It would not allow the taste of my son's friend. I closed my eyes and melted into Tristan.

"It tastes yummy, Crystal!"

Ignoring him, I tightened my grip on Tristan.

§

Moments later, we pulled up in front of my house. The roar of steel thunder was killed. Then, Tristan turned to confront me.

"What...?"

Ratliff interrupted Tristan. "Bitch, what the fuck was that back there?" he asked, storming toward me.

Tristan intervened. "Back the fuck off," he demanded, inching in closer to him.

"I think she needs to answer the question," Ratliff said, cocking his head.

"I agree." Sabol appeared at our side.

"Fine," Tristan replied. "What was that about?"

My heart was saddened and torn. Torrance was my son's best friend.

The front door flew open. Robert stood there, rifle shouldered, aiming it at the entire group. Robert's appearance brought me back to reality.

"I'll tell you later, not now," I whispered.

"Tristan, she..."

Tristan cut him off, "She said she'll talk about it later. Now back off, Ratliff."

Uwe sat on his bike, licking the blood off of the blade. "Mm, that's some good shit. Tastes like...pig, though. Interesting." He holstered the machete.

I took Tristan's hand in mine and walked past the men. I was thankful Robert was a werewolf and a cop, for he was fully prepared for anything. Most of his bullets were made of silver. At this point, though, I wasn't sure who it would and wouldn't kill.

I stepped onto the porch. "It's okay." I pushed the barrel down. "They're Tristan's brothers."

We exchanged a look of uncertainty. He kept the barrel pointed at the ground, yet, his finger remained near the trigger. His fangs glistened in the moonlight.

"Robert," I whispered, "the kids are in the house. You need to calm your beast." I patted him on the shoulder. "Come on. Let's go inside."

I walked into the house. Rebecca stood in the doorway to the exercise room, which was toward the back of the house. Jennifer, Raelin, and the kids stood by her side.

Jennifer must have sensed the anxiety for her eyes were dilated, the werewolf within her on alert. Her nostrils flared.

"Relax, Jennifer. It's going to be okay," I said.

Robert stood in the doorway.

Tristan touched his shoulder. Calmly, he said, "Put your nerves to rest, they are not the enemy, they're my brothers."

"They're all bikers, including your brother." Robert's lip curled up.

"Please let them in, they're here to help," Tristan repeated.

Tristan leaned against the doorframe, his eyes on Robert.

"I trust your judgment, Tristan. So this better not be a mistake," he said, anchoring the gun against his other shoulder.

Sabol stood before him, his dark hair a mess. He took a step closer to Robert.

"Well, are you going to let us in or not? It's your family's life we're protecting."

"You touch or hurt anybody in my family, and I'll kill you. Remember that!" Robert said, stepping back.

No one stepped forward.

"Hey, asshole, we need to get invited in," Ratliff said.

"I thought I smelled vamp blood, besides Tristan," Robert replied.

"Is that supposed to be some sort of crack?" Ratliff asked, cocking his head.

"Nah, just trying to figure out which one of you is my natural enemy. That way, if anything happens, I know which one I have to keep an eye on," Robert said, sweeping his jacket back to reveal the sidearm he carried. "It looks like it's going to be all of you."

Robert hesitated before inviting them in.

I stood with my family. The tension between Rebecca and myself was still there after our earlier confrontation. She still didn't trust me, and I couldn't blame her.

Tristan's brothers walked in, their eyes turning toward us, the women of the family. Tristan and Robert joined them. Testosterone and tension filled the air. As Tristan introduced everybody, he advised his brothers that my family was now his family.

As Ratliff stared at my granddaughters, he licked his lips.

Out of everybody, he concerned me the most. I glanced down at the girls. They were as anxious as the rest of us.

"Please sit down," Tristan said.

Much to everybody's hesitation and nervousness, everybody complied. My family sat opposite the men, who took a seat on the couches and chairs. Robert pulled in the dining room chairs, which we sat in.

Tristan stood behind me, resting his hands on my shoulders.

"As everybody knows, I have called you here for a reason. Right now, your safety is a concern, primarily the women," he said. "I apologize for the inconvenience, ladies. I have not been able to consult with any of you, including Crystal."

Great! What now?

Tristan continued, "I have already filled Robert and the Hell's Changelings in on the current updates with the U.G.S.S. and their mission."

Tisa scrambled out of Rebecca's lap, drawing Ratliff's attention.

Ratliff shot out of his seat.

Robert bolted upright, gun in hand at the same time Tristan and I blocked accessibility to Tisa.

Robert pressed the gun against Ratliff's cheek. "I'll blow your…"

"Enough…!" Tristan yelled. "Don't…!"

Christian jumped up.

I turned toward him, ready to attack. Christian stood, eyes dark, fangs bared, yet he was frozen in air. I didn't understand what happened until I turned.

Rebecca held her hands out in front of her, blocking him so he couldn't get to the kids. Using her witchcraft, she had frozen him in place above the coffee table.

But what scared me more was Sabol, who was much quicker than Christian.

Somehow, he managed to grab Tisa. He pressed her tight against his chest and caressed her cheek. She tried to pull away, but Sabol held on firmly.

Rebecca stood, unmoving. Though Christian was frozen in air, he wobbled. Her magic was weakening.

Robert glared at Sabol. "Put my daughter down," he demanded, clenching his jaw.

Sabol smiled. "Oh, but she's so cute."

"Sabol, please put her down?" I asked.

His dark hair fell over his face. "Oh, Crystal, did you think I was going to have your granddaughter for dinner?" An evil laugh escaped his lips.

I swallowed hard.

"Oh, Crystal, shame on you." He stared at me through his dark hair. "I wouldn't hurt her. As a matter of fact, I was saving her from Christian." Turning toward Tisa, he caressed her cheek and replied, "You are a cutie. I bet you would like to go back to your mom." He glanced at Rebecca.

She struggled to maintain her witchery on Christian, who wobbled in the air.

"But she does look rather occupied. Perhaps, your aunt would like to take you."

He offered her to Jennifer, who weaved in between everybody. A golden hue masked the real color of her pupils. Cautiously, she reached out, the muscles within her arms bulging. The werewolf within her threatened to expose itself.

Sabol placed her within Jennifer's arms. Nuzzling Tisa, she walked away. She pushed the other girls toward Raelin.

"Well now, looks like we have most everything under control," Sabol said. "Rebecca, can you please let Christian loose? I don't think he'll be hurting anyone soon."

Her gaze shifted to Christian, who was airborne in full throttle mode. She backed up and cast her spell aside. He crashed down atop the table, breaking it.

Angry, he hissed. The butt of Robert's gun crashed down upon his skull.

Rebecca swept her arms out and up, sending Christian airborne into the ceiling, his head bouncing off of it.

A clap of hands caught everybody's attention.

"Nice, Rebecca, very nice," Sabol said. "I thought you were a witch. Thank you for the entertainment. You know, witches are sometimes needed. I'm glad to meet you."

He extended his hand out to her. Hesitantly, she accepted it. Sabol leaned in close. Robert kept his eye on him.

"But I do detect some weakness, which is why I could not easily determine your gift. Do you not practice your witchery enough?"

Rebecca glanced at Robert. It was apparent she detected Robert's discomfort.

"Sabol, that's your name right?" Robert asked.

"Mm, yes," he answered, nodding.

"You need to back away from my wife, now."

Sabol stepped back. Smiling, he responded, "Of course, Robert, but please answer the question, Rebecca. I'm curious."

Her eyes drifted from Robert to Sabol. She hesitated before answering. "That's none of your concern, Sabol."

"Suit yourself." He looked her over. "You have a sister?"

Her eyes narrowed in on him.

"I like my chocolate spicy," he replied, winking at her.

Her jaw dropped. "You're a sick son of a bitch."

He snickered. "Nah, I just like things spicy."

Robert pressed the barrel of the gun against Sabol's cheek. "Tristan, put your brother in check, or I'm going to personally take him out." He clenched his teeth together.

Sabol's eyes darkened. "Come on, tough guy. You think that gun is going to do much damage to me. Try it. I'm not a fucking dog like you are."

"Sabol!" Tristan yelled, "You're here to help protect them, not fight them!"

Sabol hissed.

Robert threw the gun to the side. Rebecca caught it with her magic where it hung suspended in midair.

Robert screamed, "Let's go, asshole!" He lunged for Sabol.

"Robert, no!" Rebecca screamed, letting go of her magic. Christian slammed to the ground.

Robert and Sabol charged each other.

Together, the girls screamed, "Daddy!"

Jennifer pushed the girls and Raelin out the back door. Ratliff was on their tail.

I grabbed Ratliff and tossed him across the room. He smashed into the wall above the couch. Sebastian came at me. As I turned to fight him, Jennifer jumped him, wrapping one arm around his neck. The claws on her other hand emerged. She raked her claws across his chest. He screamed. Blood spilled from the wounds.

Then, Ratliff attacked me. The girls cringed.

"Get them out of here!" I screamed.

IN MIND AND SPIRIT

Time stopped everything within the house. Movement became null and void except for the presence. The spillage of blood ceased to move. Droplets hung in midair. A dark mist moved into the home from the open back door. It swirled about Raelin and the children first. Then, brazenly it merged further inside.

It flew past Crystal and Ratliff, Jennifer and Sebastian, and stopped by Uwe, who was frozen in mid-air with machete in hand. It removed the blade from his hand swirling it throughout the air. Then, onward it went to examine Rebecca, who stood alone. It wrapped around her, staying within close proximity, before advancing upon the men.

The men, all frozen in their altercation, had physical changes frozen as well, revealing the beasts within. The presence wrapped around Robert. It picked him up and placed him next to his wife. It proceeded back through the house, picked Jennifer and the children up, and placed them with Robert and Rebecca.

It continued onward to Crystal where it threw Ratliff off of her, and onto the floor. The presence hovered over her, unsure of her placement within the family. Then, it became intrusive.

It let time move only for Crystal. The second she moved, it invaded her body. Crystal's eyelids fluttered. It occupied her mind. Her beasts fought back, her adrenaline pumping harder to fight it off. It lingered inside of her, learning what it could of her.

Then, as fast as it had invaded her, it escaped, leaving Crystal writhing on the floor. The presence merged into the middle of the room, swirling like a tornado in the air.

A woman's voice echoed throughout the room. Time was slowly allowed to continue, but only enough to gain everybody's attention.

Everybody turned to the dark mist.

"You beasts, you all let your anger out on each other, instead of protecting your loved ones! How dare you! I should let you all kill each other, rebels!"

Abruptly, the mist lowered. It advanced upon each of the bikers, coming within physical contact of each one. Then, it advanced upon the last biker, Sabol.

It brushed against him. "Spicy chocolate, boy?"

His lip curled up. Something hard slapped him across the face.

Snickering, he asked, "You must be Rebecca's sister?"

Another slap, only on his other cheek. He hissed.

She flung him against the other wall. "You will not disrespect my sister and you will not disrespect me, biker!"

§

I stared up at the ghost image of a black-skinned woman who appeared in the room. Her medium length hair hung down in braids and beads, past her shoulders. She was a little bit bigger than Rebecca and me. She wore a long, flowing black skirt, and a black shirt. Chains attached the fabric where there were cutouts in the shoulders, sides, and back. Jewels and beads adorned her body around her neck, wrists, and waist.

Her image elicited a cry of enjoyment from the children. "Aunt Larissa!"

I walked into the room past Ratliff, who also stood, staring up at her.

"Sister, thank you for your services but they are no longer needed. I can take care of it from here out," Rebecca said.

Larissa stared at her. "You have barely been able to protect your own family, much less anyone else. You need to come with me, now. I'm not waiting any longer for you." She faced Robert. "I take it she's told you that she's coming to Phoenix with me?"

He wrapped his arm around Rebecca. "Yes, she has and I think it's a good idea. As a matter of fact, I think you should take Jennifer and my mother with you. At least get them out of here for a while."

"I'm not going anywhere," Jennifer butted in. "I have school and I have my friends. I'm not changing schools again, Robert."

"She does have a point, Robert," Larissa agreed.

"Yeah, but…"

Rebecca interrupted, "I agree with your sister, she needs to stay in school. I can take the children and go. As for your mother, I'm not sure…"

I blurted out, "I'm not going anywhere, either."

"Oh, so you're Robert's mother?" She moved toward me.

"Yes, I am." Unsure of her intentions, I backed off. I was disturbed by her previous intrusiveness. "Don't pull that crap with me again. I didn't appreciate it."

"What did she do?" Rebecca asked.

Larissa swirled around me.

"She pried inside my head." I backed away from the woman but she followed my every step.

She inched in closer. "I merely wanted to know who you are, and now I know much more than anybody else here. You're quite an interesting person, Crystal, or Brandy? Which should I call you? It is quite disappointing you don't remember everything."

"What the hell…?"

Robert cut me off. "Mom, don't…"

"Don't what? She's invaded my privacy and knows stuff I don't remember. That's fucked up," I said, appalled at her aggressiveness.

When I turned toward her, she was in my face. I stood my ground.

"Too bad you haven't tapped into your other beast. I'd like to see it," she said with a smooth voice. She smiled and then turned to Robert. "I'd like to take my sister and my nieces now if you don't mind. I believe they need much more protection than what these men can offer."

Uwe stared at her, his gaze following the machete she held in her hand. "I'd like to have my knife back, witch."

She tossed the machete in his direction. He caught it by the handle.

"If you wave that thing one more time around my family, I'll behead you myself. So, you better put it away."

Smirking, he slid it inside the hidden sheath.

"I'm not real fond of her traveling by herself at night. Perhaps in the morning? I'd feel more comfortable that way."

Larissa approached him. "Then it shall be. I'm not going to argue with that but I think the children should be put to bed." She walked toward the staircase. "Come, Rebecca, help me with my nieces, and you precious ones, shall come with me."

She whisked the children up, and rushed them past the men, her ghost-like figure enveloping them.

The girls giggled.

Larissa floated them through the air, and up into their bedroom.

"Go ahead, Rebecca." Robert gestured for her to follow her. "Go help your sister. The girls don't need to be in the middle of this mess."

She kissed him. "Thank you for understanding." She followed her sister upstairs.

Robert glanced at Tristan. "She'll be down in a little while."

"Not a problem." He turned to his men. "Are we going to control ourselves, now?"

"She's a strong witch," Sabol said.

"Yes, she is," Robert answered.

"But your wife isn't. Why not?" he asked.

Robert sighed and leaned against the furthest wall. "She's been busy with the kids, and hasn't had time to practice, or use her witchery, and she hasn't been able to spend much time with her sister. Larissa doesn't have any kids so she has all the time in the world to practice, unlike my wife."

The men exchanged glances. "If we ever needed a witch, she would be good. She's strong, Tristan."

"We're not dragging her family into this. We're taking care of the matter at hand and leaving them out, besides, they're going to Phoenix."

"Phoenix, huh?" Ratliff pried, licking his lips.

"How did she do that anyway, Robert?" I asked. "You know, call her sister?"

He shoved his hands in his pockets. "It's part of her magic. She can call her sister anytime. I think Katie can do it, too. Every time she wants her aunt here, she shows up. It's been rather inconvenient at times, so Larissa prods into Katie's mind to find out why she's calling her."

"Kind of like what she did with me?" I asked, sitting down.

"Yeah, something like that, only she doesn't have to be here physically, or spiritually when it comes to the kids. It's like some genetic thing."

"It's just witchery," Tristan said.

"Oh, so, that apparition was her spirit then?" I asked.

"Yeah, she's able to travel out of her body and do things, but I think there's a limitation to what she can do when she's not in human form. I don't know everything, but Rebecca does."

Tristan spoke up. "So, Rebecca can hear me upstairs right, Robert?"

"Ask her…," he started.

"Yes, I can," Rebecca yelled.

Robert smiled.

"All right, no more fucking around. I'm going to make this sweet and simple. Ladies…" He glanced at Raelin. "Since you two are friends, this includes you too, Raelin. Got it?"

"Yes," she answered.

He continued, "These gentlemen have been called here to do a job. That's to destroy the hybrids the Underground Secret Service believes Jace Templeton created. They are on the loose, and, they are killing our agents."

Our jaws dropped.

He added, "These hybrids are extremely dangerous. They all look a little different, but they all have one identical feature, *wings*. They are abnormally larger than any other hybrid. So, if you've seen anything or heard anything out of the ordinary, then you need to let me know." With a sense of urgency, he said, "Also, there is another threat, something that hasn't been substantiated yet, regardless, we believe your family is in danger, *again*."

I peered up at him. "What do you mean in danger again?"

"Let me finish, Crystal."

My fear was coming back to haunt me. I was sure I knew what it was.

"Before I say anything about it, we have to confirm it…"

I smacked my hands on the chair arms. "Dammit, Tristan, is it Jace?"

Everybody stared at me.

"Crystal, I have…"

Standing up, I yelled, "Answer the fucking question, Tristan!" I was tired of him beating around the bush.

His blue eyes darkened. "Do you want me to answer the question with nothing confirmed yet, Crystal? Should we make your entire family nervous even if it's not true?" His face hardened. "If you want me to I will, but I don't think it's necessary! What do you think?"

Anxious, Jennifer shifted her weight repeatedly.

Scared, I challenged him. "I need to know, Tristan because even if it's not true, I need my family on guard, just in case."

"Fine," he replied.

The bikers stood by, arms crossed in front of their chest.

Tristan's gaze met mine. "We have reason to believe Jace is still alive."

Robert cracked his neck. "Alive? How the hell can he be alive? We killed the son of a bitch."

Tristan turned to face him. "We believe he's a hybrid."

All thoughts of Jace scrambled through my head. I was not being paranoid. It was true, all of it.

"Jesus Christ, Tristan, couldn't somebody have figured this out before?" I snapped. "How the hell could they not know?" And just what did that mean? "Please tell me he's not coming after us again?"

Tristan took my face in his hands. "I'm not going to let anything happen to you besides, like I said, nothing has been confirmed yet. We do have a witness, though." He leaned in. "*But* it doesn't mean it's him. We're doing everything we can to find the man. Then, we're going to take him out but, first things first, we need to destroy the hybrids he created. They're destroying our agents. We think he put a hit on the U.G.S.S. We need every man we got, including the club." He pointed at his men.

"If it is him, we have the best of the best right here, including your son. Robert's been gracious enough to provide his services."

My jaw dropped and my heart skipped a beat. I glanced at Robert.

Robert nodded.

Tristan sighed. Then, he asked, "And with that, I'd like to ask you to join us."

Eyes wide, I stared at him. "What? Me? You want me to work for the U.G.S.S.?"

"Yes, my boss asked if you wanted a job. I'm not real keen on the idea, but you have talent, babe." He gave me an awkward look.

Hesitantly, I answered, "I don't know, Tristan. I need to think about it."

"That's fine. At this point, I think it's a good thing Rebecca and the children are going to Phoenix. That takes them out of the picture should something happen around here but on the same token, it leaves Jennifer and Raelin open for attack." He glanced at the teenagers. "If it is Jace, I fear he's got others watching you again but not just you, your family too."

"You know it's one thing that it's me, but my family? Our friends, her friend?" I pointed at Raelin. "She doesn't belong here, and she sure as shit can't defend herself against anybody out of the ordinary."

"Oh, she's got a few tricks up her sleeve, dear. My men have been watching her. As a matter of fact, since Sebastian is in town now, he's been assigned to keep an eye on her and Jennifer."

Raelin glanced at Sebastian. A faint smile spread across his face.

"In the evening, Uwe will help keep an eye on both of them."

Jennifer stared in horror at him.

I was trifled by the whole situation. "I don't know…"

"Trust me, everything will be fine. My brotherhood will be good to them. Won't you, boys?"

"Yes, we will," Uwe said.

Sebastian nodded, eyeing the young women.

I lowered my voice, "I don't want…"

"Shush. I know what you're thinking, but they've given me their word. Don't worry about it, and just for your information, Raelin has already stuck her nose in the family's business. She's already helped your family before. Bet you didn't know that, did you?"

I gazed back at her.

"Do you remember when your granddaughter was taken by Jace?"

I nodded.

"Do you remember the mountain lion that saved her?"

Again, I nodded.

"That was her. She's a shapeshifter."

Raelin took a step back, cowering in the corner.

"Shapeshifters can transform into the last animal they've seen, or they can change into the most common animal they've changed into. Because she's changed into the mountain lion so much, it's become natural to change into it over everything else. She saved Katie's life, so she's already put herself in harm's way. If Jace is still alive, and he comes after your family, he's also going to come after her so we need to protect her, too."

We maintained eye contact with her, reaffirming her she would be protected.

"When will you have confirmation?" I asked. The thought of Jace alive sent shivers down my spine.

"I'm not sure yet. We're hoping within a couple of days. We'll keep everybody informed, though. Rebecca and the kids will have adequate protection to her sister's house. By then, she'll be with her family and then, they will be able to provide the protection she and the kids need,"

Tristan said, peering over his shoulder at Robert.

"Thanks, Tristan," Robert replied, sitting down.

"Not a problem. Family is what's important. Which by the way means everybody in this house right now is to treat each other with respect and dignity regardless of your background and duty. Got that, guys?" He turned to the men.

"Not a problem," said Sabol, leaning against the wall. He shoved his hands in his jacket pockets.

"That also means that the children are not to be touched, unless you're protecting them, understand?" Tristan said, sternly. He leaned against one of the chairs.

The men nodded.

"Control your appetite. Eat before you know you are going to come in contact with the children, understand?"

Again, they nodded.

Robert's shoulders settled as if Tristan's words eased some of his anxiety.

"Thank you again," said Robert.

"Anytime, Robert. All I really wanted to do tonight was, introduce everybody and let everybody know what's going on. Does anybody have anything to add?"

We stood in silence.

"So, if it is Jace, why isn't he just coming after me? Why wait? It didn't stop him before."

He shook his head. "I don't know. Something is different. We're not really sure what is going on. It would be great if you could remember where his house was."

"If I remember anything, I'll let you know."

Tristan glanced around. "If anything comes up about his residence, we need to check it out as soon as possible," he said. "The U.G.S.S. is concerned he's still creating hybrids. If he is, we need to find out where he's creating these things. So, we can't just kill him without locating his lab."

Tristan paced the floor. "The hybrids he's creating are very dangerous. More dangerous than even us. They have the ability to destroy anything and everything. This is why they cannot exist. They must all be destroyed, every single one of them."

"So, I'm just curious, how can he still be alive?" Robert asked.

"Every hybrid is different. They are unique in their own death..."

With this, Tristan explained the difference in how hybrids die vs. other immortal beings.

I listened to him intently. As I did, Robert and I exchanged looks with Sebastian. He had confided in us what my third beast was—the dragon. I was fearful of it coming forward. If what Sebastian said was true, then I worried about Tristan's reaction. He had said they must all be destroyed. Did that include me?

Sebastian and Robert's gaze remained on me. Robert would defend me but would Tristan's men, if they knew what I was? And what about my lover? Would he kill me as well or would he defend me? And what about the U.G.S.S.? Did that mean they would come after me, too? I had enough to worry about with Jace and his men. Did I have to worry about Tristan's devotion, too? Did he love me enough to fight against his own and protect me? How was I going to tell him?

As I thought about this, the subject changed to the two men who saved Jennifer and Raelin's lives. I didn't pay too much attention to the conversation. The others were intent on the subject matter, but Sebastian was not. He stared at me as if contemplating on saying something to Tristan, but then Rebecca's voice was in my head.

Don't you say a word. You keep it to yourself. Talk to Tristan alone, not in front of the men. I don't trust them, and you shouldn't either regardless of what Tristan says.

I glanced at the staircase. Rebecca's soothing voice drifted downstairs. She sang a lullaby to the girls.

"Crystal?"

"Mom?"

"Mom! Hey, are you listening to us?"

I turned my attention to my family. Everybody stared at me.

"Sorry, what's going on?"

"What's wrong, mom?" Jennifer asked.

"Nothing. What's up?"

"We thought we killed Jace, right?" Robert said. It was more of a statement than a question.

"Yeah, so we already gathered that," I replied.

"What about Warrant?" Tristan asked.

"So, what about him…?" Then it dawned on me, he was a hybrid. Jace had changed him, too.

"Fuck," I muttered. My heart skipped a beat.

"He matches the same damn description that Raelin just gave of the man who saved her," Tristan said.

"Yeah, I swear that it was him, too," said Robert.

"What!" I jumped to my feet.

"I'm sorry. I don't know who Warrant is," Raelin said.

"Shit…shit…shit!" I paced the floor.

Tristan stared at me.

"He can't be, can he?" I put my hands on my hips. "Tristan?" I gazed at him. "Can he?"

A look of frustration froze on his face. "I don't know. If Jace can survive a fire, and a claw through the face? Then can Warrant? Does the same creature reside in both men? Or is Warrant's hybrid different? We already know you have another creature in there, but it has yet to surface," Tristan said.

I glanced at Sebastian. "Yes, we're already aware of that. Do you think he used the same creature?"

"I'm not sure," Tristan said. "That we don't know. If he wanted to destroy every living thing, yes. But is that his true intent? Again, we don't know. All we really know is, that whatever existed within Warrant's body also exists within you." His eyes widened. "When we get back to my place, I want you to try to pull it out."

"But I don't know how to do it." I was nervous. If it was the dragon, I worried about what Tristan would do. Shaking, I turned away from him.

"We'll work on it later," he said. "We need to talk about Warrant. If he is the same creature Jace is, he's still alive. We need to be concerned he's going to come back here. He's already turned on you once, which means he'll do it again. The fact he saved Raelin is just a one in a million chance he wasn't attuned to his beast." Tristan turned to Raelin. "You said he was running from something?"

"Yes, he was, actually both men were." She sighed. "I know it sounds silly, but Jennifer and I thought it was a deformed dragon. Fire even came out of its mouth and burned Jennifer's face."

I glanced at Sebastian.

Tristan stood behind me. "That's it. It's time to kill those winged motherfuckers, every single one of them."

§

When the bikers left, Wayne emerged from his hiding spot in the forest. He stayed back far enough to keep from attracting their attention.

He had to know everything about what was going on in her life. Crystal's protection was far too important, as it always had been.

Camouflaging himself, he followed them to Tristan's home. He used to be able to trust Tristan. Now, he was not so sure, for he knew some of the secrets that the U.G.S.S. held. Was Tristan in on it?

THE HIDDEN

Tristan threw his hands up in frustration. "Please concentrate, Crystal."

"I'm trying!" I snapped. Frustrated, I sighed. I had yet to find the way to call my third beast out and it was irritating not just him, but me.

I stood before the bathroom mirror and hung my head. "Can't we try this another time? It's just not working."

As he sat down on the edge of the bed, his voice rose. "You need to focus."

His annoyance with me only pissed me off more. I rolled my eyes and hissed, "I am!"

A voice boomed from the other side of the bedroom door. "Hey! Try pissing her off! Maybe that will call it out!"

Tristan jerked the door open. "What do you want?"

"We just want to see how it's going," Ratliff said.

Tristan came and sat down beside me.

As they walked in, Sebastian looked me over. "I don't see any changes."

"Yeah, well, she's having a hard time," Tristan confided.

"Thanks," I replied.

"So, what is it we're calling out, Crystal? What's hiding inside you?" Sebastian asked, pointing his finger at me.

"*I don't know,*" I enunciated, ignoring his implication. "And will everybody stop asking me because I have no fucking clue what it is." Until I knew for sure what it was, I wasn't going with Sebastian's idea I was part dragon.

"You sure about that?" Sabol asked.

"Yes, I'm sure about that. Just leave me alone," I said, walking into the bathroom.

I stared at myself in the mirror. Did I really have a winged creature hiding inside of me? And if so, was it hibernating? Was that the reason it wouldn't come forth?

As the men talked among themselves outside of the bathroom door, I focused on my eyes. What would they look like? I was an ever evolving creature for I could transform into werewolf or vampire. Also, I could transform into the ever-changing hybrid, which had mixed features of both creatures so I could only imagine what the dragon hybrid would look like.

Behind me, the men left the room, the door clicking shut behind them. Though Tristan had no reflection, I detected his footsteps as he entered the bathroom. Then, he touched my shoulder.

"Come, let's get some sleep. You need your rest. It will be daylight in a couple of hours."

He pulled my hair back, and kissed my shoulder.

"Do they hibernate?"

"What?" His lips moved up to the base of my neck.

"Dragons? Do they hibernate?"

"Why do you ask?" Subtle kisses lined my neck.

I gazed at his location in the mirror. "I'm just curious."

He sucked on my ear. "Yes, they hibernate. Are you worried you have one in you?"

I lowered my eyes. "Of course not," I lied.

His lips were on me again, his hands moving up to my shoulders. "I wouldn't worry, love. That's one thing I doubt you have in you."

I closed my eyes and focused on his touch…his lips. Slowly, he removed my shirt, revealing my black and purple bra—his favorite.

The corner of his lips curled up. "I'm sorry for being an ass. I just want to help you discover yourself."

Then, he slid his hands under my breasts.

"Mm, hmm…" I moaned.

His tongue slipped inside my mouth. As he released the hook on my bra, I turned toward him, my beasts rising to the occasion.

I ripped his shirt open and pushed him back against the wall, kissing him, my lips moving to his neck.

"Oh, Crystal," he moaned, pressing me harder against him.

I ran my fingers down his chest, my claws cutting his skin. Blood oozed from his wounds. As I lowered myself before him, I savored the taste of his blood, my fangs grazing his stomach, tearing his flesh even more. A thin line of blood ran out of his wound, causing my adrenaline to rush through my body.

Hastily, I pulled his pants down and grabbed his member. I took him in my mouth, running my tongue up and down it.

Moaning, he leaned back against the wall, his hand pressed against my head.

That was merely a teaser. I needed more—him inside of me.

As if he read my mind, he grabbed me, tore my clothes off, and had me on the countertop. Hard and defiantly, he entered me, his hands around my hips.

"Oh, Tristan!"

The vampire and the werewolf inside took hold. We bucked in unison, our bodies almost one and the same, as his fang cut my lip. Crimson droplets rained down, dripping onto my breasts.

Molding me around him, he carried me to the bed. He lapped up the blood, his tongue grazing my nipple. Then, the creatures within came forth.

"Oh, yes," I moaned.

I pulled him down atop me, my claws digging into his back.

The iciness from his tongue and the grazing of his fangs upon my skin sent a chill down my spine. It enticed my inner beasts.

Tristan gripped my hips and thrust hard into me.

Warmth overcame me as it started from deep within. Another thrust of his hips and his fangs pierced my flesh. I moaned. Again, he thrust. The warmth inside erupted into a boiling fire, an almost burning yet intoxicating sensation.

"Yes, Tristan!" His rhythm was gratifying yet somewhat different. Again! The fire moved within. Ah yes, I needed him! Again! I tasted him…the flesh…the blood. The fire shot up into my loins. It was painful, yet sensual. It was not the vampire and it was not the werewolf. Again! Oh, yes, pump me harder, Tristan. *It* rose up near the surface.

Tristan consumed my blood.

My head lolled back. "No, not now Tristan. You're making me weak."

Curious, he looked at me, his lips covered in blood. "Crystal?"

"It wants out." My heart beat faster, to the point I thought it was going to explode.

"Don't stop, Tristan. I need you, more so now," I said.

He thrust into me, but not like before, instead, he was more concerned about the beast.

"I need you to fuck me like you were before," I said. "Don't stop."

He slammed into me.

"Yes!" I gripped tighter onto him. Again! Yes!

She was hungry, very hungry. As I buried my fangs in him, the pain hit. It started within my loins. The pain was excruciating.

"Don't stop, Tristan…please don't stop. It's the only thing lessening the pain," I screamed. Tears flowed down my cheeks.

His rhythm slowed. "But…"

"Shut up! Just fuck me." Again, the pain increased. The pain ripped through my upper back.

"Is it coming…?"

"Yes, it is," I moaned. "It needs to feed."

He lowered his head, exposing his neck. The artery pulsated. I latched onto him, and consumed his blood, yet, it was not enough to satisfy the creature. Horrendous pain tore through the middle of my upper back between my shoulders. I wanted to scream. Instead, I bit harder into his neck to stifle the pain.

He hissed.

"Oh, it hurts, Tristan, it really hurts," I cried. Blood dribbled down my face. The pain was becoming unbearable. "I need you to slice open the skin."

"What?" He looked down at me.

"My back, between the shoulder blades, I need you to rip it open. The pain is too much. It's trying to come out." I hissed. "Please, Tristan. It really hurts."

§

Tristan stared at the dragon tattoo on her back. It bulged out. *Slice it open.* What the hell?

He placed his elongated fingernail on her back and with his other hand, he gripped her shoulder.

"Wait," she said.

"What?"

She glanced back at him. "I don't know how painful this is going to be."

"All right, so what do you want me to do?"

She grinned. "Can you? You know…?"

With a sly grin, he asked, "Do what, Crystal? You've already told me to shut up and fuck you so you might as well just say it."

She howled in pain.

Her skin bubbled up against the inside of her shoulder blades. They pulsated. Holy hell! He thought her change into a werewolf was bad, this was worse. The bubbles grew in size.

She hissed. "Tristan…!"

You know what she wants, so just fuck her.

As he entered her, her entire body shook. Holy shit! He rocked her back and thrust inside of her.

Oh, yes!

She gripped onto his thigh, digging her claws into him. Again, her body shuddered.

Her muscles around his member pulsated, tightening around him. Oh, fuck!

"Harder, Tristan!"

He slammed his manhood deep inside of her. She moaned.

Just like the initial transformation from human to beast, the first was the hardest and the most painful. Sex helped to relieve some of the pain. This is why he decided to have sex with her after her first transformation. Tristan took pleasure that she chose to do the same with this creature.

The bulging within her shoulders pulsated through the muscles. Something was aching to change.

Clutching onto her, he pierced her flesh with his fingernail. Carefully, he cut it. A third of the way down, a wing erupted from her body. It barely missed hitting Tristan's head.

§

The cut helped to alleviate some of the pain. When my wings shot out of my back, the relief was instantaneous.

Behind me, Tristan escaped what could have been a hard slap.

I could only imagine the look of surprise on his face, along with the horrifying discovery of what I was. How was he going to react?

I cringed. I feared the worst.

At least if he killed me here and now, my family would not find me dead. My heart raced.

§

Dark grayish leathery wings sprung from her back. Now, he knew why the experience was so painful. Her wings from tip to tip must have had a wingspan of about ten feet. Long veins and bone spread throughout the wings. He spread his arms out and caressed them. The leathery texture was rough.

He took a deep breath and drew in the scent of brimstone. Then, he gazed at her. Her skin, which was once soft, was rough, though not as leathery as the wings.

Though he had smelled the brimstone when he was near her, he told himself it was something else, and not her. He had been in denial, for he did not want to kill her.

"Tristan?"

Her eyes, which were once large and brown, were emerald and elongated, and full of dread. Her long dark auburn hair hung over her shoulders, hiding part of her face.

Anger and resentment filled his heart. He was angry she was part dragon, and he may have to kill her. Also, he resented the fact he didn't detect the dragon within Warrant before they changed her.

She turned away from him. In fear, he assumed, for she knew what his intentions were with the dragons. She had every right to be afraid of him, and she should be.

Tristan wrapped his hand around her throat and pulled her back into him. The fiery hot wings beat against his chest. Heat pulsated from within her, surfacing through her skin. A mist swirled up from the contact of their flesh. A thin layer of scales layered her body, including her breasts. Her rosebud nipples remained perky, keeping her femininity through the dragon-like skin.

She peered up at him, her hair brushing against his chest. Oh, how he loved the feel of it against his body. Beneath the scent of brimstone, he smelled her, the woman he cared for.

Though faint, her voice cracked. "Tristan..."

Tristan knew what she was thinking. He didn't like what he had to do, either, but, he had to kill the dragon hybrids, which included his own lover.

But did he have to kill her? Or could he spare her life? He gripped her harder by the throat. She didn't fight back which made his task more difficult. If she would have fought back, it would have made it so much easier but it wasn't.

Closing his eyes, he whispered, "Shush, Crystal."

Lord knew he wanted her alive but duty called. When he opened his eyes, her penetrating gaze met his. His nails dug into her throat.

"I trusted you...even then," she whispered.

§

Wayne hid within the forest nearby. Crystal's scream had pierced the walls of Tristan's home. Now, there was silence. Wayne dreaded it. He had done what he needed to out of protection for her and the family, and now he regretted it.

His eyes remained fixated on one window in particular—the room he presumed she was in. Did he want to risk his life to find out what was happening? And were the other men in the house? If Wayne tried to sneak in, would the other men attack him? Probably. If they killed him, his attempt would have been useless.

He was thankful his curse was not as vampire but as werewolf, for he could invade a home without invitation. Reluctantly, he held his ground and waited for the right opportunity. Dawn was on the horizon.

ANARCHY

While Robert helped Rebecca pack her stuff, he glanced nervously out of the window. He kept an eye out for Sebastian and members of the U.G.S.S. He really didn't want her going to Phoenix without him, but he knew it was for the best.

Sebastian and three unknown men met them outside. The roughest looking man, whom Robert also assumed was a biker, mounted his steel horse. The other two men followed in separate black cars. He expected them to remain more incognito, but apparently they didn't care. In a way, it didn't matter. If anybody crossed their path, they would have hell to pay.

Robert kissed his wife and children.

"Don't forget to call me," he said.

"I won't," she replied.

She and the children climbed in the car. Once they left, he went inside and got ready for work.

§

The next day, Jennifer thought about Tristan's warning to keep a lookout around her, even at school. He worried Jace hired werewolves to keep an eye on her and mom during the day out of fear they would do anything to get to Crystal, including spying on, or attacking her family.

So when Michelle and her friends caught Jennifer alone in the school bathroom, Jennifer was on guard. If Michelle started anything, Jennifer was going to stand up for herself.

As they walked in, she spun around.

Did she really know who she was messing with? Obviously not, Jennifer thought.

Michelle sneered. She took a step toward Jennifer, her hand curling up into a fist, her blonde hair falling in her face.

"Listen you bitch. I will take you down. I know everybody in this school and they'll back me up," she said, approaching Jennifer.

That was probably true, but Jennifer didn't care. She clenched her hand up into a fist, ready for a fight. As Jennifer walked past a couple of the sinks, Michelle swung at her.

The werewolf in Jennifer rose to the surface. The muscles and bone in her face shifted. The adrenaline rushed throughout her body.

As she swung at Michelle, her claws emerged, ripping Michelle's skin. Jennifer swung again, breaking her cheekbone.

Screaming, Michelle backed off, bouncing off of the wall.

Jennifer grinned. The werewolf inside was defiant and resilient.

The other girls screamed and tried to hide in the stalls.

Michelle slid down the wall, and then Jennifer jumped her, pummeling her with her fists. Her claws tore at Michelle's flesh, spilling blood onto the floor. Michelle's limp body stilled beneath her.

Jennifer stood, horrified by what she had done. Trembling, she stared at herself in the mirror. Her reflection terrified her. Her mouth, jaw, and nose had fully transformed, and her large brown eyes were set back. She touched her face, her claws fully extended. The muscles in her arms were large. Eyes wide, she recoiled.

Behind her, one of the girls snuck out of a stall and moved toward the door. Jennifer's gaze shifted, her pupils changing from brown to yellow.

The girl stopped and stared at Jennifer, her mouth agape, her eyes wide. Blood splattered her dirty blonde hair.

"I'm so sorry," she whimpered.

Jennifer turned to face her. Michelle lay amongst the backpacks on the floor, near the girl's feet.

"Where do you think you're going?" Jennifer asked.

Crying, the girl scooted back into the bathroom stall, along with half of her friends, who stood crying.

Then it dawned on her. Michelle was dead. Blood had pooled up on the floor. What would happen if somebody came in? What would happen to Jennifer? Would she go to jail for murder? Her heart skipped a beat. Stop! You can't kill anybody! But you already did! Think of what's going to happen to you!

As if the werewolf in her understood, it backed down. Hastily, she grabbed her backpack and ran out. The halls were filled with students who were eating their lunch.

She ran past everybody paranoid somebody was watching her. Her hands dripped with blood. Jennifer was scared. She knew better than to change into her alter ego, especially at school. She killed somebody.

Hadn't everybody told her to be careful? Her mother, her brother, and her sister in law. Even, Tristan had warned her to keep control of it.

As she ran down the hallway, she glanced around, stuffing her hands in her pockets. Everybody stared at her, as though they knew she killed Michelle. They recoiled from her.

She ran down another hall, passing the drama class. Fortunately, several students were dressed up for a rendition of Dracula. With the blood strewn across her, Jennifer blended in well. Hopefully, everybody would think she was part of the class.

As she continued on, she exchanged passing glances with a student wrestler. He had a strange glimmer in his eye. Yellowish eyes stared back at her. Get the fuck out of here, Jennifer!

She took one last glance at him and pressed the door open, leaving a bloody imprint on it, and emerged into the daylight. The heat from the sun warmed her.

Since she killed someone and she was gaining a lot of attention, she decided to leave campus. Trembling, she headed for her car. She wanted to leave the murder behind her. But was it murder or self-defense? She wanted to cry.

Other students stood nearby. Fear settled within her. Yellow eyes stared at her. Then, she remembered something Tristan said.

"When the wolf in you kills for the first time, others will become aware of your beast. Beware, some may befriend you, others may want to challenge you. Be alert, take control, and do not let your guard down. When others sense the killer in you and make the decision to follow you, it's called the Unity of the Wolf. In turn, this will become your pack. Even as they become a member of your pack, they may still want to challenge you.

You need to trust your instincts. Trust and respect are something you earn. You will still need to fight for the trust, respect, and honesty of your pack. Your members will come forth, and give you what you earn. But you must still be alert, for sometimes within a pack, you may find an enemy, one who betrays you. You must weed out those enemies. And if you find an enemy, your pack will back you up. They will stay with you for as long as you want them to. Trust your instincts."

Jennifer sensed the werewolves in the students who followed her to the parking lot. She feared their challenge but was willing to stand up if she had to. She was a loner, and she knew the danger, for Tristan and Robert had spoken of them.

Clouds moved in, providing a slight drizzle. Where the hell was she going to go? She didn't want to go home, and she didn't want to go near Tristan's place for she didn't want to have to explain herself to her mother, and she didn't know his brotherhood well enough to ask for assistance, even though that was one of the reasons they were in town.

A young, female teacher stood nearby. The woman had the same glimmer in her eyes. Even the teachers? Shit!

The teacher stared at her, eyes wide, glancing back at the building from where Jennifer emerged. As if knowing Jennifer's secret, she placed her hand over her heart.

How the hell? She couldn't have known. The woman ran toward the building.

Jennifer ran into the parking lot, shoving her hands in her pocket, groping for her keys. They weren't there. Dammit! She glanced back at the werewolves.

They stopped at the gate.

She fumbled for her keys in her backpack. Glancing back, she estimated there were about twelve of them.

Tristan's voice echoed in her head. *"Trust your instincts. Some will challenge you, some will follow you."*

Jennifer jammed the key in the lock, threw her bag in, and jumped in the driver's seat. She was terrified. They must have smelled the blood on her, and who was to say if any of them were Jace's hired hands? With that thought in mind, she started the engine.

She couldn't go home. Jace knew where they lived.

The passenger door flew open. Jennifer turned, ready to rip somebody apart when Raelin jumped in the passenger seat and threw the backpacks to the floorboard.

Eyes wide open, Raelin stared at her. "Damn Jennifer, what the hell is going on?" She peeked out the window.

The students ran toward them.

She cried out, "Uh, Jennifer, you need to get the hell out of here!"

"Shit!" Her heart lurched into her throat.

Jennifer put the car in gear.

From behind, a teenage boy lurched at the car. The car bounced beneath his weight as he gripped onto the rear bumper.

She peeled out, hoping he had let go, for she could no longer see him.

"What the fuck, Jennifer?" She stared wild-eyed at her. "If I'm going to be your friend, and my life is on the line like your family's, I think I deserve a valid explanation."

"I killed Michelle," Jennifer whispered.

Raelin whipped her head around, her hair flying around her face. "Holy shit! What the hell were you thinking?"

"Umm, can we discuss this later?" Eyes wide, she stared in the rearview mirror. "I think we have visitors."

Raelin turned around. Two trucks sped up behind them. "Who's that?"

"I don't know and I don't want to find out! Help me find a place to go because I don't want to take them home."

"What about Tristan's place? Isn't Sebastian supposed to be watching over us anyway?"

"Yeah, he is, now that I…"

The rumble of a bike roared up behind the trucks. Jennifer glanced up at the rearview mirror. Behind them, a group of motorcycles followed the trucks.

Raelin leaned over the back of the seat. "That can't be…?"

"No, it's not them, can't be. Tristan and most of his men aren't daywalkers, only Sebastian is."

"So, who the hell are they?"

They exchanged looks. The trucks behind her slowed, coming to a stop.

"I don't know."

A lone Harley pulled up in front of several motorcycles. They aided in stopping the driver of the trucks. Jennifer recognized the biker and smiled.

"Oh, shit, Jennifer!" Raelin exclaimed with delight. "It's…"

Jennifer interrupted, "Sebastian."

"Who are those other bikers though?"

"Friends I'm guessing. They're not the Hells Changelings," Jennifer said, wiggling her eyebrows.

As they screamed with delight, she kept her eye in the rearview mirror. The teenage drivers stepped out of their trucks.

"Yeah! Hey, assholes, you had it coming!" Raelin screamed.

Tyler stood before Sebastian, his arms in the air.

"What the hell...? Was that...?"

Confused, the girls looked at one another.

"Yeah, that was Tyler. Why would he be...?"

"Tyler wouldn't..."

She turned her attention back to the road. A large semi was in her lane, coming straight at her. No, wait! He wasn't in her lane. She was in his.

"Oh shit!"

§

Dark sunglasses hid Sebastian's eyes.

"I swear this is her wallet," Tyler said. He opened the heart embroidered wallet. "She dropped it when she ran into the parking lot. I was just trying to get it back to her."

Sebastian stared down at Jennifer's driver's license. It was hers all right. The kid wasn't lying.

Sebastian glanced up at him. "Get the fuck out of here."

"Thank you," he said, jumping back in his truck. "I appreciate it."

Sebastian walked back to the second truck, sucking at the piece of meat stuck between his teeth. Damn lunch! Why did it have to fight so much?

Behind him, Tyler pulled onto the road, leaving Sebastian and his men to deal with the teenage boys in the second truck.

"Hey, asshole!" one of the teenagers yelled.

As one of the biker's grabbed him, a patrol car rounded the curve in the road. It slowed down as it neared them.

"Great," Sebastian muttered. "Let him go!"

The biker pushed the kid back, slamming him against the side of the truck.

"Oh look, asshole, it looks like you have company," James said with a smug expression.

While the deputy's attention was on the other two, Sebastian punched the boy. The teenager flew backward onto the hood. Dammit! Watch your strength, asshole.

The patrol car stopped, and then both deputies jumped out, drawing their weapons.

"Freeze! Put your hands up!"

He raised his arms. "What's up, Deputies?"

"Who are you?" The male deputy approached Sebastian.

The female deputy stood back, the barrel of her gun aimed at everybody else.

"This is the Devils Pack," Sebastian replied. The meat came loose. Finally, he could finish his lunch.

"I know who they are. I want to know who you are," the deputy said. "I haven't seen your face around here. Turn around."

Sebastian complied. As the lawman pat him down, he said, "I don't have a weapon, man."

"What's your name?"

"Sebastian."

"Sebastian what?"

"Just Sebastian."

The deputy turned Sebastian around and continued to search for a weapon.

The teenager Sebastian had thrown, climbed off of his truck. "Hey, can we go?"

"Just stay right there," the female deputy ordered.

"You have a last name, Sebastian?"

"Nah, it's just Sebastian," he said, smiling.

The deputy got in his face. "Just Sebastian, huh? Well, just Sebastian, do we have a problem here?" His brow furrowed in. "You a part of this pack, too? Or are you out just causing trouble?"

Sebastian chuckled. "Nah, I wouldn't do that. You see, the boy and I, here, were just having a conversation. Now, weren't we, boy?"

He wrapped his arm around James' shoulders. The female deputy shifted her gun, keeping Sebastian in her sight.

James smiled. "Yeah, we were just talking, Deputy. We're family."

Sebastian cocked his head. Now, that was a good kid. He grinned. "Yeah, we're family, and family sometimes has disagreements, like we had. But everything's cool now, isn't it?"

"Yep. Yes, we are, just Sebastian," the teenager said.

"Everything's cool. Just a little disagreement, but you know, I think it's time to get back to school. Our lunch is just about over," Sebastian said, grinning.

"What's your name, son?" the male Deputy asked him.

"James…James Olson, sir. I'm the running back at the school."

The deputy glared at Sebastian. "That's right, boy. You best get back to school now. I'll *come* see you later."

Sebastian squeezed James' shoulder.

The teenager kept his eye on Sebastian. "Can I go now?"

The female deputy spoke up, "James Olson? I've seen you play. You're a damn good football player."

"Thanks, ma'am," he replied.

"Hey, when's the next game by the way? You were supposed to tell me and forgot," Sebastian asked, releasing the boy.

James smiled. "Uh, I think it's…oh damn, I forget when it is."

One of the teenagers chimed in, "It's this Friday, six o'clock."

James shot his friend a dirty look.

"Home game, right?" Sebastian winked.

"Uh, yeah. I'll see you there." He turned his attention to the male Deputy. "Can I go now? I'm going to get in trouble if I don't get back to school."

He waved the kid on. "Yeah, get out of here."

"Thanks."

The boys jumped in the truck and drove off.

"What about me, Deputy? Can I go now?"

The woman put her gun back in the holster.

"I'm not armed and as you can see, I'm not hurting anybody. I was just out for a ride, and happened to run into my cousin."

Lowering his face, he peered at the woman over the top of his glasses. "My, you are a pretty thing." He swallowed the meat. "Very pretty."

She turned to her partner. "Let's go. They're not doing anything." She climbed into the patrol car.

"You guys stay out of trouble."

"Yes, sir!" the men replied.

§

Deputy Blanch got in the car and glanced at his partner. "You all right there? You were a bit stand-offish when he complimented you."

Deputy Fuchs peeked out over her glasses at him. "He's a little creepy. He makes the hair stand up on the back of my neck."

He fastened his seatbelt. "Yeah, well, can't really do much with him."

Annoyance registered in her voice. "Why didn't you ask for his license and registration?"

"We don't need any trouble with his kind, mainly them," said, pointing to the others. He faked a smile at them through the windshield. "He may just be passing through, but they're not. The last thing I need is backlash from them if I arrest him. You'll learn, soon enough, on who you give some slack to and who you don't, around here. Besides, the boy backed him up."

"Mm, question for you on that, by the way?"

She gazed out at the bikers, who were climbing on their bikes. The roar of the pipes rumbled.

"What's that?" he asked, starting the engine.

"Why were those boys here? There are no restaurants down this way unless you drive for a while. They weren't out here to get lunch."

They exchanged looks. Something wasn't right. He looked out at the road. Why the hell would they strike up a fight with a bunch of bikers? James was the top running back at the school.

Lunch, huh? He looked around. There were no restaurants in sight.

"You agree with me, don't you?" she asked, glancing at him. "Maybe it's not the bikers we need to be worried about. Maybe it's James."

"Nah, James is a good kid," he said.

"You sure about that, Blanche? You look like your questioning it just as much as I am."

The bikes rode off in the opposite direction of the school.

"I'm not questioning your duty, Blanche. But, personally, I would have asked the bikers for their ID."

"I'm trying to keep order here. One of them is keeping the local bikers in line. Besides, I have nothing to arrest them on, even him."

He pulled out onto the asphalt, headed in the direction they came from.

"What are you doing?" she asked.

"Just going by the school, I want to make sure the young man is there like he's supposed to be."

"What if he isn't?"

"Well, then, I guess we'll find out."

§

Robert was sitting in his patrol car when his phone went off. He was expecting it to be Rebecca, letting him know they made it safely to Phoenix. As he fumbled in his pocket for it, a heavy thud hit the passenger door. He looked up. Nothing.

"What the hell?"

He gazed out at his surroundings. Nobody was around. He chambered a bullet and climbed out of his car. Stealthily, he crept around the vehicle. A foul stench hung in the air. As he walked around the passenger side, smoke billowed from the object.

Robert glanced around. No movement. No sound. He moved in closer and nudged it, exposing the human face. Oh God! It was Torrance. What the fuck? A heartbreaking cry escaped his lips.

"Torrance?"

He bent down and touched it. Layers of dead skin came loose. A burning hatred rose up within him.

"Motherfucker," he whispered.

A screech echoed through the forest followed by a heatwave. A dragon was nearby. He stared out at the woods. Screams came from somewhere in the distance.

Tristan wasn't kidding. The motherfuckers were everywhere. They didn't care if they were out in public or not. He hated to admit, but he agreed with Tristan, the hybrids had to be killed.

Robert opened the trunk to his car and grabbed his gun, the same one he killed the other dragon with. He slammed it shut, and proceeded toward the heat, leaving his phone in the car.

§

Rebecca stood on the porch, her phone in hand. Dammit, he didn't answer. She looked up at the men.

"Sorry, he's not picking up."

The girls stood next to her, chattering away. They repeatedly knocked on the door and rang the doorbell.

"That's all right."

She snapped. "Girls, stop it! These men are trying to talk and you're being rude."

The Hispanic man knelt down in front of Tisa, extending his hand to her. Tisa stepped back, bumping into Leah.

"We just want to make sure your husband and Tristan knew you made it here safely," the balding man said.

The two men who rode with her in the car wore dark sunglasses and suits. Their physical appearance reminded her of what the FBI would look like. Behind them, the two bikers who accompanied the black Cadillac to Phoenix remained on their Harleys.

Then, the front door opened. Larissa stood there with her familiar, Hunter. The two-foot long Bearded Dragon lizard sat on her shoulder.

"I'll call Tristan. You make sure you get a hold of your husband and let him know you made it here. He'll be upset Sebastian wasn't able to escort you," he said.

He glanced at the lizard. It fluffed its beard and hissed. The agent turned his attention back to Rebecca.

"You have a good day, ma'am."

"You too. And, thank you," she said.

As the men left, Rebecca turned around to find her girls playing with Hunter. As they reached for him, the lizard smacked their hands with his tail. They giggled.

"Now, now, don't get him too uppity," Larissa said, hugging Rebecca.

Rebecca's face was inches from Hunter's, whose tongue slithered across her chin.

"Yuck," she said, pulling away.

Larissa laughed. "Is he giving you love?"

She wiped her chin. "Yeah."

"It's about time you came down here. I have missed you," Larissa said. She kissed Rebecca on the cheek.

"I've missed you, too. I'm sorry I haven't come down. I've been busy…"

"With the kids," Larissa finished. "I know, I know, excuses, excuses. You have none now. It's time to socialize, have some fun, and practice some magic. Right, girls?"

The girls danced around Larissa's long flowing red skirt, screaming with delight.

"How about we go inside? You girls can play with Hunter in there?" Larissa walked inside, her strides smooth and elegant.

They ran inside.

Rebecca closed the door behind her. The darkness of her sister's home brought back memories of her mother for she had always kept her house dark.

That and the scent of…she drew in a deep breath. Apple spice? Ah, yes, the comforts of growing up at home, including Hunter, the loveable lizard.

He was also a part of the family. Oh, how he loved Larissa and the girls, and as strange as it seemed, he didn't mind the kids playing with him. This was definitely her home—all the uniqueness she had separated herself from. It was time to get back in tune with herself.

Rebecca took a seat next to her sister, who sat on the wooden cross backed chair.

Larissa's fiery burnt orange sleeves flowed down her dark-skinned arms. Her eyes were cat-like, her cheekbones high and prominent, giving her an exotic appearance.

She bent over. "Remember, this is how Hunter likes for you to pet him." She ran her hand down his back.

"He feels funny," Tisa said, her lips curling down.

"He has scales. That's why he feels funny," Rebecca laughed.

"I know, but he's neat, isn't he?" Larissa asked.

"Yeah," Tisa screamed.

"Do you mind watching the girls for a minute? I'm going to call Robert really quick."

"Go for it."

Larissa sat on the floor as Hunter climbed onto Tisa's lap. She pulled him off.

"Oh, no you don't. You'll scratch them."

Rebecca walked into the kitchen and called Robert. Five Finger Death Punch's rendition of House of the Rising Sun played on the phone. Dancing to the music, she pulled a glass out of the cabinet and poured herself a drink.

"Come on, Robert. What is taking you so long?"

She took a sip, hit the END button, and redialed his number. Music played, then his voicemail picked up.

"Hi, honey, it's me. I just wanted to let you know that we made it to Larissa's."

She peered out through the kitchen window.

"Listen, Robert, I'm really sorry for being such a pain. You know I love you and I want the best for us and the kids. As for your mother, I'm sorry about not backing you up more. I know she's a good person, I can feel it. I'm worried about her, and everything else that's going on. She's brought a lot of bad elements into our lives but I know it's not her fault."

She paused. "Call me when you get a chance. I love you." She hung up the phone and shoved it in her pocket.

"Is everything okay?" Larissa asked.

Rebecca spun around. Larissa stood before her, her daughters gliding effortlessly in the air behind Larissa. No surprise there. It was a common occurrence around her house.

Smiling, she replied, "Yes, everything's okay."

Larissa rested her hands on Rebecca's shoulders. "I think you need a Rebecca day. Why don't you go to your room and take some time for yourself? I'll take care of the kids for a while besides, I have a surprise in there for you."

Great! What was Larissa up to now? "I…"

"Don't argue. Go to your room. If you don't go, I'll make you. You know I can."

Rebecca sighed. There was no sense in fighting her. Larissa always followed through with her promises.

"Fine, but there better not be any surprise alligators or something weird in there."

Larissa smiled. "Would I do that to you?"

"Are you kidding…?"

"All right, all right. So, I've done that before. This time, I think you'll be pleasantly surprised. Promise." She held up her pinky.

"Pinky swear?" Rebecca asked.

"Pinky swear," Larissa answered.

Rebecca chugged down her drink and then walked into the living room.

"I'll be back in a little bit, girls. You listen to your Aunt Larissa," she said.

"Okay, mommy," Leah said. She mimicked swimming movements as she floated through the air.

Rebecca continued past the girls to the bedroom she usually stayed in.

As she gripped the doorknob, the sound of waves whispered through the door. Maybe Larissa wanted Rebecca to take a nap.

She opened the door. In the middle of the room, stood a naked Hawaiian man, and a massage table. Her jaw dropped and her face turned red. Without taking a step inside, she shut the door.

"Larissa!"

"Girl, get your butt in there! You know you need one! Just smile and walk in!" Larissa laughed.

Oh, hell no! "I can't, you know better than that!" Damn her to hell.

"Girl, you don't think a woman wouldn't want to take advantage of that! You best get your butt in there! If you don't, I'll force you in that room!"

Rebecca opened the door, making sure the girls were not behind her. Oh why, did she have to do this to her? Damn Larissa!

He smiled.

"Why are you waiting?" Larissa blurted out.

Rebecca spun around. "I can't..."

"Oh, don't you like Hawaiian men? Sorry, let's try something else."

Larissa waved her finger. The Hawaiian changed into a naked African-American man.

"Jesus," Rebecca muttered.

"Oh, sorry. I forgot you're not into the brothers. How about an Asian? They're really good with their hands. You know, massage wise."

She waved her finger again, changing him into a naked Asian man.

Rebecca glanced at him. "Larissa...?"

"Oops, how about a Mexican? Or a Puerto-Rican? That's right. I forgot you're into the white men. Mm, hmm, try this one on for size."

With a flick of her finger, she changed him into a naked Caucasian man.

"Can you at least put some clothes on him?"

"Oh, what, you don't want his danglies rubbing against you? You know I find it quite erotic. It makes for a good massage, something I think Robert needs to do for you."

"Just put some clothes on him, please."

"Okay," Larissa giggled. She zapped some Speedos on him.

"Oh, please, Larissa, something more than that," she pleaded.

"Fine, but I'm not putting any more on him. You need some relaxation, and if Robert can't get it done, Thomas will."

"My husband is just fine in that department. I don't need another man to satisfy me. He's just been under a lot of stress lately."

"Oh, has he? Well, maybe I'll have to make sure he's taken care of as well."

Rebecca whipped her head around. "Larissa!"

She patted Rebecca's shoulder. "I'm just saying he needs some relaxation too."

"Don't you dare." She shot her a dirty look. "I'm warning you, Larissa."

Larissa smiled. "I'm sorry, but you both need some relaxation and if you can't take care of each other, I will."

"Larissa, I'm warning you, don't you screw around with my

marriage."

Again, Larissa waved her finger. "I'm not saying I'm going to fuck up your marriage. If it gets fucked up because you let things get out of hand then it's your fault, not mine. Oh, and by the way, Thomas is dressed."

Rebecca turned around. Thomas wore heart boxers. She sighed. The door clicked shut behind her. Crap! Larissa had locked her in. Since she couldn't undo her sister's magic, she approached the table.

"Can you turn around, please?" she asked.

"Please, undress to your comfort level." Smiling, he turned away.

As she undressed, she asked, "This is strictly therapeutic, right?"

"Yes, ma'am. Whatever you want."

Rebecca sighed. "All right, then don't touch my breasts, my butt or my...you know."

"No, ma'am, I don't, please specify."

"My groin." Dressed in her panties, she slipped under the sheet. "Please don't touch my groin."

"Yes, ma'am."

§

Robert failed to search his pockets or his car for his phone until he got home. He played the last moments before chasing the dragon down in his head. He was sure he left his phone in the car. Bloody and frantic, he tore it apart. It must have slipped through a crack, and got stuck somewhere in the seat, making it difficult to see it.

He sighed. It would have to wait until morning. He had to get some sleep, so he went in the house, and jumped in the shower.

As he thought about the dragons, the soft sound of footsteps entered his bedroom. The feminine creature was roughly 120 to 130 pounds. Her scent drifted into the bathroom. He turned the water off, threw the curtain open, and stared at the open door. Nothing, at least not from this viewpoint.

He snatched the towel off of the rung and wrapped it around him. Cautiously, he approached the door and peered into the room. A tall lanky, naked blonde stood next to the bed.

A French accent rolled off of her tongue. "Hello."

He glanced around. "Who the hell are you?"

"I'm your massage therapist," she replied, taking a step toward him.

"I think you're mistaken. I didn't order a massage therapist."

"It's a gift, for you."

"Lady, you have the wrong house. You need to leave," he said, pointing toward the door.

"You're Robert Bouchard, right?" She stopped before him.

"Yeah, but…"

"I was told to come here," she said, running her finger down his chest.

He flinched.

She smiled. "You look like you're ready for a massage. Come."

He took a step back. "Who sent you?"

"Larissa."

Oh, cripes! Of course, it all made sense now. Only she would pull something like this. He rolled his eyes.

"You can go now, you're not needed." He walked over to the door and motioned for her to leave.

"Oh, but I can't until I perform my duty."

"Well, your duty is done."

"But it hasn't been performed." She pouted.

He shook his head. "Just tell Larissa it's already been performed. It'll be our secret."

"I can't lie. It's not who I am."

He deliberated on what to say. "You're not my type. So, I wouldn't want you working on me anyway."

"I can be anything you want, Robert. Just take a pick."

The blonde transformed into a brunette, a redhead, an Asian, a Hawaiian, and then a Hispanic.

"Uh, that's pretty cool," he stammered.

"It's part of Larissa's magic."

He cleared his throat. "Uh, yeah, she's good with that."

The woman transformed into his wife, making her appearance even more awkward for him.

"Whoa! Shit!"

He backed into the wall behind him.

"I can be your wife. Do you like?"

He scratched his head. "Uh, yeah, but that's a little creepy there. I don't care for that."

Her voice changed into his wife's.

"Really? I thought you would like this. Don't you find me sexy?" She walked up to him, her breasts brushing up against him.

Holy shit!

Every inch of her body was identical to Rebecca's, including the birthmark on her upper thigh. She wasn't his wife, yet she was. She ran her finger down his chest. This wasn't good.

She whispered, "I want you, Robert."

No, this wasn't right. "Dammit Larissa, get this woman away from me!" he screamed.

"Oh, but honey, I want you."

He leaned back, bouncing his head off of the wall. She pressed against him, her hand sliding down to the towel.

"Mm, aren't you excited? You're so hard." She ripped the towel off of him, exposing his manhood.

"Larissa, get this woman away from me, or so help me, I'll get you back!" He pressed harder against the wall.

Her lips found his neck.

"Goddammit Larissa, I'm not fucking kidding! Get this bitch away from me!"

She latched onto his chin. "Are you calling your wife a bitch?" she sneered. Larissa's face replaced Rebecca's.

"No, because she's not my wife, now get the fuck out of here, Larissa!"

He grabbed her by her shoulders and pushed her back, enough to create space between them. "Get her the fuck out of here! This isn't funny."

He snatched a pair of pajama pants that lay on the bed. "Dammit, Larissa! Why the fuck do you...?" As he put them on, he turned and found himself alone.

Sighing, he sat on the bed, cradling his head in his hands. "That really isn't funny, Larissa."

From behind, the woman touched his shoulders.

"Dammit," he snapped. He attempted to get up but she firmly held him down.

"I'm sorry, Robert," Rebecca said. "Relax, I'm dressed."

He glanced back at her. He knew it was still Larissa's creature but at least she had clothing on. Her hands kneaded his shoulders and neck. Groaning, he closed his eyes. Pain radiated from the trigger points.

"Now, that I can use, just a good massage, no come-ons or sexual innuendos please," he said. Another trigger point sent a wave of pain down his back.

§

Dazed and confused, Jennifer wandered past the front of the car looking for Raelin, but she was nowhere to be seen. Dizziness overwhelmed her. She stumbled, but caught hold of the hood, barely maintaining her balance, and glanced up at the windshield. Blood stained the glass and the hood. She looked down at the ground. Raelin had to be out here somewhere.

A patch of flattened and bloody grass caught her eye. She presumed Raelin had been ejected and had come to rest there but why would Raelin, if wounded and in pain, not come to check on her? Jennifer speculated Raelin lost a decent amount of blood. If this was the case, then she wouldn't get very far.

Maybe she headed back to the road looking for assistance. Jennifer turned. Her Mustang was demolished but it was the least of her concern, instead, she needed to find Raelin.

She climbed up the rocky and muddy incline to the road. Her wounds were healing up. Again, she was thankful for her alternate side. Since her first transformation, she found her body healed quickly.

She wiped at her face. Dried blood was crusted to her skull. She dug her nails into it, pulling away pieces of pasted blood. Her hair fell in her face, sweeping across the mud on her skin.

As she scrambled to the top, Michelle drifted into her mind. Jennifer was a murderer. Then, her mom popped into her head. Had her mom gone through these same emotions? She needed somebody to talk to, particularly her mom.

Jennifer glanced at the road. No sign of Raelin. The wind picked up. It plastered her hair to her face. Hastily, she pulled at her hair.

"Raelin!" she yelled.

Only the birds answered.

"Raelin!"

The wind howled. Then came the rain. She couldn't walk down the road in this weather, not dressed like this. She would need her parka, which was located under her seat, and her wallet. Then, she could follow the road into town.

Still dazed, she trudged down the steep decline, narrowly avoiding a couple of falls. Then, her foot caught a loose rock, throwing her off balance. She stumbled, and then slid, slamming into the side rear fender. It took her breath away. Her knees gave way, and she fell face first into the mud.

Rain pelted the trees above her. She struggled to get up, her eyes falling on the jagged rock.

"Dammit."

The driver's door was still open. She reached into her backpack and struggled to find her wallet. No! Oh, hell no! Her eyes widened. She drove her hand deep inside. It had to be here.

Something rustled in the leaves. She snapped her head around. Something was there yet there was nothing. The scent of a carcass wafted by. An animal had recently died, which meant one thing, the killer was nearby.

She slid into the driver's seat and gazed into the forest. Rain drummed against the car. Slowly, she reached for the door handle. Movement to the right caught her attention. Something large lurked behind the brush.

Was it a dragon?

Her hand enclosed around the handle. It moved again. No! Wait! There was more than one! One! Two! Her alter ego leaped to the surface as something attacked from the driver's side.

§

The patrol car cruised through the high school parking lot. Deputies Blanche and Fuchs scanned it, noting the trucks they stopped were not in the parking lot.

Fuchs glanced at Blanche. "Well?"

He sighed.

"Dammit." He pulled into a parking spot and killed the engine.

§

Ms. Evans, the teacher who had been around when Jennifer left the campus, stared at Michelle's dead body. She drew in a deep breath, picking up the scent of the four other girls who had been in here with Michelle. The most notable was Cindy Keller. Ms. Evans approached one of the stalls. Ah, Jordi Newnan and Lexia Anderson had cowered in there together and the scent of another lingered to her left, Brit Saxon.

A girls' voice came from the doorway. "Is somebody actually working in here or can I come in?"

Ms. Evans approached the door, careful to avoid stepping in any blood. She hated this. If there was a time to be able to lock students out of the bathroom, it was now. But due to school rules, they couldn't have locking doors to the bathrooms. So, she had taped up the outside of the door to keep students out.

The teacher poked her head out, careful not to rip the *Do Not Cross* tape from the walls.

She smiled. "I'm sorry, you'll need to use another bathroom. I'm waiting for maintenance right now."

"I really need to go, though. Can I come in, please?" The girl leaned in, and whispered, "I think I started my period."

Ms. Evans whispered, "I'm sorry sweetheart. I understand the issue. Trust me, I do but I can't let anybody in here right now. It's pretty nasty, if you know what I mean."

The girl frowned. "I can't wait, though. And really, I don't give a shit what the toilet looks like. You're a woman, you should understand my situation. Whether you're willing to let me in there or not, I'm coming in."

The girl started to push through.

Ms. Evans put her hands on her shoulders. "All right, I'll let you in, but there are conditions."

§

Deputy Blanche and Fuchs walked into the principal's office. Four girls stood in there, their phones in hand. Fake blood was strewn across their clothing. The second the deputies walked in, the girls glanced at them.

"Should we tell them?" one teenage girl asked another.

"Nice, looks like you girls are ready for Dracula," Fuchs said. "Love the costumes."

"They're not costumes," one said. The girls exchanged looks.

"Yeah, we should."

As one of the girls approached Fuchs, the principal's door opened. Mr. Sanford, the principal, stopped in the doorway.

"Well, hello, Blanche, Fuchs." He shook hands with the deputies. "I'd like to say nice to see you, but I'm not sure what warrants your attention, so I'll just say hello."

"Hello, Mr. Sanford. We just need a minute of your time…"

"Mr. Sanford…"

"Now, just one second. Is it nice to interrupt someone when they are talking?" Mr. Sanford said to the girl.

"No sir, but…"

"Then you can wait just a moment," he said, pointing at her. "Blanch, Fuchs, come in my office. I'll be with you in a minute, girls."

Blanch and Fuchs followed him in his office. Behind them, the girls began whispering to one another.

THE CLEANER

"Are you kidding me?" the teenager asked. Ms. Evan's covered the girls' eyes and walked her to the cleanest stall.

"No, I'm not. I told you it was pretty nasty. Can't you smell it?"

"No, thank God. I have a damn cold. I can't taste anything, much less smell anything."

"Well, then you should be thankful."

Once the girl was in the stall, Ms. Evans shut the door behind her. She blocked the door, so the girl could not walk out. The blood wreaked. It drew the werewolf within her to the surface. Thank goodness she had detected the scent on Jennifer. With that, she was able to track down Michelle's body.

As soon as she found it, she called the cleaner. The body and the blood had to be cleaned up right away. Heavy footsteps entered the bathroom. Ah, yes. The cleaner was here.

§

Wayne pushed open the front door to Tristan's house. It was dark, so there was no telling if Tristan or one of his men were lurking in the shadows. So he had to be careful. His keen senses were on alert.

The scent of her blood and sex wafted down from an upstairs bedroom. Gently, he shut the door, cutting off one of the few things that could kill Tristan...sunlight. But Tristan was not the only one he had to worry about, he also had to worry about the bikers. The daywalker had already left for the day, so he snuck in to check on

Crystal.

Wayne scanned the room.

Unlike most vampires, the windows were not painted black, nor were they boarded up with wood, instead, they were boarded up with steel plates.

Wayne kept an eye out for Tristan and his men as he followed her scent up the stairs to the bedroom door. As his hand curled around the doorknob, he glanced back at the dark house, expecting one of the men to attack him. Nobody was there.

Gently, he pushed the door open. His jaw dropped. He was mortified at the blood covered walls.

§

The cleaner, Odesso's blonde hair was pulled back into a short ponytail. Upon entering the bathroom, he knew something was amiss. Ms. Evans was not alone.

In the past, she had never allowed another to step foot within the perimeters of his job. Today, she did. That irritated him. She knew better.

Why the hell would she betray his mission?

Huffing, he approached her. One of the stall doors was shut behind her.

With a questionable look, his eyes settled on hers. "How are we doing today, ma'am?"

She gazed up at him and then let her eyes trail over her shoulder as if requesting his gaze to follow hers.

"I'm doing well. As you can see, there's a bit of a mess to clean up."

"Mm, yes, there is."

As he glanced at the floor, he sensed her eyes undressing him. Though, he wouldn't mind the pleasure of her company, now was not the time, so he dismissed it. Right now, he had a job to do, and the girl in the stall was interfering with his time. He jutted his chin toward the stall door.

"Sorry, there's a young lady in the stall. It was an emergency."

"Is there a guy in here?" the girl asked.

"Yes, miss," Ms. Evans replied. "I told you I was waiting on maintenance."

He frowned.

Apologetically, she said, "Sorry."

§

Ms. Evans glanced at the mirror. Even though she knew he didn't cast a reflection in it, she wished he did. It would be one of the few ways she could stare at his amazing body without him knowing it.

Odesso was a unique and private man in the immortal world. Nobody knew much about him. From what she understood, he hated his curse yet loved his gift.

She wanted to learn more about him, in more ways than one.

Just then, the stall door opened. Quickly, she covered the girl's eyes.

"Really, Ms. Evans, it's totally unnecessary for you to do this. I'm sure I've seen worse."

"No, honey, I really don't think you have," she said, escorting the girl out.

When she re-entered the stall area, he asked, "Are we alone now?"

"Yes, my apologies, sir."

She wanted to stay and watch him do his job, for she admired his gift. There was nobody in the world quite like him.

Nobody.

"I'm sorry I can't stick around while you clean. There's something I need to tend to." It was one of the only times she ever had to dismiss herself.

Unbuttoning his shirt, he gazed up at her. "What is it that's so important?"

"I'm afraid there were witnesses."

"Really?" he replied.

"They're mortal, so they're probably at the principal's office."

He sighed. "Well, then be on your way. Oh, and Ms. Evans, please hurry back here with them. We don't need the mortals involved in this anymore than necessary."

He removed his clothes and laid them over the side of the sink.

Tattoos of every kind adorned his chest, shoulders, arms, back, buttocks and legs, from crosses to other symbolism from every religious and ethnic background.

Other tattoos that had no visible representation stood out on his body. He had so many, that some of the tattoos overlapped others, yet, they were still identifiable.

"I'll be right back," she said.

With that, she hurried to the principal's office.

§

Odesso turned to the mess before him.

Clenching his fists, he pulled forth the powers within. Every tattoo that adorned his body visibly pulsated on him, each with its own distinct shape and physicality. The colored tattoos lit up. As he channeled on one tattoo, in particular, it pulsed, and moved forward, coming off of his body.

He focused on the black and morbid-looking leech. As Odesso licked his lips, the leech licked its lips. He was hungry—the leech was *hungry*. Odesso channeled his energy into the creature as it morphed into a living being. The large creature slid along the floor, sucking the blood from it, cleaning it with its three mouths.

Odesso was thankful for his gift for he hated his curse. It was a way for him to avoid killing as much as possible. Instead, he would let his gift bring him the blood he needed to survive. The leech slid forward, moving onto Michelle.

§

Ms. Evans walked into the principal's office, her eyes falling upon the four teenagers she was looking for. They sat in the chairs near the principal's door.

"Hi, girls," she said.

"Hi, Ms. Evans."

Ms. Evans glanced at Mr. Sanford's door. It was closed. This was good. It meant he was busy.

She smiled. "Um, can I see you girls for a moment?"

The office staff was busy with students and other tasks. They didn't even notice Ms. Evans and the girls.

"We're waiting for Mr. Sanford," Cindy replied, her face pasty white.

"Well, it looks like he's busy for a moment. This really won't take long."

"It's important," Brit whispered.

"Well, you can come back, if it's that important," Ms. Evans said.

"He's got two deputies in his office right now. We should probably talk to them," one of the other girls said.

Ms. Evans smile faded. "Really? Well, I guess they will be busy for a while. You do realize when the sheriff's office comes in, it can be a couple hours or so."

The teenagers exchanged looks.

"Besides, it gives you time to clean up some of the fake blood you have all over you. I'm sure the drama teacher doesn't want you walking all over the school like that. Some of the other students might think it's real blood, and might freak out. We don't want to scare them off, now do we?"

The best way to get them to comply was to make them feel guilty about something, like wearing the blood, fake or not. She wanted to get on their good side.

"Yeah, I guess you have a point," Cindy said.

Brit smacked her friend in the arm. "What are you saying?"

Cindy shot her a dirty look. "I'm just saying, we don't need to scare everybody, that's all."

"Tell you what, I'll write you a note for your next class, or even escort you here. By the time we're done, the sheriff's office will probably be done, too, and if it is really that important, the principal will escalate it. What do you say?"

Hesitant, Lexia stepped forward. "What is it you need help with?"

"Come, I'll show you." Ms. Evans held the door open.

§

Wayne cringed. Almost everything in the bedroom was covered in blood. He glanced around, looking for any sign of life. Nobody was in the room, yet he detected Crystal's scent. Where the hell was she?

The floor creaked beneath his foot as he moved neared the bathroom door. A strange odor from inside the bathroom caught his attention. It was wet, but dank. Mud? The door was shut.

Wayne inched the bathroom door open. It was darker than the rest of the house. The smell in here was atrocious. The overly dank scent engulfed the room. An image in the mirror drew him further in. As he approached the mirror, he realized it was his own reflection. Then, something more bizarre caught his attention, it was in the bathroom tub.

Wayne turned toward the tub. It was full of mud. The sides and the outer edges of it had a different substance on it. He knelt down and swiped his finger across it. It was pasty. His heart lurched into his throat. It was blood!

He reached inside, grasping for what he was sure was inside—Crystal. Hastily, he wrapped his arm underneath her and pulled her up. Crystal's lifeless face stared up at him.

A knot stuck in his throat. No! She was not supposed to die! He pulled her up further, wrapping his other arm around her hips. He pulled her in tight against him. Mud spilled out over the floor.

"Brandy! No, Dammit, no!"

Tears of anger and resentment filled his eyes. Her head rolled against his chest.

"Brandy, no, baby, no!" Wayne cried. She slid into his arms. Tears ran down his face. "I love you, baby. I've always loved you."

He ran his hands over her face. "I love you, Brandy," he whispered. "I'm so sorry I left you and the kids. You've always meant the world to me."

As he kissed her on the lips, something moved downstairs.

Wayne couldn't fight all the men by himself, so he escaped through the bathroom window. He would have to wait for them to leave. Once they left, he would grab Crystal and take her home, for he was not leaving without her.

§

"Where are we going, Ms. Evans?" Brit asked.

"Down the hall a bit," she said, pointing.

The bell rang. Students filed into their classrooms. As they neared the bathroom, the girls glanced at one another.

Jordi stared at the bathroom. "I really should get back to class, Ms. Evans."

Ms. Evans caught her apprehensiveness. "Really, Jordi, this isn't an option anymore. You and your friends are going to help me whether you like it or not."

"Yeah, Ms. Evans, I have to get back to class, too," Cindy replied.

They stopped near the entrance. Brit started to walk away.

The werewolf within Ms. Evans rose to the surface. She grabbed Brit by the upper arm and threw her backward into the partition, separating the stalls from the outside corridor. Brit struck the wall. Her head bounced off of it as she fell to the floor.

"What the…?"

Ms. Evans interrupted Lexia. "Now ladies, no excuses, otherwise, you're not going to like me. File into the bathroom now."

Wide-eyed and slack-jawed, the girls stared at her.

"You can't do that," Lexia said, her voice breaking up. "You can't touch us, Ms. Evans."

Cindy rushed to Brit's aid. "Holy shit!"

Ms. Evans advanced on the girls, walking them backward into the restroom. She wasn't going to put up with their teacher-student regulation crap.

Odesso walked up behind Lexia, grabbed her, and with a quick snap of her neck, silently pulled her behind the partition. Cindy was too busy with Brit to notice her disappearance.

Jordi turned toward Lexia, "Lex…"

Odesso re-appeared behind Jordi, clasped a hand over her mouth, and pulled her behind the partition.

Ms. Evans knelt down next to the other two. Brit lay, dazed and limp, on the floor while Cindy tended to her. Ms. Evans rested her hands on Cindy's shoulder.

"Cindy, I really shouldn't have let my anger get to me. Why don't you check on your friends, and I'll take care of her?"

"I think you hurt her really bad, Ms. Evans."

Ms. Evans stroked her cheek. "Nah, I'm sure she's fine. Listen, your friends are in the bathroom. They were pretty upset. Why don't you go check on them? I'll take care of Cindy."

Reluctantly, Cindy walked around the partition.

"Oh my…" Two solid thumps followed.

Ms. Evans grabbed Brit by her wrist, pulled her around the partition, and dropped her. She ripped the girl's blouse off, then walked back around. No witnesses. She used Brit's shirt to clean up what blood there was on the floor and then walked back into the bathroom. It was dark. Odesso had cut the lights, probably hoping no students would cross the tape.

As her eyes adjusted to the darkness, he pulled her into him.

"Well?" His voice was haggard as if he just ran a mile up the road.

His eyes were red, his features rough, and his fangs bloody. The smell of the girl's blood was upon him. It enticed her. She was hungry.

"Well?" he urged again.

"Nobody was even paying attention in the office, so there's nothing to worry about." The smell enveloped her, bringing forth her beast.

"Good. Now strip."

"Why?"

"You're hungry, aren't you?"

"Yes," she whispered. The smell was invigorating.

"You don't want to get blood all over you, do you? Not in the middle of the day."

"No, I don't."

"What about other...?" She looked toward the doorway.

"Don't worry. It's dark. Nobody will come in here."

With urgency, she stripped and laid her clothes next to his, glancing at the open doorway.

"I'm still worried about somebody walking in, though," she said.

Something slammed shut. It echoed within the bathroom.

"Did you close the doorway?"

"Yes," he answered. "Is that better?"

"Yes."

Odesso stepped out of her way allowing her access to the girls. Her night vision coupled with her hunger for blood took over. She started toward them when he moved up behind her, wrapping his arm around her waist, and pulled her back into him. He pressed his cheek against hers.

"Everything in here must go, and I mean *everything*." He brushed her hair away from her face.

Ms. Evans grinned. "Perhaps when we're done, we can get cleaned up together?"

§

Mm, yes, that was definitely a possibility, but Odesso didn't want to tell her yet.

"Come back to me when you're done," he said, letting go of her.

He found the mutation into her werewolf erotic. She was a muscular, strong and intriguing creature, who's genetic curse brought beauty to his eyes. Though he cursed his own disease, he still found others absolutely fascinating, particularly the women. Just to watch them transform was a thrill.

Her jaws snapped shut on the one girl who was still conscious, Brit. Within seconds the girl was dead.

Odesso let his werewolf take over. It was one of many of his beasts. From there, he and Ms. Evans consumed the girls remains. All that was left was bones and materialistic shit, that he would dispose of.

Once he changed back into his human form, he lunged at Ms. Evans. He didn't give her a chance to transform, so he caught her by surprise. As he wrapped his arms around her and clamped his mouth down on the back of her neck, she shifted into her human form.

He shoved her face down, grabbed her hips, and jerked her back, plunging deep inside of her. She gasped. Blood spilled down her breasts. She rocked back in succession with him.

There was something very naughty about banging her at the school, something they found immense pleasure in, but this was the first time they enjoyed a full meal together. Odesso found it rather kinky and erotic. She was oh so tantalizing. He admired the exotic way she moved when she was on top of him, her stealth when she was in her human and wolf form, her beauty and her sultriness. He wanted to be inside her all of the time for she was one of the few women who had ever really rocked his world, so he had to admit there were times when he thought about commitment with her but it never failed, every time he did, something always came up, whether it was an argument or a bickering over a *fuck* location. Was it that difficult to come up with a *fuck* location? He didn't think so. So, she proved to him just what he didn't want, commitment.

He pumped her hard and rough, just the way she liked it. Their rapid speed escalated to a progressively climatic fast pace.

"Oh, Odesso."

Oh, hell. Maybe, they needed to keep up with the bickering after all. It made for an interesting relationship.

As she sat back against him, he thought of her past. He had respect for the woman. For a female teenage werewolf who was coming of age, Ms. Evans was resilient. She wound up in a fight with another girl over a boy the girls liked. Needless to say, the other girl wound up her first kill.

Five boys who happened to be at the bonfire that night raped Ms. Evans. They had left deep claw marks in her that it took a full day for them to heal, so she said. Now every time he looked at her back, he thought of them.

Despite his lack of commitment, she had his respect. He kissed the wound he had left on her. He was a piece of shit. Why the hell could he not commit to her? She was stunning, intelligent, amazing and a great lay. What else could a man ask for?

Contemplating his question, he picked her up, and propped her up against the wall, pushing himself inside of her. She moaned.

"Next time, beautiful?" he said, gyrating inside of her.

She smiled. "Oh, I love how you do that. Are you busy later?"

"I have a job to do, but give me a call, and I'll see what I can do."

"Mm, please don't tell me it's another woman?"

He chuckled. "As a matter of fact, it is, but it's not what you think."

"Why don't you give me a call if it doesn't take too long?"

He smiled at her. "I just might do that."

§

Deputies Blanche and Fuchs climbed into the car. Rain pounded against the hood.

"Well, I guess we're going to have to keep an eye on him," Blanche said.

Fuchs glanced at him. "I think we need to go to the home game. What do you think?"

"Mm, I think that's a good idea."

"And not just for him," she added. "I think we need to keep an eye on that biker too. There's something about him I really didn't care for."

§

Robert awoke in his bed. "What the hell?"

He glanced down. Pissed off, he jumped out of bed, looking for his wife's clone.

"Bitch, where the hell are you?"

Cool air swept in from somewhere within the house. It brought a female voice in along with it.

He grabbed his gun from the nightstand. Carefully, he slid around the doorframe.

"Hello! Is anybody here?" she yelled.

It wasn't the clone, but it was familiar.

"Robert? Crystal! Somebody!"

The pitter patter of female feet came from the downstairs hallway. Robert peered over the stair rail. He didn't see her. Quietly, he walked down the stairs. He knew that voice. Who the hell was it?

As his feet hit the floor, Raelin came out of the darkness, her face bruised and swollen, her clothes tattered, torn, and stained with blood.

"Raelin?" Robert lowered his gun. "Holy shit, are you all right?" He moved toward her. Then, he stopped. Even though he wore underwear, he covered his man parts with his hand.

"Somebody came after me," she cried. Tears streamed down her dirt ridden face. "I tried to go back for Jennifer, but they chased me away from the car."

"Who? And where's Jennifer?" he asked, his brow furrowing in.

"I don't know. We got in a car accident." She wrapped her arms around her chest. "I'm scared, Robert. I think they followed me here. I didn't want to come here, but I didn't know where else to go. I'm sorry."

Shit! Jennifer! As he turned to run upstairs, he noted the rips across the girl's shirt.

"Why don't you go change into some of Jennifer's clothes while I get dressed?"

§

Tristan stood in the bathroom, glancing around. His eyes had settled on the tub. Nothing was out of the ordinary, yet the scent of another man was in his bathroom.

"Come on, Tristan! It's time to hunt!" Sabol yelled.

"Yeah, do we need to come in after you!" Ratliff screamed.

"I'm coming!" Tristan replied.

He scanned the bathroom one last time before leaving his bedroom, hoping the guys wouldn't notice the blood on the walls but he should have known better. They picked up on everything.

"Is she that good?" one of the men asked.

Tristan avoided the question as he pulled on the door handle. Before he could shut it, Sabol pushed it open.

"Wow, Tristan…"

Tristan slammed the door shut.

"You got yourself a wild one there."

"Where is she?" Sabol asked.

"She's sleeping," Tristan answered. It was none of their business.

"Sleeping? Are you sure about that, Tristan?" Ratliff asked. "With the amount of blood in there, it looks like you killed her."

Tristan frowned. "Of course, I'm sure about that."

Sabol confronted Tristan. "Where is she?"

Tristan stared at Sabol. "Why are you so concerned about her?"

"I just want to make sure she's trustworthy."

"Oh, you can trust her." Tristan wasn't up for his shit.

"I'm surprised you didn't clean that mess up." Uwe looked Tristan over.

"I have a cleaner coming over to take care of the mess," he responded.

"Cleaner? Really?" Sabol cocked his head. "Do you want one of us to stay behind and make sure it doesn't get into anything?"

"No, the cleaner will be fine," Tristan replied.

"Do you really trust everything the U.G.S.S. says or sends over?" Sabol asked.

"No, not everything," Tristan answered. "But I trust him."

Just then, Tristan's phone rang. It was Robert.

§

Latin hip-hop music blared from the gym's dance room. As Rebecca walked in, her reflection stared back at her.

"You'll have fun, sis!" Larissa walked around her sister. "The instructor is hot!" Larissa growled. She pointed at the Latin teacher, Manuel.

Rebecca rolled her eyes.

"All right, everybody, let's get this class moving!" he yelled. "Let's stretch it out."

Rebecca turned her attention to the dance instructor. He reminded her of someone. Was it...? Hmm...? Oh yes, he was Sabol's twin, only in Latin form! She flashed her pearly whites at her sister.

Larissa glanced at her. "What? What the fuck you looking at?"

"Your Latin dream up there reminds me of someone. Take a wild guess who."

Larissa studied him. "Oh boy, would I like to fuck him," she whispered.

Rebecca stared at her, wide-eyed. "Huh? What was that, sis?"

"I didn't say nothin'..." Her eyes trailed over his body. "I don't know, sis. Who does he remind you of?" She followed the instructor's movements.

"Come on, think about it. I know you'll agree with me once I tell you."

Larissa bit her lip. "Girl, I don't know."

"Yes, he does. Think *spicy*." Rebecca made sure to imitate Sabol's voice.

Larissa's brow furrowed in. She was deep in thought when it struck her.

"Oh, hell no."

"Yes, yes."

"No, no! Now, that's not funny, Becky. You bitch, how could you?"

"Look at him. Seriously, he looks just like him."

"Uh-uh," she said. "Becky, you're a bitch. You just totally ruined my vision of Manuel. You know I had this whole dream of being in Costa Rico with this man, and you just totally fucked it up. Fuck you very much," she said.

As Larissa spun around, she slapped Rebecca's arm.

Rebecca laughed. "You think you'll ever get together with him. I mean you have Manuel on a pedestal. How about Sabol? He looks just like Manuel, only the white version, and Sabol does like *spicy chocolate*."

She and the class shook their hips.

"You have one advantage already. Sabol already likes you, and he doesn't even know you."

"Hmm, we'll see about that."

Larissa gave her the evil eye.

"Keep it up, Becky."

Rebecca laughed. "You know you need to get laid. Probably, just as much as I do."

Oops! She was enjoying herself a little too much. Rebecca bit her lip.

With a twist and a spin, Larissa leaned into her. "What? You and Robert aren't…"

"I don't want to talk about."

"Oh, no, no you don't! You started this. Now, you're going to finish it. Robert isn't giving you the ole'…?"

"Ladies, ladies!" the instructor yelled. "I don't want to hear about your sex life! Keep it to yourselves!"

They nodded.

Larissa's head spun. "Seriously, you two aren't…"

"Ladies, keep your voices down!"

Several women glanced at them.

"Sorry, my sister has a big mouth," Rebecca said.

"What?" Larissa spat.

All but one woman turned their attention back to the instructor.

"All right, maybe this isn't the time to talk about this," she whispered.

The woman looked Larissa over.

"Hey, why don't you mind your own business," she snapped.

"She's sorry about that." Rebecca glanced at her sister. "What the hell got into you?"

Larissa's voice rose. "Fuck Sabol? Are you kidding me?"

"Ladies! Do I have to ask you to leave? One more outburst and I will!" the instructor yelled.

"Hmm, that's bullshit. I can't believe you said that, and now my Manuel is yelling at me because of you."

"Come on, sis. Calm down." Rebecca giggled. "Let's Zumba."

Outside of the aerobics room, a man with shoulder length dark hair glanced at them through the glass wall. Rebecca figured he was just another gym member, so when she spun around and he wasn't there, she didn't think much of it.

§

Larissa's friend, twenty-one-year-old Kendra, a young black woman, sat on the floor of Larissa's house with Rebecca's girls. Her dark hair was wound up into a tight bun. She glanced from one girl to another.

"Show me what you can do with these?" she asked.

She threw a handful of gemstones up into the air. The gemstones froze in mid-air. Kendra smiled. Hunter sat nearby, his head cocked. Then, the gems swirled around in circles.

The girl's eyes widened. They squealed in excitement.

"Good job, girls! Now, who made them stop?" Kendra asked.

Leah was the first to speak up. "I did."

"No, I did," Katie said.

"Uh-uh, it was me," Tisa screamed. Pouting, she folded her arms across her chest.

Kendra rubbed Tisa's back. "It's all right, Tisa. There's no need to get upset besides, I think it was all of you. You work well as a team. That's good."

"Well, we try, but Tisa doesn't always work with us," Katie replied.

Kendra laughed. "That's okay, sweetie. She's still young. Now, who made them spin?"

Again, the children bickered over their accomplishments.

Sighing, Kendra shook her head.

"You all are very special. Remember this. Now, what else can you do with them? Show me?"

The multi-colored gems lit up one at a time and then two at a time. Eventually, all of the gems lit up. Some of the gems jumped up and down.

Using her powers, Kendra turned on the stereo, which was across the room. The girls bounced to the music. Before she knew it, the gems rained down on everyone.

"Concentrate on the gems, girls. You need to keep them up. You can still dance, but only if you can keep the gems in the air. You need to make them all dance."

Katie stood, and wiggled her hips to the music. Momma would be proud of them. Now, they were multi-tasking. That was a huge achievement. The gems whirled about in the air.

"You girls are doing great." Kendra clapped her hands. Tisa and Katie looked at her, losing their concentration. A few gems bounced off of Kendra's head.

"Oh, hey, watch it there. You're supposed to be keeping an eye on them, not me."

"Hey, watch this," Leah said. "I'm gonna make Hunter dance."

"No, not Hunter."

"Yeah, Hunter!" they exclaimed, jumping up and down.

The gems poured down on her. The girl's magic whisked Hunter up into the air and bounced him up and down.

Kendra bolted to her feet, captured him, and cradled him against her chest. The girls stopped and stared at her.

"But we were having fun," Leah pouted.

"I know honey, but Hunter will get very sick. Lizards are not meant to dance. I know it looks silly, but he can get hurt, just like you can." She rubbed Hunter's back. "Now, let's pick up these gems. It's late, and you all need to go to bed."

"Aw, but we don't want to go to bed," the girl's pouted.

§

The cleaner needed no key for Tristan had left the back door open for him. Odesso entered the dark house, keeping an eye open for anything unusual or out of the ordinary. In his line of business, anything was apt to happen. Drawing in a deep breath, he inhaled the scent of testosterone, estrogen, vampire, werewolf, brimstone, sex, dragon and blood…lots of blood. He was told she would be the only one home, but she was not. There was another male inside…a werewolf.

Odesso moved toward Tristan's bedroom. The male's presence lingered near her. This wasn't good. Tristan did not tell him there would be another near her, not within proximity, but in heart. Odesso sneered. He had no desire to be in the middle of a love triangle.

Odesso's hand slid along the bedroom door. He cocked his head…listening. He took another whiff. Then, he pushed the door open.

Blood was strewn about the entire room.

Someone moved in the bathroom so Odesso headed toward the door. It was shut. One thing at a time. The male inside would be dealt with first.

He stopped outside the door. Using his curse, he detected the man kneeling down before the tub, that was until the man detected his presence.

§

After the men left, Wayne snuck back into the house. As he reached into the bathtub, a male presence approached. It was not Tristan. It wasn't any of the bikers, either. This was his only chance to get her out of here, so he decided to gain the upper hand.

When the man stopped outside the bathroom door, Wayne ran at it. It slammed open and hit Odesso. Both men fell to the floor, Wayne atop Odesso. He buried his fist in the man's face as his werewolf struggled to take reign over his body.

Odesso shoved his arms straight out, throwing Wayne up into the ceiling. Pieces of the log cabin style home broke free from the ceiling. Odesso bolted to his feet. The fully transformed werewolf landed before him.

Odesso ripped his shirt off, exposing his tattooed body to the beast. It snarled at him. Saliva dripped from its lips. Fangs bared, the werewolf stared at him, studying his movements.

He egged the beast on. "Come on, motherfucker!" The beasts within him crept to the surface. "Come on, you piece of shit! You want a piece of me!"

It hunkered down, readying itself for the attack. The claws curled into the floor, leaving deep scratches within it. It reared up on its haunches and growled.

"Come on, you piece of shit! What the fuck are you waiting for?" Odesso yelled, bracing himself for the impact. Instead, the werewolf backed up. "Come on, or I'm going to come get you! What the fuck are you waiting for?"

The tattoos pulled away from his skin and circled him, each lighting up.

Wayne didn't like it. The man had to be some type of sorcerer, so he tried to maintain control of his beast, for it didn't like the colors, nor the smell. Damn sorcerer's and their magic. Unless he could gain the upper hand somehow, he was unlikely to defeat the man.

The man's words echoed in his head. *"Come on, or I'm going to come get you! What the fuck are you waiting for?"*

Wayne waited.

And, the sorcerer waited.

The man was becoming more pissed by the second. His flush face reddened. Wayne wasn't stupid. He wasn't going to attack like others of his kind. If he did, chances are the man would kill him instantly.

"All right, asshole! Fuck you, then! I'm not waiting on you! I have things to do, and you're in the way! Whatever you have going with this woman is between you and Tristan, not me! So, I'll let him handle it!"

One of the tattoos resembling the Ying/Yang symbol stopped in front of Odesso. A wave of energy shot out from the symbol toward the werewolf. Wayne tried to dodge it, but was slammed into the wall, and forced to change back into his human form.

The sorcerer approached him.

"Tsk, tsk. I see you control your creature very well. That's good."

Wayne fought the energy force.

"Hmm, now what should I do? Should I leave you here for Tristan? Or should I take you with me? If I leave you, the bikers may come back and kill you themselves." He glanced around at the blood on the walls. "But if I take you with me, I'll just tell Tristan I found an intruder in his home." He looked Wayne over. "I think I'll take you with me. I'm sure Tristan would prefer to do the dirty work himself. In the meantime, will you stay there for a moment? I have some cleaning up to do."

The tattoos circled around the sorcerer's body. Finally, it centered in on a tattoo of a leech which came to life.

Wayne recoiled. He tried to speak, but the energy force did not allow him to talk.

It maneuvered around the room, sucking up the blood from everything, including the walls and the ceiling.

As Odesso walked into the bathroom, Wayne struggled against the energy force. A third tattoo resembling a coffin appeared. It opened. The coffin lengthened into a human size casket. It settled on the floor next to Odesso.

"Well, I guess it's time to get my hands dirty now."

Odesso stripped out of his pants, folded them, and laid them on the counter before he knelt down and reached into the bathtub. The woman was inside. He wrapped his arms around her and pulled her out. Mud dripped everywhere. As he slid her into the coffin, his hand scraped against something on her back.

"What the hell?"

He rolled her toward him and studied her back. The space between her shoulder blades had two long lacerations along the inside of the shoulder blades.

He gasped. "Oh, shit, Tristan. What the fuck did you do?"

He laid her down in the casket and covered her with mud from the tub. The mud not only masked the smell of the blood, but helped to soak it up, and keep her hydrated despite her condition.

Odesso cleaned up and got dressed. With one hand he lifted the coffin and walked it through the door.

Wayne stared at him.

"Who are you to her?" Odesso asked, stripping the force shield away from Wayne's face.

"It's none of your business."

Odesso shook his head. "None of my business? When it concerns to Tristan, it is my business. Now, I'll ask you one more time, who the hell are you?"

"*Fuck you*," Wayne said. He didn't care who the man was, especially if he was associated with the U.G.S.S.

"Fine, have it your way?"

The tattoo of an electric chair circled around the sorcerer.

"Listen, asshole, you're one of the few who have seen just one of my talents. Do you really want to push this further?" Odesso raised his eyebrow.

Wayne hissed. "Kill me, I don't care. She's the only woman I've ever cared about. Now, she's dead thanks to Tristan." Anger fumed inside of him.

"Well, we'll see if she's truly dead. I need to get her back to the lab, so I can take a look at her, and you my friend, are coming with me."

The leech consumed the last of the blood.

"Lab? What lab?" Wayne asked. His heart skipped a beat.

The man ignored him.

"You, come," he demanded. The leech crawled onto Odesso's body, where it transformed back into a tattoo.

Odesso peered over at Wayne. "Now, it's your turn."

He pulled Wayne, and the force field back toward him. Wayne wouldn't be able to resist him, no matter hard he tried.

"What the hell are you going to do with me? And what fucking lab are you talking about?"

The force field spun Wayne around so his back was to Odesso. "You really shouldn't have fought me so much."

Shackles appeared. They bound Wayne's wrists and ankles to prevent him from running away. The silver burnt into his flesh. Wayne hissed.

"If I were you I wouldn't fight so much. I have much bigger issues, so I won't have any problem killing you."

Hesitantly, Wayne backed down, allowing Odesso to escort him outside. A black hearse waited behind the house. First, Odesso packed the coffin in. Then, he shoved Wayne in next to the coffin.

THE HUNT

Raelin led Tristan, the Hell's Changelings, and Robert to the Mustang.

The front window and the driver's window was broken, but Jennifer was nowhere to be seen. The flattened pile of grass where Raelin had fallen was matted with blood. Everything inside of the car was wet from the rain.

Robert stared off into the distance, surveying the scene of the attack. Raelin cried as she recounted the details of the accident. Behind him, the rustle of leather and chains moved. He glanced back. Sebastian pulled her in close to him and consoled her, resting his chin on her head.

"Do you know anybody who would take her?" Sabol asked.

"No, I don't. The only person I know of would be Jace or his men."

Tristan and his men inspected the branches.

"Well, we know they're werewolves. How many would you say, Ratliff?"

Ratliff looked around. "It's a pack, so it's kind of hard to tell, maybe five or six, maybe more. It's kind of hard to tell because of the rain."

"In order to cover more ground, I suggest we split up, except for her of course. She stays with you Sebastian," Sabol said.

"Not a problem," he replied.

"Hey, Sebastian?" Christian nodded. "Just be careful which head you think with while you're out there."

Sebastian cast him a dirty look.

Christian eyed him. "Seriously, man. I see the way you've been looking at her. Keep that thing in your pants."

"That's enough," Sabol snapped. "Hey, girlie, why don't you go with Christian instead," he said, motioning toward him.

Christian whipped his head around, his wet hair splashing Sabol. "I don't need any chick slowing me down, especially one who's mortal."

"Because I said so," Sabol said. "I don't need Sebastian running around with a hard-on."

Sebastian frowned. "That's not funny, man. I'm not into…"

Raelin threw her hands up in the air. "Hey, don't I get any say in this?"

"No!" they answered.

"This isn't fair! I should have some say…"

Ratliff interrupted her. "Keep it up, missy, and I'll personally take you home, where you belong. This hunt isn't for pussy little teenage girls like you," he spat. "Now, why don't you run along and play with…whatever the fuck it is you girls play with nowadays!"

"She's not going anywhere alone," Robert intervened. "They chased her to my house, now she stays with us."

"Agreed," Tristan replied.

"Yes, agreed," Sabol said.

"And personally, I think she should remain with Sebastian," Tristan replied.

Everybody looked at him.

"The rest of us need to be ready for battle. Her being with Sebastian is a good decoy, especially since he has a hard-on for her," Tristan said.

Raelin wrinkled her face.

"Sorry to be blunt, Raelin, but we need you in on this." Tristan pointed his finger at Sebastian. "No fucking around, and I'm not kidding either. I'll be the first to stuff your dick down your throat if you pull something stupid."

Sabol grabbed Tristan's shoulder. "Glad to see you're acting your normal self again." He smiled. "Now, did you hear Tristan?"

Sebastian glared at him. "Yes, I did."

"Good, now Raelin, you're going to stay with him. Just keep your nose to the ground, and let him know if you smell or see anything familiar. Got it, shapeshifter?"

She nodded.

"Now, if he pulls anything stupid, just yell for one of us. We'll keep an ear open. If we hear you, we'll come running."

Uwe touched her shoulder. "But if something attacks you, shape shift and get the fuck out of there."

Again, Raelin nodded. "All right."

"Before we split, I want to remind everyone that the low grounds and lakes are probably flooding over. I don't know where these wolves are hiding, if they are even still out here. Once we find Jennifer, we alert the others, and get the girls out of here," Tristan said.

§

Wayne tried to open his eyes, but they were heavy, along with his head. What the hell did the sorcerer do to him? He was lethargic and had to force his eyes open.

The room was cold and white. What the hell? He strained against the spell the man cast on him.

A lone casket lay on the table in the center of the room. He struggled to look around. Lining the wall to his right were human size steel enforced coffins that stood on end, only they were set upon a mechanical device which kept them off of the floor. The head of the coffins had plate glass, allowing others to see inside, or vice versa in his case. Then it dawned on him, he was inside a coffin.

Eyes wide, he glanced back at the casket on the table. Dried mud caked the outside of the coffin. It was the casket the sorcerer had put Crystal in.

Just then, the door to the room opened. The Sorcerer and a pudgy man wearing a doctor's coat walked in. They shut the door behind them.

Odesso began to undress. "My apologies, but I don't like to dirty my clothes when I work."

Wayne closed his eyes and leaned back.

"Whatever you say."

§

The casket lid creaked open. As Odesso pulled Crystal out, mud spilled over the side of the coffin, his arms, and onto the floor.

"Are you sure this is her?"

"I'm positive," Odesso answered. He laid her down on the silver medical table and wiped some of the mud from her face.

"It does kind of look like her. Does Tristan know she's here?"

"No, but it looks like we might have a slight problem."

"What's that?" Through thick glasses, the man studied her facial features.

"Somebody needs to look at her back. She's got some wounds back there."

"Huh? Did you say wounds?" He glanced up at Odesso as if he wasn't listening.

"I think you need another pair of glasses along with a hearing exam."

Odesso shook his head. The agency didn't need a mortal in here, especially one who didn't listen for shit.

"That's not what you said," the man replied.

"I was saying we have a problem. She has wounds on her back. It almost looks like…oh fuck it, I'll show you."

Odesso rolled her toward him, exposing her back to the man.

"So, what were you talking about?"

Odesso sighed. "Look…" He pointed to her upper back. "What the hell…?" He wiped the mud from between her shoulders, exposing only bare skin. Crystal's wounds were gone. "She had wounds."

"Well, what kind of wounds?" The man stared at him.

Odesso laid her back down. "Her wounds healed."

"So?"

"Shit!" He glanced at the door. "I need to talk to Tristan. Strap her down!"

He threw his clothes on and headed for the door.

"But…"

Odesso gazed back at him. "I said to fucking strap her down before she wakes up! She's not dead, she's alive!" With that, Odesso ran out of the door.

§

Inside the coffin, Wayne opened his eyes and peered out at the man who stood over her. Alive? Tristan buried her alive? If she were human, she would have died buried in the mud but if she were immortal and he buried her in the mud, it would have helped to heal her wounds, unless, Tristan wanted to mask the smell of her blood. Why would he do that in his own home? He wouldn't have. So, he must have made her immortal.

§

Firelight caught Robert's attention. He approached the camp where a woman sat with her back to him. At first, he thought it might have been Jennifer but as he drew nearer, the backless dress revealed the woman's dark skin. He glanced around. Nobody else was nearby.

Maybe she had seen Jennifer.

He turned his attention back to her. With her back to him, the woman stood and untied the dress string that went around her neck. The dress fell.

A lump formed in his throat. Did he dare approach this woman?

"Come here, Robert."

Robert peered up at her, her seductive eyes enticing him to move closer. Don't look at her! Close your eyes! Rid yourself of this vision.

"You're seeing things," he told himself.

Opening his eyes, he approached the camp. Wait a minute! It was Larissa. Damn woman.

"Dammit, Larissa, would you stop the bullshit?"

The woman cocked her head. "What do you mean, Larissa?"

The tone of her voice made him stop mid-stride. Only a woman or a wife...?

"Rebecca?"

"Yes, it's Rebecca."

He swallowed hard. "My wife?" How could it be? But, of course, only a witch could...?

"Of course, I'm your wife. I wouldn't be anybody else's wife, now would I?" She propped her hands on her hips. "I wanted to check on you. That, and well..." She batted her eyes. "I thought you might want some..."

"This really isn't good timing, honey." Nervously, he glanced around, his face flushed. He didn't want the others to find him like this.

"Why not?"

When he turned around, she was in his face.

"Damn, that was fast," he said.

Lightly, she ran her fingers over his eyes. "I've been studying with my sister."

"I see that," he whispered.

"I love you, Robert."

He was worried this was another one of Larissa's tricks. She loved to test his loyalty to his wife by putting images in front of him to see his reaction.

"I love you too, Rebecca."

Hesitantly, he touched her, half expecting her body to dissipate before him. So, when he touched her solid form, he recoiled.

"Whose body are you using?"

"The lady whose husband drowned in the flood," she answered.

He frowned. "Oh God, don't do that."

"Would you rather me leave her here to mourn over her husband?"

Oh, no! No. He shook his head. "No, honey. It's just wrong." He was surprised she would do such a thing. So, her sister must have put her up to this.

"She was alone. Her husband and another couple they were with, drowned in the flood."

"Oh God." Again, he shook his head. "It's just not right, though."

"I know it's not, and you know I normally wouldn't do this." She wrapped her arms around his neck.

"Yes, I know."

Their lips touched. "The kids are asleep and I want you."

Oh, shit! Not now. "Dammit, I can't right now."

Her lips moved to his ear. "Is it because you're hunting?"

"No, it's not that."

A branch broke. They gazed into the woods surrounding the camp. A pair of reptilian eyes stared at them.

Her voice cracked. "Robert, what's that?"

"You need to go now," he demanded.

He turned toward it as Rebecca grabbed his shoulder. "I'm in this woman's body. I can't just leave her."

He looked at her. "I told you to get out of her body and go."

Remorsefully, she stared at him. "And what happens to her?"

Robert had nothing to say, for he didn't know what would happen if she jumped out of her body. He didn't know how all of the witchery worked.

"Fine, get her body out of here, somehow, someway but get the fuck out of here, *now!*" he screamed.

A branch fell from the tree. It broke beneath the weight of the hybrid dragon.

Rebecca's eyes widened. "Robert, that's a..."

"I know, honey. Now if you and your sister can find a spell to help get rid of these dragons, or find something to deter them, please do."

The dragon moved in closer. It had no tail.

"Holy shit! What's wrong with that one?" she asked.

"They're hybrids, honey. Looks like this one might not have taken to well to the experiment. Stop asking me questions, and go home!"

As Robert turned, it ran at them.

"Robert, be careful!" she screamed, running to higher ground. Her movement drew the dragon's attention. It ran after her.

"Goddammit! Over here!"

It ignored him.

"No!" He ran after it. "Run, Rebecca!"

§

Rebecca ran. Maybe she could cast a spell to ward it off.

She started to turn around to use her magic, but it was moving too fast. Fire erupted from its mouth. She changed course and ran around the tree. Behind her, the branches caught on fire, the heat warming her back.

As she spun around, Robert attacked the dragon. The werewolf within him came forth. Her jaw dropped. The dragon's head reared back.

"No," she whispered. She had to do something.

Then, an unknown male voice whispered, "Witch..."

She expected it to be one of the Hell's Changelings, but it was not. David clamped his hand over her mouth.

§

In werewolf form, James rushed Jennifer, slamming her into the tree behind her. One of the small limbs stabbed her in the back. She cried out in pain. As his jaws snapped at her, Jennifer drove her arms in between her and James, crossing them, trying to create distance between them.

His teeth gnashed together, barely missing her face. She looked for a friend among the werewolves, instead, she found enemies. They closed in on her.

James claws scratched and dug into her skin.

The more she fought him, the further the branch dug into her back. Tears spilled down her cheeks. His face inched in closer. She was losing the battle.

If she could change into her werewolf, maybe...but the agonizing pain reminded her she wasn't going anywhere. Tears streamed down her face.

Then James growled, peering over her shoulder as if something held his gaze.

She glanced back. Nothing.

James's head snapped back, once, twice, three times. He flew back and struck the ground. It was as if an invisible man were punching him. Was it Tristan?

Tristan's invisible body materialized. He kicked James in the head. "Would you like to be my dinner, asshole?"

James growled.

Tristan kicked him in the stomach. "Get the fuck out of here!" he screamed. He glanced at the others. "All of you! This alpha is nothing but trouble."

The pack backed off. Then James stood, his gaze on Tristan.

"I'm serious motherfucker. I'll drain your body dry, and then feed it to your friends."

James loped off, his head hung low. Once he neared his friends, they scurried off.

As Jennifer pulled free from the tree limb, Tristan approached her, studying her wounds.

"This will heal and so will the rest of your wounds," he said. "You and Raelin really need to be careful. Your curse could get you killed."

"It was an accident…"

"You really need to use that," he said, tapping her on the nose.

She wrinkled it. "Thanks for helping me."

"Come on, let's get you home," he said, whisking her up in his arms.

Jennifer howled in pain.

§

Fred's heart raced. Alive? His anxiety kicked up. She was alive? His hands shook. Oh, how he regretted taking this job. Odesso told him she was dead, so he had no problem meeting him at the U.G.S.S. laboratory but now he stood over the woman whose reputation he knew well. She had killed a number of people when she fought in the underground circuit. Now she lay before him.

His heart leaped into this throat. Fred pushed his glasses up and nervously grabbed one of the leather straps that was attached to the table. Gently, he laid it over her ankle. Calm yourself, Fred. He drew in a deep breath.

He glanced up at her face. Please God, let her stay in whatever coma state she was in. Fred grabbed the second strap which had the steel hoop on it. Oh, silver. That was good! If she had werewolf in her, it might weaken her.

He fought to control his shaking hands as he looped the other strap through the hoop, and tightened it. One down, three more to go.

§

Wayne watched the man strap her leg down. Hell, if she had a reflexive movement, the man would hit the ceiling. His nervousness was obvious.

Wayne searched for an internal latch, digging into the casket lining.

§

Trembling, Fred fumbled with the strap, dropping it on her leg. His heart leaped out of his chest. As he reached for the table to steady himself, he missed it, and fell over sideways onto the floor, scrambling to his feet. Bile rose in his throat.

Bolting upright, he stared at her. No movement. Slowly, he approached her, grabbing the strap from where it was attached to the table. It dragged across her skin. Movement caught his attention. He peered up at her calf—it wasn't the leg that moved, but her muscles.

Stop wasting your time. The sooner you get this done, the less chance you have of her waking up while you're doing it.

Hustling, he grabbed the other strap, his fingers brushing across her ankle. He fed the strap through the loop and pulled it tight. He jumped back, fearful she would awaken. No movement. Two down and two more to go. Now, it was time for the more difficult part—strapping her arms down.

As he walked up near her arms, he glanced down at her muddied breasts. He would love to touch one. Then, he could brag to his buddies about it at their next poker game. They always had such great stories. But did he dare? What if she woke up?

Something grazed his hip. He flinched.

Did she move? He glanced down at her hand. It was still. Movement—not her hand but her face. Was she awake? He couldn't tell. The mud covered most of her face.

Fred leaned in closer.

A facial muscle twitched.

He recoiled. Dammit Fred, get your shit together and get her strapped down. If you don't, she's going to wake up and kill you. As he grabbed the strap, her finger twitched.

§

Ah! There's the locking mechanism.

Wayne gently pushed on the casket door. It didn't budge. One more turn with his claw and the door gave way. The man stood with his back to him.

§

The strap fell on her wrist. Fred rubbed his eyes. This was getting ridiculous. Shaking, he picked up the strap and put it into the loop. Something clicked behind him.

Stop it, Fred! It's your imagination.

Not unless... He glanced at the steel door. Nothing.

No! Wait! There was something there! He glanced up at one of the caskets on the opposite wall. A human reflection stared back at him. It advanced on him.

What the fuck...?

He started to whirl around. Then, something grabbed his wrist. Shit!

The stranger bared his fangs.

Fred turned around. Crystal was in his face. Fangs bared, she latched onto him.

"No..." he screamed.

Crystal's claws penetrated his chest. Behind him, the stranger buried his fangs in Fred's neck.

§

Wayne glanced up at Crystal as the man fell in a crumpled heap at his feet. As she fed on the man's heart, her gaze shifted to Wayne. He had never seen her like this before, her needs were so primal.

§

My beasts were hungry. So, the man's heart was enough to suffice me for now. As I took another bite, my eyes fell on Wayne. I stopped chewing.

Kill him! Drain his body dry…but wait, how the hell could he be here? Jace popped in my head. Jace must have made Wayne a hybrid, too. That was the only explanation.

Had Jace put the dragon in him, too? Or was it something else? I cocked my head.

Wayne held his hands out before him as if surrendering. "Crystal, listen…"

I threw the heart at him.

He moved, barely avoiding it.

I slinked forward.

His voice was smooth. "You need…"

This may be your only chance to get even with the son of a bitch. I lunged for him.

He took a step back, slipped, and fell to the floor.

I struck out at him, shredding flesh from his chest.

"Crystal…"

I struck again. Only this time, I caught him in the face. Then Wayne caught me and threw me to the floor.

"Dammit, Crystal, listen to me," he whispered, rolling atop me.

As I slashed at him, he caught my wrist. I hissed.

"Brandy, stop fighting me and causing a commotion, or you're going to get us both killed," he whispered, glancing up at the door.

The blood from his facial wound dripped onto my face. I licked it up. It wasn't enough. I snapped at him. He recoiled.

"Oh, you are hungry, aren't you?"

His wound was healing and his pupils turned into a golden hue.

"Do you want my blood, babe?" He lowered his face, barely keeping it out of reach. "How hungry are you?"

"I'm weak, Wayne," I said. "Feed me, please. I need more blood if I'm going to get out of here."

I needed his blood. If not his, then the dead man's. Later, when I had the chance, I would kill Wayne but, right now, I needed my strength.

"You do as I say then, all right?" he asked.

"Yes," I whispered.

His jaw muscles clenched, the werewolf within him on guard, ready to kill if it had to.

"I don't trust you right now, so I'm going to hold you down while you feed. Got it?"

I nodded.

With one hand he gripped both of my wrists and held them down above my head. He lowered his face, his unwounded cheek grazing mine.

Our eyes met.

Sternly, he said, "Don't try anything stupid or I will kill you, dear."

"I won't," I whispered, jerking my arms. No success.

His grip tightened. "I told you not to try anything stupid."

"You know it's out of habit, asshole."

Since I couldn't wrap my arms around him, I used my legs instead. It was the only way to pin him against me. I ran my tongue over his throat, and down his neck.

He moaned. Then, his body relaxed.

Could this be bringing back old memories for him? If so, this could work to my advantage. I latched onto him, his blood filling my mouth. He tensed up and grabbed my chin with his other hand ready to push me away if needed.

Wayne growled. Hair sprouted from his hands. Agitated, his beast fought to take control. It didn't like this situation any more than I did.

My beasts pushed to the surface, though I struggled to maintain control. The battle of power and control between our creatures aroused me, yet filled me with the need to fight him. Memories filled my head.

I stood next to Wayne in a wedding dress. The preacher spoke of marriage vows. I turned to the man I loved, Wayne. He smiled, his eyes never leaving mine. We exchanged rings. When our lips met, I thought I was in heaven.

That night, he made love to me in a bed filled with rose petals. He fueled the fire within. I succumbed to him, giving him full reign to take me however he wanted. It was the first time he had bit me. Though it was painful, I still trusted him. His fangs deepened with every thrust.

I slipped one hand out of his grasp. As he fought to keep me pinned, he rubbed against me, his manhood hardening and bulging against his pants.

Suddenly, his hand slammed down into mine, his claw penetrating my palm. I hissed. Blood spilled from the wound.

The time I spent locked up in a cell by this man pained me but with the thought of our honeymoon in mind, he fueled my desire.

My other hand slipped from his grasp but before he could catch it, I wrapped my arm around him and dragged my talons down his back.

Wayne growled, his fangs piercing my neck.

Moaning, I melted into him.

"Oh, Brandy," he moaned. "I still desire you."

He gripped my hips and pulled me into him. His manhood filled me up.

"Oh, yes, Wayne," I moaned. "Fuck me."

His hips bucked against mine.

"Harder, deeper, please."

Another thrust.

"Oh, yes…"

"You feel so good," I moaned.

Firmly, he gripped my hips, thrusting harder into me as the honeymoon played in my head.

§

Woodrow sat in the leather chair, his eyes on the crystal ball. It gave him Wayne's point of view on everything, including Crystal.

Their minds had connected. She was remembering her past, only because Wayne was having sex with her. It was one of the few things that would help her to remember.

§

Crystal was remembering her past. That was what Wayne needed—for her to recall everything. Though he might be considered a monster for fucking her here on the lab floor, it was one of the few things which would help her dredge up her memories.

He loved her and he still wanted to be with her but he wasn't sure if she wanted him considering everything he had put her through. Wayne couldn't blame her if she didn't but he did what was necessary for the protection of his family.

He thrust deep inside of her.

Regardless of the fact she was with Tristan now, she was still Wayne's wife. Tristan had defied him by going after Crystal, so one way or another, Wayne was going to remind her of her life before Tristan. Once he helped her regain her memory, he was going to share everything with her. Then, he hoped she would make the right decision.

§

He curled me up into him.

"Oh, Wayne…" I *held him against me. I didn't want to let go. "I love you."*

"I love you," I moaned.

"I'm sorry for everything, baby. I never meant to hurt you."

Our eyes met.

A wave of release overwhelmed me. And him? He was fucking me? In the throes of passion, anger consumed me. As we came together, I had the desire to kill him.

I lashed out. He caught my wrist, his eye on the door.

"I know you want to kill me but can you just wait? We need to get the fuck out of here. We need each other right now. We have visitors."

"You're a dick," I spat.

APPEARANCES

Footsteps on the other side of the door caught my attention. As we bolted to our feet, the door flew open. Five large men stood in the doorway. They were all dressed in Army style uniforms except for the Mexican, who wore dress pants, a black button up shirt, and a sports jacket.

"He's expendable!" he screamed. Then, he pointed at me. "But get her alive!"

As the men advanced on us, Wayne pushed me behind him.

One man walked each side of the room while the other three stayed near the entrance. One of the men jumped on the table.

As the blond man on the table lunged at me, two of the men advanced on Wayne. Another man to the right, ran at me, dropped, and slid across the blood on the floor, attempting to take my legs out from under me.

I jumped up, my foot connecting with the blond man's face. Pain ripped through my upper back. New wings sprouted, only they were larger, darker, and had streaks of red, purple, and amber in them. They held me suspended in air.

The blond man fell backward onto the medical table. The man who slid on the floor collided with the steel coffins which lined the walls.

Everybody stared up at me.

"What the fuck…?"

Wayne punched him, driving him backward into the wall, and then Wayne's werewolf emerged. As the second man lunged for him, Wayne jumped him.

I turned around, coming face to face with the blond man. Shit! The blond man punched me sending me flying backward into the coffins. As both men rushed me, I snapped my wings out. One wing struck the second man and sent him flying into another wall.

The blond man hissed, revealing his razor sharp teeth at the same time I struck out with my talons, gouging out his eyeballs. He screamed. Then, I ripped his heart out of his chest, letting his lifeless body fall to the ground.

The other man crouched down, as if ready to attack.

Wayne's growl echoed within the room followed by a mauling. Then a hard impact from the side threw me into the coffins; at the same time, the man lunged for me. I fell to the ground and spun around.

Wayne struck at two vampires, one of them being the second man I had been fighting. Airborne, Wayne's jaws clamped down on the vampire's throat. Shrieks filled the room. Blood rained down on me. The three of them crashed into the coffins, making them sway.

I bolted to my feet. Blood soaked the floor. Against the furthest wall lay a headless body. His decapitated head lay next to him.

Movement in the doorway caught my attention. The large Mexican ran out of the room. Oh hell, no! If he had anything to do with this, he was a dead man. I ran after him, slipping on the crimson colored floor.

§

Once David took off with the woman, Rebecca left her body. She wanted to help the woman, but her children were her priority.

In the other room, Katie awoke.

Her muffled cries caught Rebecca's attention. She tiptoed into their room where she found Katie sitting up in bed. Tears dripped down her face.

"What's wrong, baby?"

She rubbed her eyes. "I had a bad dream."

"It's all right honey, momma's here." Rebecca laid down next to Katie and pulled her in close. "I'm sorry you had a dream, honey. We need to change that."

Katie curled up against her mom.

"Will you tell me a story?"

Rebecca smiled. "How about the butterfly story?"

Katie's eyes glistened. "I love that story."

§

The woman David grabbed lay on a table in the dimly lit room, her body disemboweled, and the top half of her skull cut away. Woodrow pulled her brain out.

David stood at the foot of the table. "Did you get the witch?" he asked.

"No, but I got something even better."

"And what's that?"

"I tracked her to a house in Phoenix," Woodrow said. "She's living with her sister, and she has her children with her."

David frowned. "The kids? I don't want anything to do with the kids."

Woodrow stood, brain in hand. "Oh David, I've learned things about them. They will all be very helpful in my quest, and this includes the children."

Woodrow walked around the table. "Get rid of her. I need this table cleared so that I can finish my mission."

"Where's Jace?" David stared at him. "And what do you mean, your mission?"

"Jace is busy." Woodrow leaned over the table. "He has me taking care of things right now. Just do as I say. By the way, is Ezzie locked up?"

David rested his hands on the woman's legs. "I thought you took care of Ezzie. You told me you were going to do it after you talked to Jace. Where is Jace? I need to talk to him."

Woodrow's eyes darkened. "I told you Jace is busy. He doesn't even want to see me right now. Go check on Ezzie."

"Since when did you start giving commands?"

Woodrow sneered. "Jace put me in second command David. I have things to do. I found one of our men with Crystal."

David jabbed the woman's leg. "I don't give a fuck. Where is…" He did a double take. "Wait…what?"

"Wayne is not only the man who held Crystal captive, but he's also her ex-husband." Woodrow took a bite out of the brain.

David cocked his head. "Really?"

"Yeah, and now I need to track our other former captive, Warrant. Once Wayne focused in on Crystal, he lost all track of Jennifer. So, I have Warrant looking for her."

"Jennifer? She's the daughter right?"

"Yes, she'll come in quite handy as well." Woodrow shook his bloody finger. "But get to work. Jace will be back in a while. In the meantime, I've got something to do."

"Before you leave, I have some bad news."

"What's that?"

"Several of our hybrids have been killed."

"Fuck!" he snapped. Woodrow's eyes darkened. "Are you kidding me?"

"Yeah, Tristan, Robert, and some biker gang are out there, killing them."

"What biker gang?" he asked. Angrily, Woodrow slammed the brain down on the table, squashing it.

"I think they're called The Hells Changelings," David answered.

Silence.

"Who the hell are they?"

"I don't know."

"I haven't heard of them." Woodrow sighed. "They must be from out of town."

Their eyes met.

"Hey, it's Arizona bike week, isn't it?"

Confusion settled on David's face. "Yeah, I think so. Why?"

A bloody grin crossed Woodrow's face. "The Warlords of Satan are probably in town. You know where to get in touch with them."

David rubbed his bald head. "Are you sure you want me to contact them? They're a messy bunch."

"Yes, I do."

Son of a bitch! Why was Jace not around to oppose this suggestion? Why should he follow Woodrow's command? And where the hell was Jace?

§

I tucked my wings in as I ran down the corridor. Footsteps echoed through the hall after me, and then Wayne slammed me to the ground. We slid across the floor, crashing into the closed door before me.

"Dammit, keep it quiet, will you? You're going to piss off everybody in here," Wayne whispered.

He backed off enough for me to spin around. I was still angry about earlier, so I punched him in the face.

"Jesus Christ, I wish you were mortal right now. You're a stubborn bitch."

I whispered, "Fuck you, Wayne. You've done nothing but destroy my life."

He grabbed me by the throat, his claws digging into my skin. The anger in his eyes pierced my soul.

"Really, have I? Because I recall you bearing my children, our beautiful babies. Jennifer and Robert took very much after the beauty of their mother, and I presume much of your stubbornness as well."

Warm liquid dripped from the puncture wounds he left.

Rage turned his face red. "Tell me, Brandy, Crystal, whatever the fuck you want me to call you now, how the hell would I know anything about you or our children? How the hell did I know Robert's birth date? How would I know your name?" he spat. "Huh, Crystal?"

My hatred of him boiled deep inside. "Why, Wayne? Why would you do this to me? If I was your wife, how the hell could you put me in such a position? Did you really love me, or was I just a piece of the puzzle to help you get what you want?" My voice rose. "Why Wayne? Tell me!"

"You're getting a little loud, and this isn't the time," he whispered.

"You always tell…"

His hand clamped over my mouth. "Baby, do me this one favor, shut the fuck up? This really isn't the time or the place. The men, or creatures I should say, aren't real fucking nice in here. We need to get out and now. I guarantee they have people on their way…"

Footsteps echoed beyond the closed door.

"And there they are…" he begun.

We glanced at the closed door.

He whispered, "You'll get your chance to get even with me if you so desire. But right now, you need to back me up. I'm your only chance of survival."

He peered up at the door before helping me up.

His brow furrowed in. "By the way, what the fuck are you?"

"In your words, I don't have to explain that right now."

I glanced at the doors in the hallway.

"All right," he replied. "How high can you fly?"

"I don't know. That was my first time in there."

"Okay. Well then, you may need to use your gift once we get out of here."

Wayne shoved open a door. "Let's go."

"Where does that lead?"

"You'll see."

I glanced up at him. "You know this place?"

"Yes, very well, unfortunately," he answered. "Let's go."

He led me into the room and shut the door behind us. A door echoed in the corridor we had been in. If we didn't do something soon, they were going to find us. He engaged a large circular lock on the door.

"Do you think that's going to keep them out?"

"There are twenty steel rods inside this door. That should keep them at bay for a little bit. Now, shush," he answered.

I shut my mouth and followed him through another door. He engaged another lock similar to the first. As he spun around, I stepped in front of him.

"Are there some clothes around here I can use? I really don't want to be running around here naked."

He looked me over. "You shouldn't be ashamed of your body. Except for the mud, you still look fantastic."

"Hey, asshole…"

"What are you concerned about, you're with your husband."

He proceeded past me.

"I think you mean ex-husband."

"Actually, you're still my wife. My death certificate was a fake."

My mouth dropped.

"Your marriage to Chris wasn't exactly legal because you and I were still married."

My eyes narrowed in on him. "What?"

"Which also means you're committing adultery by sleeping around with another man."

He unlocked a round steel door, revealing a tunnel which led upward. When he turned around, I slapped him.

"I guess I deserve that," he said, wiping the blood from his mouth.

"Oh, and much more," I replied, climbing into the small, concrete tunnel after him.

He locked it behind us. At this point, there was no avoiding any physical contact with him as he maneuvered around me. It was awkward and surreal as we moved onward.

After a couple of turns, we reached a ladder which was barely out of reach.

"Here, let me help you," he said, grabbing my hips.

Regardless of my anger, our tryst had brought back memories of him. This wasn't helping, and neither was his close proximity.

I peered over my shoulder at him. "Do me a favor, Wayne?"

"What's that?"

"Don't touch me. I can do this on my own. Second, you're distracting me."

"All right, but let me go first." He brushed past me. "When we get out of here, there is a creek toward the left. Head toward it. We need to wash up, or every creature known to man will smell us."

"Okay." I nodded in agreement.

He grabbed the bottom rung. "By the way, I still love you."

Our eyes met.

The horror of my captivity was still fresh in my mind. "You're still an asshole."

His eyes dropped. "I understand but when we get the chance, I'll explain everything."

I followed him out of the tunnel.

Visions of my captivity and fighting played in my head. I didn't need this again.

The clank of steel reverberated overhead, and then fresh air wafted up my nostrils. Where the hell was I? And how the hell did I get here?

As I emerged from underground, something hit me. It sent me reeling head over heels down the hill and into the freezing creek. Above me, Wayne took on full transformation of his alter ego. A female creature which was half dragon, half werewolf advanced on him. It reared back on its hind legs. Fire shot out of its mouth.

"No! Dammit, no!" I screamed.

Wayne was not going to die, not here, not now. As I ran up the hill, my wings shot open. Wayne rolled down the hill past me, on fire and shrieking in pain.

"Bitch! Leave him alone!"

She turned, her eyes narrowing in on me.

Scales erupted on my flesh, encasing me with a hard defense. Fire shot out of her mouth again. I ran into it toward her and slammed her into the mountainside which hid the laboratory where I had been. She struck out, her talons raking across my chest.

As I grabbed her by the throat, the beasts within me emerged—the werewolf head, the human body, and the dragon talons.

She swung at me, her talons raking my arms, as I pinned her down and locked my jaws on her. With one bite, I nearly decapitated her.

After tossing her to the ground, I turned to find Wayne lying wet, next to the creek. He had already made it into the water and now he lay next to it, drying off, his burnt flesh healing.

I walked down the hill and into the water. The rain had turned the creek into a river.

"Are you all right?" I asked, looking him over.

"Yes, I am," he answered. "You know you put on quite a show."

Water glistened off his chest. "Though I enjoyed watching you fight when you were human, I'd kind of like to see you fight as an immortal."

Of course, he would. I rolled my eyes.

I dipped below the water surface and scrubbed my hair. It wasn't the cleanest water, but it was better than nothing. As I broke the surface, Wayne slid into the water.

The night air was cool and brisk, but the heat from my beasts kept me warm. I scrubbed my chest.

"Don't even think about it."

He waded toward me. "About what?"

Firmly, I answered. "About getting off on this."

The intensity of his eyes changed. There was a smug satisfaction in them. I imagined he was glad to have me back in his life again. Arrogant bastard. His eyes dropped as he moved in closer.

I sunk lower, enough to cover my breasts.

"I remember watching you shower at home. You're a beautiful woman."

"Stop it with the sentimental bullshit, Wayne. You held me captive and beat me. What the hell was that all about?" I snapped.

"We'll discuss all that once we get away from here. You need to wash up so we can leave."

"Then get away from me. I can handle this." I turned my back to him.

His breath was on my neck. "You missed a spot in your hair, hon."

"No, I didn't."

"Yes, you did. Now, shush, and let me take care of it."

In the prison, Tristan had washed my hair, not Wayne. At that time, Tristan was my only source of compassion. Now, it was Wayne. I peered back at him.

"If you try to drown me…"

"I wouldn't do that to you."

I allowed him to comb the blood out when a sense of déjà vu

overwhelmed me. Tristan had been behind me, now it was Wayne. He had caressed my wings, had made love to me, now…

I jerked and spun away from him.

He backed off, holding his hands up. "I didn't do anything."

It was Tristan's fault. He was the last person I was with before this place…whatever the hell it was.

A curious look arose on his face. "What's wrong?"

Confused, I mumbled, "Tristan…" But why? My heart hurt.

"Tristan did this to me." Confusion and nervousness aroused my creatures, and not in a good way.

The muscles in his jaw twitched. "What do you mean? What did he do to you?"

"We were making love when I made the change…when my wings came out for the first time," I said. My heart skipped a beat. "He said they had to kill the dragons…and he tore my wings off."

The crease in his forehead deepened as he narrowed his eyes in on me. "What do you mean, ripped your wings off? You have wings right now."

Wait! What? They grew back? I glanced at my new wings.

"What's going on?" he asked.

I rubbed my forehead, confused. I didn't know what to think.

His pupils turned amber. Another twitch of the muscle.

"I don't know. I don't remember anything after that. Why would he do that, though?"

"I think it's time we get out of here. We're in dangerous territory. It's not wise to talk here."

Oh, how my heart and soul hurt.

"Why don't you fly us out of here?"

"I haven't flown before."

"I don't care," he replied. "The territory around here is closely watched. I think it would be wiser to talk somewhere else."

In agreement, I wrapped my arms around him. I was ill. Tristan had hurt me just as much as Wayne had. He had torn the wings from my back and purposely brought me here. Why?

Now, I held the man whom I had married. Why should I give Wayne retribution for the hostility he took upon me? Both the men whom I had cared for and trusted had intentionally hurt me.

Why the hell should I give either man retribution? My heart ached.

I spread my wings out and took flight. If I had no family to worry about, I would become a free spirit, and leave this life behind me but it was my family and Tristan that kept me here.

Hmm…Tristan? Was I too trusting with him?

Apparently, Wayne had trusted him at one point, too. After all, Wayne had recommended I seek Tristan out when he let me go, yet Tristan betrayed us both. A discussion was in order, rather sooner than later. Preferably now.

Once I was low enough to the ground, I dropped Wayne. Then, I landed, tucking my wings in. The scales on my body thickened, hiding a good portion of my breasts and private female parts.

Ah-ha! Now, I didn't feel so naked.

Beside me, Wayne wiped the brush off. "That was a nice abrupt landing."

I kept my chin up. "Sorry, Wayne, but you're on my shit list."

Nodding, he approached me.

I flicked my wing out and slammed him into a tree. Leaves and pinecones rained down on him.

Annoyed, he said. "All right, I get it, you're pissed."

He brushed leaves out of his hair.

Enraged with fury, my beasts surfaced. They lashed out but not before Wayne grabbed me and slammed me into the tree.

He leaned into me, his face red with anger. "You want to hit me, go ahead. You want to beat me, go ahead. What I did was wrong? But I did it for the protection of my family."

I sneered.

His amber pupils fixated on mine. "Go ahead. I deserve it. I won't fight you," he said, holding his hands up and backing off.

I drove my fist into his face, once, twice…on the third punch when he didn't fight back, I became annoyed.

Hissing, I spat, "Come on, asshole! You had no problem hitting me before. Why not now?"

No answer. Instead, he stared at me, his hands at his side.

"Damn you!" I spun around, walking away.

Wayne jumped me.

"Asshole…"

He covered my mouth. "Shush, there's somebody over there."

Bullshit.

"They'll think we're lovers," he whispered, his lips on mine.

Oh hell no, this was not happening. One more damn excuse.

Leaves rustled. To my right, somebody hunkered down in the brush. Somebody was watching us. The scent of his leather jacket wafted by. Oh, shit, this wasn't good. It was the Hell's Changelings.

I pulled Wayne in closer to block the man's view. Wayne stiffened against me. Memories flooded in again.

"You mean the world to me, Brandy," Wayne whispered.

He nibbled on my earlobe.

"You know that, don't you?"

"Yes, I do," I smiled, staring into his golden pupils. I ran my hand over his stubbly beard.

"I'll do whatever I can to protect you."

"I love you, too." He was the love of my life.

He smiled, revealing his fangs. His hands, which remained human, sprouted hair.

I nuzzled against him.

Stop it! I needed to hide from the Hells Changelings, not reminisce about our love life. I nuzzled into his thick fur. What…wait? Oh, shit, this wasn't good.

Almost in full transformation, he took a protective stance over me. Growling, he lowered his muzzle.

The scent of the bikers drifted in toward us. It wasn't the entire group but it was enough to endanger our lives.

My beasts took reign over me, primarily my dragon, and because it was her, my life was expendable. Damn them!

§

Gothic heavy metal music blasted over the sound system in the bar. The long-haired bartender grabbed a glass and sauntered over to the blonde woman who was sprawled over it. He jerked her head up, forcing the blood to spill from her neck and into the glass he held.

She was almost drained, but he knew his customer well. He liked the last bit of crimson fluid from his victims. Then something splashed in the cup. Droplets of blood splashed onto the floor. Nice! Victor would enjoy that piece of her. The bartender turned and set the glass down in front of the big biker.

Victor smiled, threw some cash down on the counter, grabbed the drink, raised it, and nodded.

"Thanks for the topping."

"Not a problem, man. Enjoy!" The bartender moved onto his next patron.

Victor chugged his drink down and swished the topping around in his mouth. Savoring it, he walked away.

Unlike his brotherhood, he preferred to keep himself clean. Others said he wasn't a biker because he didn't let his curse dirty him up but he thought otherwise.

He crossed the room to the pool tables, where he spied a woman moving toward the gang. Smiling, he licked the last drop of blood from his upper lip.

She was gorgeous. Her long blonde hair swirled around her breasts, her medieval corset and black mini skirt barely hiding her feminine assets.

In the corner of the room, the biker club smiled, all focused in on the virgin who approached them. Oh boy, this really wasn't the type of place mommy and daddy would want her. She was barely of age, had an angelic face, and could be easily mistaken for being underage but Victor knew she was not for she carried herself much different. The blonde was confident but nervous…sensual but not overly sexual. Her make-up was a little overdone, more so than what he liked but everything else about her was perfect.

As she approached the table, the men's eyes fell on her arm. The smell of blood was in the air, her blood. It was fresh and vibrant. The puncture wounds from the needles revealed her major at the university, phlebotomy.

Snake's tongue slithered across his lips, his small beady eyes fixating on her body. As he jumped to his feet, she recoiled and ran into Victor who moved up from behind her.

Her eyes darted away from Snake's tattooed face to Victor, who appeared beside her.

"What are you doing, brother?" Snake snapped.

Victor's brow furrowed in. "I was watching her from back here, brother. Find another woman, someone who's more your type. This pretty little thing doesn't want to fuck around with something as nasty looking as you."

"What do you like, lady? Hmm, you want that piece of shit? Or do you want a really bad boy?" Snake asked with a shit eating grin. His long, straight red hair fell in his face.

Her eyes fell on the tattoo on their left shoulder—a red horned devil skull with two rockers, The Warlords above the image, Of Satan below it.

"What's wrong, bitch, you afraid of me? I know you wanted a piece of me, come on, girlie," Snake continued.

"Shut the fuck up," Victor responded. "Let me buy you a drink, lady."

She stammered, "Uh, I made a mistake. I thought you were somebody else."

She turned to flee but Victor caught her hand. "I know you want a drink."

Their eyes met.

A deep voice boomed, "Shut the fuck up, Snake, and you brother…" Saber wrapped his arm around Victor's shoulder. "…don't have time for a piece of ass. Sit down."

"But…"

The blonde ran off.

Saber pushed Victor down into his chair before sitting down next to him. The tall broad chested man announced, "We got a hit."

"Ah, who is it?" Richard asked.

"David called, said Woodrow executed the hit. We get paid half upfront, half when the job is done."

§

The blood from Jennifer's wound stained her and Tristan. She had been worried the scent of her blood would attract predators but thankfully, it had not. The moment Tristan set her down on the patio she caught the stranger's scent.

Firmly, Odesso said, "We need to talk."

They turned. The patio was empty.

Tristan glanced around. "O…"

"Shh, Tristan."

Eyes wide, Tristan shut his mouth and walked across the patio.

"Tristan…?" Jennifer started. Shaking, she rubbed her arms.

"Let's keep the child out of this," Odesso said.

There was nobody within sight. Goosebumps spread across her skin.

"Why are you here?" Tristan asked.

"Like I said, we need to talk."

Jennifer stared at the edge of the patio. Was the man hiding on the other side? And who the hell was he?

She took a step toward the edge.

"No, Jennifer," Tristan whispered.

Headlights appeared in the near distance.

"Go inside," Tristan ordered.

It was a truck. Tyler's truck?

"Tyler?" she muttered. Why would he show up here? And why so late? Curious, she ran down the steps.

"Who's Tyler?"

She stopped, mid-stride. "He's a friend from school."

"Tristan, we need to talk. Now!" Odesso demanded.

When Jennifer glanced back, Tristan was gone.

"Tristan?"

Since the headlights were shining on the patio, she started around the side of the patio.

Tyler turned the headlights off and yelled, "Jennifer!"

Shit! She backed off.

Tyler stepped out of the truck. With a curious look on his face, he asked, "Are you all right?"

"Uh, yeah, I'm fine." She was glad to see him yet she was concerned about Tristan and the stranger.

Who was the other man? Why did he need to talk to Tristan at this time of night? Why was Tyler here? And where were the Hells Changelings? Weren't they supposed to be helping? And where was everybody else? There were too many questions and not enough answers.

Tyler smiled.

Maybe she would take Tyler inside, so Tristan could talk to the stranger. Wait…bad idea! The stranger's voice had been urgent. She didn't want to be around if anything happened. So, since she was safe with Tyler she decided on a walk around the two-acre property instead.

"Uh, would you like to go for a walk?" she asked.

A gentle push urged her on. Tristan? She looked back. The porch was empty, but it was not. Invisible, Tristan stood behind her.

"Sure." Tyler wrinkled his nose. "Do you smell something?"

"No, I don't." She shoved her hands in her pockets.

He glanced around. "Hmm, maybe there's a dead carcass nearby."

Another gentle push.

He sniffed the air. "Is somebody here?" He glanced around.

"My mom's boyfriend is wandering around here somewhere. Maybe out back," she lied. Then, she spied something in his hand—her wallet.

He caught her looking at it. "Oh, hey you dropped this at school. I thought you might need it, so I thought I'd bring it over. I know it's kind of late. Sorry about that."

Smiling, she took it from him. "Thank you. That was very sweet of you."

"You're welcome." He smiled.

A stronger push moved her forward. All right, she got the hint.

"Hey, let's go for that walk," she said.

§

Once the teenagers were out of sight, Odesso revealed himself. "Glad to see we're alone. We don't need the woman's child in danger now do we, Tristan?"

He turned to face Tristan, but Tristan was nowhere in sight.

"Tristan?"

No answer.

"Tristan, reveal yourself," he demanded.

Only silence answered him.

"Son of a bitch," he muttered.

AN EYE FOR AN EYE

I tried to hide my face so they wouldn't recognize me but chances are they would recognize my scent, and considering the position I was in, they would probably say something to Tristan.

As I rolled over onto my stomach, my wings snapped out, wide and fast.

Wayne hunkered down, his eyes on the men.

The bones within my face lengthened and my teeth grew sharper. The muscles within my body grew larger, taking on the full appearance of the dragon.

Shrieking, I reared up on my haunches. It echoed within the mountain walls. As my gaze fell on Uwe, Ratliff, and Christian, I took a step forward.

Uwe wielded his machete as Wayne jumped. The blade sliced the air, barely missing Wayne.

Then, Ratliff and Christian rushed me. I lashed out with my wings, the claws on the end of them ripping their flesh. As I whipped them back, the claws struck Christian, ripping part of his face open.

Then Ratliff moved in. As he swung at me, I stepped back and allowed him to move in, rolling and maneuvering back with his punch. It was then that he lost his momentum and fell down the hill.

Smoke filled the air from the forest fire down below.

By then Wayne had descended upon Uwe. As the blade circled around, the werewolf fell to the ground, sliding into Uwe's feet and knocking him over backward.

Wayne scrambled to his feet but Uwe still held the machete, only it lay above his head. Wayne lunged for his throat.

§

The Warlords of Satan hid in the darkness outside of the biker bar waiting for David. When David arrived, he came alone, hiding beneath a dark dust jacket and cowboy hat.

Snickering, Saber got off of his bike. The motorcycle club remained on theirs.

He slinked up next to the wall where he scooped a swab of Skoal out of the container and dipped it in his mouth.

David approached him.

Saber glanced around. Another MC stood outside the bar, their eyes on David. Three of the bikers took a step forward. Saber smiled. Maybe he needed to show them who was boss.

David stared at them.

Regardless whether this was their territory or not, Saber emerged from his hiding spot, sneering at them, exposing his fangs, ready for a fight.

David hissed at the other motorcycle club.

One of the elder bikers smacked the prospect in the chest. It was his way of telling him to stand down. They nodded at David and Saber, who stepped into the shadows.

David greeted Saber with an envelope. Opening it, Saber skimmed through the cash.

"There's a list inside," David said.

He raised an eyebrow. "A list?"

"Yeah."

"That raises our price," Saber said.

Snake approached.

"I know that and I know your prices."

Saber passed Snake the envelope. "Count it. And look the list over."

§

David glanced at Snake. God, he was an ugly motherfucker. The snake tattoo drew unwanted attention, something Jace and his men were against but then, of course, they were the Warlords of Satan. They didn't live by the same rules Jace and his men did.

"Where's Jace?" Saber asked.

Firmly, David answered, "He's tending to business."

"Really?" Saber glanced at Snake.

A suspicious look crossed Snake's face.

"Yeah, really."

Saber spit out a swab of chew.

David scowled at him. "Is that enough there, Snake?"

Saber folded his arms across his chest. "How many do we have?"

Snake looked the paper over. "Seven."

"Seven…hmm, that's a lot."

David grinned. "Yeah, well, we have other things to do. We figure you guys could do the dirty work."

Saber snickered.

David adjusted his hat. "By the way, we were wondering if you knew another MC by the name of the Hell's Changelings? Does it sound familiar?"

Snake and Saber exchanged looks. "Yeah, it sounds familiar."

"Why are you targeting another biker club?" Snake asked, eyeballing the bad man.

"They're getting in the way," David answered.

"Who ordered the hit?" Saber spit again.

Tired of the questions, David answered, "Jace did,"

Saber scowled. "I don't see Jace ordering a hit for a motorcycle club."

David knew this was suicide, regardless if he was vampire or not.

"They're killing our hybrids."

"Hybrids?"

Again, Snake and Saber exchanged looks. "What do you mean…hybrids?"

"That's for Jace to tell you, not me. Ask him when you see him again. I'm only the messenger. Remember bring us the heads when you're done."

David lowered his hat and walked away.

§

"I don't like this," Snake said, frowning.

"Neither do I. Something sounds fishy."

"Well…?"

242 • Lynn Mullican

"He's paying so we do it but remember, he who gets in the way gets killed, too. No excuses and no witnesses, I don't care who they are," Saber stressed.

Snake nodded. He followed Saber back to the motorcycles.

"You know the rules, Snake." Saber climbed on the motorcycle. "With that said, we keep an eye on David and Woodrow."

"You got it."

The motorcycles roared to life.

§

I held Christian in my talons when something struck me from behind. I whirled around. A long silver chain spun through the air. I lashed out, but it was too late. The chain Ratliff held wrapped around my neck. The spikes on the chain penetrated my skin, the silver burning my flesh.

I tossed Christian aside and turned to face Ratliff. He wrapped his arm around the chain and pulled me inward, strangling me. I fought to get a grip on the chain, but I lacked the ability to get a hold of it with my claws.

Beside us, Christian fell on Wayne and Uwe, his head arched over Wayne's back. As Uwe swung the machete, Wayne backed off. The blade came down on Christian's neck and severed his head.

"No! No! Christian!" Uwe scrambled to his feet. "Christian! No, dammit, no!"

As Uwe cried over his friend, Wayne turned toward me.

I tried to pull away from Ratliff, unintentionally tightening the chain, along with Ratliff's grasp on it. Before I knew it, Wayne lunged for Ratliff, knocking him off balance. The chain fell from his grip.

The moment I took flight I snatched Wayne up and whisked him away.

§

Woodrow entered the bedroom where Rebecca and the girls slept. The easiest one to remove was the youngest, Tisa. Sleeping, she molded into Woodrow's arms, and then he moved onto Katie, who was wrapped around her mother. He crept up next to the bed and wrapped another arm around Katie. She too melted into his arms. Then, he moved around to the other side of the bed where Leah slept.

Since Leah was the oldest, he expected her to raise a commotion. With the witchcraft he learned, he created a third arm and slid it beneath the child. Quickly, he picked her up. It wasn't going to take much to convince mom to come with him, now that he had the children.

His voice filled Rebecca's head. "Wake up, woman! I have your children!"

Rebecca rolled over.

"Let me sleep, Robert. It's your turn to take care of the kids," she murmured.

"Rebecca!" he yelled in her head.

Her eyes shot open.

In the dimly lit room, the stranger stood by the door, holding her daughters like Robert would hold them. She bolted upright, her heart racing.

In the other room, Hunter awoke and scuttled about.

"Who are you? What are you doing with my girls?"

He grinned. "It's time Rebecca. I want you too."

"No…" Wait! He had a third arm. What the hell…? Nobody had a third arm unless you were…

No!

Robert? Larissa? Her mind shifted from one to the other. Hunter?

§

Larissa's eyes shot open. There was a heaviness on her chest, and it wasn't just Hunter, who pressed his foot against her face.

Rebecca's mind connected with hers. Then, Rebecca and the children vanished from the house.

§

As Robert walked home, Rebecca implanted her last memory in his head, that of the kidnapping of his wife and children.

"Rebecca? No," he muttered. "No!" he screamed.

Robert doubled over.

Pain ripped through his heart. Tears welled up. Anger fueled the drive in him, pushing him deeper into the woods. He would kill anybody who got in his way.

§

"Start talking, Wayne. I'm done with this bullshit!" I demanded.

We stood face to face in a cave.

His pupils dilated back and forth as he focused on calming down.

"I need to relax first."

"No, just fucking…"

He pulled me in tight, his mouth on mine. I tried to push him away as the memories flooded in.

Blackness consumed me. Voices whispered in the dark room.

"I need you to wipe their memories, along with the rest of the family. They don't need to remember me," Wayne said.

"But Wayne, you're their father and she's their mother. At least let them have something."

"I don't know…"

"At least think about it."

"It would be better this way. This is for their protection." Wayne's voice trailed off.

I broke free of his hold and shoved him into the stone wall behind him.

"Stop it, I'm sick and tired of you doing that. You're such an asshole." I ran my hand through my hair. "Tell me the truth! I'm not waiting anymore. And no more lies!"

A different conversation interrupted the memory in my head.

"Remember that no what matter happens to me, I love you and the kids. You mean the world to me."

The memories wouldn't shut off now.

"You're right, you deserve to know everything," he said with genuine concern.

He took my hands in his. "I want you to understand, though, that I still love you."

I shook his hands loose. "That's nice, Wayne. Why don't you prove it?" I snapped.

He lowered his gaze. "I'm sorry for everything. I really am."

Sighing, I sat down on a nearby rock. My stomach churned.

"I was in law enforcement…I uh, worked for the U.G.S.S., the Underground Secret Service."

My jaw dropped. His words echoed in my head. Dammit, is that how he knew Tristan? Did he know Warrant?

He continued on.

§

"I was following you so I could give your wallet to you," Tyler said. "Well, earlier that was. I lost sight of the Mustang, and couldn't find you after that."

"Oh." If only he did find her, she may not have been attacked by James. And Raelin? Where the hell was Raelin?

"By the way, you really should get a truck. A truck is much more conventional up here."

She laughed. "You sound like my brother."

"Good minds think alike." He laughed. "Mustangs are nice, but trucks really are more durable up here."

"So, where do you live?" she asked.

"Not far from here."

"What's not…?"

"Where are you going with that piece of shit?" James screamed.

Cringing, she stopped. No, please no, not him. She hesitated, then reluctantly turned around.

Tyler's gaze narrowed in on James. "Who are you calling a piece of shit there, fairy?"

"Tyler, don't…," she whispered.

"What? You like this guy?" he asked.

"I used to. Not anymore." She grabbed Tyler's arm. "Come on, let's go."

James stood, his arms folded across his chest. "You know, I'm not deaf. I can hear you."

"Can you, dude?" Tyler asked. "If you can, tell me what I'm saying now." He mouthed the words, *Fuck you, asshole. Go find a slut to bang.*

James smirked. "I'd rather bang a slut. At least she knows what she's doing. That virgin wouldn't know how to suck…"

Tyler took a step toward James, breaking Jennifer's hold. "Apologize, asshole!"

"Stop it." Jennifer grabbed Tyler's shoulder.

James egged him on. "By the way, did she tell you I nailed her to the tree earlier?"

She glared at him. "You're an asshole."

"I thought you said you wouldn't do her type. Hmm, a little hypocritical, don't you think?"

"Fuck you, Tyler!" James spat. He took a step in Tyler's direction.

"Tyler, can we go?" Her heart beat faster like it was going to burst out of her chest.

"Do I need to kick his ass?"

As much as she wanted Tyler to do it, she said no. The Hell's Changelings came to mind. They needed to get out of the forest for she feared running into any dragons, much less the biker gang who would be in pursuit of them.

"Just take me to your place. You can do it another day," she said.

Tyler bit his lip.

"I really enjoyed nailing you, bitch. That felt really good, just driving it in you like I did. Oh yeah…" he said, gyrating his hips.

Fuck him! She turned, ready to attack him but Tyler was quicker.

They exchanged a series of punches before James fell over backward, Tyler atop him.

Jennifer took a step toward them when Warrant grabbed her from behind, clamping her mouth shut.

"Shh, be vewy, vewy quiet. I'm hunting little girls."

§

I stared out at the drizzling rain, my arms crossed over my chest. Wayne touched my shoulder.

"I'm sorry. I understand why you're mad at me and you have every right to be. I only did it for our family's protection. I didn't think it would ever come to this."

I had nothing to say. Too much time had gone by and too much time had been lost, especially with my children. I had him to blame.

Tears of blood flowed down my cheeks.

"I hate you." I found a seat deep within the cave and sulked.

He bowed his head and gazed out at the rain. "Who changed you?"

I looked at him. "Tristan and his friend, Warrant. We didn't know Warrant was a hybrid, though. Either way, it wasn't his fault."

"It's never our fault, Brandy. It never is. We get stuck with these curses, and we have to learn to live with them." He looked back at me. "What about the kids? How are they doing?"

"They're great. I couldn't have had more beautiful children. Oh, and Robert's married to Rebecca. They have three gorgeous girls; Tisa, Katie, and Leah."

He took a seat across from me. "I have granddaughters?"

"Yes, you do, and they are absolutely gorgeous."

He grabbed my hand. Our eyes met.

Sorrow filled his eyes. "I'd like to meet them. I really miss the kids." The look on his face was sincere.

"I'll see what I can do, okay?"

"Thank you."

"We'll need to make sure the kids are all right with it. It's been a long time and I'm not sure how comfortable they will be," I replied.

"I understand. But will you talk to them, if not for you or me, but for them?"

"They may freak out. So, you need to be prepared for some hostility from them."

He nodded. "I understand. Thank you."

"You're welcome." I peered out at the rain. It was still drizzling. I folded my arms across my chest. "By the way, your granddaughters are half werewolf."

He raised an eyebrow. "Great," he said. "I know Robert's one."

"Yes, and so is Jennifer."

"Shit, I had really hoped I didn't pass it onto them." He hung his head.

"Well, you did." I was beginning to hate the beasts within me.

"There's no need to get snippy with me. You were desperate to marry me, so we got hitched. Shit happens," he snapped.

"You mean children happen, not shit happens. Don't get pissy with my either, Wayne. This is the last thing I wanted for our kids," I retorted. I paced the floor.

"Same here, so stop blaming everything on me. Fucking is a two-way street. There was a fifty percent chance of it happening."

"Fucking? Nice, Wayne," I replied. The rain was dying down.

An excruciating pain hit me hard, deep within my loins. That was the second time tonight. What the hell? I doubled over. It wasn't just my loins, but my heart. It hurt.

"Are you okay?" He stood.

The wolf within crawled to the surface.

"Oh, God," I hissed. Tears streamed down my face.

Groaning, Wayne doubled over in pain.

"Wayne...?" I looked up at him.

He gritted his teeth. "No, Dammit, no...." His pupils changed color.

"It's the kids, isn't it?" I asked.

"We need to find Jennifer," he hissed.

A hard rapid thumping beat in my ribcage. "It's Rebecca…and the girls, too?"

Hollowness filled my chest. Anger replaced the hurt. The change into my werewolf was rapid and painful.

Growling, he moved past me. I followed him into the woods.

§

With Christian's head in hand Ratliff and Uwe met up with Sabol at Tristan's house. Sabol glanced from the decapitated head to the smoking leather Ratliff wore.

Sabol's jaw dropped. He stared at Christian's head. "What the hell?"

"Some damned werewolf *she* was with, got him killed," Ratliff spat.

"*She*? Who's *she*?" His eyes narrowed in on Ratliff.

"That bitch of Tristan's. She was cheating on Tristan with this asshole," Uwe hissed.

Sabol's voice deepened. "Where is *Crystal*?"

"She took off with him."

Sabol cocked his head. "She got away?" He looked Ratliff over again.

"We have a problem, Sabol," Uwe interrupted.

"And, what would that be?"

"She's…"

Interrupting Ratliff, Uwe smacked him in the chest and pointed to Sebastian, who emerged from the forest, covered in blood.

Sebastian glanced from one man to another. Smoke rose from Ratliff's clothing. He did a double take. Questionably, he stared at Ratliff, unaware of the head Uwe held due to his position.

"What the hell happened to you?" he asked.

"I'll tell you later. What's going on?" Ratliff asked. "Where's Raelin?"

"I don't know. I got in a fight with a dragon, and she took off." Sebastian shook his head. "I can't find her." He exchanged looks with his brotherhood. "What's going on here?"

"For starts, I can't find Tristan, Jennifer, Robert, or Raelin. Crystal's missing too," Sabol answered with an irritated tone.

Ratliff and Uwe hissed at Crystal's name.

Sebastian looked at them. "What's that for?"

Sabol glanced back at the other men as he walked past Sebastian.

"Kill her."

Sebastian whipped his head around. "Are you sure, Sabol? I mean, she's Tristan's woman."

Sabol eyeballed his men. "If I said to kill her, I meant to kill her. Should anybody question her disappearance, we blame her death on the dragons, plain and simple."

Ratliff and Uwe grinned.

Sebastian walked around Sabol, his gaze dropping to the head in Ratliff's hand. His mouth dropped open.

"You can blame Tristan's bitch for this," Uwe announced.

"We find Crystal, and we kill her, along with the werewolf," Sabol demanded.

"Yes, Sabol," Sebastian answered.

"Her body disappears…for good. I don't want to find a trace of it."

"I see you all agree."

They nodded. Then, they followed Sabol into the forest surrounding Tristan's home. Something shrieked in the forest, alerting them to her whereabouts.

TO DIVIDE AND CONQUER

One down, another one to go. Warrant's brain faltered again. The sharp pain intensified. He stopped. Why? Why did it do that? What the hell had Jace done to him?

Violently, he shook. Warm fluid ran down between his legs. Oh, how he wanted to die. This wasn't fair. He was a good man, always had been. Dammit, stop! Stop!

The voice reappeared in his head. Fucking wimp! Pussy! You're not the man you were. Get used to it.

His body went rigid and his brain wavered, bringing him back to his task. Get the other woman…the mother! Uh, Crystal, yeah Crystal! By the time you capture her, Woodrow and David will be back. Stay on track, and don't let her get the best of you. Beat her if you need to but don't kill her. Woodrow wants her alive.

§

The shriek of a wounded animal caught the teenager's attention. Tyler glanced up. Jennifer was gone.

"Jennifer?" He gazed back at the spot where she had been.

James chuckled. "What's wrong, your girlfriend, disappear?"

Tyler growled, "Where is she, you son of a bitch?"

James chuckle turned into an evil laugh.

Tyler raised his fist. "I'll kill you, asshole."

"Wouldn't you like to know?" James grinned.

That was it! Tyler was done with this jackass. He held him down as his fingers transformed into claws. They merged within James scalp.

James struggled beneath him. As Tyler stood, James tried to gain his footing. The skin on Tyler's hand fused together with James's head, so he couldn't escape Tyler's clutch.

"Until you tell me where Jennifer is, I'll just have to drag you then." He dragged James, heading in the direction Jennifer had been.

The rumble of motorcycles echoed through the woods. He headed in their direction, concerned they might have taken Jennifer.

§

The stench of burnt leather drifted by. Not them! Not again.

Wayne growled.

As I spun around, a werewolf slunk out of the brush. Warrant's scent was in the air. Warrant? No, not…

Warrant attacked, driving me backward into the tree, his jaws latching onto my shoulder. I howled in pain.

Then, Wayne jumped him, knocking him to the ground. Warrant struck back, his claws digging into Wayne's chest as Wayne fought back.

I shot to my feet. My human form took over, the scales on my skin thickening to hide my feminine assets. The crack of branches caught my attention.

As I looked up, The Hells Changelings emerged from the brush.

Ratliff's gaze fell on mine.

"Son of a bitch," I muttered. I covered my wound and hauled ass.

The rattling of chains and the smell of burnt leather followed me. As I neared a shack, Ratliff latched onto me, grabbing me by my shoulder. Blood poured from my wound. I howled in pain as he pinned me against him.

Then from out of the darkness, other bikers emerged from the forest. Did the Hell's Changelings bring on more bikers? Yet, the patches were different. They had to be another biker club. Were they Tristan's friends? Or were they enemies?

One of their bikers appeared with a tight grip on Raelin, her head hung low, her hair in her face.

My jaw dropped. "Ah….no, no."

Ratliff tightened his hold on me.

In the nearby distance, Wayne and Warrant continued to fight, which must have caught the attention of the biker club.

"What's with the fight?" Saber asked.

"Don't know," Sabol answered.

Sebastian eyed Raelin. "Who's the girl?"

"Oh, the girl," Bruce said. "Found her wandering through the woods, said she was going home. I wonder, though, what drives a young woman to wander the forest in the rain all alone. I find that rather odd, don't you?"

"Don't know," Uwe answered.

There were seven of them, and there were only four of the Hells Changelings. They might be able to hold their own, but it might be a challenge. Had I not been a dragon, and determined Tristan's adulterous girlfriend, I might be able to help them, instead, they were ready to kill me.

"Who's the woman?" Saber asked.

"A friend," Ratliff answered.

"Mm, looks like we interrupted a gang bang here," Snake said, approaching.

Kneeling down, he caressed my cheek with his dirty hands.

"Don't touch me, you freak," I snapped.

His slithery tongue slipped out of his mouth and up my cheek. "Mm, you taste…What is it I taste?"

A confused expression came across his face. "You're not human."

"No, I'm not," I whispered, wrapping one hand around his neck.

As my fingers evolved into talons, I pulled him into me and slammed my other hand through his chest, ripping his heart out.

That was all it took for the biker clubs to fight.

Once Ratliff let go of me, I assessed the situation. The tattooed man hadn't been much bigger than me, so I stripped him down and put on his clothing. Then, I turned my attention to Raelin, who lay still on the ground, her attention focused on the bikers.

Then, something rustled behind me.

Tristan whispered, "Crystal?"

Turning, I sneered at him. "Fucker."

As if surrendering, he put his hands up and moved toward me.

"Stay away from me, Tristan."

"You don't understand…"

Somebody grabbed me from behind.

Then, Tristan lunged at us. The three of us tumbled to the ground. As Wayne charged Tristan, Warrant attacked. Talons extended, I struck back but not before his claws sliced open my midriff. Another swing from him sent me flying back against the old shack. It buckled from the impact and fell beneath me.

Blood poured down my face while I struggled to get to my feet. A hand grabbed my leg, swept me up, and slung me over an embankment down into a six-foot-high block wall.

Wincing, I scrambled to my feet and climbed the wall. Pain reverberated throughout my entire body. At the top of the wall, I slipped, fell and attempted to get up again when I fell into a swimming pool.

§

Tyler pulled James along with him, his claws still embedded in the dancer's head. From afar, he stopped and sized up the house before him. A block wall separated the backyard from the forest.

Tyler pressed James against a nearby tree and extracted his claws from his scalp. Blood poured from his wounds.

James cried so Tyler clamped his hand over James's mouth to shut him up.

"Now, you're going to do me a favor and keep quiet. If you make any noise, I'll kill you and your family. Don't piss me off, I know where you live."

James glared at him.

"Don't give me that look either, I'm not dicking around."

James lowered his eyes.

Tyler left him and continued on toward the house, deciding it was best to look for a door other than the front.

§

I glanced about the backyard. Nobody was around. A circular hole was broken out of the block fence on the side of the yard. It was as though something broke out of the yard, not into the yard. How odd!

Then, I turned toward the house and my jaw dropped. Was it the house where Jace had kept me captive? No, it couldn't be. Could it?

Scowling, I looked for the steps. What the hell...? The pool had a severe algae problem. The water was brown, slick and disgusting.

As I found the steps, I ran my hand through the water. I scooped up mud. Too much dirt and rock had found its way into the pool. It was as if somebody intentionally filled the pool with it. But why?

I leaned in closer. Something shone near the deep end of the pool. Wait! Two semi-circular things shone beneath the surface. They moved. What...?

Beyond the block wall, something moved. The fights were moving closer to the house. I needed to move my ass...then the huge snake-like creature broke the surface of the water. I bolted out of the water.

Then, Warrant, still in werewolf form, bounded over the fence and jumped me. We crashed through the sliding glass door.

I jumped over the kitchen island. The werewolf slunk around it while the snake slithered around the other side.

I leaped up on the island at the same time Warrant jumped up at me. I threw a kick. It connected with him but the impact threw me off the island.

§

Rebecca's witchery had brought Robert to this strange house. He was confident she and the children were inside, so he looked for an alternative way into the large house rather than the front door.

§

Raelin ran in Crystal's direction. If there was anywhere safer to be, it would be with Crystal for she did not want to be alone. Carefully, she moved through the forest. She considered changing into the mountain lion but if she had to change back, she did not want to wind up naked.

"Oh, daddy, I wish you were here with me," she whispered. She gripped her cross necklace. "I know you'd protect me."

Tristan and Wayne, both bloody, barreled past her. The rampage of men headed in her direction. Her heart raced as she ran for her life, scrambling through the hole in the block fence. Then somebody latched onto her hair. She screamed.

§

As Tyler inched the door open, somebody pressed a gun against his temple. Tyler froze, glancing back at Robert.

Eyes wide, Tyler put his hands up.

"Who the hell are you? And what are you doing here?" Robert

glared at him.

Tyler cleared his throat. "You live here, man?"

Robert demanded, "What's that to you? Why are you here?"

Tyler turned toward him.

"I'm a Deputy. Don't fucking move." Robert pressed the barrel harder against the teenager's head.

Tyler bit his lip. "I'm just here to help a friend."

"And that would be?"

"Dude, are you really a Deputy? Because if you are, then she needs your help?"

"Yes, I'm a Deputy. Now, I asked you, what is her name?"

Tyler swallowed hard. "Jennifer...Jennifer Bouchard."

Robert blinked. "What makes you think she needs help?"

"Because that asshole over there..." He pointed where he had left James but James was no longer there.

"Dammit, she disappeared, and this asshole said she was probably here. Look, I don't know what's going on, but I think she's in trouble. It's kind of been a shitty day, and I'm just trying to help. I like her...and I don't want anything to happen to her."

Robert cocked his head. He looked him over. Even though he didn't know him, he believed him, for the most part.

"What's your name?"

"Tyler, Tyler LaRue."

Robert lowered the gun.

Tyler lowered his arms and let out a sigh of relief. "Fuck man, you're intense. What's your name, Deputy?"

"Robert Bouchard."

He smirked. "Seriously? Are you like her brother or something? You don't look old enough to be Jennifer's dad."

"Actually, I am her brother." Robert backed off of him.

They exchanged looks.

"Okay, so well then, do you like, have my back?" Tyler asked.

"Yeah, I do, and by the way, you can help me find my wife and kids while we're at it because I have a funny feeling they're here."

With a confused look, Tyler replied, "Sure, no problem."

Robert pushed the door open.

"So, like what the hell is going on?"

"Long story, I'll have to explain later." He glanced back at Tyler. "You know how to shoot a gun?"

"Yeah," Tyler smiled. "I grew up shooting guns."

Robert pulled a gun from his ankle holster and offered it to the teenager.

"You'll be my backup. I don't want you shooting unless you have to." He got in the boy's face. "*Got it?*"

Tyler looked him in the eyes, nodded, and took the gun. "Got it."

He followed Robert into the house.

Something crashed and a scream echoed through the empty hallway.

§

Sebastian whipped his belt off. The sides of the belt opened up, exposing razor sharp blades which flared out. He snapped the belt, slashing Richard across the face, the blades cutting across Richard's forehead, each slicing deeper into his scalp.

Sebastian whipped the belt again. This time, it wrapped around Richard's neck. As he jerked it, it ripped deeper into the biker's neck, decapitating him.

Then Raelin's scream caught his attention.

§

A constant hum in the dark room drowned out the noise from the rest of the house.

The eyes of the witches had fallen on the children who were confined in the small cell.

Leah and Tisa curled up together while Katie fell into a comatose state, closing herself off from her sisters and the witches who lurked within their prison cells.

Tisa and Leah cried, curling up into a ball next to Katie.

The witches gripped onto the cell bars and hummed an eerie but soothing song which calmed the girls some.

§

The Warlords of Satan biker sliced the air with his knife. Raelin ducked as the blade skimmed past her. Losing her balance, she fell to the ground, barely missing falling into the pool.

A silver chain whipped out, wrapping around his neck and

decapitating him. His head rolled into the pool, along with the body Sebastian kicked into it.

As Raelin struggled to breathe, a huge snake slithered out of the back door. It struck out at Sebastian, driving him backward into the pool.

The snake-like creature disappeared into the pool behind Sebastian.

With nowhere else to run, Raelin ran into the house, one of the bikers on her heels

§

David stepped into the hallway leading to the room of cells. The sound of running footsteps resounded on the floor above him. He glanced up. Crystal was here, just as Woodrow wanted, but she brought company.

The witches humming in the room to his left was annoying.

"Shut the fuck up in there!" he screamed.

They didn't listen. Fine, so be it. At least they couldn't use their witchcraft within these walls. That included everybody else, except for those Woodrow determined otherwise.

§

Jennifer fought the straps that bound her. She really didn't want to change into her werewolf, so instead, she tried to use her canine strength to break free, but she was useless.

A cold hand patted her on the forehead.

"Calm child, your powers are useless here. Only mine will prevail."

Jennifer stared up into Woodrow's dark eyes.

"My family and the bikers will kill you," she spat.

He chuckled. "Those bikers won't last long, and neither will your family. Our minions will take care of them."

Cold steel pressed against her forehead, burning her skin. The half-moon bracket was made of silver, one of the few things that could kill her. She whimpered.

Smoke from her burnt flesh loomed in the air above her.

Hissing through gritted teeth, she spat, "I'll kill you."

His words cut the air. "Relax, you'll be reunited with your family soon. Your family is already here, including the little ones. You'll see them soon enough."

She fought the straps and silver bracket that bound her, but without her inner beast, she knew she wouldn't win.

"What the hell do you want?" she screamed. Tears streamed down her face. "What do you want from us?"

His lips brushed her ear. "Your family."

"Oh God," she muttered.

"Oh, he can't help you," Woodrow replied.

Jennifer struggled against the restraints.

"There's no use struggling."

Why couldn't she conjure up her werewolf?

"Please let us go, please," she whimpered.

"Oh, I can't do that. I need your family, including the witch and her children. You see, each of you has something I need but thanks to your family and your friends, I'll have to make some sacrifices just to rid the house of some of you."

Jennifer's eyes widened. No!

"No!" she screamed, fighting harder against the restraints.

§

I ran through an unknown section of the house toward a metal door at the end of the hall with Warrant on my heels. A metal door?

I had expected his claws to rip me wide open, instead, he hit me with a fist. I lost my footing and fell. Then, he reached down, grabbed me by my shirt, and slammed me against the wall. Damn him. I struck back, expecting my claws to form. Instead, I hit him with my fingers, bending them back. I screamed.

Hissing, he punched me in the stomach.

I doubled over in pain. What the hell was happening? Our powers were useless. If I was going to assume my beastly forms, it would have to be outside the house.

Warrant threw me against the metal door, slamming my face into it.

§

War wounded and bloody, Tristan and Wayne's battle raged on, driving each other to higher ground to pursue and win the battle.

Tristan flung Wayne into the air but as Wayne came down, he struck a nearby tree, the large branch breaking beneath him. As they fell, the branch busted a hole in the roof and Wayne fell through into an empty room.

§

Robert and Tyler stopped in one of the hallways. A metal bang came from one direction, and a crash from the second floor of the house.

Robert motioned for them to split up. He headed upstairs while Tyler headed for the bang.

§

"One more time, asshole, and I'll kill you!" Tyler aimed the gun at Warrant. He was ready to shoot the stranger if he hit the woman one more time.

Warrant had Crystal pinned to the metal door, his hand wrapped around her throat.

He peered back at the teenager and hissed, "I suggest you back off and mind your own business, kid. Get the fuck out of here!"

Tyler glanced at Crystal. Another crash came from directly above them. Part of the ceiling caved in. Wood and debris rained down on them. Neither Crystal nor Warrant moved.

"Don't think so, asshole. Let her go."

"Not happening, kid."

§

Sabol crashed through the roof on the other end of the house, followed by Saber.

Behind them, Uwe followed with machete in hand, ready to take Saber's head off but an appearance and a kick from Manson, another Warlords of Satan biker, sent Uwe falling through the hole.

§

A gunshot went off on the first floor followed by a woman's scream.

Wayne threw the door open. Robert stood at the end of the hallway, his gun aimed at him.

Wayne hesitated. Tristan was right behind him, so he decided it was best to deal with Tristan, and then help Robert. At least Robert had a gun to protect himself in here. Wayne had nothing.

Whatever hellhole Wayne was in, did not allow him to use his curse. Tristan came up fast behind him. Now, he would have to fight Tristan man to man, no vampire, no werewolf curse involved. Even better!

He stepped back into the room, driving an elbow into Tristan's nose, spun around, and delivered another fist into Tristan's face, pushing Tristan back into the moonlight.

Tristan's fangs erupted from his gums.

Now wait a goddamn minute.

Tristan rushed him. As he left the moonlight, his fangs disappeared.

If Wayne could get the son of a bitch near the hole, his curse would come back and he could kill him. Whatever magic the house held disappeared near the hole, which told him that the magic was held by the house or something within it.

Tristan stuck him in the ribs with a fist.

Or maybe he just needed to create more holes, thereby defeating the supernatural effect it had but, in doing so, he needed his beast.

§

Raelin ran past the kitchen and into the hall where she came to an abrupt halt. Tyler stood in the hallway with a gun.

Warrant grinned. "My, my, who do we have here?"

Tyler glanced back. Raelin stood in the hallway behind him. Then somebody hit his wrist. Son of a bitch! Wrong move! He shouldn't have looked away.

As he turned around, a biker ran up behind Raelin. The gun fell from Tyler's hand.

No!

Tyler turned, ready to fight the man, but it was too late.

The woman struck Warrant in the kidney. As he doubled over, she wrapped an arm around his neck and kneed him in the lower back. He fell to his knees.

Tyler dropped to the floor and grabbed the gun, turning to shoot the biker in the chest.

Screaming, Raelin clamped her hands over her ears and pressed herself against the wall.

§

With Warrant on his knees, I snapped his neck.

When the gun went off, I glanced up. One of the bikers from the other biker club fell against the wall, clutching his chest.

"Put another bullet in him," I demanded.

The teenager glanced back at me. "We need to save bullets besides I think that one will kill him."

"Put another fucking bullet in him," I demanded.

He glared at me. "Look lady…"

"Put another…"

The biker grabbed Raelin.

"Listen to me, kid!" I snatched the gun from him and aimed it at the biker. Dried and fresh blood coated the man and his clothing. He pulled Raelin in tighter to him.

"Go ahead, bitch, shoot. If you don't kill her, I will."

Raelin squirmed within his arms as he tried to hide behind her. He took a step back and pulled her along with him, a blade perched in her ribcage.

I took a step forward. I didn't have a free shot at him without striking her too. I kept my finger a hair off the trigger and followed them.

"Let her go!"

"Sorry, can't do it. You better stop, or I'll stick this knife in her."

I stopped, took aim, ready to nick her arm to put distance between them when a bullet took the biker and Raelin down.

"Raelin…?" I whispered.

She didn't move.

I inched forward, swinging the gun to my left and peering around the corner. Another shot rang out. The bullet grazed my arm.

"Shit!" I covered my wound.

"Mom!"

"Robert!"

"Did you just shoot!"

"Yes!"

Robert ran to my side. "Shit, mom, I'm sorry. I thought you were somebody else."

"Check on Raelin. That biker had her."

Robert tossed the biker aside and checked for her pulse.

"She's alive." Carefully, he looked her over. "Have you been shot?"

Trembling, she stammered, "No, I don't think so."

Robert helped her sit up.

"No, I think I'm all right."

"Good, now let's find the rest of our family, and that includes you, Tyler," Robert said. "You're helping."

"No problem."

Tyler wrapped my forearm with a piece of fabric from the biker's t-shirt meanwhile Robert made sure the biker and Warrant were dead.

Eyebrow raised, Tyler asked, "What the hell is going on around here, anyway?"

"Well, our family is in danger for starts," I said, looking back at him. "Who the hell are you anyway?"

"I'm a friend of Jennifer's," he answered.

"Oh, okay," I muttered, turning back to Robert. "Why the hell can't we tap into our beasts right now?"

"I don't know," Robert answered. He gazed past us. "Where does that door go?"

"Beats me," I answered.

As we approached the metal door, something crashed through the roof and both floors, breaking beams and structural posts. The house shook from the impact. The floor caved in, taking everybody from the second floor down into the basement.

§

Victor got to his feet again. Where the fuck was that piece of shit? He scraped the mud from his jacket, climbed on his bike, and looked around. The scent of the creatures combined with death all around them made it difficult to decipher who was where.

His bike roared to life. So, did the debris in the darkness. The leather clad creature's face was wolf-like, its fangs overly large for the mouth. His jacket was gone, and his t-shirt was ripped to shreds. It exposed the human but massive muscles in his torso and arms.

Victor gnashed his teeth together and shot forward, ready to run Ratliff over but Ratliff jumped up and pulled Victor off of it, his clawed hand penetrating Victor's face.

Victor struggled to free himself when a large tree branch struck him in the back. It continued through into his heart.

Ratliff climbed on Victor's Harley, riding back to the area where they had originally met up, and turned the motorcycle around. He revved the engine up and leaned into the bars, gunning it, acquiring the speed and momentum he needed to get the motorcycle off of the ground at the top of the hill.

"Yeah, vamp it up, bitch! Woohoo!"

The force of the impact took half of the roof off where the two holes were already, breaking some structural beams and posts. Half of the second floor caved in. The impact from the combined structural components broke open part of the first floor. The hole to the basement swallowed up Ratliff and the motorcycle.

§

Contained within his own prison, Jace lay on the table, strapped and recovering from yet, another surgery. Only this time it was to release the creature contained within him.

It had been a process but Woodrow was learning. It took a combined effort of medicine, science, and witchery to hopefully unleash the beast within Jace. With the witch's efforts, Woodrow was able to not only cast a spell on the house restraining the gift of the immortal but to also use it against them in return for not sacrificing their lives, at least not yet.

Meanwhile, Jace stared about the dark room, his gaze focusing in on the hanging light above him. Crystal was on his mind. Was she pregnant with his child? He needed to know for sure.

Noises in the house caught his attention.

§

We had barely made it through the metal door when Robert disappeared. As I turned to face Robert, the door slammed shut.

"What the hell was that?" Tyler mumbled.

"Robert! Robert!" I cranked on the door handle. It wouldn't budge.

"Uh, ma'am, you might want to lower your voice."

I glared at Tyler. "You don't think the sound of that crash made a difference?"

I pushed at the door, throwing my shoulder into it. "Robert!"

Raelin touched my shoulder. "Crystal, maybe he's…"

The door flew open, smashing into me and throwing me backward into Tyler and Raelin as we fell down the curved stairwell.

I scrambled to my feet, my gaze traveling up and down the

staircase.

Raelin fought to get up. Blood oozed down the side of her head from a severe head wound. Once on her feet, she looked up at me, staggered, and then toppled down a few more stairs where she came to rest. Tyler was nowhere to be seen.

I ran down after her and checked her wounds. Raelin's condition wasn't good.

"Hold on," I whispered. "I promise I'll be right back for you."

I smoothed Raelin's hair back. A faint smile crept up on her face. Her eyes were not as bright as they once were. That worried me. I kissed her gently on the forehead.

§

Robert took blow after blow from Ezzie's fists after the surprise fall from the first floor. Hurt and weak, he lay there, trying to catch his breath. Nearby footsteps echoed in the room. He was not alone with his assailant.

"Damn bikers. Why the hell can't anybody get the job done right? I guess I'll have to take care of them myself," David sighed.

David glanced over at the motorcycle. Moonlight illuminated the bike as if it were the star of a show. He reached down and pulled it off of Ratliff.

"Hello motherfucker," David spat.

Using his foot, he rolled Ratliff over onto his back. Moonlight shone down upon Ratliff's face.

He grinned. "Good thing your mortal right now, it only makes it easier to kill you."

Ratliff's hand shot up, razor sharp claws gauging David's flesh. What the hell?

Ratliff shot to his feet, snarling. The motorcycle fell from David's grip. It caught the illumination of the moon, casting a glimmer across the room onto Robert and his assailant.

Ezzie leaned in close to Robert, his fangs glistening in the moonlight.

Robert's facial muscles twitched, transforming.

David screamed and so did the hybrid Robert latched onto, as he pulled the transforming beast into him. Wings erupted from its back, battering him.

§

Hoping to take an alternate route into the house, Sebastian discovered the low window after killing the snake and slipped inside. The surrounding darkness hid the details of the small lab.

Labored breathing came from the left of him. Jennifer laid on the table. Keeping an eye out, he approached her.

§

The witches pressed their faces tight into the cold steel. Some turned to peer at the door. Others kept an eye on the girls.

The long blonde haired witch spoke up. "Hey there, what are your names?"

With teary eyes, wet cheeks and a flushed face, Leah looked up at her. She wrapped her arms tighter around her sisters. Mommy always taught them not to talk to strangers, so she kept her mouth shut.

"It's all right. I won't hurt you. What's your name, little one?"

The witch's dark eyes focused in on the oldest. If she could convince the older one to trust her, then the others would follow.

§

Larissa and Hunter tracked Rebecca to the house. They stood in the trees. Evil and black magic lurked within the walls.

She used her witchcraft to seek out the sinister one who held power over the house. There were other witches inside. Some were nice, and some had black hearts.

Their darkness bothered her. She had to get her family out of there before the witches regained their powers. In order to do that, she would need assistance.

Larissa glanced at Hunter, who sat on her shoulder. She would call upon his power, too.

§

In a dark room beneath the floor of the house, Rebecca lay confined to a table, her wrists and ankles strapped down by metal clamps.

"Awaken, Rebecca! You're needed."

Her eyes opened.

Woodrow used his magic to unlock Rebecca's clamps.

Against the coven's wishes, he had learned the witches' witchcraft. If anybody were to find out what they taught him, or what he did, they would be killed.

Rebecca's witchcraft had become stronger since her visit with Larissa. Using his magic, Rebecca's, and the other witches, he would be able to use it against everybody else in the house, and by confining her daughters, it would give him the control he needed over Rebecca.

The witchcraft, along with Jace's alter ego, would give he and Jace the ability to annihilate anyone and everyone, including the U.G.S.S. The only one they wanted alive now was Crystal.

Rebecca was their next creation. What a beautiful specimen…and perfect bait. No better way to kill her family than by her own hand.

Rebecca stood, draped in a white peasant dress.

"Help me kill everyone, Rebecca. Just not Crystal…not yet. If you don't kill them, I'll kill your kids. I won't think twice about it."

Her eyes were cold and almost lifeless as if she were under his spell.

§

I halted at the bottom of the staircase. My mouth fell open. We were in a war zone.

The moon shone through the hole in the ceiling. Men fought all around me. In one corner, Saber had Sabol pinned to the floor. Manson and Uwe exchanged fists near them.

Uwe reached for his machete but his sheath was empty.

As I looked for it, my eyes fell on Wayne and Tristan. They fought to my right.

To my left, David lay on the floor, a large hole where his heart had been. Ratliff scrambled to his feet, David's heart in his hand.

Behind David and Ratliff, Robert lay atop Ezzie in werewolf form, thrashing and killing Ezzie.

Tyler ran across the room and disappeared down the hallway.

Ratliff stared at me. "Dragon, your dead!"

"Shit!"

§

Tyler came to a stop in the hallway, slamming into an invisible barrier before him. Rebecca stood in the hallway with a blank look on her face.

"Who the hell....?"

She threw her arm forward, sending him flying backward across the basement, his head rebounding off of the concrete wall.

§

I called unto my beasts but they lie dormant. Cursing, I ran upstairs with Ratliff in pursuit.

As he left the moonlight, his fangs disappeared, leaving him without his alter ego.

Robert's werewolf disappeared and reappeared as he ran through the light of the moon after Ratliff.

I ran past Raelin, up the stairwell, and threw open the metal door, coming to an abrupt stop as I teetered on the edge of the hole. The moonlight shone past me into the basement below. The floor beneath my toes gave way, sending me spiraling forward.

Before I knew it my wings burst out, smacking the walls surrounding me. I gazed up at the ceiling. Above me, the distinct shape of Uwe's machete stood out. It lay on the top floor, the blade protruding over the hole.

The house had to be destroyed, otherwise, nobody would be able to escape it. The roof was still intact, keeping a portion of the house deep in shadows.

My dragon took the lead. I shot upwards, breaking open more of the ceiling and roof. As I flew out, I grabbed Uwe's machete. Wood and debris fell in behind me, blocking the hole to the basement.

§

Larissa found Rebecca...only it wasn't really her sister. As she located her, Crystal crashed through the roof.

There was a problem inside, but Larissa couldn't get in without becoming defenseless. She ran up to the house, laid Hunter on the ground, and proceeded on using Hunter to get inside.

§

Rebecca appeared in the room. An air of magic surrounded her, drawing everybody's attention.

"Rebecca…" Robert whispered.

She was even more beautiful than the day they met. Only this time, her eyes were cold and deadly. A mysterious presence lurked in the darkness behind her.

§

Jennifer struggled against her constraints. "Who's there?"

Nobody answered.

"Who's there?"

Sebastian came around the corner. "Shush."

Jennifer was growing weaker. Tears flowed from her eyes. As she struggled to look up at Sebastian, hope filled her heart.

"Oh, Sebastian," she cried. "Get this clamp off of me, it hurts. It really hurts."

"All right, try to relax," he said, examining the clamp. He winced. The damn thing was burnt to her skin. "Okay, this isn't going to be easy. It's burnt to your head."

"Oh hurry, please get this off of me."

He pried at the clamp. It didn't budge.

"All right, I'm going to have to climb on this table with you."

"I don't care, it hurts."

He took his jacket off, climbed on the table, and grabbed the clamps. Groaning, he pulled on them.

"Why can't I change into my wolf?" she asked.

"I don't know. I can't use mine either," he groaned.

The muscles in his upper body bulged against his shirt and sweat coated his flesh. It moved. Relief settled in. He was going to get this off of her.

"If I get this off, it's going to hurt like a son of a bitch. I'm just warning you now."

"I don't care." Tears fell down her cheeks.

§

"That's it, sweetheart. You can do it. I have faith in you," the witch said, smiling.

Leah crawled to the door.

"All you have to do is open it. He forgot the lock on it, so you can open it."

"They're special," another witch said. Her silver hair fell in her face.

"Shut up, old woman, we don't need to give them a reason to back off. If we get out of here, we take them with us."

The witches leaned forward.

The blonde witch urged Leah on. "Come on, sweetheart."

Leah opened their cell door.

"Good girl," the witch said.

The others leaned in closer, each calling to Leah.

§

Woodrow emerged from the darkness behind Rebecca and wrapped his hands around her midsection.

Robert glared at him. Control it, Robert! Don't let him get the better of you. Wait until you won't risk any danger to her or the children. Where the hell were the girls?

His heart raced.

"It sucks when you lose your powers, doesn't it?" Woodrow asked. "Saber, Manson, I think you guys could have done a much better job than what you have. Looks like you guys are going down with the rest of them."

Saber shook his bloodied fists. "Fuck you, Woodrow. I'll kill you, and I don't need anybody else's help."

Woodrow hissed. "Really, you think so?"

Woodrow disappeared and then reappeared behind Saber, his hand taking on the appearance of a long sword. He held it against Saber's throat.

The others froze.

"Does anyone else doubt me?" Woodrow asked, exchanging glances with everyone.

Everybody remained silent as the sword sliced across Saber's throat, spilling blood at Rebecca's feet, decapitating the man.

"Kill them all Rebecca, even your husband!" Woodrow demanded.

Robert's jaw dropped. He was horrified. Rebecca was not a killing machine, nor would he allow her to be made into one.

"Rebecca, no!" he screamed, taking a step toward her.

Tristan snapped, "No, Robert, that's not your wife…not anymore!"

Wayne's eyes lit up as he peered up at his son. "Robert? Robert Bouchard?" he asked, his voice raspy.

"What's it to you?" Fear and anger, along with sorrow and dread filled Robert's heart. Tears filled his eyes.

"Son?"

"Dad?"

His brow furrowed in as he turned toward Wayne. Then Rebecca appeared in his face. Yet somewhat human, her slender hands turned into mangled talons, and her mouth opened into a large gaping black hole, covering most of her face.

Rebecca reached up to touch his tears.

Brazenly, he touched her hands. A burning sensation shot through his hands, decaying his skin, and spreading up his arms.

Eyes wide, Robert begged her to tell him where the kids her. As he pulled her into his arms, Wayne tackled him, breaking his contact with Rebecca.

§

Sebastian tore the clamp from Jennifer's forehead, ripping the skin from her forehead, and toppled over backward onto the floor.

A blood-curdling scream escaped her lips.

§

I struggled to gain flight. What the hell? Something was wrong with my wing. It must have been from the impact it took inside the house.

Shit!

I crashed into the roof, wings open. The roof collapsed, breaking most of it open to the battle below.

The crash sent wood, beams, and debris flying throughout the basement. It crushed most everything in its wake. Dust, dirt, and blood flew up, spraying everything and everybody.

In the commotion, Uwe and Manson advanced on Woodrow. Before they had a chance to attack him, Woodrow waved his arms, throwing the bikers up into the ceiling, but due to its weakness, they crashed through it and out of the house into Ratliff and me.

The four of us collided in mid-air. I lost my grip on the machete and dropped it.

Below us, came a crash and then two voices bellowed down the hallway below, first Jace, and then Jennifer.

§

Due to the destruction of the roof, it allowed those who had been human to tap into their inner beasts and their magic, which also allowed Larissa and Odesso, who tracked Tristan to the house, to get inside of it while Hunter searched for the girls.

There were few vampires who had the conviction and the willpower to learn witchcraft. They didn't need it but any other form of paranormal knowledge was an advantage for them. Some of the underground loners looked up to them as Gods or leaders, someone they could learn from. Most of these Gods or Leaders were generally rogues, and they were destined to become criminals.

Odesso recognized it for what it was.

The first warning sign was how Woodrow blocked everybody from using their powers. The second was the high amount of magic Odesso sensed inside. There were witches, and Odesso couldn't find them. They had to be locked up or contained elsewhere within the house.

As he assessed the situation, he spied Tristan close by, yet, his eyes locked on Woodrow. Tristan was the least of his problems right now. The rogue vampire had to be dealt with. The house fell apart as he evaluated everything and everyone.

Werewolves, vampires, and a witch were nearby. He stopped. Only sorcery could defeat magic. With that said, he needed a diversion. As his tattoos swirled around him, he called upon the magic of the gothic style mirror tattoo. Odesso used it to create live mirrored counterparts to each person within the room and placed them before their human counterpart.

While the mirrored twins were created, Jace ran into the room. Beneath the moonlight, veined human colored wings sprouted from Jace's back. Then, he took flight and disappeared through the roof.

The gargoyle and griffin tattoos emerged from Odesso's body and turned into life-like size living creatures. They targeted Woodrow, who transitioned into Rebecca, and switched places with her. Odesso's creatures roared, shaking the house.

Rebecca and her twins advanced upon Odesso. Another beam crashed to the floor, barely missing the triplets. Dust flew up.

Odesso and his creatures went after the trio. Again, the house shook. Uwe's machete fell through the roof as the triplets merged into one and then split again, switching up their positions.

The gargoyle to Odesso's left slashed at one replica of Rebecca, ripping her chest open.

Behind them, Robert struggled to escape Wayne's grasp on him.

"No! Rebecca! No!"

Wayne held on tight to Robert, burying his son's face in his chest, muffling his son's cries.

The griffin to Odesso's right leaped on another replica of Rebecca. It slashed at her face.

Odesso knew which was the true Rebecca.

He cast aside the Rebecca who stood in front of him while the other replicas struggled to free themselves.

With no warning, his griffin turned into a stone statue.

"Protect that one!" Odesso yelled, pointing to the one in the middle of the room.

The machete fell, the blade dipping down while the gargoyle and the replica he had cast aside rushed the mortal Rebecca.

"Are you sure you have the right one?" the replica asked.

Odesso knocked the replica to the ground and peered up at the gargoyle.

"Yes, I'm…" When he turned back to her, she was gone.

"I'm over here, sorcerer."

The one he had just been in contact with had merged into the trio of Rebecca's. He frowned. Then more Rebecca's popped up, turning everybody else into her replica.

Some, Odesso recognized as the men due to their position before the fight.

Before him, a fight ensued between a gargoyle and some of the replicas. The gargoyle scrambled with them as some of the replicas fell to the floor. The gargoyle slashed out, slicing them open when a glimmer caught Odesso's attention. The machete arced downward toward them.

Odesso snapped his head around. The gargoyle split open, its guts spilling onto two Rebecca's. Then one of the replicas climbed inside the gargoyle and brought it back to life. Another Rebecca latched onto another replica and merged into one.

Then, another Rebecca climbed onto the gargoyle and pulled back on its wings. It reared back. As it did, the blade came down, striking Rebecca's throat. Blood spilled down her chest.

Robert's screams filled the room.

As the blade slid down her side, Odesso grabbed the machete. The gargoyle bucked, throwing Rebecca off and into the hallway, where she struck the wall.

With one swipe, Odesso took the gargoyle's head off. The headless beast disappeared. In its place was Woodrow's decapitated body. Odesso kicked the head away from it.

As he glanced around, everybody transitioned back to their original bodies, leaving only one Rebecca, the one who lay in the hallway.

Robert escaped Wayne's clutches and ran to his wife, crying. Behind him, a beam from the first floor caved in. It crashed down upon Larissa.

Another crash came from the hallway where Robert and Rebecca were. Jennifer's scream followed. Above her, the ceiling gave way. Cries and screams from women and children penetrated one of the doors in the hallway.

Another loud crack caught Odesso's attention, only it came from above. His eyes widened as one of the main structural beams gave way and came crashing down.

§

A strong invisible force had thrown us away from the house toward the canyon.

I crashed onto the ground and slid over the edge, grasping onto a bush branch. Another body came flying. It was Ratliff. He slammed into a canyon wall behind me and plummeted into the darkness below.

One of the Warlords of Satan, Manson slid past me and over the rim, His fingers dug into the rock a couple of feet away from me when Uwe crashed into us, casting us into hell.

As I fell into the canyon, I struggled to straighten out my wing. It wasn't working. Shit! Then somebody slammed into me and bounced me off of the canyon wall. It was Ratliff! His blood red eyes stared into mine and his fingers dug into my throat.

"Dragon, you will die!" he hissed.

"Fuck you, Ratliff!"

He slammed my head against the mountainside. Blood poured from the wound.

"Cheating whore, you deserve to die!" His fist connected with my rib. "You don't deserve a man like Tristan!"

"Maybe you should worry more about Uwe. He's headed for his death, asshole! You know he can't fly!"

"Shit!" As quick as he had come, he disappeared.

I fought to stay afloat. Dammit! I snapped my wings out, hoping for a crash landing at least. It was better than death. Blood dripped down my face. Then, the wind picked up, driving me faster toward the ground. No, this was not happening. Water splashed below, once, twice...and then Ratliff was in my face again. Only this time, he drove me spiraling down backward toward the water below.

He grumbled, "Not so tough now, are ya?"

"Asshole, are you trying to kill me or...us?"

I clung to him, embedding my talons in his back.

Behind him, Jace plunged toward us, his wings out wide. My jaw dropped. No, not...! Then, impact. Water splashed up over us.

§

The witches stood amongst the rubble, unmoving. Pieces of the ceiling had fallen into the cells, killing some of the witches upon impact. Overhead, the moon cast its light into the room, the cool night air leaking in.

The blonde witch glanced at the silver-haired witch.

"You all right over there, old lady?"

The older woman hissed. "Yes, I'm fine. What about the little ones?"

"I think they're all right. Just shaken up."

She glanced over at their prison cell. Scared, the oldest girl had run back into it to join her sisters. She couldn't blame the child for she would have done the same thing.

Then, she turned toward the lock. It popped off.

In the prison cell next to her, the redhead elicited an excited cry. "Looks like we have our powers back."

As the coven snuck out of their cells, the blonde approached the girls. With a gentle voice, she called to them.

"Come along, little ones. We'll take care of you."

Crying, the girls remained curled up together.

Since the children didn't seem appreciative, the blonde became annoyed. With an irritated tone in her voice, she snapped, "Very well, I don't need you to volunteer."

The blonde swirled her hands around an invisible ball, and threw her palms out toward them, forming the invisible ball around the children. They floated up and out of the cell.

"It's all right. You're coming with us," she said with a smile.

"Ah, look, he's cute," the redhead said.

The witches turned to gaze at the lizard who stood near the door. The silver haired witch stared at him. "How did he get in here?"

"I don't know, but I'm taking him with me." The redhead lowered her hand to Hunter.

Hesitantly, he slinked up her arm to her shoulder.

"He's probably scared."

As the witch made googly sounds at him, he peered over at the girls, who in turn smiled at him.

The witches then peeked down the hallway before proceeding onward to where Rebecca lay unconscious against the wall, debris atop her.

"What do you think?" another asked.

"We'll bring her with us," the old woman said.

She flipped her wrists, levitating the woman up, and into a vertical position. They continued past Robert and Jennifer who also lay on the floor.

Bodies lie buried beneath the rubble. Most of the witches hurried out of the house while the old woman and the brunette stopped to look everything over.

"Well, what do you think?"

"Leave them be. I think most of them are dead," the old woman said.

The brunette raised an eyebrow. "You don't want to double check?"

"No, look at them. Most of them look like they've been crushed or even staked," she said, pointing to a biker. "I think that one caught part of the broken beam. Let's get out of here. We'll take the woman and the children."

The witches camouflaged themselves with the forest colors and disappeared into the night.

§

Manson drifted downriver, the blood dissipating within the water around him. At the bank, Uwe laid half in and half out of the water. Behind him, Crystal and Ratliff floated nearby, her arm awkwardly entwined with his body and her wings expanded around them.

Voices echoed within the canyon. Unsure of who they were, Jace crept into a crevice in the rock. Death was in the air, and it was only the beginning.

Behind him, something splashed in the water. It was time to move on!

ABOUT THE AUTHOR

LYNN MULLICAN was born and raised in Phoenix, Arizona, where she currently resides with her husband and three adult children. She has woven her fascination with the paranormal into written works including short stories, dramatic plays, poetry, and full length novels. In *Bad Elements: The Hybrid Unleashed,* she incorporates years of knowledge in self-defense and martial arts.

www.ingramcontent.com/pod-product-compliance
Lightning Source LLC
Chambersburg PA
CBHW060357180626
46817CB00007B/2457